THE
PILOTS

RANDOM HOUSE NEW YORK

THE
PILOTS

RICHARD
FREDE

Grateful acknowledgment is made to the following
for permission to reprint previously published material:

Elsevier, Amsterdam: Excerpt from *Elsevier's Dictionary of Aeronautics*, 1964.

Farrar, Straus and Giroux, Inc.: Excerpt from *Geography III* by Elizabeth Bishop.
Copyright © 1972 by Elizabeth Bishop. "Night City" appeared originally
in *The New Yorker*.

Harcourt Brace Jovanovich, Inc.: Excerpts from *Wind, Sand and Stars*
by Antoine de Saint-Exupéry; translated by Lewis Galantiere.

Harper & Row, Publishers, Inc.: Specified two lines from "Crow's Nerve Fails"
by Ted Hughes.
Copyright © 1971 by Ted Hughes.

Random House, Inc.: Excerpt from "Evening Hawk" from *Selected Poems 1923–1975*
by Robert Penn Warren.
Copyright © 1975 by Robert Penn Warren.
Excerpt from *The Random House Dictionary of the English Language*.
Copyright © 1966 by Random House, Inc.

Library of Congress Cataloging in Publication Data

Frede, Richard.
The pilots.

I. Title.
PZ4.F852Pi   1978   [PS3556.R37]   813'.5'4   77–5997
ISBN 0–394–46232–7

Manufactured in the United States of America
2 4 6 8 9 7 5 3
First Edition

To my wife
BARBARA
and to our sons
MICHAEL ARI
and
BENJAMIN DOV
the three points of my compass
With love

Do not boast about the tempo of technology. The final, essential questions are not altered by technology. They remain. Even in the most modern airplane you travel forever with yourself—your mood, your misery, your world-weariness . . . the ultimate questions still stand before your soul today, as they always have. Take heed that your flight does not carry you beyond that which is essential, but closer to it.

—Carl Sonnenschein

CONTENTS

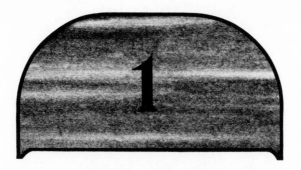

NIGHT
FLIGHTS

Technology, after all, is still man's handiwork; man is
the one to watch.

—Michael J. Arlen
From The New Yorker

A single engine beating.

Three o'clock in the morning of the first day of the new year. Hilary —the name he had chosen for himself and taken legally—lay in it tentatively. New time seemed to him dangerous with possibilities. So much could go wrong. He was twenty-six years old.

His one-room apartment was dark and cold with night and winter. The window was partially open, but there was an acrid taste to the air. At odd moments the radiator made bumping and hissing and sighing sounds, but it produced no heat.

The young woman who lay beside him probably didn't know she was there. He envied her her numbness. Decerebrated, she seemed exquisitely comfortable—while Hilary felt helpless and afraid. The feelings came on him whenever he felt alone, whether or not there were other people about. He felt insistently like getting physically inside her again. But he was afraid that if he woke her she would say real things. What these things might be, he did not know.

He considered his present doom: driving a cab the rest of his life. He considered the frozen dinners with which he made do, all the while waiting for the telephone to ring with a call from his agent or a letter to arrive with some message of hope—a promise of a job, money, fame, even love.

Crazy thoughts, Hilary thought. Residue of bad gin, result of slow sobriety.

It is a particularly bad night of the soul among many bad nights of the soul. He remembered feeling this way in bed as a child—helpless. But *then* he had been waiting to grow up. When he was grown up everything would be all right: he would be able to take care of himself, be in charge.

Sitting beside him at the bar where they had just met, the girl hadn't believed him at first. "You mean you're the one in the commercial?" she had said. "The one who says to the girl, *'I will if you will'*?"

Then she had looked at him. "You really are," she said, "you really are. Wow, you must be famous."

Grown up, in charge. He had grown up and become Hilary. A couple of hundred dollars a month, after agent's commission, for a television commercial that he had done a year before and that soon would not be shown any more. Going to bars to find girls. Driving a cab three days a week. The rest of the time working hard to get a reading, an interview, his photographs looked at . . .

He had been drinking martinis when she had come into the bar. A solitary celebration of New Year's Eve. They had begun to drink martinis together. Later, her eyes shiny and her head unsteady, she had said, "Say to me, *'I will if you will,'* the way you do on TV."

"I will if you will," he had said.

"I *will,*" she had said, and they had gone down the street to the one-room apartment, to his bed.

January, a month for beginnings. But to Hilary it seemed a sad month, a time when, forced to look backwards by the occasion of the new year, he perceived emptiness and failure.

A large aircraft was low on its approach to La Guardia. Hilary's night-filled room shook from the nearness and harmonics of the aircraft's engines. Beside him the girl did not wake. When the sounds of the engines were distant and then gone, Hilary heard her breathing.

While they had been drinking the martinis, they had had the prospect of a whole new year before them. Now they were in the new year and it was no different from the old. There was nothing he could control.

Another heavy aircraft passed above his building on its approach to La Guardia. The engines dominated the night, rattled the room. In a few seconds, silence.

Hilary looked up into the darkness of his room. He saw himself up in the night sky, an instrument panel aglow in front of him, *in control.* In control of every aspect of his life. That's what being a pilot is. There would be nothing he would be afraid of any more if he were a pilot. How could there be? Pilots are not afraid.

He saw strong, knowing fingers. His own. They move without hesitation, they move with command and vitality, move to the engine controls, grasp them and . . .

He thought of warmth, of summer. He had been offered work for the summer at a theater in Cornwall, New Hampshire. Only a few weeks' work, and at minimum pay; but out of the summer city where failure is magnified by the heat.

He decided that if nothing broke for him in New York by April, he would go up to Cornwall early. There was an airport in Cornwall. He would find work—any sort of work—and he would take flying lessons.

This simple resolve gave him great comfort. He would be unafraid. He felt strong. He thought of himself in the black sky now. A stewardess—otherwise the same girl of so many of his fantasies—enters the flight deck . . .

After three in the morning of the first morning of the new year. Now the sky above Hilary was silent.

2

"La Guardia Approach, Jetstar Four-two-zero. Say again, did you want me to squawk on one two hundred? . . . Okay, sir, negative both targets, we don't see them."

"La Guardia Approach, Eight-seven Yankee's lookin' . . . Eight-seven Yankee's on a headin' of one-seven-zero . . . Okay, we're all lookin'. And Eight-seven Yank has our traffic . . . We got 'em . . . "

"La Guardia Radar, Two-six November with Information Uniform. We're at five thousand, proceeding on a heading of one-three-three degrees . . . Yes, sir, it's sure shakin' my teeth. Next year I hope to be safe in bed. Good night, sir."

"Okay, expect vectors, and Victor Four-four-five for now, and we have the traffic . . . Yes, sir, it's more than light turbulence up here. Allegheny Three-seventeen."

"Okay, good night, and thank you, sir. And happy new year."

3

Earlier, as Hilary had stared into a martini in the lonely bar, Perry Sullivan, first officer of New EnglandAir Flight Five-one, had looked out into a night sky that was clear and weightless and full of celestial illumination. The winter ground was starkly white beneath the darkness.

Five-one—727 jet service from Atlanta Municipal to Boston Logan via Washington National and New York La Guardia—was on its last leg and maintaining relatively low altitude for the short flight between New York and Boston. As a result of its altitude, Five-one was experiencing a certain amount of buffeting—enough to make some of the passengers nervous, Perry thought, imagining the long, dark cabin behind him, its occupants illuminated only by the narrow projections from overhead reading lamps. The FASTEN SEAT BELTS sign had been left on. The captain, Jack "King"

Kahn, had told him to request a higher altitude. Perry had called Air Traffic Control and done so. There might be less turbulence at a higher altitude.

"New EnglandAir Five-one," said a voice modified by electronics.

Perry said, "Center, Five-one."

"New EnglandAir Five-one, climb to and maintain one-three thousand. Cross Norwich at or above one-one thousand."

The captain nodded at Perry and made some adjustments of power settings and trim. Perry said, "Center, Five-one leaving nine for thirteen. Cross Norwich at or above one-one thousand."

"Affirmative, Five-one."

Perry glanced at the distance-measuring-equipment readout. "Sixteen miles to ORW, Captain," he said.

The captain nodded. ORW—the radio signal letters for Norwich—was their next checkpoint, mandatory reporting position, and course change. The aircraft trembled, calmed itself, and then trembled again. The climb continued. Through eleven thousand and on. The night seemed to pass the windscreen visibly. But Perry knew this was not so, there was not even any cloud. The aircraft was jolted with some severity. Perry thought again of the passengers behind him. He thought of Laura, his wife of a year. A little over a year ago she might have been one of the stews back there. There were times now when he wished she still were. The thought made him feel guilty. But there were times when . . . *Screw it,* Perry thought, I can't figure it out now, here . . . The VOR needle moved and the indication of TO was replaced by an indication of FROM and Five-one had passed over the ORW navigational station.

"Give Center a call."

"Yes sir," Perry said. "Center, Five-one. We're level at thirteen."

The airplane was trimmed up and on autopilot, signals from the VOR stations guiding the flight to Boston perfectly without either pilot having to look outside the aircraft. Kahn said, "Congratulations."

"Thanks," Perry said.

"Got your Air Transport Rating and your upgrade training and all set to be a captain."

"That's what they tell me."

"What are you graded in now?"

"The 227."

"Well, it doesn't give you too many routes to bid. But the routes'll give you a hell of a lot of weather."

"I picked up a relief selection—One-six-five."

"That'll be like home for you, won't it? New York, Cornwall, Lebanon and turn around. You live in Cornwall, don't you, Sullivan?"

"Yeah. Learned to fly there, too. When I was a teenager. My folks used to spend summer vacations near there."

"How old are you now?"

"Thirty-four."

Kahn said nothing. Perry thought of his own youth and luck, both of which he acknowledged. He would be the youngest captain on the line, and that at a time when other lines weren't promoting—or even hiring—but were bumping full captains back to copilot and laying off copilots to make room for captains. Young and lucky, Perry thought, though maybe not so lucky in love.

"I've been *flying* thirty-four years for this airline," Kahn said. "I guess, all in all, I've been lucky to fly for as long as I have. Fly professionally. You never know when the physical's going to catch up with you. At your age I don't suppose you think about it much. I didn't at your age."

· "I think about it. Passing three physicals a year? I think about it. Look what happened to George Detwiler."

"Now, George Detwiler, there was a brilliant pilot. Thirty-eight years old and a light colonel. Would have made colonel and had his own squadron by the time he was forty. He and I used to rent lightplanes and go off to the boondocks and go fishing together a couple of times a year. You ever run into him now?"

"Not any more. He keeps to himself."

Kahn nodded. "He doesn't do any flying at all? I mean, take a lightplane up once in a while?"

"No. Not that I've heard," Perry said.

Kahn nodded again. "New York, Cornwall, Lebanon. That's not a route to you, then, that's home."

Wouldn't it be nice if it really was, Perry thought.

"Virgil Yancey was dead by then. When you started to fly."

"Yeah. Though they called it Yancey Flying Service. Still do."

"You must have flown with Ev Goodsom."

"Sure. It was his operation by then. Still is. Ev was my first instructor. Later I even had some lessons from Falun Aigborg."

"Christ, I'dve liked to have had some flying lessons with Falun Aigborg. By God I would."

"Ev soloed me. There at Cornwall. And, of course, I did all my cross-country work out of Cornwall. Then later, after I got my commercial, I flew some charter work for Ev. Mostly to New York. Yeah, I guess I'm not unfamiliar with the route."

"Then probably you won't get lost."

"Probably."

After the landing in Boston, the rest of the crew deplaned for the terminal building. Perry lingered on the flight deck finishing some of the secretarial duties of the copilot, work which normally he would have completed in the flight operations office. But a step from the flight deck was a step closer to Laura, and Perry was reluctant to take it.

A few hours ago he had been enjoying a sunny afternoon in Atlanta. Now he was set to earth in Boston. Ninety miles from Cornwall, ninety miles from Laura. Set to earth too swiftly, Perry thought. His car was out in the company parking lot. When he got in it and started it up, he'd be less than two hours from Laura. And already he felt the strain. *Captain* Sullivan was timorous about going home.

4

"Center, I'm not interested in holding that long here. So I think we'll just divert to Chicago long as we got the fuel."

"Kennedy, this is Speedbird Three-four, can you assist me? I can remain in this hold until twenty-two hundred, but there's no reason to do so unless I can expect approach clearance within the foreseeable future."

5

Jonah Jaquith saw that Sylvia Raab was startled. She was looking across the living room to the entrance archway where George Detwiler was solemnly shaking hands with Barney Raab.

"When I sent the invitation, I never thought he'd possibly come," Sylvia said. "I don't think he's been anywhere for—"

"For a long time," Jonah said.

Sylvia and Barney Raab, who owned a twin-engine airplane which they both flew, had invited only pilots to their New Year's Eve party—friends and acquaintances, professionals and nonprofessionals, whom they knew from the Cornwall airport or who had flown in from other places.

Jonah watched George Detwiler walk away from Barney Raab and go to the bar. Barney looked perplexed. From across the room he turned toward Sylvia and shrugged. He picked up his drink and came over.

"I just tried to engage him in some idle conversation," Barney said. "Nothing serious."

"Like what?" Sylvia said.

"Inertia navigation. Man appears out of almost nowhere, you don't want to put him on the spot with something personal."

"Never mind," Sylvia said, "*I'll* see if I can make him feel at home."

She started making her way through her guests, smiling and offering comment as she went. All the talk that Jonah could hear was of flying.

Barney held out his hand. "I've only just heard, Jonah—my wife never tells me anything. Except how to fly the airplane." The two men shook hands. "Wonderful news. When's it to be?"

"Doc Glynn says sometime in July."

"Any preference, boy or girl?"

"Like Yvonne says, just healthy."

"That's the best wish of all." Barney nodded across the room. "Would you like to meet Delaney Howard?"

"Our new competition? What do you think? I wondered about him. I watched his hangar go up last fall. Then it just sat there unoccupied."

"He just got out of the Navy."

Barney took Jonah to a man of about thirty who was standing with a woman of about the same age. The woman's face showed strain, perhaps even fear, Jonah thought. The man's face suggested that he'd had a very pleasant life and he looked forward to more of the same.

Barney said, "Betty, Del, I want you to meet Jonah Jaquith. Jonah's our local flight instructor, one of the best teachers of a skill I've ever known. He also flies charters if you need to go someplace."

Del Howard laughed. His wife smiled carefully. Jonah shook hands with them. "Right nice to meet you," Howard said. "I hope we'll be friends."

Howard, Jonah thought, was finally a reality, like bad weather. "Welcome to the friendly skies of Cornwall," Jonah said.

"I reckon it *is* goin' to be friendly competition," Howard said. "Hell, when I came to look things over last summer, your boss told me he'd refer any business he couldn't handle over to me."

Now that will be something, Jonah thought, a day when Ev Goodsom refers business to someone else. "You going to offer instruction as well as charter?"

"No. Howard Air Charter consists of one airplane and that's an Aero Commander. We're a passenger carrier only."

Jonah nodded. He saw Howard's business as a threat to his own employment and thereby as a threat to his unborn child, and he didn't particularly want to help Howard, but he said anyway, "I don't see how you can survive on charter alone. I don't think *we* could—at Yancey. We need to offer instruction."

"Oh, I know it's goin' to be rough. At least to start with, till I get known."

"Barney said you were Navy Air. What were you flying?"

"S-2D Trackers. Antisub stuff. We carried acoustical search equipment and a couple of homing torpedoes or depth charges."

"Carrier-based?"

"Yes."

"To my mind," Jonah said, "that's the most hazardous flight duty in the world."

"Some think so," said Howard.

"Someone told me they lose one or two guys a month off carriers."

"*He left it,*" Betty Howard said suddenly.

Howard went on leisurely. "It happens," he said. "Fuel exhaustion. Screwed-up approach. Severe weather. Bad luck. Like I tell Betty," and he put his arm around his wife, "if I could hack carrier duty, charter is going to be a picnic."

Betty Howard's face relaxed. The tight smile disappeared, and in that new quiet Jonah saw a pretty woman. She said, "We'll have a home. We've never been in one place for more than a year. We have two children. They need to grow up in one place."

"How did you pick Cornwall?" Jonah said.

"Well, I grew up down South, but I flew out of the naval air station at South Weymouth for a while and I used to drive around a lot, you know, all over New England, and I just had this feeling about the area. Later I got it in my mind to do like Betty here wanted and quit the Navy, seein' as how I'd already seen the world, you know, but I hadn't seen much of my family. Anyway, I had enough money for a down payment on a fair charter plane, and enough to start a mortgage on a hangar and, well, I have a friend who's a demographer—he teaches demography at Harvard—and I went to him about a year ago and asked him could he employ his brains and the all-fired computer and find for me a place in New England that needed an air charter service. And Cornwall was its name. Though, like my friend said, maybe y'all don't need *another* charter service, leastways not right now, but he said the area in the vicinity of the Cornwall airport has the greatest growth potential of anyplace in New England."

"I moved here, and there's a lot of other industry coming, too," Barney said.

"There's a whole *bunch* of factors," Howard said. "So here we are. *Eager to go where you want to go.* That's the company motto."

Barney said, "Just don't be too eager to go anywhere till you get used to our New England weather."

Howard smiled at his host. "I've flown in weather from time to time."

Yvonne Jaquith looked over to where her husband Jonah was talking with Barney Raab and the new pilot, Del Howard. Yvonne did not enjoy being with pilots. She had married Jonah in spite of his occupation.

Sylvia Raab had joined the three men and was smiling and saying happily, "I *told* Barney the left engine sounded funny."

"*Inspired* technological description: 'the engine sounds funny.' Besides, all the gauges were right where they should be."

"Yes, dear," Sylvia said, "and then the engine goes *pop,* just like that, a little sound pop . . ."

Yvonne tried to ignore the conversation. She was becoming anxious. All they do is talk about what went wrong, Yvonne thought. No wonder I'm nervous about Jonah. Oh, they make jokes about it, but all they seem to talk about when they get together is what went wrong. Bring two pilots together anytime and within five minutes they'll be discussing disaster. Or at least near disaster.

"Blew a jug coming back from—" Yvonne heard. It was Jonah.

From another part of the room, *"Oil all the hell over the place . . ."*

Then she began getting the full, multichannel effect. Voices came in from all over the room: "Thought I might have busted the gear, so I gave it full power and . . ."

"Didn't see it till it almost took a wing off me . . ."

"Lost *both* VORs *and* communications capabilities and . . ."

Jonah!

Ev Goodsom found himself in the curious and surprising condition of getting drunk, something he hadn't done in sixty years. Well, once. Years ago with Yancey. On bootleg stuff. That Yancey had brought in from Canada. Couldn't find anyone to deliver it to. Had one hell of a two-week party out of that, more girls than you could shake a stick at. Jesus Christ. Never drank anything but beer before or since. And never got loaded. Got a hell of a good buzz on from time to time, but never, *never* got drunk.

Falun Aigborg was making him drink, Ev thought. He was just across the room, Falun was, but Ev could not look at him, had not even said good evening to him yet, and it was nearing eleven o'clock.

There were ties between Ev and Falun, God knew there were ties between them. From way back. At a time when none of them could even imagine someday being able to look back so far. Christ, Falun wasn't just one of the early pilots, he was one of the earliest ones, Falun was. Went back even further than Yancey. Yancey dead now and Falun dying.

Earlier in the evening Falun's wife Marion had taken Ev to another room and told Ev that Falun was dying. "You and I and Falun and Dr. Glynn are the only ones who know," Marion had said. "I'm not going to tell Falun that I told you. He doesn't want to burden anyone. But you're his oldest friend." She had closed her eyes then and it had seemed a very long time to Ev before she opened them again.

"How long has he got, Marion?"

"At the very outside, the end of summer."

And now Ev was almost drunk, almost ready to go over and greet his old friend and former partner and sometime instructor, almost ready to wish Falun a happy new year.

Ev had his mug refilled. And then he looked over at Falun, acknowledged their mutual presence for the first time that evening. Acknowledged his own cowardice in the face of Falun's dying. Falun looked back, smiled, and made a small gesture at Ev with a cigarette. Still smoking. Not that it probably mattered now—Falun was dying of emphysema and lung cancer. The one precluded the medicants for the other. Falun had been smoking a couple of packs of cigarettes a day as far back as when they had chased the same girls there for a year or two and even flew the same airplane for a while, as far back as when Falun'd had a little money—but not much—saved from his years of flying, and Ev had had almost none but access to some that wasn't his, and Yancey'd had what had seemed like a considerable amount of money from the rumrunning, back when Yancey had first started talking about the fixed-base operation, Yancey Flying Service, that the three of them had started—how long?—nineteen thirty-eight, thirty-two years ago.

Ev went over to Falun.

Falun had been large, but narrow in features—strong, fast, hard, and narrow. Quick reactions. My God, the time when he pulled them out from a certain takeoff collision. But now his face was puffy, no angle in it or to it, all roundnesses. Breathing hard and smoking just as hard. "I'm a little shaky, Ev. That's why I have to sit. It's just temporary."

And Ev thought, as he shook hands, that he might be catching death from Falun.

Sylvia Raab said, "Jonah, have you seen George Detwiler?"

"I tried to talk to him. But it was . . . difficult. He kept looking around. I kept thinking he was looking for someone."

"I think he left—he just left without saying goodbye to anyone."

"Who didn't get here tonight? Who could he have been looking for?"

"Ben Cain and Adele Fortune are the only ones. God knows where Ben has got himself to. And Adele, of course, couldn't leave her ski-instructing up north. I didn't think she could."

"Or would," Jonah said. "She was happy to get away from here this fall."

Jonah heard the voice of his employer, Ev Goodsom, rolling across the room. The voice was a combination of hoarseness, crustiness, and curtness. Scared students, but worse, put off some prospective students entirely. Nothing to it really but having had his ears ruined by the old engines and poor radios. Pounded by all those decibels from the engines hour after hour and day after day, the tissues of the inner ear had suffered permanent damage. Between the diminished sensitivity of his ears and the communications habit left over from having to *shout* over the oldtime radios in order to be understood or merely received, Ev maintained an awesome level of sound even in casual conversation.

"Christ," Ev was saying to Falun in a voice that sounded like a loud reprimand, *"Ben Cain,* for Christ's sake! Who *the hell* would have thought it? Jesus Christ, not me. Ben Cain flying the Caribbean? Alone? In a single-engine aircraft? Christsake, three years ago Ben was afraid to solo."

Jonah edged into the conversation next to Ev. "Yeah, but he came out for his lessons," Jonah said. "Scared shitless half the time, but he always showed up for his lessons. I've got to hand it to a guy like that. He can play on my team any time. And he did solo, Ev. You want to remember you bet me he wouldn't, but when I told him to go, he went."

"Oh, he soloed all right, and cost me ten bucks, but I saw it, I saw the fear. Then he was afraid to fly to *Portland, Maine,* for Christsake, on his first cross-country solo. A whole hundred and forty miles each way. Christ knows how many miles of *open ocean* he's trying to fly now. And to tell the goddamn truth, I'd think twice about doing that with *two* engines."

"Has he made it?" Falun said. "Has anyone heard if he made it?"

"No," said Jonah.

"Christ, no one even knows if he left Florida," Ev said. "We know he got that far."

"Jonah," Falun said, "did you ever wonder why he went through all that —that fear? Did you ever wonder why he went through all that to fly?"

"Adele and I used to talk about it. We both gave him lessons, you know. Adele—Adele got to know him better than I did. She said he'd told her he'd dreamed about flying all his life and he couldn't help it if he was scared of it too. He said one part of him did it in spite of another part."

"Yes," Falun said. "Or *for* spite of the other part—the fearful part."

"Could be," Jonah said.

"There have been a lot of fliers like that," Falun said. "Some keep flying, some don't."

"Ben's been flying for three years now," Jonah said.

"How old is he?" Ev said. "Is he thirty yet?"

"Twenty-seven."

"He moved here from New York, if I remember," Falun said.

"Yeah," Ev said. "Just before he started taking lessons. Course he was pretty goddamn upset when he got here. Making about twenty million dollars on his first art show, that upset him pretty bad."

"Surprised him, anyway," Jonah put in. "Kid, twenty-three, twenty-four years old, suddenly making all that money, everybody talking about him and his work, top of the art world in New York—"

"He sure as hell ran from it fast enough," Ev said. "Cornwall isn't the art center of the universe."

"He wanted to live around here. All right, he was scared, too."

"I read somewhere he gets between five and ten thousand dollars for a painting and more for his sculpture," Ev said. "He must find that even scarier."

"Adele thinks he's more frightened of screwing up his work than he is of killing himself in an airplane."

"Adele talks a lot," Ev said. "I'm fond of her, but right now I'd say she talks a lot." He started to raise his mug to his lips but then put it down without drinking from it. "Ben Cain," Ev said, "flying the Caribbean solo. Jesus Christ. Who would have figured it? You just couldn't figure Ben for that."

"Ev." It was a few minutes before one and Yvonne had asked Jonah to take her home. She was upstairs getting her coat. "Well, Ev?" Jonah said.

"You becoming a partner in the business? I've been thinking about it," Ev said, and looked away.

"You've been saying that for a long time, Ev. You've been saying that for a very long goddamned time."

"I've got to see Mrs. Yancey. It'll all be up to her."

"Then go see Mrs. Yancey."

"She's not going to understand. She'll think it's money out of her pocket."

"Don't shit me, Ev. The widow of Virgil Yancey isn't going to understand about a man flying and getting paid for it?"

"You're getting paid for it."

"Not very goddamned much, I'm not. I could make more as a worker in a factory—as Yvonne keeps pointing out. A hundred and fifty dollars a week, Ev. With a baby coming. And Yvonne's going to have to quit teaching, so that hundred and fifty a week is going to be all there is. A hundred and fifty a week, Ev, and who does most of the flying? I've kept track since last summer. I've done over ninety percent of the charter flying and *all* of the instruction since Adele took off for the winter. When was the last time you flew a charter, Ev?"

"I fly almost every day, Jonah."

"Not for hire you don't. You leave that to me. So who's bringing in the money you and Mrs. Yancey take out of Yancey Flying Service? Who, Ev?"

"My money helped start this operation, God damn it, and don't you forget it, Jonah."

"Yeah. Well, your money's not what's keeping it going. My flying is. And don't *you* forget it. For three years I've been carrying this operation—"

"Adele—"

"Adele flies summers. When there's too much work for me alone. I want part of it, Ev. I've been flying for you for ten years now. I want what I earned, what you said I'd get if I stayed with it. Remember? 'Stay with us, Jonah, and I'll see to it you're part of the business. A partner,' you said."

"I've got to talk to Mrs. Yancey."

"Talk to her."

"She's got to be approached in the right way."

"Approach her, Ev."

"Suppose she wants you to invest money? Suppose she wants you to *buy* in?"

"Right now, without me, there *is* no Yancey Flying Service. Approach her with that."

"But suppose she insists you've got to *buy* in?"

"I'll take care of it."

"How?"

"None of your fucking business, Ev."

"Where are you going to get backing? Who's backing you? Someone wants into *my* business?"

"*Your* business?"

"Mine and Mrs. Yancey's. Who is it?"

"Talk to Mrs. Yancey, Ev. Talk to her about my coming in with you."

"Like I said back in the fall, Jonah. I'll talk to her about it in the new year."

"This is the new year."

Ev looked at Jonah. "You could come up with the money?"

"I could come up with the money."

"Who's backing you, Jonah?" Ev took the cigar out of his mouth. "I have a right to know. Who is it?"

Jonah was silent.

Ev put the cigar back in his mouth. "Yvonne's waiting," he said.

6

Mrs. Virgil Yancey took down the bottle of bourbon from the shelf in the den closet. Once a year, on New Year's Eve, she drank a shotglass full in measured memory of Yancey. Virgil Yancey, her husband, the hero, whom she despised for that last flight of his, that *heroic* flight, despised quite as if he were still alive—though she had loved him intensely even to the last moment she had seen him alive. That had been in this house when he had paused in the doorway before going over to the airport. Paused in the doorway and looked at her.

Drinking bourbon was not Mrs. Yancey's favorite way of remembering Virgil Yancey or of invoking his presence. But it had been one of his favorite ways of invoking himself. She drank the bourbon. She did it for the same reason she remained in this house and sometimes listened to the airplanes going out and coming back, though when she tried to look at the reason closely, it eluded her entirely.

The single shot of bourbon in her was creating both warmth and mild protest, slight nausea, the smell of its past presence rising from the empty glass like Virgil Yancey reentering the room, this room where, when not flying, he had sat at his desk and drunk his bourbon and water and pondered for many long hours whatever it had been that Virgil Yancey had pondered for many long hours year after year.

She replaced the bottle. It was not yet eleven o'clock. She decided to watch the news before she went to bed—to find out what sort of year the new one might become.

7

"Good evening. Fighting has broken out on many fronts in Vietnam. In spite of a three-day new year truce earlier announced by the Vietcong, numerous instances of large-scale combat have been reported. Earlier today, after four B-52 raids and several ground clashes initiated by the Allies to secure positions, the American command announced its own twenty-four-hour cease-fire . . . President Nguyen Van Thieu achieved a major political victory today when he recorded strong support in the South Vietnamese House of Representatives. Protest by some members of that legislative body is also reported . . . And this just in. Vice President Spiro Agnew has interrupted his Asian and South Pacific itinerary and is in Saigon for an unscheduled visit. More as that story develops . . .

"Those five gunboats which left Cherbourg, France, mysteriously almost exactly a week ago—well, those ships are docked in Haifa, Israel, tonight after a secret three-thousand-mile voyage across the Mediterranean. France currently employs an arms embargo against Israel . . .

"A second trial has been ordered by the Army for Staff Sergeant David Mitchell, who is accused of having assaulted with intent to murder thirty Vietnamese civilians at Song My a year ago . . .

"President Nixon promises a balanced federal budget. That story coming up in a minute . . ."

8

"All right, sir, out of one-seven thousand . . . Roger, ident."

"Okay, Boston, Two-twenty-five, good evening. And happy new year."

"Cornwall Area Radio, One-one Romeo. Listening one-zero-niner."

"Uh, say again? . . . Three-three Alpha. I've got about twelve stations on here, Bradley. I'm unable to read you except as background . . . One-nineteen-four? Roger."

"Boston, Whiskey-Echo-Golf, we'd appreciate Flight Following if possible. And we know it's not your problem, it's New York Center's, but you'll appreciate we need to get this flight in as expeditiously as possible."

"Okay, and the logbook is clean . . . Okay . . . And we'll take forty going out."

"Worcester Tower, Fourteen Charlie. Heck of a peculiar angle of wind down Zero-two. Can we go around and have Three-three instead? . . . Roger, full stop short or long of second intersection. Fourteen Charlie going 'round."

9

Ben Cain's eyes were closed and he was staring into his own fear.

He lay on a bed in a motel near Palm Beach International Airport and, in his mind, looked down at the sea from the cockpit of his single-engine Piper Cherokee and wondered if he would ever be in his house in Cornwall again. He thought of the house, his home isolate and now deep in snow, all that long way back in New Hampshire. And such a long, long menacing way still to go, still to fly. And refly if he was lucky.

The flight had started back there in his studio. One late afternoon in October, Rupert Zur had called from Connecticut. "We're off this evening. I'll be back and forth, I daresay, but we'll largely be in Geneva until the holidays. Then St. Thomas. Now look, boychick, Madelon has it in her head to make New Year's Eve there, at our place. Why don't you come down? It would make an interesting little flight for you. Think about it. How is the work?"

Ben had looked around his studio. He had promised his dealer enough material for a show in May. He had enough work done for half a show. A half-assed show at that, Ben had thought. Nothing was good enough to leave his studio. Not in Ben's mind.

About his work he felt a desperation and sometimes even a panic. The very success of his work jeopardized him. The altitudes to which he had to climb merely to get to where he had already been were so extreme. They were altitudes to which few others had been at his age. Or at all. It seemed impossible that he would be able to get back there time after time . . . As he worked, every decision seemed a matter of life and death. He could not sustain himself in the fierceness of that emotional weather.

"What of my designs, boychick, how are they coming?" Rupert had asked Ben to submit designs for the courtyard and lobby of an office building he was going to start putting up in Manhattan in the spring.

"I have them," Ben said. They comprised the single piece of work he had been able to complete during the entire summer and fall. Possibly because the money was already promised to someone else—to Jonah, all of it. Not the smartest investment he would ever make, but Jonah had asked Ben to back him in buying into Ev and Mrs. Yancey's flight service; then Ben had become interested in going partners with Jonah, possibly reorganizing Yancey Flying Service or even starting their own flight service if necessary. Thirty thousand dollars was what Ben would receive for the designs if Rupert accepted them. A small fraction of that if he did not.

"I am delighted to hear that, Ben. So. All the more reason for you to come to St. Thomas. We may combine business with pleasure and discuss your designs there."

Ben had thought of the days upon days when work had been left incomplete, and of the recent days when work had not been begun at all. Jean Bera, a racing-car driver, had once said, *Only those who do not move do not die, for they are already dead,* and Ben had recalled that.

"I think I'd like to try that flight," Ben had said. And thought: And when I get back, after *that,* everything will be simpler, there won't be any problems to it after that, and I'll be able to get my work done. If I survive that, I can do anything. It would make him different inside.

"That is so good, Ben. Come for Christmas week. Madelon I think has a little letch for you. It will excite her to have you around the house."

The little aside had surprised and stimulated Ben—Madelon was a frequent actress in his sexual fantasies. He had not, though, entertained thoughts of a real Madelon and a real episode with her.

"Actually, she tweaks me with you, boychick. To her I think you are *la vie bohème.* Whereas I am the stodgy businessman. She says, for instance, I make flying an airplane seem like double-entry bookkeeping—that is how well I am able to remove the rapture from life."

"Madelon exaggerates."

"I am afraid so. Rather badly. Ah, well, we shall discuss it all when we see you in St. Thomas. You will come Christmas week?"

"Some time that week."

"Cable when you file your flight plan. I'll meet you at the airport."

The late-afternoon sky was a glinting blue—the thunderheads had passed —and the sliding screen doors to his balcony let the sound and the smell of the ocean into his motel room.

The preparation of the flight plan. He remembered putting it off again and again, like a work he felt he was not ready for yet, and then finally spreading the charts on the floor of his studio. And the overwhelming exhaustion that had come on him then.

He had lain on the cot there and looked down on the charts for a very long time—shapes of pale yellow and pale brown, islands, interrupted the sea of white emptiness of the maritime charts like a few jigsaw pieces strewn widely on an unpainted canvas. He could almost imagine he was overflying what he looked down on.

He had gone to the Jeppesen Airway Manual binder in which he had placed the special contents for a Caribbean flight. He had studied approaches to any airport that might be useful to him and determined the probable prevailing winds from the runway layouts. He had noted where his grade of fuel was available and where repairs. He had studied the exacting intersections and reporting points of the radio chart for the Miami/Nassau area where he would first leap out, and then he'd gone on to "Entry Requirements." After that he'd closed the manual and put it aside.

All you have to do, he had told himself as he looked down on the charts laid out degree-to-degree on the floor, is plot the course out over the islands. And measure the distances landfall-to-landfall and figure out how much altitude you'll need for a glide to safety if the engine quits. Though there'll be a lot of places where you won't be able to get that altitude—without using up your emergency oxygen or running into cloud. And figure your headings and no-wind elapsed time point-to-point. It'll be beautiful out there over the water—greens and blues and shiny towering white cumulus . . . And all you have to do is plot the course out there and . . .

Leave from Miami and go to Bimini or direct Nassau? From Miami at all? One hundred and seventy-three statute miles of water that way, seventy-nine minutes over water, though with Bimini and Andros standing by at thirds a little off course, but probably close enough for emergency use. Island hop from the start? Palm Beach International to Grand Bahama, direct Treasure Cay Radio Beacon on Grand Abaco and then almost a ninety-degree right turn to Southwest Point and then over to Northern Eleuthera, only sixty-four miles and twenty-eight and a half minutes of open water . . .

There were options that carried him mile by mile and minute by minute and degree by degree out over the expanses of the water, where there were limitless options but no assurance of options to return if he made the wrong decision now: there in the safety of his studio.

All he had had to do was decide his course and chart it.

The great lassitude had enveloped him.

I'm afraid, he had thought, and thought now in the motel room. A single-engine airplane. All that open water. The most shark-infested sea in the world. Barracuda. I *am* afraid. Just as I was when I started flying. The fear grows less only a little bit at a time. And only by flying, never by just thinking about it. The others *are* pilots—Jonah, Adele, old Ev, poor George Detwiler—*but I'm not. I still fear too much.*

Three years of flying. Four hundred hours of it since he had first touched the controls of an airplane, since those early hours when, Jonah or Adele beside him, he had first gotten an airplane into the air *himself,* himself *flown* an airplane. And now the winter endlessness of the overflight of Chesapeake Bay, gray, cold, spotted white with darting chop; the excruciating endlessness of the overflight of the beautiful and eerily motionless swamps, hideous with peril; and now here.

At home then, in the studio, he had rolled on his side and looked down on the white expanses of the charts, and he had begun to measure and compute and draw and compare and guess and justify. He became inquisitive and then connected; and then intrigued. He began to believe and to hope. Ben began to think that he might accomplish and survive the flight.

The results of all the work in the studio back home lay on the floor of the motel now, a jagged path of pieces of charts taped together and a binder of figures—headings, altitudes, frequencies, distances, minutes en route per leg, estimated fuel consumption, emergency alternatives. Out on the beach he had been studying his calculations all afternoon.

He heard the shrill of a jet aircraft's slow-flying in off the water on an approach to Palm Beach International.

He looked at his watch. Five o'clock. Time for an early dinner.

The bar was open to the ocean. The air was warm, turned yellow by the beach, blue by the sky. Ben ordered a tall rum drink. He had also calculated how many ounces of alcohol it would be safe for him to drink without residual or toxic effect very early the next morning.

Women were coming up from the beach, light frocks pulled over their bikinis or wound against their bodies. A few children were seated together, given colas and Shirley Temples, then left to themselves.

An attractive woman looked around the vacant places at the bar and then sat next to Ben and ordered a drink.

"Hi," she said.

"Hi," Ben said.

"Nice day," she said.

Ben nodded.

"I noticed you," she said. "I watched you on the beach all afternoon, and a question occurred to me."

Ben smiled at her.

The bartender placed a drink in front of her, and without looking away from Ben she picked it up, took a sip, and then put it down. "What I decided to find out was, what were you studying so hard?"

"Life and death."

"What?"

"Figures," said Ben.

"Figures?" She glanced down her dress and laughed. "Are you any good at them?"

"I hope so."

Ben looked at her hands, at her wedding ring.

"Pay no attention," she said. "Merely a memento. Left over from happier times. Different times, anyway."

Ben got up.

"Did I scare you?" she said. "Did I scare you?"

"Early day tomorrow," Ben said.

"Early? How early can early be? It's only five-thirty right this instant. It's still early right now."

"Thanks," said Ben.

At dinner he ordered carefully, plain food, nothing that would be likely to give him gas at altitude or other intestinal difficulties out over the long water the next day.

He thought about the woman at the bar, the sun and salt-water smell of her. She had excited him, but it would have meant staying up with her, drinking with her, being with her as late as she wanted or needed him to be—if he had understood the invitation, if he was to be his gentleman to her lady. It would get very late.

After dinner he went back to the bar and ordered a double brandy. The earlier women, including the one he had talked with, were gone. There were couples now, and the few lone men and women were dressed for the evening rather than for the beach. The women were quite lovely. He felt the brandy trace its way through him and he felt a concurrent insistent desire to be with a woman. Not just to get laid, Ben thought, but to . . . what?

To feel himself reassured of life, the continuing of his own life. As if some gentle lady could reassure him of that simply by her presence naked to him.

Ben got up to go to his room and sleep. The woman from the beach was coming in, alone. She wore a deeply cut flowered dress. She smiled at Ben.

He felt like going over and over the charts, the flight plans, the estimates, the calculations. Instead, he set them up in his flight bag for the airplane. He packed everything else except the clothes he would wear the next day, the toilet articles he would need in the morning. He went back to the flight bag and got out his J-AID manual and under "Meteorology" looked up the restricted telephone number for U.S. Weather Bureau Aviation Weather in Palm Beach.

"Weather Bureau, Farrell speaking."

"Hello," Ben said. "I'm a pilot, aircraft number Eight-niner Niner-zero Whiskey. I'd like to go Palm Beach–St. Thomas, via West End, direct Treasure Cay, direct—" and Ben gave him the rest of his route. "I'd like to get off at ten hundred Zulu." Six A.M. "I intend to go visual all the way."

The weatherman left the telephone for about two minutes. When he came back he said, "Okay, sir, it looks like you've got it." Nothing unusual expected along his route, just the usual late morning and afternoon cumulus build-ups. "You realize this is only a twenty-four-hour area forecast."

"Yes, I do."

"Okay, sir. Have a good flight. Give us a call in the morning."

"I will. Thanks."

Ben hung up, but he didn't go to bed. He sat there and thought of the girls he might call. There were so many girls he wanted to talk to suddenly. He felt like calling Adele and telling her about his great journey, a flight longer and more exacting than any she herself, instructor or not, had ever made. He knew the ski area where she instructed skiing in the snow months, the lodge where she lived. He had stayed there himself, skied there; he could visualize the room in which she lived, for he had slept with her there once, the first time, the previous winter, a night of completeness for him. He had waked up while it was still dark, aware that she was already awake. Her eyes were open, but she had not acknowledged him.

"Aren't you going to say anything?" Ben had finally asked.

After a while Adele had said, "I wish you weren't staying here. I mean, in my room."

Jesus Christ, Ben had thought, not knowing *what* to think.

The features of the motel room were still just discernible from the little remaining light outside. Earlier he had closed the sliding glass doors and turned on the air conditioner. He lay down and heard the air conditioner turning, his mind reciting, *Palm Beach Radio one-fifteen point five, Miami Beach Radio is one-twenty-six seven, squawk as proscribed: make sure going to penetrate Air Defense Identification Zone within three minutes of es-*

timated time of arrival . . . Crooked Island to Salina Point on Acklins Island is thirty-one statute miles, it'll take fourteen minutes plus, maintain six thousand or higher. Know where you are. If lost, go up, fly wide, and look for light water. Light water means shallows, shallows mean land . . .

It was still early. Just after seven P.M. The sky through the glass doors was now a deep blue, the sharp bright white crystal of a star penetrating the blue, and Ben again thought that the success of his work endangered him, took him to those *altitudes* of endeavor. Will take him to that *altitude* above a shark-infested sea. With so little to maintain him there. The thin turning of a blade in his hand on a piece of work, the laboring of a blade above the sea.

Everything is dangerous. Ben wondered why no one else had discovered this. Or if they had, why they didn't admit it. Or how they lived with it.

He wanted to sleep. It would be a long night and he wanted to get it over with. But the thought of the next day was so quickening his body could not find a restful place on the huge bed . . .

Through a long night of brief sleeps Ben was startled awake by a noise in the hall, by the turning of the air conditioner, by silences. The long water stretched before him, and the sound of the air-conditioning unit reminded him of his mortality, reminded him that a mechanical unit could stop.

If you have to ditch, ditch to the west of land and remember the Beaufort scale for judging the seriousness of the wind and remember that the foam goes into the wind. If you can see the foam. Keep the knife handy, ditch to the west, and remember dark blue or dark green is deep water, shallow water looks clear, shoals indicate the good side for ditching, shoals appear green or yellow or both and seem to lift out of the water at you. Keep your options open. There are good Low Frequency signals from West End International and from Grand Bahama and from Treasure Cay. LF from Great Inagua, too. A litany of obsessive information that had insisted itself upon him like undigested food, like voices in his mind, all through the long night in the motel room. *Acklins Island to Great Inagua. Get fuel Great Inagua and use radio beacon. Eighty-seven statute miles, forty plus minutes. Need fourteen thousand the stretch for glide to land. Won't go for it—have to save oxygen for emergency use only . . .*

When he got up in the darkness of the morning to dress, he found he had the beginnings of a cold from the air conditioning. He thought he might not fly that day—altitude changes with clogged ear channels could be exquisitely painful.

"Shit," Ben said to the silent walls of the room. *"Fuck it."* And he got dressed.

[23]

When he taxied out he was the only thing moving on the expanse of the airport. The sky directly overhead had become blue, the horizon was orange and hazy yellow. The runway lights were still on and his cockpit was dark enough so that he had turned on his instrument lights to a low level.

He finished his runup, the only aircraft proximate to the runway.

"Palm Beach Tower, Cherokee Eight-niner Niner-zero Whiskey is ready for takeoff."

"Eight-niner Niner-zero Whiskey, cleared for takeoff."

He moved the throttle forward slightly and moved out on the runway. Lined up with the broken white line coming at him, he gave the engine full power. "Niner-zero Whiskey rolling. Request straight-out departure."

"Straight-out departure approved, Niner-zero Whiskey."

"Niner-zero Whiskey."

Ben slipped the microphone onto its clip. The engine sounded terribly loud, as if it were laboring. Ben held the airplane on the runway and then, as the takeoff roll smoothed, he lifted off. The sound of the engine diminished. He built up speed and then decreased the angle of his climb and reduced power. The air was steady, the instruments in front of Ben equally steady. He changed frequencies, talked with Palm Beach Radio. At altitude he reduced power again and leaned the fuel mixture till he got the rpm's and rate of consumption he wanted. The engine sounded subdued, a peaceful companion doing its work.

He was out over the water.

As always, it is easier in the air.

The feeling of apprehension continued, but it was for the time subdued, like the sound of the engine, there but not dominant. The stronger feeling was one of satisfaction, of exhilaration.

Ben had no intention of going all the way in one day; there was a certain sense of security in that. Today he would island-hop, never be over water for more than forty or so minutes at a time, top his tanks down at Eleuthera or Long Island, and then fly on to Matthew Town on Great Inagua at the end of the Bahamian chain and spend the night there before going out over the longer waters to Haiti and Santo Domingo and on to Puerto Rico and then St. Thomas.

He is tucked in with his survival gear, knife at hand, twice the amount of fuel he will need for his several legs to Eleuthera. Life jacket, covered raft. Dehydrated food. Water. Solar still. Sea anchor and paddle. And noted on his flight plan that he had on board flares and a distressed aircraft beacon and was transponder equipped.

Remember to wedge the door open before ditching. A shoe will do it, they say. So that when the aircraft's down in the water the pressure of the water won't hold the door absolutely closed on you.

He had attached strings to the survival gear so that he could pull it in-a-piece out the door once he was out.

The sky is bright, the sun yellow-white and well off the horizon. Day now, not only morning. Grand Bahama is behind him. He turns southeast from Great Abaco and the sun slides from in front of him to a hot feeling on the side of his face. His eyes unsquint slightly; the salt sweat and tears in the corners of his eyes from looking into the sun begin to go away. There is talk on the radio now. It gives Ben the pleasure of company, the implication of assistance, should he need it.

Ben looks down again. A different place. There is a clutter of useless, meaningless rocks turning the moving water white. Not entirely useless or meaningless. If he went down here and could swim to them, he could climb up on them away from shark and barracuda. And there is a clump of sand below. Unbelievably small to withstand so much water. White in the sun. Technically an island. Ben is contrite as he overflies it—a place of providential refuge if the engine quits. He flies on. A rusty shipwreck. Brown. A long metal hull rising from glinting, clear water, the yellow sand of the floor beneath it clearly visible . . .

Squinting from behind his sunglasses and through the glare of the water thrown up into the sky, Ben scanned for other traffic . . .

Ben looked below. He was overflying an immense blue hole. He felt he was being sucked down into it. He checked his altimeter, which was holding steady. So too the airspeed. He remembered another pilot telling him about almost flying into the water because he thought he was flying the horizon. But there is no horizon: blue meets blue in haze. *Keep checking your instruments.* He makes five-minute position notations—there is no backup radar in the Bahamas. *If you get lost out of sight of land, have a search plan ready in your mind. Remember: don't chase a cloud shadow thinking it's an island off in the distance.*

Ben hears the missed beat, hears the silence of the engine quitting, looks down at the blue hole which is sucking him down. Nevertheless the engine continues to turn, the rpm's remain steady, the temperature gauges and oil pressure are where they should be, the fuel supply in both tanks is positive, encouraging even: possible. Another five-minute notation . . .

His mind continues to study the sound of the engine. But then Falun's voice comes to him and Ben hears Falun say, as if he were an absent instructor in the cockpit, "It is not engine failure but the crisis in the

[25]

individual which finally kills." Falun's remembered voice repeats the words in concert with the beating engine.

... Coming up after Long Island, just past Deadman's Cay, on Crooked Island, fifty-three statute miles or twenty-three point five minutes of water, *but can off-fly Long Island for the first twenty statute miles or nine point five minutes. Keep nine thousand or above for glide ratio, figuring zero wind component.* There is motion in the air now. From the angle of crab he is holding, Ben figures a slight breeze from the east. Deadman's Cay—this is the one which Ben, with his sense of the ironic, dislikes approaching, to pass out from over, onto open water: does it augur? Ben flying along conscious of the flotation equipment behind him, a knife which he had honed strapped to his right leg in case the raft in the back seat inflated in the air and jammed him and the controls into the panel. It *had* happened, pilot and aircraft into the sea. He had been told to have a knife where he could get it quickly and puncture the raft.

It is hot in the cabin.

He is suspending himself above the waters, the long waters, like a spider suspending itself from its own thread, Ben suspending himself from his own knowledge, hanging there over the long waters, and progressing. Alone. Alone. No land in sight. He gets weather on unicom from other aircraft around the Bahamas. He tells them what it was like where he has just come from and what it is like where he is.

"I've got cloud bases at about five thousand," he says.

His voice sounds amazingly calm to him.

Later he hears a voice from a ground station say, "We have a pirep from that area. The pilot reports cloud bases at five thousand," and Ben knows he was that pilot.

Sonofabitch, he thinks, *I'm a goddamned transoceanic* authority.

Now there is no straight-line flying. With bases at five thousand he is dodging clouds in order to still keep as much altitude as he can. *Christ, see the boilers building up.* Darkening sky. Looking up ahead, an island darkened by the clouds above it, shadow-covered by the clouds, dark green from the shadow, bright sea around it, but clouds pushing down on it, cloud base pushing down to about two thousand, clouds that lifted from the island that morning, island raining its own moisture on itself, subtle mist rising, cloud tops gleaming at the edges in the sunlight, dark as old city snow at the base, Ben steering carefully around it all, spending time, fuel, altitude.

Another island under dark cumulus build-ups. Runway of an airport aglare from a peculiar angle of sunlight upon it. Everything else dark from cloud.

Great Inagua. Matthew Town.

Well met, runway.

He decides to go all the way this same day.

He lands. His shirt is immediately wet against his body. He pops open the door as he taxis for the little motion of air it brings into the cabin.

Go on now. While there is the will. The joy. Or the numbness against fear.

Ben stands in the hot sun, the ramp glaring, and waits for the Customs and Immigration man to come to him and take his papers and inspect the airplane.

Safely down. Waiting.

He wants to take off while he feels he still wants to. And he wants the Customs and Immigration man not to show. So he, Ben, can stay there. Safely on the ground. Challenge no altitude, no distance.

Climbing out from Matthew Town he looks down at the geometry of the stone remnants of an abandoned plantation. He is fixed by it. He has filed and gotten a message off to Rupert, *Estimating St. Thomas 2100Z.* He looks away from the plantation and out to sea.

Then more of the five-minute position notations, as if he had never landed, been on earth again, the little circles and rectangles and X's stretching out from West Palm long across the water—*no,* Ben thinks, stretching out uninterrupted now from his mind in his studio in November in New Hampshire to here where he holds himself above the sea, passing out from Great Inagua Island, seventy-eight statute miles and thirty-seven minutes of water coming up, Cuba a distant seventy statute miles off to the right, Ben hoping some Cuban fighter jockey or radar operator doesn't get a funny idea about him out here. Hoping he knows where he is and that where he is isn't inadvertently some Cuban restricted zone. Or the Atlantic Fleet's weapons range. Still, it would be comforting to see a ship out there.

But there is nothing. Not even a horizon.

He concentrates on the instruments. He remembers Adele sitting next to him, back in his student days, tapping on the panel with a pencil. *Concentrate on the instruments.* Adele tapping her pencil, as if he were a schoolchild. Ben thinks of Adele undressing in front of him to model for him. He thinks of the sweet dry grass and the fallen leaves and the fragrance of a warm day just the past fall. All of his tension is concentrated between his legs. He is alone with it in this cabin over the sea.

He has an astounding thought. Over the sea or not, it is as if he had never left New Hampshire. *He is in the same place: his cockpit.*

But then he is startled into terror by what is happening to him.

He can't understand it: *everything is wrong.* He can hear it in his ears, feel it in his gut. The engine screams it, his insides, the *skin* of him warns him against death. A figure inside himself is pointing at the instruments. He has everything screwed up: *he is in a dive, he is losing altitude terribly fast, he is in a steep bank, he is almost out of altitude, he* . . . He is so low he can see the surface of the water coming up at the windscreen. Ben wills himself onto the instruments. He is plummeting and turning. Rudder and aileron to get himself straight, shove the nose down, jam on full power, and when he is straight and diving directly for the water Ben pulls out so abruptly he thinks he hears the wingspar break. But the airplane is together, the engine calms as he reduces the power, the instrument needles settle to normal positions, and he climbs out as if there had been no interruption, as if the sky and the sea, by invisibly meeting, by depriving him of a horizon, had not conspired to kill him and nearly done so.

The circles and rectangles and X's and time notations extend themselves. Haiti. *Haiti,* for Christsake. *Dear Mr. Cain: For overflying or landing in Haiti you are required to obtain a special flight permit which* . . . He has never been here before and he knows exactly where he is. That always amazes him.

Below him a mangrove swamp, inhospitable.

And yet he is still in the same place: his cockpit. And that amazes him. He has not gone from one place to another so much as he has transported his world to the sky over the coast of Haiti.

Across Santo Domingo and now the landscape has no reality for him. It's as if it existed only in his mind and his mind was experiencing some geographical phantasmagoria. Fatigue and heat crowd his body. His body flies on in the airplane. But he himself has withdrawn to some tiny cockpit in his mind.

He sucks on hard candy. An ex-fighter pilot, George Detwiler, had taught him about how quickly it revived the mind and the spirit in flight.

Out over water again, the Mona Passage, eighty statute miles . . . But then he begins to feel aware again, as if he had slept all that distance immediately behind him and now awoke, all his faculties alert: there ahead, soft on the horizon, Puerto Rico.

Thirty-nine minutes flying just inland of the Puerto Rican coast—and given the choice would it be better to go down in jungle or sea?

. . . The sea is ahead again, the jungle at the end of Puerto Rico dropping away in what appears to be a falling wave of steam. Ben looks at his flight plan: *Puerto Rico to St. Thomas,* fifty-two statute miles, twenty-four minutes, but off-fly Culebra halfway there for ten of those miles, four and a half of those minutes. The circles and X's and time notations stretching out twelve hundred and fourteen miles: nine hours and twenty-four minutes in the air, early morning to late afternoon, the approach plate for Charlotte Amalie, Truman Airport, St. Thomas, on his lap for reference, the VOR tuned up on one-oh-eight point six, needle pointing straight up, *dit-dit-dit dah dah* clear in the cabin speaker, avoiding restricted and warning areas, flying outbound from SJU (San Juan), one-fourteen zero, and then STT (St. Thomas VOR) and then the airport in sight.

Christ. Journey's end.

"St. Thomas Tower, this is Cherokee Eight-niner Niner-zero Whiskey."

"Cherokee Eight-niner Niner-zero Whiskey, St. Thomas Tower, go ahead."

"Niner-zero Whiskey is coming up on your VOR. Request landing instructions."

"Niner-zero Whiskey . . . Runway nine . . . cleared for straight-in approach . . . "

The wheels bumping down just as if on any other runway, the same sensation to it, as if he'd been shooting touch-and-go's at Cornwall. But suddenly hot in the cabin, humid, sky graying up. He had been here once before. But then it had been as a passenger on an airline. Before he had ever imagined he would or could become a pilot, much less fly the Caribbean. Have *his own* airplane, fly *here.* Humid heat now. He cracks the door, turns off the runway at the intersection opposite the windsock.

"Niner-zero Whiskey, contact Ground Control one-twenty-one nine."

"One-twenty-one nine. Thank you, sir, and good day." Ben switches over. "Ground, this is Cherokee . . ." and listens and then taxis again. Rain soon, it looked like. "And Ground, would you cancel my flight plan for me? Eight-niner Niner-zero Whiskey is VFR from Matthew Town, Great Inagua . . . "

My Christ, I did it. It's done.

Then Ben is standing unsteadily by the wing of his airplane as the tanks are filled. He is more physically exhausted than he had anticipated in any way, his legs actually unsteady beneath him, the hard surface beneath his feet *pushing up* at him; he can feel the pressure of it against his feet, in his thighs, into the base of his spine—a good feeling. Ben is a little light-headed, gasoline fumes in the warm, gray, humid air, white wing beneath his hand. Rupert is coming out to him in the rapid, short-gaited way of his, smiling, making a brief allusion to the flight, as if Ben had just flown down from Cornwall to Danbury, Connecticut, to stay overnight with Rupert and Madelon, Rupert's voice seeming to come from some place where Ben isn't; there is much talk of the party to come, of Ben's sketches for the lobby and courtyard, of the extraordinary *creature* Madelon and Rupert have found for Ben; Rupert is jealous of Ben's situation, the opportunity to be with such a woman, caress her. Rupert is so overcome with the sexual stimulation he is experiencing he feels that he and Ben should have a drink —certainly Ben could use a drink after such a flight crossing the Caribbean by himself? and in a single-engine airplane in one day. Rupert is astonished at Ben's audacity. He must be more careful. And now that drink.

But first Ben gets up on the wing and back into the cabin, sits himself again into the interior he thought he had left, having forgotten this final business, his legs and buttocks and back aching from the repeated posture, Rupert sitting himself beside Ben in the copilot seat. Ben goes through the checklist visually even though he knows it by heart and even though all he wants to do is start the aircraft up so that he can taxi it to a tiedown area. He speaks the words to himself as he accomplishes each little physical task ... And starts up. He taxis and goes through the shutdown procedure, and after they have climbed out Rupert stands to the side and watches him as he ties down the airplane.

Then they have a drink. What an excellent idea, Ben thinks, as if it never would have occurred to him, as if Rupert had come up with an idea of greatness. Indeed, Ben is a little light-headed.

The drink, a strong rum punch, seems to sober Ben. The light-headedness diminishes; he hears Rupert's voice more immediately. Into his second drink he feels himself sitting on a chair on the ground, his body beginning to forget the vibrations of the airplane, his ears beginning not to hear the engine any more, the chill sweat of his shirted back against the plastic upholstery gone, dried.

"Thirty-two years old, I believe. Just the perfect age for a young man. Part American Indian. Cherokee, I believe. *Hah.* Like your little airplane. But you will see. The most extraordinary eyes I have ever beheld. Any man would desire to look into them."

"And what does Madelon think of your infatuation?"

"Oh, Madelon would like those eyes. She is quite otherwise satisfied with her own face and with her own legs and breasts and etceteras, but Madelon would like those eyes. She is quite clear on it."

Rupert nods. Ben laughs. The seriousness of it. Madelon *would* like those eyes. As if they could be purchased like her cosmetics and fragrances and clothes.

Rupert does not once mention the woman's name. He goes on about her.

But Ben's mind has flown a little way off.

My Christ. I did it. It's done.

No, says another voice in his mind. *Half* of it is done.

10

"Yeah, I readya, but ya faded out . . . Okay, one-one-zero for vectors and we're out of two-five."

"Center, this is Sixty-seven Sixty-eight. Do I look pretty good on the centerline of Victor Four-twenty-seven? I'm trying to check the VOR reception."

"Seventeen is at flight level one-nine-oh . . . No, sir, we've been here, just checkin' in."

"Charlie George leaving twenty-one for fifteen, and thank you, sir. We'd like to get even lower before Albany if that's practicable."

"Yes, sir, Kilo Hotel is military . . . No, sir, we're just chuggin' along here, makin' flight pay, eatin' up the taxpayers' money, same as always . . . Okay, Kilo Hotel changin' frequencies."

II

Adele Fortune is a woman in orbit.

She could have been at a party, among her fellow ski instructors. Instead she is in darkness, in bed and alone in her room at the back of the lodge. It is not yet midnight and it is her birthday almost to the minute. Her birth *moment,* Adele thought. The realization makes her terribly uneasy.

She saw a photograph in her mind. She was nude . . . rising from a bed . . . like something gossamer born aloft by the simplest breeze, a cradle of air . . .

Adele liked to pretend that when she could not actually fly, her soul could leave her body at her will and fly for her. It was a fantasy she'd had as a child and she liked it well enough to keep it. She knew that what she pretended was not real, but it made everything so easy, so simple, to think that way sometimes.

She was flying an airplane. People were looking up. Everyone she knew. *But I'm not coming down, people. Not just yet.*

She rose up above New Year's Eve, up into the night sky all blackness and stars, lifting herself into it in an airplane. She felt mighty. She felt gratified and exhilarated. She felt strength infusing her muscle tissues. It spread out through her body and permeated her legs and shoulders. She felt her blood all warmth and joy. She looked down at the people below. She could no longer see them. Earth itself was darkness. She climbed higher.

The wind made a clatter against the side of the old wooden building. If it hadn't been for the wind—the bitter rampage of northwestern air that always followed a New England winter storm—Adele would have been flying. She would have been away from New Year's Eve.

Adele remembered the first time her soul had flown away from her when it had not been at her own bidding.

Another night. A boy named Spencer. A proper gent. She had been at Radcliffe and he at Yale. He had courted her since the spring dance at which they had met. He had courted her through a summer of letters and into a fall of football games and dry fragrant leaves in warm sunshine. A proper gentleman, he had never more than kissed her lips and touched her always properly covered breasts.

Adele had felt something which had distinguished her from other young women: she had felt *revered* by Spencer's care of her. But she had also felt an almost humiliating disappointment in herself—because of Spencer's lack of physical response to her.

And then, over the Harvard-Yale weekend, in a motel outside of New Haven, Spencer very properly fucked her. She had been drinking, no question: bloody marys at a party in the morning—she remembered the room had been sunlit and warm and she had worn a gray tweed skirt and jacket and a bright-yellow cashmere sweater—and beer with the sandwiches at lunch; a grasshopper before going to the game, screwdrivers from a gallon glass jar at the game, Scotch at the party after the game, a Scotch before dinner at the restaurant, wine with the dinner, and a stinger, pressed on her by Spencer, after dinner. She hadn't, as she recalled—but recall was difficult —drunk much of what had been handed to her all day. Not drunk much, but had been drinking somewhat all day.

And back at the motel. In her room. More Scotch. With Spencer and his friend Mark. Spencer's very best friend. Down from Harvard. She remembered getting excited and happy and laughing and dancing with each boy. Everything had felt so warm and affectionate. And then Spencer had undressed her. She had known it was happening. She had known that what was happening was somehow not usual. But it had had no significance for her. She remembered that she had felt unexpectedly liberated and sovereign without her clothes in the presence of the two boys, the two young gentlemen. Then Spencer, ever the gentleman, had invited his friend Mark to fuck Adele. That's what he had said. Adele didn't remember much of that night exactly, but she remembered Spencer's words exactly.

Spencer: Mark, don't you think Adele's attractive?

Mark: Sure, Spence. She's beautiful.

Spencer: Mark, why don't you fuck her?

Mark: Hey, Spence, I mean . . .

Spencer: I mean it, Mark. Why don't you fuck her?

Mark: You mean it?

Spencer: Go ahead. I mean it.

Adele had listened to this exchange with some distant curiosity as to how the conversation might develop, to what conclusion it might lead. It still did not seem of much moment when Mark had undressed himself. Mark had had difficulty maintaining an erection. It being her first time, Adele had watched with interest—from what seemed to her, at the time, a distance. Not being able to maintain an erection, Mark had gotten angry. Adele couldn't understand why he was angry—he was supposed to be enjoying himself. And she was supposed to be experiencing . . . something. Spencer just sat in a chair across the room and watched. He seemed not to be experiencing anything either, seemed peculiarly unmoved. She remembered that later in the darkness Spencer had tried to do something, but she didn't remember what, or to whom. Both boys were in bed with her then. She remembered that it was as if she had suddenly come back to consciousness. Aware of presences. Consciousness and terror had spread through her simultaneously. She had held her tongue with her teeth to keep from shrieking. During the night one or the other of the boys had touched her, manipulated her, tried something. She had remained motionless. In the gray morning light the boys had left. Her muscles were by then suffering spasms from the exertion of motionlessness.

Adele had always wondered how it could have happened that way. How she could have *let* it happen that way. Often she had thought of herself as a victim. But as she'd grown older she had begun to suspect that she had been a conspirator.

Four in the morning, midnight gone, the new year begun.

Adele has slept, she thinks.

Spencer and Mark never came back, Adele thought. What an *insane* thing to feel funny about, as if *she* had done something wrong to them or been a disappointment. Whatever. Adele often came upon what she considered to be queer turns in her mind. She wondered if other people had the same experiences within *their* minds. She had decided that most people probably dismiss the peculiar turns and pretend they're not there.

Hello, Spencer. And hello, Mark. And hello, you little bitch who let it happen.

She thought of Ben, sweet Ben, who would not have her. She thought of D.G.—and her mind skipped quickly past him. She thought of Sam, a man she had known in New York. That had gone on for two years, but Sam had been married. It was funny, his *marriage* had given their *relationship* stability. And when finally he had left his wife, packed, walked out one night, come to Adele's little apartment on East 72nd Street, she had said *No!*

That was when she had left New York—when her lover had left his wife and come to her. She had given up good money modeling—the only girl who was currently active then who had been on the cover of *Vogue* two times in one year.

She had long straight blond hair and a slim body. The agency people and photographers who used her regularly said it was her lips, the turned-down smile, together with the wide, childlike quality of her eyes that made her such a good association for their fashion- and female-oriented wares. Dependence in the eyes, command in the mouth. Innocence and experience. Fear and passion. Weakness and strength. Passivity and activity.

In her mind Adele is flying an airplane. She is on final. She pulls the yoke back. For a full stall landing. Up until now she has been in full control, absolute authority. Now she must wait and see what happens. *Ora pro nobis.* It is the only time in flight that frightens her. *Clunk.* She is down. Controls are applicable again. But for that second or so, she had been sitting there virtually without control, subject to the airplane, wind, temperature . . .

Radcliffe. Married and divorced the same year, her junior year, played hell with her grades. Poor D.G. His sensitivity had made him so appealing. But it had been craziness.

D.G. had taken her on a picnic down to the Cape. He had prepared the picnic himself—pâté and cold shrimp and cold chicken, a salad and bread and cheese and strawberries, a bottle of splendid white wine and a bottle of champagne as well. He had gotten a Victorian picnic basket from somewhere. D.G. had been very proud of it all. He even had a Victorian carving knife which had belonged to his grandfather and to his father and which his mother still used on formal occasions. D.G. had deftly taken apart the cold chicken with it. Then he had sat and sipped at his wine and turned the knife slowly in his hand, the blade flashing and glinting in the sun. He had been talking rather somberly about how Adele already wasn't taking very good care of their child—staying up late at night, eating junk food, being friendly with the wrong people. Adele had been terribly amused. She thought he was making fun of himself—the self-serious father-to-be. They were sitting up on a sandy bluff. There were boulders below, and then the beach ran smooth and flat to where short waves fell quickly, line after line of them. It had been quite chilly; spring was not really there yet. Adele was three or four months' pregnant and was enjoying the little vacation from Cambridge and school. She was laughing when D.G. had become angry, furious at something, and she could not understand what. But he had gestured at her with the knife—short, jabbing gestures, as if to underline what he was saying. Then he ran at her with the knife, and in backing away from him, she had fallen down the bluff and struck a boulder. D.G. said he had run at her to keep her from backing off the bluff—a misunderstanding.

But when, the next day, she had been in the hospital hemorrhaging from the miscarriage, he had come up to her room and pulled out every needle they were feeding her with before anyone except herself even knew he was in the room—he had yelled at her that she was losing the baby through the tubes, on purpose. And then she had signed the papers on D.G. She knew she had *had* to, but it often made her feel ugly bad that she had done it. Though D.G. was out and in his mother's custody now. He had called her since getting out. Last week, at Christmas. And then he had said he was embarrassed because he had nothing to say.

"That's all right, D.G.," Adele had said.

D.G. had said nothing.

Adele wondered sometimes if she *makes* them crazy, some of the boys she has known.

After the two-year lover she had looked for someplace to go, away from New York, and she had thought of Cornwall. She had spent summers there all her life. Her family had a camp, as New Hampshire people called such places, on a lake. A house long since sold.

Adele turned and embraced herself beneath the covers. Cold air.

She had been a certified ski instructor at eighteen, the only person in all of New England to qualify for and take the USIA precourse, otherwise the full instructor's course, at fourteen. Soloed a sailplane at fourteen, earliest legal age. Private, Multi-engine, and Seaplane on her sixteenth birthday—earliest. Flight instructor earliest at eighteen. *Why so fast, Adele? Why? Run run run.* She asked this often and did not have time to think of the answer. Freshman at Radcliffe at seventeen. Raped, so to speak, shortly thereafter. Married at twenty. Divorced at twenty. Lost a pregnancy at twenty. Graduated at twenty-one. Earned fourteen thousand dollars modeling in New York her first year there when she was twenty-one. Had averaged four thousand a year in Boston modeling part time for an agency there through her four years of college. Earned twenty-eight thousand her second year in New York. Was going to make more her third year, but left, abandoning her lover.

Back to Cornwall. Where she had known warmth.

Flying for Mrs. Yancey and Ev Goodsom.

Father and brothers gone now, father dead, brothers dispersed, unremembered mother dead in childbirth—Adele's.

No wonder it seems like life and death sometimes, Adele thought, thinking of a man on top of her, inside her.

She thought of Ben. She touched herself. Removed her hand. *Not* on your thirtieth birthday. Don't be an adolescent on your thirtieth birthday.

My God, it's the night my mother died thirty years ago.

Adele projected images upon the darkness above her. She felt cold and alone. The total aloneness made her shiver. She thought of Ben.

Adele never felt alone with Ben—but she never felt *together* with him. Maybe because she was a few years older, Adele thought. But Ben . . .

Adele felt warmth and found that, in her mind, she was looking at remembered photographs of herself. The air had been still—she could feel the warmth of it against her unclothed body. She had felt so secure being photographed by Ben. As if nothing bad could happen, as if the happenstance of the world had been suspended just then.

A warm day in September this past fall, the feeling of heated moisture in the air, a pleasant invisible cloak, an affectionate and gracious and sunlight day. Dry fragrant leaves on the ground, her bare feet crackling them. She knows she is going to enjoy sex with Ben, going to make it this time. She luxuriates in the extension of time preceding their lovemaking as *click . . . click . . . Now move over there . . . Now touch that leaf . . .*

She craved warmth now. In her mind she went through the photographs to remember, never having shown them to anyone else. Ben had never shown them to anyone else either.

Adele sees herself: high contrast black-and-white evening dress, the top of it hanging from her waist, her upper body bare, walking through the tall grass, her skin unnaturally white in the way Ben had printed the photograph, the sky behind her a contrasting gray that outlines her against it.

Another photograph: meadow grass, tall to her knees, she is nude, an old house distant behind her, very distant, the black-and-white evening dress a jagged thing on the grass, like metal, and three-quarters to the camera, Adele is holding her long blond hair (white, as Ben prints it, against the become-gloomy sky), holding it up and brushing it. The blackness of an approaching thunderstorm overhangs everything. Her body is starkly white in the sunlight from the horizon. It is a startling photograph to the model.

Adele presses her fingers against herself, removes them, thinks of Ben, thinks of the photograph, touches herself again.

She thinks of the girl standing there nude in the air and feels warm, but thinks of her there combing her hair, unprotected, her evening dress jagged upon the ground, combing her hair, and Adele feels sorry for the girl, pities her, so alone, so unloved, photographed but untouched, touched by the air only . . .

She thought—there in the bed at the back of the lodge, the covers like covers she remembers from when she was a little girl—I love that girl, I wish I could take care of her, she is so *needful* and no one knows her needs and how sad she is . . .

Climbing in the air now toward sleep, touching herself, taking her hand away. She thinks, knows, she flies to get away.

12

"Understand you have Maintenance listening. Very good. Number two HF set not very bright. And number two VHF set intermittent and not very desirable . . . No, we think it's the aerial loading unit. It will tune up but not transmit . . . That's affirmative, number two HF set."

"Okay, sir, we'll go down to seven, and we're proceedin' direct Cornwall . . . We're showin' twenty west of Cornwall . . . Ident . . . And we haven't picked up our clearance yet, we'll be lookin' for our IFR into Boston."

"Yes, sir, will do. And we're estimating our arrival at about—in about ten minutes. And we were wonderin', you guys got anythin' to eat down there? . . . I say again, is there anythin' open at your airport this time of night to get somethin' to eat?"

13

". . . Former President Lyndon Johnson said today that he would have won in sixty-eight if he had chosen to seek the Presidency again. Mr. Johnson said that the Democrats lost the Presidency because, in the middle of the election campaign, Hubert Humphrey made concessions to Vietnam doves.

"I'll be back with sports in a moment."

14

When George Detwiler got home, his deepest awareness was of his son Randy's absence from the house. Stop thinking about it, he told himself. He got a can of beer from the refrigerator and then went back into the living room and sat on the couch. It was not yet midnight. The Raabs' party had been a disappointment—Adele Fortune had not been there, so George had left early. The beer went unopened—George was distracted by Guy Lombardo on the TV set, though he didn't hear the music. He was back in the alert barn four years ago to the night.

Four years ago this night, George remembered, he had been one of the two on five—one of the two pilots on five-minute takeoff capability.

It had been the last night he would ever be on flight duty, though he had not known it then, the last night he would ever fly an Air Force aircraft, the night before January 1, 1967.

He had been a thirty-nine-year-old lieutenant colonel of an elite radar fighter-interceptor squadron flying F-106's. The squadron was part of Aerospace Defense Command, and its mission at George's base was to intercept possible incoming enemy aircraft from the north over Canada and from the east over the Atlantic. Detect, identify, attack, and destroy. He'd been there for almost three months, and he'd had reason to believe that within a year or so the squadron would be his, along with a full colonelcy.

He hadn't been back from Vietnam for very long. The *100 Missions North Vietnam* patch was on the arm of his flight suit. For him the patch celebrated something that was over and done with, like the entries in his log. And with all the other things George felt about it, he had felt pride, pride in himself as a pilot. That went back to when he had graduated from college an Air Force ROTC second lieutenant and had been sent to flight school and to his surprise had found—English major and psychology minor—that he liked to fly, was very, very good at it, and was, to his amazement, shock, and pride, not a nice little good boy who stood quietly off to the side, but bloody-minded. When the occasion warranted.

Or permitted.

It had surprised him and given him deep pleasure that he could kick up a fuss himself—and that having kicked up a fuss himself he could be better at it than the other guy. "I don't go for this shooting-up-villages shit at all," he had told Ceil. But he hadn't told her the rest: *Personal combat. That's what the fighter pilot wants. The ultimate test of his skill.*

George remembered getting home from Vietnam and discovering that some of the people—more than he had expected—disliked him for having been there, fought there, risked his life there. For them. All the time you were protecting them. And they thought you were dirty or something for it. For Christsake, they gave you an assignment and the assignment was to go someplace and risk your life to protect them and then some of them hated you when you got back. Shit.

George thought of something happy. He remembered the first times he had had a high-performance aircraft to himself. He remembered the sensations and visions when, ecstatic, he rolled the airplane and made the horizon and clouds and earth and up and down and the world and the *universe* do what *he* wanted them to do.

He looked over at his telescope. In a while he would have a look at the goddamn universe.

When he had been back from Vietnam for a while George had run into a college classmate; the two of them had gone drinking in a bar one night, and George got to thinking about those beautiful early hours in high-performance aircraft and had said, "The picture of the fighter pilot, you know—it's one of someone who's always drinking and wenching. But really, it's not that way. We try to be good at what we do, we work at it, and what a fighter pilot wants to do is fly." The drinking had gone on, a lot of it. The classmate was a civilian whom George liked and whom he wanted to like him. The classmate was opposed to the U.S. involvement in Vietnam, and all through the drinking, he kept after George about it until George said, or at any rate had *heard* himself saying, "If I had to dig down in the morality of it, I'd stifle in the abyss. I'd suffocate. I'd expire. There's no *handles* to get hold of in it." Because he believed it, or because his friend wanted to hear it and then they could leave the subject? George didn't know. *But the goddamn bastards who sent him there*—like his classmate, who at least had let it happen—and despised him for going, and then pretended it wasn't any of their responsibility.

Guy Lombardo caught his attention. George saw himself in bed as a child, secretly listening to it all on a radio—New Year's Eve!—and eating peanuts, all of it happening in his own bed, even Times Square. *Christ, that Randy were in* his *bed tonight,* George thought.

The little living room resonated briefly with the rumble of huge locomotives heard from a distance. SAC B-52's, George knew, flying north from Westover Air Force Base in Massachusetts, some of them certainly going up to the polar icecap, there to spend New Year's Eve, nuclear-laden, circling. He thought of Randy again. Oh, Christ, Randy.

Over the polar icecap if there is a moon and no cloud cover, you could see the blue whiteness beneath you. In Vietnam his last flight had been in shimmering and smoke-filled low-altitude air. The high-altitude air, where they mainly flew, was as crystalline as anywhere above the earth. Except when the flying telephone poles, candy-wrapped in stripes, broke out from white cloud beneath. Or came gunbarreling up from green below. The green of the jungle and the sometimes pure blue of a narrow little river in it. George could not remember having seen a pure-blue river ever before.

George heard the quiet sound of the television across the room, the Royal Canadians playing "Auld Lang Syne." Midnight. He remembered the can of beer. There was a pop and hiss as he opened it. High pressure rushing into lower pressure. Rapid decompression. George remembered the inflight RD he had had. Hell of a thing. Hell of a thing. Forty thousand feet or so and there was a sound like dynamite going off in the cockpit and sonofabitch there was a fog in there under the canopy like you couldn't see your faithful instruments or your loyal gloved hand or God's own outside. Something had gone bang on him and he was sitting in an aquarium filled with smoke and there was the God-*awful* sheer *temptation* to raise the ejection-seat handgrips and propel himself out of the deadly fucking thing, but George hadn't done that or made even a twitch in its direction. The *boom* had been pressure escaping from the cockpit at high velocity, and the smoke had been condensation, the moisture in the cabin air frozen to infinite crystals by the sudden below-zero temperature. So George had slowed up, checked his air hose, gone on emergency oxygen, went through the other procedures in his mental checklist, and gone on down to twenty-four thousand quickly. And home.

Got home one hundred times. Sometimes it didn't seem possible.

He lay back on the couch. Getting to sleep under the canvas in Vietnam in the hot night was often like getting to sleep in a hospital room the night before they're going to cut into you. George remembered the air being close and somewhat fetid. The little stench of fabric decaying from moisture and heat and bacterial process. That was like the smell in the ward in the hospital, too. Though the ward was air conditioned. There had been smoke in the cabin. And red warning lights. The temperature had gotten painful. And then the gear couldn't be gotten down. *Unnecessary jettison tanks, keep the approach normal,* could they hear him on the ground? he couldn't hear them, was that emergency equipment down there or just maintenance stuff? *all right, the speed brakes did seem to have gotten open,* so bright and sunny and *usual* down there like none of this was going on, push forward and *shoulder harness feels locked,* ALL RIGHT! Throttle off fuel switches closed keep the canopy on and KEEP THE APPROACH NORMAL KEEP THE TOUCHDOWN NORMAL AND AND *DRAG CHUTE NOW!* and hit the master and—

There had been titanic sound, attitudes of vision frightening and incomprehensible, and then the amplified sound of his own breathing. In the great stillness. The hospital.

George had stayed. Flown again. One hundred missions altogether. And then he had gone home.

George remembered some of those nights at home—not in this home but in the house he and Ceil had owned. There were nights after he had been back home for a few days when he felt glacier cold. They had not been nights that he had been prepared for or ever experienced before. It was mid-August and ninety degrees in the bedroom sometimes, and he felt struck through with cold. He would lie in bed at night and think that there was something huge and menacing out there. Threatening more to Ceil and Randy than to himself. He had taught himself numbness to it. But sometimes it broke through anyway. And then he *felt* it out there, stalking approaching. And then Ceil had disappeared and he had never flown again.

15

Three o'clock in the dark and cold of the morning.

Deep under blankets and quilted covers, Yvonne Jaquith felt content, unafraid, her flesh still warm from Jonah having made love to her. *At least this night is safe,* she thought, *and tomorrow. At least this night is safe from Jonah having to fly. And tomorrow, too. Jonah has tomorrow off. There won't be any time when I'll be afraid.*

She heard Jonah off somewhere in the house and wondered what he was doing.

Never mind that the temperature outside was twenty-five degrees below zero, the night covered Yvonne with warmth, she felt safe in it, it was a friend protecting her, protecting them all, herself and Jonah and the little unborn baby, and she went to sleep.

Jonah had gone down to the basement to look in a box where he had hidden toys for the baby. A plastic fish with colored beads inside it for the baby's bath. Gotten at La Guardia during a long wait for charter passengers—it used to be, before he had begun looking for things for the baby, that he had wandered the corridors and stores of airports without motive. A stuffed animal from an overnight in Philadelphia. A paperweight with a snowstorm inside it from Montreal. An expensive music box from being weathered in three days in Cleveland. Airplanes he has carved and painted to hang like mobiles in the baby's room. Many other things. Jonah sees them in his mind without opening the box. Then he opens the box and looks at them anyway.

He went back upstairs. Turned out the basement light and went into the baby's unfinished room, a room he was adding on to the house himself. He was in darkness then, but soon the starlight off the snow illuminated the unfinished room enough so that he could see the naked studs. It was cold there, no insulation stapled in yet. Jonah thought about a year from that moment, the baby asleep in the room, the heating duct completed, insulation and wallboard in, everything brightly painted, the crib just there . . .

After a while Jonah looked out into the distance of the night. The wind was so strong it looked as if it were blowing the stars across the sky.

"It's late, Jo. It's *too* late."

Jonah, asleep in bed beside her, heard Yvonne's voice in the darkness before he realized the telephone was ringing.

"It's almost *five,*" Yvonne said.

Between sleep and wakefulness he reached out to her. He turned to hold her and in turning became awake.

"Jo? Jo? Please, not tonight, everything seemed so *safe*—"

"It's okay, honey."

"Don't answer it, Jo."

Her hand caught his as he turned from her to reach for the phone. "Don't," she said.

Her voice was quiet. Jonah heard the quiet it left about the room. *"Don't,"* he heard her say again as he reached for the telephone and picked it up. "Hello," he said.

"Hello? Jonah, Harvey. Harvey Sauer."

"Yes, Harvey," Jonah said to Cornwall's chief of police.

"Jonah, I wouldn't call you at this ungodly hour if it wasn't necessary, you know that. How's the missus doing, by the way?"

"Fine. What is it, Harvey?"

"I've got to pick up two people in Poughkeepsie."

"At five in the morning?"

"Right away. They were just apprehended, and right now the cops're willing to waive extradition if we come get 'em right away."

"Harvey, it's rougher'n a cob out there."

"Look, I've had a call out for these characters for weeks. Well, one of 'em ran a car into a storefront over there. Some one-horse town near Poughkeepsie, some jerkwater place with just three cops on the whole force. Anyway, the night man picked them up. They weren't in much condition to resist, man says they got banged up a little, but he thinks they're shot up on drugs."

"What'd they do back here?"

"Well, not *them,* as far as I know, just *him.* He passed a flood of bad checks here. Got away with it because of his poppa, of course. But Poppa won't make good. So the kid's lookin' like a felon."

"What kid?"

"The Whittier boy."

"Gilbert Whittier's kid?"

"The same. Good family, Jonah. You know. Old stock."

"Sure." Owned the bank. Big in state and local politics. "I see." Sauer could call Ev. Ev and Whittier were buddy-buddy sometimes. There could be considerable pressure for Jonah to make the flight. "I see."

"Thing of it is, Jonah, I wouldn't ask you to come out like this, but right now they're willing to come back. Tomorrow they might fight extradition and make us go through all the proceedings, involve the governor and all, and then we'd have to go down there God knows how often, me and the city attorney—"

"You calling me just to save some driving time? A couple of trips?"

"It's not just that, Jonah. Those three cops down there, they haven't got the facilities to keep these two. They don't know anything about drugs. They just want to get *rid* of them."

"Poughkeepsie."

"You can find it, I know you can."

Jonah laughed.

"The thing is to get these people back here while they're willing to come."

Jonah said nothing. He let the receiver lie on the pillow a few inches from his ear. He looked at Yvonne. She was looking at the ceiling. He felt empty.

The voice from the receiver on the pillow was small and harsh. "I'll remind you, Jonah, that you're a deputy. I can order you."

Christ. He had become a deputy so he could sign for blood. When there was an emergency need for a certain type and he was sent off to pick it up somewhere. So a cop like Sauer wouldn't have to go along on a flight just to sign for it.

The small harsh voice from the receiver said, "Jonah? Jonah?"

Jonah picked up the receiver. "This is an emergency?"

"What do you mean, Jonah? Emergency—"

"Part Ninety-one eleven of the federal air regulations stipulates that you can't fly a passenger who is under the influence of drugs. Unless he's under a physician's care. Or except if it's an emergency."

"Why, yes, you might deem this an emergency. I deem it such."

"You home, Harvey?"

"Yes, sir."

"I've got to check the weather. If that wind's as strong as it was before, I just won't go."

"I can accept that."

"I won't take a chance of bending a bird for anyone. Not when I'm riding in it."

"I understand. Shit, Jonah, remember I'm going too."

"Okay, I'll check weather. If you don't hear from me in ten minutes, I'll meet you at the airport in half an hour."

Jonah hung up and turned to Yvonne. She had her eyes closed now and did not respond to his attention. He picked up the telephone and dialed the Flight Service Station in Concord and got the weather along his route. The winds were calming, but were still at twenty-five knots and from three hundred degrees, a hell of a quartering wind—take an hour plus to get there, maybe come back like a bat out of hell. The cold was still extreme. Jonah filed instrument flight plans for both the departure and return flights.

The flight attendant read back the plans and then said, "I've got a pirep for you. Air Canada pilot reports he encountered light to moderate chop descending through nine thousand in the Hartford area."

"Thank you," Jonah said.

"Have a good flight. Happy new year."

"You too. A happy new year."

Jonah hung up.

Yvonne had turned away from him. *"You're going to fly people who've been taking drugs?"*

He sat on the side of the bed motionless.

There was silence.

Jonah got up and dressed.

16

Three in the morning, cold splitting the night. George Detwiler, in his living room, Scotch and soda at hand, peered deeply into the outside darkness through a tripod-mounted telescope he had bought for himself a few weeks earlier. Every night, when visibility allowed, he had been at it. That there *were* craters on the moon and that he could discern them from his own living room gave George feelings of awe and astonishment which others derived from certain religious experiences. In the blackness out there, the surface of the moon was a brighter whiteness than any sunlit snow he had ever seen. George's eye scanned the craters and seas and mountains of the moon as if he himself were overflying them in a space vehicle. The moon was as close as a town seen from the sky. It more than filled the telescope's largest lens, moving across the lens as he tracked it. He felt that the moon was like most aspects of his life now, moving out of close observation before he had had the chance to properly examine them.

He picked up the Scotch and soda and drank. He rarely drank much, and in the past three years he had drunk less than ever—ever since he had discovered how easy it was to drink. But he had dozed somewhere around this New Year's Eve midnight, and when he awoke in the empty house, his son Randy's absence had been like an excruciating wound; he had begun drinking at first to numb the pain and then simply for company. As he had drunk and become calmer, he recognized that the pain did not belong to the wound at all—that, indeed, there was no wound—but that what he had been feeling had been *fear,* and the turmoil of fear, fear that he would never see Randy again, and that he himself would remain forever as alone as he was when he awoke from having dozed off. The alcohol subdued all that, and then it became a pleasant companion to spend part of the night with.

George drank some more and set the glass down. Through the telescope he searched the universe, his eye and mind confounded and enthralled by what he encountered: a fugue of stars and blacknesses and darknesses and lights . . . and of white shapes moving and terrible emptinesses.

What George has decided he must do for himself is find shape in the void.

This he must do if he is ever to escape his certain knowledge of the brutality of life—and of the randomness of that brutality. He must do this if he is ever again to sleep past five in the morning, the chill hour neither dawn nor night when he awakes knowing that he is nowhere, that anything can happen, and that he is helpless, helpless even to protect Randy, as he had been helpless to protect Ceil.

Randy had wanted to spend this New Year's Eve at a friend's house. George lacked an excuse to keep him at home. After the boy had been picked up by the friend's father, George had lain down on the couch in the living room. It had been late afternoon. Lying there, he felt his heart begin to tremble and build speed. He thought of his invitation to the Raabs' party. He got up and showered and dressed and went to the party. He had not been to a party in three years.

Three years ago Randy had been six. George had been thirty-nine. Ceil had been thirty-three. The year had been nineteen hundred and sixty-seven reckoned in Christian time. George now knew many of the other years it had been as well: what Jewish year, what lunar Chinese and Vietnamese, what Japanese. It had been the first month and the fourteenth day. George had looked at all the dates and numbers for pattern, significance, meaning, *anything* . . .

George had had some deferred leave coming. Both he and Ceil loved to travel, but not to places where their friends or neighbors might go, not to places where they would know what to expect. They had decided to go to Beirut. A week in Beirut and then a week in Istanbul. And then back home. But Ceil had never come back home.

They had left Randy with Ceil's parents and gone to Beirut. They had been walking through a crowded street in Beirut, holding hands, when George had felt Ceil's hand slip from his. He had looked to her instantly. But he never saw her again.

George's commanding officer had allowed him parcels of compassionate leave—a few days at a time—and George had found military transport he could deadhead on, so he had been able to return to Beirut six times. George had been unable to give the authorities and other organizations anything upon which even to base a speculation, and they in turn had been able to find out nothing about Ceil Detwiler's disappearance. Nothing.

When George had finally come home to stay, he had developed tachycardia and was grounded. They had put him in operations, a desk job. Not the place for a pilot, not a reasonable environment for a man who had spent eighteen years flying airplanes. What they had in mind was that Lieutenant Colonel George Detwiler should be given every opportunity to stay in another two years until he had earned his full twenty years' retirement benefits.

But the tachycardia got worse. It hammered in his chest and in his mind. He could not stand for any length of time some days, it so weakened him. Getting up in response to a need to urinate, he would feel faint, as if hyperventilating in his first high-altitude emergency class. He would lie down again until absolute discomfort forced him to try to get up again. By the age of forty he was no longer a member of the Air Force. He had an early retirement and a medical discharge with a partial disability. He quit anything to do with pilots or with flying. He had already, even before his discharge, entered law school. There seemed to be reason in the law.

George, at his telescope, set a drink down and thought, I want to know what's out there.

Behind him, across the room, the tiny orange light of the heater in the aquarium came on. It vaguely illuminated black shapes hovering motionless near it.

And behind him there were voices in the night and static and music. George listened to foreign countries at night. At first, when he had built the shortwave receiver three years before, he had waited for Ceil's familiar voice —from somewhere, anywhere—had waited for her name, news of her. Now the original impetus was only semiconscious. He listened every night, but now he just waited. The insults of the People's Republic of China, the always stately music from Cologne, the mainland-aimed propaganda from Havana, popular music from the Netherlands, Cairo explaining, New Delhi justifying, Seoul protesting, the BBC carefully examining what everyone else had to say, small and comfortable news from the Caribbean, sinister announcements in sinister vocabularies from places not identified—George listened to them all, for some small thing might suddenly be of use to him, some very little thing: in a droplet of water under an electron microscope they say you can see the structure of the universe. George made himself another drink.

He looked through the telescope into the night again. He felt as if he was looking out from an airplane and controlling the aircraft's attitude with the declination and ascension cables. On into the night. He felt airborne, as if he is roaring through nowhere alone.

George stood up and sipped at his drink. The living room he was in did not feel like his. It never has.

George's eye looked inward at memories and outward at space. He shook his head. He didn't believe in God. In Vietnam he had ceased to believe in God. What George had been doing there George'd had to do, and it was right for him to have done it. But God didn't have to do it, did not have to allow it. Therefore there was no God—maybe something else, some other force, a storm of malevolence somewhere in the universe, but no God.

George remembered Korea—when he had still had a concept of God— the world and other aircraft spinning round him and away from him and at him as if he and his shiny bright fuselage were fixed in space, the eye of God, forever observant and unmoved and unmovable, the eye of God, but not the hand.

The hand is his own. And it is very good at what it does. Fly an airplane. Among the best, the very best.

All the while the eye of God watching, approving. But connected to nothing. It is cerebral approval, intellectual approval. The universe is numb. Excellence is all.

But finally excellence too was nothing.

George looked deep into the icy blackness where *he sees nothing.*

At four, George Detwiler went to bed, not drunk at all, finally, but cold. He imagined a bird flying up into that icy blackness—some black night bird struggling to get home, climbing, climbing . . . and falling to earth again, frozen, homeless.

Five in the morning and George Detwiler awakes with a dread of the arbitrary and vagrant upon him.

He stares up, sees death, fire, mutilation, kidnapping, sudden disease, accidental suffocation, loss.

He has dreamt of a dog, a missing dog. Ceil's dog had not come home the day before they had left for Beirut. She had almost stayed home to wait for it to return. It never had. This afternoon Randy's dog had not come home.

He turned on the lamp at his bedside and dialed the Larsens', where Randy is staying.

"Steve."

"George, something . . . ?"

"No, I just want to check on Randy."

"Randy? George, it's . . . George, it's *five in the morning.*"

"I know. But I wanted—"

"Look, George, if you're drunk, you might just as well lie down. Get some sleep. Let the rest of us get some sleep."

"I'm not drunk, but never mind that. Steve, would you just go check on Randy, take a look at him?"

"Randy's sleeping in the same room with Hank, and there hasn't been a sound out of them for hours."

"Yes. Would you just look in on Randy for me please, Steve."

George heard the sound of the telephone receiver being put down abruptly upon a hard surface.

There is silence. George hears himself breathing, listens to the self-destroying swiftness of his heart, feels it beating within him, the life sustainer that is the killer within him, feels the beats of it in little pulses of nausea in his stomach. It is an emotionally inspired condition, he knows. He does not know how to turn off the emotion.

"Randy's all right, George."

"Did you hear him breathing?"

"Did— Yes, George. I heard him breathing."

"Thank you, Steve. I know this was . . . imposing, on my part."

"It's all right, George. Now—"

"Just one thing, Steve. I want to pick up Randy as early as possible. What time do you think you'll be up over there?"

"Jesus, George, *I* don't know. We're just going to sleep till we wake up. That's what we *planned*, anyway. You come by about nine, I'm sure the boys'll be up by then, even if we're not."

"Okay, Steve. Thank you. Good night. And happy new year."

"Yeah."

George lies down. In the darkness he sees fire creeping through the Larsens' house. He sees a diseased rodent in the room where Randy sleeps. He gets up, begins dressing, seeing himself in a few minutes in his car waiting outside the Larsens' house, watching, trying to protect.

17

At the airport the wind swirled condensation from his breath as Jonah got out of his car, a rusted compact station wagon. Harvey Sauer, already waiting, got out of his personal sedan and locked up.

"Christ, what a way to start the new year," Sauer said. "Pretty windy, huh?"

"Harvey, I just hope you don't puke all over Ev's brand-new airplane." Jonah glanced again at Sauer. Sauer was in full uniform. "Got your gun with you, Big Chief?"

Sauer ran his right-hand fingertips down the crosspiece of his Sam Brown till his fingertips rested on the flap of his holster, the butt of a revolver underneath.

"You keep that thing right where it is," Jonah said.

"What you got there, Jonah?"

"Airway manual. Thermos of coffee."

"No, that other stuff."

"Towels."

"For what, for Christsake?"

"For cleaning up. Case someone doesn't draw himself a sic-sac fast enough."

Jonah and Sauer rolled the aircraft out of the hangar and onto the ramp. They went back and laboriously closed the hangar doors. The wind was painful.

Then, settled into the cabin of the Skymaster, they were out of the wind, but the cold was very much with them. The aircraft swayed in gusts of wind; there were creaking sounds from the fuselage, groanings from the wings. Jonah didn't hear them. Sauer heard them too well.

Jonah said, "This fucking cold." He handed Sauer the checklist to give Sauer something with which to occupy himself. "Read it off, Big Chief." Jonah, in his mind, was already several places down the list, but he didn't allow his hands to move. Sauer cleared his throat and began to read. Jonah began to do and to reply.

The checklist went without interruption until Sauer said, "Auxiliary fuel pump switch."

"On high," Jonah said.

Sauer stopped and looked at Jonah. "It says here low."

"This is a subzero start, Harvey."

"But it says here—"

"You do it different. C'mon, Harvey, if you want to get back by next New Year's. I'm freezing my ass off."

Sauer said, "Ignition switch."

"Okay, just a second." Jonah hand-primed the engine eight times and advanced the throttle for a higher-than-normal fuel flow. "Okay, you sonofabitch, *start*," Jonah said and he hit the ignition switch and hand-primed swiftly twice as the engine tried to engage itself in its power cycle.

Then it had caught and Jonah brought back the power to a low-normal setting and threw the fuel pump switch to OFF and watched the white needle of the oil pressure gauge move slowly up and into the green arc within the proscribed thirty seconds. He glanced at the oil temperature gauge. As he expected, the oil was showing no temperature at all.

The procedure of command and response and reply was repeated for the rear engine. *It* caught, smoothed, and held. *"Sonofagun,"* Jonah said with

[49]

admiration. The second oil pressure needle climbed into the green. There was still no oil temperature in either engine. "I guess we're ready to taxi," Jonah said.

He released the brakes and taxied carefully. A wind like this could flip them over on the ground. Jonah managed the ailerons and elevators with great care to diminish the lift the wind was trying to put under the flying surfaces.

Braked short of the runway, Jonah completed the runup and the rest of the "Before Takeoff" checklist. He tuned up the radios and set his radio navigation course. The airplane was buffeted heavily by sudden chops of air. Jonah saw that Sauer was gripping the bound checklist with both hands, his knuckles gone bloodless from the strain of bone against tissue. Jonah set the altimeter.

Jonah glanced across the instrument panel once again, looking for an errant needle. Sauer stared straight ahead. Jonah checked the outside visibility—runway lights clear in an arrow shape pointing away from the windscreen, dark but lightening sky, no horizon. He set the instrument panel illumination so that it was low enough not to interfere with perception outside the aircraft.

"Hold tight and say your prayers, Harvey," Jonah said, smiling for Sauer, "this is going to be a flight you can tell your grandchildren about."

"I hope so."

Jonah looked at his watch. Seven minutes after the hour.

He moved the aircraft out on the runway, his left hand on the yoke, right hand fisted over the throttles, no careful turning down the runway to line up, not with *that* bastard quartering wind, but carrying power as he turned, turning so abruptly and carrying so much power that the sideloads dipped Jonah's side of the airplane *into* the attacking wind, and then first moving forward, *Okay, okay, no roughness,* engines building without hesitation or interruption, fuel flow adjusted, the wind jabbing, *punching,* sharp reports from the exterior of the aircraft, the wind wants to lift it off, turn it over, Jonah holding it down, holding it on the runway and insisting on its direction, *60* mph indicated, *65,* almost got thrown, maybe quit this shit right now, go home and back to bed, *70, 75,* normal takeoff speed but Jonah holds the aircraft on, it's brute strength he's using now, no finesse at all, *holds it on* and maintains direction, *80,* still on the runway but won't stay on much longer, and *85!* and he hauls the yoke back violently and the whole aircraft, not just the nosewheel, jolts into the air, *"Ohhh"* dragged out of Sauer's throat by the minor G-load, violence of maneuver, fear, and the aircraft being pushed sideways and into the ground except that Jonah, now that the aircraft has lost contact with the ground, adds firm aileron and rudder and turns the aircraft directly into the wind.

Gear up.

They rise swiftly and are staggered by gusts of wind.

They are being *savaged*—Jonah has already reduced power to the normal twenty-four inches and 2600 rpm. But it is still too much. He reduces again and lowers the angle and rate of climb.

This is somewhat better. The stars don't dance as violently on the windscreen. The lap belt and shoulder harness are not as stressful against the body. The brief instants when visual and aural and kinetic senses are scrambled, the stomach clutched by nausea and then released, are fewer.

Jonah looks out. The sky is black above, stars piercing and crystalline, ground illuminated below, starlight on snow. Houses can be seen, black blocks; fields, irregular shapes of whiteness; night forests, stands of trees, are irregular shapes of blackness such as a child might draw. *His* child, Jonah thinks. He thinks of Yvonne, of his house, down there behind him.

Jonah checks his instruments. Leaving four thousand. He adjusts the trim for less nose-up attitude. Now that he has the altitude for radio communications in this irregular terrain, Jonah activates the boom mike in front of his lips.

"Cornwall, this is Skymaster One-four Two-two Charlie," speaking very slowly, knowing that his voice is being distorted by the varied pressures on his body caused by the turbulence in which he is flying.

"Aircraft calling Cornwall Area Radio, say again."

"Cornwall, this . . . is . . . *Skymaster*"—they are pitching *up* again and the word is strained from within him—"One-four Two-two Charlie—" And then abruptly *down,* beneath the night, the belts' strictures making speech difficult. "I say again, Skymaster One-four Two-two Charlie."

"Skymaster One-four Two-two Charlie, I read you now. Go ahead."

"One-four Two-two Charlie is instruments Cornwall to Poughkeepsie . . . H——y——gah——rrrr clearance?" the turbulence misusing Jonah's body and the voice that tries to emerge from it.

"Standby one."

Jonah studies the wind. He cannot see it but can see its delineation. He examines its sudden midair shapes and contours on his instruments. It causes him some worry.

"Skymaster One-four Two-two Charlie."

"We're here."

"I've got your clearance."

"Ready to copy."

"Roger, ready to copy. ATC clears Skymaster One-four Two-two Charlie to Dutchess County Airport as filed via—" and he repeats what Jonah has asked for. "Climb and maintain ten thousand, report leaving seven—"

Jonah listens and then reads back the clearance. "And we were off at zero seven."

"Two-two Charlie, contact ATC Boston Center on one-one-eight zero-five at this time."

"One-one-eight zero-five. Thank you, sir, changing frequencies."

Jonah reaches for the communications knob, and as he does so, they are ballooned brutally upward. Two hundred feet. Little extra climb there, Jonah thinks, hoping the wings stay on. Sauer is rigid.

"Relax, Harvey, fighting it makes it worse," Jonah says, knowing the advice can't be taken.

"Yeah," says Sauer, barely.

The winds of the night are flooding: they boil and crest and cascade and crush, and then they pitch the nose up toward the stars. The airplane is almost standing on its tail, the engines almost soundless in this attitude, and Jonah jams everything forward—throttles, yoke. And then they are relatively at ease again, relatively straight and level. Harvey's eyes are closed, his jaw is set tightly, and sweat runs down the pale white skin of his face.

"Boston Center, Skymaster One-four Two-two Charlie is with you, instruments, Cornwall to Poughkeepsie."

And immediately: "Skymaster One-four Two-two Charlie, what is your present heading and altitude?"

"Two-two Charlie is coming up on the Keene VOR, inbound on a heading of two-five-five degrees and we're just coming through six thousand."

"Roger, Two-two Charlie, squawk ident eleven hundred."

Jonah reaches out to the transponder, which will enlarge their blip on the controller's radar screen. "Two-two Charlie squawking eleven hundred."

"You just about over the Keene VOR?"

"I'm getting a From indication right now."

"Roger, Two-two Charlie, radar contact. Maintain this frequency, report leaving seven."

"Report leaving seven, yes, sir, and I'd like to amend my flight plan and stay at eight instead of going to ten."

"Two-two Charlie, altitude change approved, climb to and maintain eight thousand, report reaching."

"Two-two Charlie for eight, and we're just coming up on seven."

Bang! Aircraft driven *down*. Jonah rights it, hand loose on the yoke, riding the ups and downs, not fighting them and placing increased stress on the wings and control surfaces.

"We can go back if you want," Jonah says to Sauer. "No harm done."

"Keep . . . going." Sauer is staring straight ahead.

The night is still black out in front, the wind smiting vigorously as if to propel them into an abyss or fling them disastrously into the stars. Sauer cries out, then is silent again. Jonah feels that he is *aiming* the aircraft through the night rather than flying it.

"Boston, Two-two Charlie is ten DME out of Pawling, still at eight, and I'd like to begin our descent now."

"Two-two Charlie, cleared to descend pilot's discretion unrestricted to Dutchess County Airport via flight plan route, maintain VFR."

Jonah acknowledges. He puts the mixtures on rich and closes the cowl flaps. They begin their descent.

"Two-two Charlie, Poughkeepsie Flight Service Station requests you give them a call when you're within range. Their frequency is"—Jonah has already noted it for himself—"one-twenty-two point three."

"I'll give them a call now," Jonah says. Reaching to change frequencies Jonah glances beside him and thinks that Harvey's muscles are going to ache bitterly tomorrow from the tensions they have been loaded with this late night. "Hey, and Boston Center, a happy new year," Jonah says.

"Is it still that? Yeah, I guess it is. Same to you, Two-two Charlie. You're coming back this way soon, I see."

"Yeah. This is just a quick turnaround in Poughkeepsie, so I guess I'll be working you on the way back."

"We'll be talking."

"Okay, Two-two Charlie leaving your frequency at this time."

"Change of frequencies approved, radar contact terminated at this time." Jonah calls the Poughkeepsie Flight Service Station.

"Two-two Charlie, a law officer wishes us to inform you that the runway lights at Dutchess County have been turned on as you requested and that your passengers are waiting. For your advisement, winds at Dutchess County are currently from the southwest at twenty knots, gusting to thirty. Runway Two-four indicated. No reported local traffic. Altimeter three-zero four-zero."

"I've got the runway lights in sight and I'm about eight out for Runway Two-four. Thanks. Two-two Charlie."

The night seems to have steadied down, the lower they get. Jonah watches the engine temperatures carefully and carries power even as he descends slowly. Sauer is peering ahead, his body no longer quite so rigid now that the runway lights are in sight. Jonah checks to be sure that he placed the mixtures on rich when he began the letdown. He decides, once again, that because of the wind he won't use any flaps. In spite of the reported strength of the surface wind, he notices that the severity of shock is growing less and less as they descend. Maybe it's smoothing out with the shift from coercive northwest flow to steady southwest flow. Maybe the ride back won't be so hairy. Fuel selectors, LEFT MAIN front engine, RIGHT MAIN rear engine. He ticks it off in his mind. Harvey seems to be settling down. "The next mind-boggling noise you hear will be, I hope, the gear going down," Jonah says. Nose high into the night, carrying a lot of power, but speed down to 130 indicated, Jonah lowers the gear. There is a sound as if of a great animal exhaling, a seeming pause in their progress through the air, and then a huge *snap* and silence. The green gear-down indicator light goes on. Jonah has already lowered the nose a bit to compensate for the added drag caused by the gear. They settle on down toward the runway lights as if their flight had never known anything but a benign passage such as this.

18

Nine o'clock of a warm and gentle evening on St. Thomas. Rupert and Madelon Zur's party was just beginning, though no guests had arrived yet. Ben stood alone on the stone terrace outside the living room. He was looking down on the long black sea. The night was extreme with stars, and Ben was thinking of the Caribs and the other ancient sea wanderers who navigated canoes with those stars.

He looked back to the living room to see if any guests had arrived, or the promised woman. Rupert was strict in a tuxedo. Madelon wore a severe pants suit of green silk. It displayed the contours of her body almost as exactly as nudity. It was a promise of sexuality and sensuality. She was bending to float exotic flowers in lacquered Oriental bowls. Sensuality closed in upon Ben . . .

He letched. Flying did that to him. Tension did it. Madelon did it.

The feeling of the heat of the day was a burning sensation on his skin. A rum drink was cold in his hand. A warm breeze brushed his face. The sea down below, running on the sand, was a soft sound talking to him . . . *hush . . . hush . . .*

He looked out across the long black water. It seemed entirely friendly now, benign, not a danger to it.

All that way to here on this stone terrace above the black and glistening sea, to here on St. Thomas on New Year's Eve. So long a way to come. It seemed impossible that so long a way could be safely retraced. *Christ, it seems like you can't do it twice,* Ben thought.

He had come so very far in one day. Yesterday.

The night before last at this hour I was still trying to go to sleep. In that motel room outside of Palm Beach.

Ben's glass was empty. People had gathered behind him in the living room. Others were arriving. When she entered the room, Ben knew it. She *was* extraordinary-looking. Black hair lifted, golden skin. Ben had never seen skin quite that color, as if the pigment of an egg yolk had been admixed. She wore an ankle-length yellow paisley skirt and golden sandals. The skirt was flat across her stomach, tight around her, cut below the navel. Her midriff was bare to her breasts. The matching yellow paisley top had long fluffy sleeves, but it was cut wide at the shoulders and deep to the breasts. She stood beneath a large black-and-white oil which Rupert had paid ten thousand dollars for and which had been the first work of Ben's that Rupert had ever purchased—before he had ever met Ben. As she talked to Rupert, she looked up at the painting. She was all gold and yellow beneath the soft black sculpture of her hair. She seemed to turn from the painting to look at him out on the terrace. But of course she could not see him out in the darkness, the light from the living room didn't reach to where he was standing, and she could not know he was there. There was an Oriental look to her eyes, a look of sadness and of acceptance, as if she often cried.

"Doris . . ." Rupert said.
Doris. *The sea.*
She took Ben's hand. Her fingers *held* his hand, her eyes looking at him. Asking?

Madelon stood alone with Ben. They were on the terrace. They were brushed by lantern light. Some couples were dancing nearby, but Ben and Madelon were alone. It was almost midnight.
"She is most beautiful, is she not?" Madelon said.
"Yes, she is," Ben said.
"I believe she is on loan to you. But of course I am only guessing."
"On loan. I don't think I understand."
Madelon exaggerated her European accent. "You Americans are *so naif.*" She looked at Ben sternly, then smiled. She rested her arm on Ben's shoulder. Her fingertips just touched the back of his neck. "But I think I will come visit you myself, dear Ben—in the spring? Would you enjoy that, do you think? Being with me?"
"You and Rupert are always welcome."
Madelon looked at Ben. She was amused. "You are not naive at all, are you, dear Ben? No, you are not. Now I see. You are a diplomat."
Madelon kissed Ben, lingered against him, and then left him.

Ben felt as if he and Doris had already experienced some sort of intimacy with each other. Doris also seemed to possess that knowledge.

Ben danced with her on the terrace, his hand on the warm, firm skin of her waist.

Ben took her hand. Not innocently. It was foreplay.

They had somehow become alone on the terrace.

At midnight she kissed him with her full mouth and then looked at him, smiling, eyes of sadness gleaming, looking into his, and she held Ben firmly, as firmly as he held her, their bodies separated only by the fabric of their clothes, and Ben's hands fell to her buttocks and pressed her against him.

Doris.

The sea.

19

Lined up on final approach for Runway Two-four, Jonah is about two miles out when he sees the twin rotating beacons flashing on top of the waiting police cruiser. It is parked on the ramp outside the terminal building. Jonah adds a little nose-up trim. They are being jostled by a steady chop now, but nothing like the duress which beset them earlier. Two-two Charlie makes its way as directed. A little more nose-up elevator trim. Speed just under one hundred. A little hot, but he's not using flaps to slow him. Just over the threshold of the runway, Jonah eases back on the yoke, his right hand gentling the throttles back. He rounds the aircraft gently upward. The mainwheels touch, hold, screech. Jonah settles the nosewheel to the runway. The aircraft slows with little braking. They turn at the intersection of Runway Three-three, the landing roll long since spent, a model landing, though the beneficiary of it, Chief Sauer, is unaware of the accomplishment to which he has just been treated.

"Well," says Jonah, taxiing toward the terminal ramp, toward the flashing blue-white lights, black car on floodlit white ramp, "well, we're down."

"Yeah," says Sauer. Jonah notes him. An even and reclusive man, Sauer is visibly wearied. His exactingly cut uniform seems worn and misused. Sauer steadies himself with his hand on the top of the panel. He unclips his harness, tests his body with motion. "Good job, Jonah."

"Tell me, Harvey. If you'd known it was going to be that rough, would you've come out anyway?"

"My job," he says, and then is quiet.

It probably wouldn't have been his job if it wasn't old man Whittier's kid out here, Jonah thinks. Jonah calls the flight service station and cancels his flight plan. "Down one-eight," he says.

There are three policemen waiting for them outside the cruiser now. One of them is an old man; the other two are in their early thirties. They are backlit by the ramp lights. Halos blossom and diminish behind their heads as the beacons flash. Facing them, the aircraft already aimed into the wind, Jonah sets the brakes and moves the mixture controls to IDLE CUT-OFF, the fingers of his right hand then rapidly traversing the instrument panel as he throws switches to their OFF positions. The engines miss, struggle, and are quiet. There are the sounds of the instrument system winding down in the otherwise silent cabin: whisperings, shrillnesses, slowly abating. Jonah sets the controlwheel lock in place.

He climbs out. The cold is abhorrent. He had gotten a little sweaty flying the airplane. Sauer is talking to the old man, the other two leaning against the cruiser. There is wire mesh between the front seat of the cruiser and the back. Two people are in the back seat. There is a rhythm to their physical encounter with each other. Sauer is looking at some papers the old man has handed him. Jonah goes back to the airplane, gets out the thermos of coffee, and pours himself a cup. Steam blossoms up. He recaps the thermos and goes back to the conference of law officers.

"He's a sweet one," the old man is saying. He is looking intently into Sauer's once-again-reclusive face. Jonah becomes aware that as far as the old man is concerned he's dealing with the chief of police of a big force. Air transport and all that. Harvey has twenty-six men on his force. Policing about twenty-five thousand people. Harvey signs the papers.

"They're animals," says the old man.

"Why do you say that?" says Sauer, handing some papers back and keeping a set for himself and inserting them into his shirt.

"You'll see," says the old man. "They'll show you good," he says, not without some discernible pleasure. "They'll show you good," he repeats. The two other policemen laugh. Sauer glances at them, and they stop laughing.

"I'll accept the prisoners now," Sauer says.

The old man nods. One of the other two unlocks the back door of the car. At first the two inside remain there. "Out," says the policeman who unlocked the door. "Come on in and get me!" says a youngish male voice from within. And then Jonah hears frantic laughter.

Jonah thinks of his wife at home in their bed, of their baby, the little child who will be born. Jonah knows nothing of drugs, and he is frightened.

"Harvey," Jonah says, "I don't know about flying people in this condition."

The other policeman steps forward. No, he's not even thirty. "Uh . . ." —searching for a word—"uh . . . *Captain*, I'm a private pilot and I try to read up on things that concern me, as a policeman, you know? And I've read quite a lot—extensively, you might say—about drugs, and I'd say if these prisoners want to go with you, you shouldn't have any trouble. I mean, I guess it's kinda *bouncy* out there tonight, and these two are still happy and high. I expect they've been smoking grass all night, maybe taking some uppers or something like that, and I expect they'll be just *the most* relaxed passengers. Better'n someone sober and sane in wind like this." He swallowed. The old man was looking at him.

"I don't know," Jonah says, "I've got no experience in this."

"I'll handle them," Sauer says.

"In the *air?*" Jonah says.

"Can I look at the inside of the plane?" the younger policeman says.

"Sure," says Jonah, wanting time to think and think again. They walk over together.

"Actually, I just wanted to tell you something," says the younger policeman. "See, I wouldn't want the others to know, but I've smoked some of that stuff myself, you know, just to see what the effect on others might be. You know?" Jonah nods, not knowing. "And what I found was, if it hits you right, it can get you into a relaxed state, and happy. That's the way those two strike me as being now. I think they'll be pretty relaxed passengers if you want to take them."

"You people sure want to get rid of those two, don't you? Let me ask you this. What if they come down hard and get paranoid on me at seven thousand feet?" He walks back to the cruiser.

Sauer says, "Well?"

"If you can coax 'em into the airplane before my ass freezes off, I'll see how they behave."

Finally the two inside the cruiser are getting out. The girl is probably not yet twenty. She wears an open coat. Her skirt appears to be as high as her crotch, and the upper part of her dress has been unbuttoned at the chest. She seems insensitive to the blowing cold.

The male is about twenty-two, twenty-three. His blond hair is uncut and unkempt rather than purposely long. The skin of his face is extremely white. His eyes are small and sharp, the pupils so intense Jonah is conscious of them from several feet away. He wears a high school warm-up jacket.

"Nobody told me I was gonna have to *fly.*"

"You said you wanted to go home," the old man said. *"Son,"* he added sternly.

"I didn't say I wanted to go home. I said I wanted to get out of this shitty little town of yours. I didn't say I wanted to *fly* out."

"You already flying, baby, sugar," says the girl.

"That's sure as shit," says the young man. "Nobody gonna make me fly nohow, how's that?"

"Nohow," says the girl and they both laugh frantically.

"I'll get these bums into—" Sauer starts to say.

"No *way,*" says the boy.

"C'mon, Conrad, your father asked me to come down and get you."

"My father?"

"Yes, Conrad."

"That prick? That shit?"

"Now you show some respect, son!" says the old man.

"Why?" says Conrad, looking at the old man. *"Why?"*

The old man looks away.

"Hey, old man, do you *know* my father, somethin'?"

"No."

"Then you don't know what the shit you're talkin' about, old man. Do you?"

"Get these animals out of here," says the old man, not to anyone in particular.

"Hear that, Lou-Ann, the law says we're ann-eee-mules."

They giggle.

"I guess that's why we fuck so good," the girl says.

Sauer looks at one of the papers. "Lou-Ann *Ralsan.*"

"That's what she said," the old man says.

"I don't know the name," Sauer says.

"There's a Ralsan mailbox out my way," Jonah says.

Conrad looks at Jonah. "We*llll,* hi-deee-*ho,*" Conrad says. "Mr. Jonah Jaquith, the famous aviator and sky chauffeur, the very same himself. And the top of the mornin' to *you,* Mr. Jaquith."

"I don't know you," Jonah says.

"No, sir, you don't. Indeed, it has not been your privilege. But you know my dear old daddy, I believe you aviate him about the sky and hither and yon and so forth from time to time. I have seen you from a distance, as they say."

Jonah looks at him and he looks back at Jonah. Jonah sees something that surprises him: *questioning,* indecision, uncertainty.

"Lou-Ann, honey, you ever ridden in a airyplane?"

"No," she says sullenly. "And I hope I never do."

"Lou-Ann, honey, if I said so you would."

"If you said so, Con."

"Lou-Ann, I believe this could be a thrilling experience for all concerned. I hate to admit it, but I've never ridden in a airyplane either. Let's try it."

"If you say so, Con."

"I feel like soaring with the birds, floating with the clouds, and all that shit."

"If you say so, Con. Will you keep a finger on it for good luck, Con?"

"I sure will keep a finger on it for good luck, Lou-Ann."

"I got my own good-luck piece *I'm* gonna be holdin' on to," she says. She holds out an open hand toward Conrad's fly and laughs.

Conrad laughs. "Not too *tight,* now."

"Animals," the old man says, looking away.

"No one's goin' to be holdin' on to anything but themselves," says Sauer, taking two pairs of handcuffs from off his belt.

Conrad backs away. "No. *No, sir.* I'm not goin' in no airplane with handcuffs on."

"You'll go any way I decide you go," Sauer says quietly.

"Then you better get extradition papers, shithead, you pig."

"I don't believe I need them now. The prisoners have already surrendered to me."

"No handcuffs!"

The boy is terrified.

Jonah walks Sauer several yards away. "I can't fly 'em in handcuffs, Harvey."

"What the shit, Jonah?"

"The FARs prohibit the transport of anyone in handcuffs by air."

"What do you do, Jonah, stay up at night and memorize that stuff?"

Jonah says nothing.

"Christ, Jonah, no one has to—"

"I don't care if anyone has to know or not. Aside from my own feelings that I won't have anyone in an airplane *I'm* flying wearing handcuffs, if those kids ever testified that I flew them that way, I'd lose my license."

"Who's going to believe them if I say—"

"I won't do it, Harvey."

"You want two junkies loose thousands of feet—"

"I'll take my chances. They don't look anything more than beer high to me, no matter what they've been using. Now let's pack this up if we're going, I'm goddamn cold."

Jonah walks over to the Skymaster, Sauer looking after him. Jonah hears Sauer quietly say, *"Shit,"* but he continues to walk to the airplane. Jonah leans into the cabin, unclips a flashlight, turns it on, steps back out into the cold, and begins a slow walk-around inspection of the aircraft, now looking with special attention for structural damage from the severe buffeting: a popped rivet, a broken cotter pin. He shakes the wings, pokes the beam of the flashlight into an access, and checks an oil level. He gets back in the airplane and sets up the cockpit for the return flight. With the tailwind, and carrying a little more power now that the air seems to have become less violent, Jonah thinks he can make it back in forty-five, maybe thirty-five minutes. Sauer is talking to Conrad and Lou-Ann. Conrad is moving the weight of his body rapidly from foot to foot. Lou-Ann still doesn't seem to have felt the cold.

When they come over, Conrad and Lou-Ann just stand there looking in, Sauer behind them, expressionless. After a moment Jonah helps Lou-Ann and then Conrad into the two seats immediately behind the pilot and copilot seats. He gets them harnessed and buckled up, and offers them coffee. "No, *man,* you got to realize we're *already* high, and we *don't* want to come down, that right, sugar baby?"

"Sure is, daddy."

Jonah briefly wonders to what additional extent they may be subject to hypoxia by whatever drugs they have in them. He thinks about the drugs. "You realize I'm the only one who can fly this airplane," he says.

"That's okay, that's okay," Conrad says. "We *need* you, I know it. Anyway, I got my own flying to do," and still looking at Jonah he puts his hands on Lou-Ann's breasts. Then he smiles at Jonah and pushes Lou-Ann's skirt up. Jonah turns and gets into his own seat. Sauer climbs aboard. In a few minutes Jonah has the aircraft all buttoned up and taxiing. At the edge of each wing he can see a small glow from the navigation lights, left green, right red. Sauer is glum next to him, staring straight ahead. Short of Runway Two-four, Jonah completes his runups and then gets his clearance relayed from the Poughkeepsie Flight Service Station. He taxis out to the runway and lines up, wind settled enough so that he needn't be abrupt about it this time. Then they are rolling and then they are lifting off into blackness.

On the ground the old man watches the aircraft climb. Quickly the shape of it is lost in the blackness. But the red and white rotating beacon on the top of one of the tail fins flashes at him, wink, flash, wink, flash, diminishing with the sound of it, and then it seems a long way away, changing direction, a star in a sky now empty of stars. It is a new year, and the disappearing star makes the old man feel that perhaps there were other things he might have done with his life, not *better* things, but *other* things, occupations which might have involved him with the things which have always given him wonder.

Quit of the runway by several hundred feet and heading southwest into the night and away from home, Jonah turns, climbing, first to the south and then to the east and then somewhat to the north. It is as if by the turning of the airplane he has rearranged time. There before them morning is spreading up the eastern sky, brilliant deep blue, pale at the horizon. The airplane is jolted—sharply but not severely. *"Whoo—ee!"* says Conrad, "this is more fun than *downtown.*" The boy and the girl giggle. "This has got to be almost as much fun as fucking."

"Shut your dirty mouth," Sauer says, looking straight ahead.

"How you *talk,*" Lou-Ann says, giggling.

They both giggle.

"Hey, cop," Conrad says. "You want to see her tit? I got her tit out." He laughs.

"Look but don't touch, cop," Lou-Ann says. And laughs and laughs.

Sauer continues to look straight ahead.

"Boston Center," Jonah says, "this is Skymaster Four-one Two-two Charlie. Good morning and hello again."

"Two-two Charlie, Boston Center. Welcome back to our all-night radio show. You missed some real good jokes and stuff."

"I'll bet I did." He and the controller exchange information and Jonah activates the transponder, squawking ident.

Crosses Pawling, morning climbing into the sky. In a little while Jonah will need sunglasses, flying straight into the sun almost. He dials in 055° on the VOR. A little bank and the needle remains centered. The air is steadying up quickly. Thin fingers of cloud are beginning to gleam in the bright light, a low pressure area trickling in from the southwest. Orange in front of him now. He begins to feel tired. Can he actually be feeling *heat* from the morning sun? A sun so low?

Frantic laughter from behind him.

Sauer turning around to see, Sauer saying, "Cut that shit out," raising a hand, Jonah reaching out to him quickly, *"Cut it out, for Christsake, Harvey,* you want to have a fight, wait till we get on the ground."

Laughter again from the back seat.

"Fiddle with the radios or something. You can switch over to Chester for me if you want to. One-one-five point one."

Sauer leans over. "He's got his hand on her cunt, I swear, and she's got her hand inside his—"

"Fiddle with the radios, Harvey. Make love, not war."

"Oh, yeah. Those two didn't make some war tonight."

There is renewed roughness in the air as they begin letting down over the hills of New Hampshire east of the Connecticut River. Jonah calls the Cornwall police on unicom and lets them know he's in range.

They are in brightness, blue light of morning, as they let down and, minutes later, find the black lines of the Cornwall runways in the white snow. The boy and girl have been silent for some time. Jonah wonders if they are awake. Jonah closes his flight plan with the Cornwall VOR and sets up for his landing, the airplane startled in its flight as the gear locks down, but the air more stable, airplane sinking beneath them, carrying them lower, long dock of runway lined up and coming up at them, near end seeming to widen, a little adjustment of throttles here and there, of rudder and of aileron, coming down, runway coming up, all human silence in the cabin and . . . *down,* moving along the dark runway between the runway lights and banks of snow, *cowls* open, *flaps* retracted, adding power to taxi to the hangar.

Jonah swings around in front of the hangar and goes through the shut-down procedure. The three passengers are silent. Two young policemen are walking toward them from the police car. The instruments whine down.

Sauer gets out. Jonah turns in his seat. Conrad and Lou-Ann are unbuckling. Conrad looks at Jonah, leans forward and looks at the instrument panel, *stares* at it.

"Come on," Sauer says from outside.

Conrad and Lou-Ann get out.

Still they are together—Conrad, Lou-Ann, Sauer, and Jonah. The rear doors of the police car cannot be gotten open, their locks have frozen. The two young policemen are working on them with cigarette lighters. The other four stand together, as if still constrained by the Skymaster's cabin space. Conrad is again staring, now at the airplane. Lou-Ann is feeling the cold upon her. She appears desolate. She looks at Conrad, then back into the cold, then at Conrad again.

Conrad is still looking at the airplane. He says quietly, simply, "That was fantastic."

Jonah says nothing.

A rear door to the car has been gotten open. Conrad and Lou-Ann get into the back, like little children who have been trained.

Sauer says, "There's no charge against the girl. You can take her home after you get him downtown."

"Call his father?" one of the young policemen asks.

"I'll take care of it," Sauer says.

The doors are shut and the police car is driven away, no lights flashing.

"If the boy's father wasn't such a big goddamn stick, we wouldn't've been out tonight, right?"

Sauer says nothing.

"How much money is involved in the bad checks the boy wrote?"

"Eight, nine hundred dollars, so far," Sauer says.

"Oh, boy. *Huge* criminal. Got to go charging around through the night

[63]

after him. You know how much this flight is going to cost the city, Harvey? Maybe two hundred."

"The old man is paying."

"You were just along as a private citizen, right? Except for your uniform, right?"

Sauer looks away.

"What about the local charges back there? Stealing a car, possession of a controlled drug, smashing up that store?"

"Somebody over there must have owed some political favors to someone over here who owed Gilbert Whittier some favors. I would guess, anyway. No one's going to tell *me* something like that, you know, Jonah. So the charges were never even brought 'long as I hightailed it over there and relieved them of Conrad tonight. And long as old Whittier pays the damages."

"You jailed him. Why doesn't the kid get off here?"

"I don't think his old man wants him to."

"Jesus Christ."

Sauer looks away.

Jonah goes over to him. *"God damn it, Harvey!* I don't have to fly trips like this. Fuckin' *phony* emergency!" They look at each other. Sauer looks away again.

Yvonne hasn't slept.

Now the wind has stilled somewhat and she has heard the sounds of an aircraft. She thinks it's the new one, the Skymaster, though she has only heard it a few times. Since marrying Jonah she has come to know which sounds belonged to the Cornwall airport and which belonged to the airlines and which—as unfamiliar as the children of strangers—belonged to nothing to which she was attached.

Now that she knows he is safely back, she feels anger, anger that he has put her to so harsh a night, so much worrying and waiting. But he hasn't landed yet, she thinks: *What if he crashes because of my bad thoughts?*

Jonah comes into the bedroom quietly. He is so tired he feels the cold now even inside himself. Yvonne is asleep. He had known it would be all right once tiredness entangled her and she slept. He sits in a chair and begins to remove his boots.

20

"And Clipper Two-oh-five is out of three-five-oh."

"Uh, you wanted fifteen hundred on the transponder?"

"If you want this for a turnaround flight right off, I've got some items for you . . ."

"I thought you had somethin' real good for us like direct Kennedy or somethin' like that . . ."

"This morning we recorded a message from an aircraft in distress, a foreign jetliner over the Atlantic, and we wondered if you had anything further and if Search and Rescue might want the message?"

21

Ben awakes to a hot breeze filled with the smell of the sea.

He is in Doris' bedroom. It is airy, brilliantly lit, the hot day and sunlight coming in through windows that have no glass, even their shutters pulled back. Ben can see the ocean, light green in toward the shore, darkening to thalo green near the horizon, white foam sparkling and glinting in the sunlight. He hears the sounds of the sea falling on the sand not far from the windows.

Beside him, nude, Doris sleeps, flesh made lighter in this light, and also shadowed reddish and brown, like the burnt pigments thinned to glazes, her breasts and pelvic area white. Tall, boughless trunks of palm trees are black silhouettes seen through the windows against the shining sea. Their green leafy tops glisten in the sunlight, move, glisten, still and move and glisten again. Hot breeze on his naked body, smell of sea, look of sunlight, nude Doris beside him.

Doris is the most satisfying and satisfied love partner he has ever known. Her nudity arouses him, the look of her is what has always been in his imagination, but so unclear he has never seen her before, even in his imagination.

Rapid heartbeat, slight headache from the night before. He listens to the sea, measures his heartbeat and the distant pain in his head against it. He is calmed by the sound of the sea, heartbeat gentled, pain removed.

Doris. The sea. Of the sea.

He sighs.

Doris awakes.

She holds herself against him, puts her hand upon his erection, kisses him. She kisses his face, his chest, his stomach, her black hair falling on his skin, her breasts touching his stomach, genitals, thighs. She takes him in her mouth.

He closes his eyes.

He is upon the open ocean. He is looking up from the surface of the sea. The sky is bright and blue and cloudless and empty except for a single airplane high above. He hears it, a single engine beating, sees its shape small and black against the sky. He sees himself there high above himself, traversing the open sea.

He wills himself not to come. He wants to wait forever for ever.

He looks up at himself high above and feels himself sucked into the seas.

WINTER
FLIGHTS

Basically, airplanes get us into places and situations man wasn't designed for.

— (Captain) Robert N. Buck

22

"Cornwall Area Radio, Zero-niner Golf, can you give me anything on that front between here and Detroit?"

"Cornwall Radio, I understood there wasn't any of this junk till the Albany area, but we just stuck our nose in it, so we made a one-eighty and we're holding about ten miles west of the city of Cornwall, so would you kindly take our numbers for an IFR flight plan . . . Roger, here we go. Ten-ten Alpha is a Lear jet . . ."

"Yeah, we were pickin' up ice at thirteen, but we're okay here at nine."

"Cornwall, Bonanza Seven-one Bravo is missed approach, returning to the VOR for holding before we try again."

23

Jonah stepped out of the door of the small frame building that housed Yancey Flying Service. Behind him Ev had been yelling at someone over the telephone.

But now Jonah stood in a cold, gray stillness. The air was motionless. There was not a sound in it. In the distance a flashing white high-intensity beacon signaled that because of limited visibility the airport was closed to all traffic save IFR traffic—aircraft operating on instrument, rather than visual, flight rules.

Jonah looked across the field to the low, brick airline terminal. The ramp in front of it was empty. The morning flights from New York City and Albany that usually would have been in at this hour either had been canceled or were being delayed by weather.

The cold, gray stillness was forewarning of an overflooding weather system. Jonah looked at it. It was toneless, without variation. The sky was the same blank grayness at the horizon as it was directly overhead. Students' lessons had been canceled.

Jonah's ears were sensitive to the stillness, but he was hearing Dr. Glynn. Dr. Glynn had been on the phone for him just as Jonah had come into work at eight o'clock. Dr. Glynn had not called him at home—and that troubled Jonah.

"Jonah," Dr. Glynn had said over the telephone, "could you come by my office at five this afternoon, perhaps?"

"Something wrong, Doc?"

"I'd like to discuss your wife's condition with you. Not to worry, but I'd like to discuss it with you. And if you will, let's keep this to ourselves just for now."

The words and the sounds of the words were very clear in all the stillness out under the sky.

Jonah looked down the field and saw another figure motionlessly studying the grayness. At that distance and in that light the figure looked like a black statue, something wrought in iron. Delaney Howard was standing in front of his own hangar. The hangar doors were closed, Howard's aircraft shuttered away inside. The hangar doors had been mostly closed, Jonah thought. For weeks. Since the sign *Howard Air Charter* had gone up. Howard had turned his head and was looking at Jonah. He nodded at Jonah. Then he went back into the hangar through a side door.

24

Delaney Howard pushed the ill-fitting door closed and he was in his office, a cubicle of plywood and wallboard and two-by-four pine studs which he himself had built into the interior of the aluminum hangar. He turned on the radio.

"The time is eleven-seventeen, the temperature is twenty-eight degrees, and it's snowing heavily here in Midtown Manhattan. Norm Kent says more snow this afternoon, continuing this evening, and diminishing towards daybreak. But expect an accumulation of about a foot. Hello, I'm Jane Tilson Olsen and these are the stories we're following this hour on News Update . . ."

Delaney Howard was dissatisfied with the carpentry. Nothing fit exactly as it should. Joins were not snug, corners were visibly not right-angled, the frame was too tight for the door, and no matter what surface he planed, the door would not shut unless he urged it with his shoulder.

"Israeli jets strike near Cairo. William Colby, chief of the Vietnam Pacification Program, testifies before the Senate Foreign Relations Committee as

it continues its investigation of Operation Phoenix . . ."

Del Howard looked around the little room and thought what a miserable impression it would make on a potential customer. If the customer got the suspicion that Del's airplane was anything like Del's office, the customer would just naturally *git,* if he had any brains at all. The impression this room makes, Del thought, I'd be better off without it. For a moment he thought of taking an axe to it.

When I make some money, that's the first thing I'll do, he thought. I'll rip this out and I'll get me a real carpenter in to build me a real office. In his mind he added on a small but comfortable and impressively appointed waiting room outside the hangar and butting up against his office door.

When I make some money.

But there had been no customers. None. Not one. Not in . . . not in . . . It came to just about seven weeks since he had opened for business on January second. Bad weather, lack of local contacts, no local reputation yet. *That's* what I *have* to get, Del thought. A local reputation. *Somehow.*

"President Nixon says that Vietnamization is on schedule and that the situation in South Vietnam is most encouraging. Frank Sinatra testifies in Trenton about what he may know about the Mafia—nine months after he was first subpoenaed to do so . . ."

Del sat on a chrome-bodied and red-cushioned secretary's swivel chair. It was the only piece of quality in the office. The plain, yellow-varnished oak desk in front of him might have belonged to his second-grade teacher back in Tennessee. Two aluminum garden chairs with a Formica table between them occupied a corner of the room an arm's length away. There was a large glass ashtray and some aviation magazines and *Time* and *Newsweek* on the table. A plant of some sort—he couldn't remember the name—that Betty had given him on *opening day* stood in another corner. Near it, a photograph of his squadron taken on the deck of a carrier. An oil painting by Betty—a cumbersome and self-conscious attempt at flowers in a vase—hung over one chair. Directly in front of him there were two pictures his children had made for him to wish him well. *Flye with Dadye hees the beste. Goode luck Dadye* from Mark, who thought most words ended with an *e,* and *I love you, you are the best Daddy ever, you will fly us to everything we want, we love you, good luck* from Sheryl. Below the kids' pictures, a portable radio. He hated it all, except for the pictures from Betty and the kids. And the squadron photograph. And the radio.

"The Chicago Seven jury is in its fourth day of deliberation and the defense is asking that Judge Julius J. Hoffman declare a mistrial . . ."

Waiting from seven in the morning till nine at night for someone to walk in or for the telephone to ring, Del had discovered that the radio had the unlikely ability to pick up an all-news station from New York City.

[71]

"The Senate is delaying on the Carswell nomination . . ."

On the corner of the desk there was an empty bottle of champagne which Del and Betty had drunk the night before the day the business opened. Betty had kissed the label hard and the lipstick imprint of her lips remained on it. She had written the date on the label with a felt pen and put an exclamation mark after it. To their mutual surprise they had made love there in the office that evening.

Now Del had the idea he wanted to go to bed with Jane Tilson Olsen. She said, *"Cassius Clay would like to leave the country, but only long enough to fight Joe Frazier . . ."*

Del had conceived his fantasy affair with Jane Tilson Olsen after a number of days in the hangar when there had been no customers, not even a visitor, and the telephone had not rung for any business purpose. He had begun listening to the news all the time. He had gotten the idea from her voice that Jane Tilson Olsen was a wonderful woman. He had attached a face and a body to her voice—from someone he had known once, but whose name and relationship to his life eluded him. Perhaps a girl from a magazine, perhaps someone from television or the movies, perhaps a woman he had known somewhere briefly.

On board ship he had always, *always* been with people. At home he was with his family. The only times he had ever been alone in his adult life were when he was flying. But that was different. Flying alone was different from being alone. Now he was alone all the time. It seemed to him that *being alone was his work.* And he hated it.

25

Jonah left the gray and quiet and went back into the waiting room of Yancey Flying Service. As soon as he opened the door Ev's voice came at him like something out of a public-address system. "The *legendary* Bucky St. Jean a *pilot?* Good pilot? Jesus Christ. Let me tell you, Sullivan. Tell you about old St. Jean."

Perry Sullivan was sitting back with his chair tipped against the wall and his feet propped up on a coffee table. The table was littered with flying and business magazines and ashtrays. Falun Aigborg was looking across the room to a wall where a number of air charts had been carefully butted together to make a single air chart of all of New England and the tangential geographic carpet running several hundred miles to the north, west, and south. Lucy, Ev's young secretary, was typing. Perry held a paper container of coffee in both hands and watched Ev. Ev had taught him to fly, but Perry was now a captain on an airline and he no longer deferred to Ev. He smiled as he listened to Ev, his body supplely relaxed in the tipped-back chair.

"I'll tell you about Bucky St. Jean. With *all* his reputation. I used to fly with him, see him fly, back with, back in the days of, God rest his soul, Virgil Yancey, who taught me to fly. Let me tell you about Bucky St. Jean. Once there was, oh—say they said it was a bird. A duck. It looks like a duck. It honks like a duck. It walks like a duck. It swims like a duck. Everybody *says* it's a duck. Even the *experts,* the ornithologists, for Christsake. What no one *notices* is that the fucking animal can't fly."

Perry wore rumpled and oil-stained chino slacks and a lumberjack shirt and brightly shined fur-lined halfboots. Perry, Jonah thought, had been spending a lot of his offtime at the airport recently. He had a J-3—an old Piper Cub—out in one of the hangars, and kept it in meticulous mechanical and cosmetic condition himself; of course he flew the airplane when conditions permitted, but a lot of his time at the airport was being spent just lounging around Ev's waiting room.

"The goddamn honeymoon must be over," Ev said. "What d'you think, Falun? You think Sullivan's honeymoon is over?"

It seemed for several seconds that Falun would not answer, that perhaps he had not heard. Then he spoke quietly. "I sincerely hope not." Then he looked off again at the huge air chart that hung on the wall behind Perry. The scale was such that it was almost like looking down on details of New England from fifteen or twenty thousand feet on a perfectly clear day. *I'll never do that again,* Falun thought. For a few seconds the thought alarmed him. But then a composure, like a sedative, overtook him. The composure was something that had come to him unsought months ago for the first time —months ago when Dr. Glynn had told him he was going to die soon. Unsought that first time, Falun was able to summon the composure almost at will now, though he did not know from where.

"How come that wife of yours never goes up in the J-3, Sullivan?" Ev said. "Is it you or the airplane she doesn't trust?"

"Hey, Ev, your pot's hangin' out," Perry said.

"God damn it, *I know.*"

Jonah was the only one near enough the windows to see the silver sedan approaching—Gilbert Whittier's Mercedes. Jonah turned his back on it.

He looked around the room. Not much by most peoples' standards, but pretty good for a small flight service at a small city airport. Jonah had seen worse. Most pilots had seen worse at bigger fields with bigger operations.

The large central room—the room they were in—had accumulated its furniture rather than been furnished. But the carpeting was wall to wall. A glass display counter held pilot and flying-related items for sale—logbooks, manuals, computers, navigation plotters, government publications, sunglasses, beer and coffee mugs decorated with airplanes. A coffee maker, its red light aglow, sat on a table in a corner. Next to the counter and near a window and the door was a gray metal desk where the secretary worked. A unicom transmitter—the airport's advisory radio—was near the desk, and on the wall by the door was an open or hotline telephone to the central flight service station in Concord, New Hampshire. On the walls were a number of photographs of pilots and airplanes. Grinning student pilots who had just soloed standing by their airplanes, more restrained pilots who had just earned their licenses. There were photographs of Ev and Yancey and Falun, some of them sepia-toned and going back to the leather-helmet-and-goggles times, and a photograph of Falun when he had landed at the North Pole. A bulletin board displayed government notices to airmen. There were posters admonishing airmen against everything from drinking the night before flying to failing to make a proper preflight inspection of an aircraft.

Four doors led off the room. One went to a storage and file room, another to a toilet, and a third to Ev's own small office, an empty wooden room with some photographs, some trophies, a plain wood desk, and a telephone. Ev spent most of his time in the big room. The last room contained a seminar table, chairs, a screen, projectors for both slides and movie film, and a wall-wide blackboard. It was, in effect, Jonah's room. Three nights a week he taught there—Private Pilot school, Commercial school, Instrument Rating school, and sometimes Instructors' school. He was able to earn about two thousand dollars a year in additional income doing this. The carpeting was wall to wall in that room, too.

Jonah just didn't understand it, the wall-to-wall carpeting. Ev spent almost no money on the things Jonah knew would bring students in. But a couple of years ago he had put in wall-to-wall carpeting.

Jonah watched Gilbert Whittier park his car. Then he looked up at the perfectly blank gray sky, and in his mind he checked the weather systems to the west and south. *I'm not going to fly today,* Jonah thought, and he wondered if he could hold on to that resolve—even if it meant losing his job.

26

Jonah had known Gilbert Whittier, *Mr.* Whittier *the banker,* ever since Jonah had been a child. Known him by sight, anyway. Then Jonah had grown up and become a pilot; after a while, he had gone to work for Ev Goodsom and had begun flying Gilbert Whittier on charters. Once Jonah had brought them back with a burst engine cylinder and oil obscuring vision through most of the windscreen, and Whittier had instructed Jonah to address him thereafter as Gilbert.

Whittier was short and angular. He wore a dark gray suit, as always, and a sensible narrow tie.

His companion was physically his opposite. And also his opposite in haberdashery. The man was in his late fifties or early sixties. Florid, with brilliant white hair combed back over a pink scalp. The hair had waves in it. He wore a black-and-white-checked suit and a wide tie of yellow and gold bands. His shirt was white and there was a blue-and-white-flowered hand-kerchief in his breast pocket. He was tall, stocky, and robust. He looked as if he had just come in from a football field, dyed his hair white, and dressed to go out. Jonah swore to himself he knew who the man was, but he couldn't give him a name—even though he could hear the man's voice before he spoke, and every inflection in the voice.

Whittier's entrance was abrupt, and so was what he had to say. "Jonah, this is Congressman Lyman Dougherty. I'd like you to run him over to Sky Ridge Lodge just as quick as you can. There's a little bonus in it for you."

Jonah shook his head.

The congressman seemed to be watching him with care. He damn well ought to, Jonah thought, and he began to place the man. Not a New Hampshire congressman. But he was chairman of a most important and influential House committee—though Jonah couldn't remember which one.

"Now, Jonah," Whittier began.

"No," Jonah said.

"Ev?" Whittier said.

"Why don't you go preflight Two-two Charlie, Jonah?" Ev spoke very quietly.

"Because Two-two Charlie isn't going anywhere. Unless someone else is flying it."

"No one else is flying it," Ev said. "Go preflight it."

Jonah paused. Okay, here was the confrontation. He walked over to the wall chart and began to point. "There's a front stretching from Ottawa, here, down to, anyway, somewhere here in West Virginia. It's snowing like hell in Albany. Here's Sky Ridge, back here behind the front, back here in the Catskills. And nothing around it but high hills and I'll bet overcast right down to the ground. I got the northeast aviation weather half an hour ago, Mr. Whittier, and I'll bet you you couldn't get into Sky Ridge with a seeing-eye dog. And radar."

Whittier said, "I spoke to the people at Sky Ridge just minutes ago. They say they can see the length of their runway and beyond."

"Their runway's only twenty-five hundred feet."

"They say you can make a VOR instrument approach off of *two* VORs. De Lancey and Hancock. They tell me the approaches are in your Jespersen manual."

"Jeppesen. Yeah, they're in there. I've used them. But I'm not even going to *try* to use them today."

Whittier said, "If you'll forgive me, Jonah, I call that gutless."

The room was quiet.

After a while Whittier said, "Ev?"

Ev said, "Jonah, why not give it a shot?"

Jonah said, "Ev, why not give it a fucking shot yourself? You're licensed to fly. You're licensed to fly on instruments."

Ev was silent. But he remained looking at Jonah. Then he said, "You're the better pilot."

Jonah sat down and looked at the huge chart on the wall. The congressman was looking at him, but the man Jonah was particularly aware of was Falun. Falun seemed to be looking into Jonah's eyes.

"No," Jonah said.

"Well, you better fucking well think that through twice," Ev said.

Jonah got up and went to the chart. "Congressman," he said to Dougherty, "let me give you a little lecture on weather. Maybe it'll save your life."

The congressman laughed. "Well, I'm always glad when someone wants to do that."

"It's not as if this meeting were something you might pass up attending," Whittier said to Dougherty.

"I know. But I hadn't thought of killing myself to get there."

"You might think again."

"Whittier," Dougherty said, "*you* think again. Mind whom you're talking to. And shut up."

"Mr. Congressman, I *know* who I'm talking to. And I know it's in your best interests to skedaddle over to that meeting. You know it, too."

Dougherty looked at the chart of New England. As if he were already flying over it. "Well, maybe we ought to give it our best shot," he said, "try it once. We can come back here."

"You'll never get back in here," Jonah said, "and I swear to you, you won't get in at Sky Ridge."

Ev said, "Jonah, you've got a baby on the way. Maybe you've gotten kind of cautious."

"Ev, I'll give you a little lecture on weather, too."

"There's them that fly in it and there's them that don't," Ev said.

"You and me, Ev," Jonah said evenly, "we don't fly in it."

Ev said, "Just say I don't fly in it any more. When I was your age and had your reflexes, I flew in anything. This is nothing."

"Well, now, Congressman," Jonah said, "let's have a look at this situation. We'd fly from our radio navigational facility here—our VOR—to Albany and its VOR. That's ninety-four miles into a headwind." Jonah used the circular slide rule that is the pilot's computer. "Let's say thirty-three minutes. 'Course, there'd be en route delays because of the weather and other traffic."

Falun was still watching Jonah. Ev had gone over to a window and was looking out. Whittier's lips were pursed together. The congressman was pleasantly attentive. Lucy, the secretary, had turned from her typewriter and was also watching and listening.

"Now when we're here over Albany we take a little turn to the southwest and we're on Victor Four-forty-nine. That's a highway in the sky. A radio navigational highway. We just follow that over to De Lancey VOR, let's see, seventy-one miles and . . . say, twenty-one minutes to fly it, and there we are, over De Lancey VOR, just spitting distance from Sky Ridge Lodge. Let's see—eight miles.

"But it'd be more realistic to say it'd take us an hour and a half to get to De Lancey and then some more time to get cleared down to shoot an approach to Sky Ridge. Then I guess we'd try the approach two or three times—if the weather gave us the chance. But my guess is you won't be able to see anything. My guess is things will be a lot worse than that, and here's the clincher why I won't go. That in there is probably just plain saturated with ice. It's just sitting there waiting to wrap itself around an airplane. You know anything about what happens to an airplane enveloped in ice, Mr. Congressman?"

"It gets heavy. It can't carry the ice and so—"

"That's the least of it. What happens is that the ice spoils those nice clean aerodynamic lines the designers went to all the trouble of figuring out. The wings lose more and more of their ability to lift the airplane. You can put on full power and still go down. The way you come down—well, Mr. Congressman, you wouldn't want to be inside. And neither would I. So that's why I'm not going. The best thing to do on a day like this is just go sit down somewhere and have a beer."

Ev said, "You could go over. If it's the way you think it is over there, you could just turn around and come right back. First sign of ice, climb out. It's a warm front, isn't it?"

"Yes, it's a warm front, Ev, and no, you damn well know better than that, *don't you, Ev?* Warm air overriding cold air. The result is ice and snow."

Ev looked back out the window and said nothing.

Jonah went over to him and spoke very quietly. "What the fuck's going on, Ev? Does this guy Whittier own you or something?"

"Why don't you go over and have a look and then come back if you have to?" Whittier said. "Jonah, I'll give you a personal two-hundred-dollar bonus just for going over and having a look."

"No. Thank you, but no. Look, Gilbert, there's a front over there and it's just going to overflow us here like a great big wave and flying visibility here's going to be zero-zero in a very short time. Two, three, four, maybe five hours. Meantime, look down here in the New York City area. Kennedy's down. La Guardia's down. Newark's down. Nothing's flying there. Because there's a nice little low pressure area that's been moving up the coast for a couple of days and now it's just getting inland to Hartford, not so far from here, right? Last time we had systems like this converging, nothing was open east of Cleveland or north of Washington. That's okay if you've got a four-engine jet. We don't. We don't have that kind of range or time."

Jonah found his heart beating. In his mind he had just made the flight to De Lancey—and it had frightened him. He was glad and almost surprised to be in this room on the ground.

"Thank you, Mr. . . . ?" Congressman Dougherty said.

"Jonah. Just Jonah."

"Thank you, Jonah, that's as good a summary for a layman as I've heard. And my committees have heard a lot of summaries for laymen."

"Ev?"

"Yes, Gilbert."

"What about this new fellow down at the end of the field?"

"Delaney Howard?"

"Yes. He any good? Any good for weather like this?"

"I'd say so. Fellow had to make a lot of instrument approaches to carriers and he's still with us."

"Call him up, will you?"

27

Delaney Howard stood facing the wall chart in Ev Goodsom's waiting room. His hands were on his hips and he was studying the topography of the Catskill Mountains on the chart as if he were looking down at the real thing.

"I'll tell you this, Mr. Whittier, Mr. Congressman, I been callin' in and makin' weather checks all day, jes like any good ol' pilot, and I'll tell you this for sure: that is one fine ol'-fashioned mess over there where you want me to go."

"Will you go?" Whittier said.

"I'd like to know what the weather is right now."

"Use my hotline," Ev said.

"All right. I'd like it also to talk to someone over there at Sky Ridge Lodge, if that can be done."

"You can do that," Whittier said.

"I don't know," Del said, after he'd completed his calls. "If I do solely by the briefing I got from the flight service station, I wouldn't go. Just be a waste of time to go over there. Have to come right back. But the man at Sky Ridge Lodge says he gets breaks in the ceiling of fifteen hundred feet—"

"Measured? What did he measure it with, Del?"

"He didn't say, Jonah. And too, he's got over two miles' visibility from time to time. The approach plate says what you need is twelve hundred feet and two miles for my class aircraft."

Jonah said, "He says he gets it from time to time. What's to say you're going to get both visibilities at the same time?"

"What's to say *not,* Jonah?" Del was getting angry. "You already turned this flight down, right, Jonah?"

"Right." Del turned from him. Jonah said, "While you're waiting for the two miracles to happen simultaneously, you're icing up."

Whittier said, "Now, Del, I just want to run over the figures for you one more time, quickly. Your regular charter fee plus two hundred for going over there and another three hundred if you actually get Congressman Dougherty down there. That's satisfactory, isn't it?"

"Everything is fine, sir. You're most generous."

"Well, then, you'll want to be getting started, won't you?"

Jonah said, "Get the check in advance, Del. Get it made out to your widow. I'll see that it gets deposited myself if you want."

"Get the fuck out of here, Jonah," Ev said.

"Okay, Jonah," Del said, "I wasn't goin' to say anythin', but I guess I will. Y'all're chickenshit and y'talkin' chickenshit. I suspect you got your own reasons for wantin' me not to make this flight, 'cause it makes you look bad you didn't take it. I suspect your own job might be in jeopardy 'cause you refused a flight that another pilot's gonna make in your stead. Now I've heard enough of you. No more, Jonah. Lest I get truly angered. Then I will cream you, Jonah. I swear, any more words from you and I will make you hurt *real* bad."

28

Some fifty miles to the north of Cornwall, Conrad Whittier lay on his bunk in a barracks at Attridge State Correctional Facility and, awake, dreamed of flying.

There was snow beginning to fall outside. He could see it through a barred window. The other occupants of the barracks—all of them, like Conrad, male first offenders below the age of twenty-five—were at their jobs. They all had relative freedom on the grounds—a farm where the winter months were spent learning and repairing machinery—but once in this barracks it was a real lockup. In a number of ways it was worse than the cell they had put him in in Cornwall. At least he'd had the cell to himself back there. Before the cell there had been the flight from Poughkeepsie to Cornwall. He had flown that flight, what he could remember of it, over and over again. Thinking about flying produced a flush of emotion that felt good all by itself.

His father, the eminent Gilbert Whittier, had not come to see him once while Conrad had been in the cell in Cornwall. He had been in the courtroom when Conrad was sentenced and had spoken to Conrad's lawyer afterwards, but he hadn't spoken to Conrad. Nothing new there. That went back to when Conrad had been five or six, when his mother, whom he rarely ever saw again, had left his father.

When he was being moved to Attridge, Conrad had gotten Chief Sauer, who was driving him to Attridge personally, to stop at the airport. It had been on the way, only a moment.

"Well, hi," Jonah Jaquith had said to Conrad.

"Didn't expect to see me again, did you?" Conrad had said.

"I guess I didn't. Not for a while."

Conrad had laughed. "No, not for a while."

It had been a gleaming blue January day, cloudless. Glistening drops of melting ice and snow fell from the edges of the flying service building and from the hangar. Three bright-hued light aircraft stood almost wing to wing on the other side of the fence, facing away toward pine hills and sky. A mechanic whistled as he walked toward a metal-bright gas pump. Conrad had felt, like a physical presence, the absolute blueness, the absolute tranquillity of the sky.

A white, low-wing, single-engine airplane kept taking off and coming around and landing again. The engine would become as soft as a motorboat idling in the distance and then there would be a sudden outburst of sound and the airplane would race along the runway again and hurtle up into the sky.

A single-engine high-wing airplane glided down almost without sound and touched the runway with a little shriek of rubber. It taxied over and the propeller stopped. After a while the door opened and the pilot got out.

The pilot was a woman, and Conrad thought she was one of the most beautiful women he had ever seen. Her beauty seemed to stab him and release a spring of loneliness in him.

"Sonofabitch!" Jonah Jaquith had said. "*Adele!*"

The woman had grinned. "I got lonely for all you boys, so I decided to fly down for lunch."

"Well, all right!" Jonah had said.

The woman had smiled at Conrad. He had gone over to the fence that separated the parking lot from the ramp and the field. It was a sturdy fence made out of steel tubing and quarter-inch wire mesh. Conrad had leaned against it. It did not give against his body. In spite of the days he had already spent in a cell, he had felt his first terror of prison.

"You motherfuckers," Conrad said.

"*What's that?*" Sauer said.

Conrad was silent.

"Get in the car," Sauer had said. "*Get.*"

Conrad had shrugged, turned his back on the airplanes. The airplanes didn't exist. When he got to the police car Conrad had turned to look at Jonah Jaquith. "Lou-Ann tells me your old lady's gonna have a kid."

Jonah had nodded.

"Take care of it," Conrad had said.

They said Attridge wasn't a bad place to be, and maybe that was so, but it was such a complete fucking bore. Conrad was supposed to have been repairing the teeth on the bucket of a backhoe. He had spent two days doing the same work over and over. Then he had just walked away from the repair barn and come back and lain down on his bunk. They'd find him, punish him one way or another. Conrad didn't give a fuck; it would be more interesting than repairing teeth on a fucking backhoe bucket.

He looked up and didn't see the dull yellow ceiling. He saw the blueness of the sky that day they'd stopped at the airport on the way here. The blueness glared and shimmered above him. He watched it and stared into it, thinking to tumble into it, to dissolve and vanish in it, and then to reappear cool and at ease within an airplane diminishing into the cool blueness way far away, going far, far away.

Watching the airplane flying away he felt something in himself which he cherished and with which he had only sporadic contact.

He thought of Jonah Jaquith's not-yet-born kid.

29

"Hello?"

"Hello, Adele."

"My God, it's—"

"The Phantom Ace."

"Ben!"

"Tell me you love me."

"Ben, *dear,* where *are* you?"

"According to the sectional I'm in Las Vegas."

"I thought you were in the Caribbean."

"I was."

"Well, what about Las Vegas?"

"I just took this left turn at New York City and—I wasn't sure whether I'd get you. I figured you'd be out skiing."

"It's snowing like a bitch here. There's always snow in Stowe, right? All the lifts are shut down. There's a big front moving in from the west right now. What's it like there?"

"It's morning. Bright, sunny, warm. Actually, I haven't been to bed yet. I lost seven hundred dollars last night. It took me all night to do it, but I did it. I was playing blackjack and at first I was down, then I kept even for a couple of hours. Then I had a late dinner and when I came back I started winning like crazy. So I started betting ten and twenty-five dollars a time and that's how come I'm down seven hundred dollars and feeling poorly. How would you like me to come visit you?"

"Why aren't you home, Ben? How come you're in Las Vegas?"

"I told you, I took this left turn at New York and—"

"Why?"

"I was on my way back home from the Caribbean and I was coming up on Westchester and I decided to stop off and see some friends there. They said come have dinner and stay over."

"This call is costing a lot of money, Ben. I just *realized,* you're calling from Las Vegas."

"After dropping seven hundred dollars, this is nothing."

"It's making me nervous."

"Then why don't you let me come and see you?"

"How did you get to Las Vegas?"

"I flew."

"Yes, but—"

"The morning after I stayed over with those friends in Westchester?"

"Yes, Ben."

"Cornwall was socked in. Everything to the north and northwest was freezing rain and snow and shit like that."

"So you went back to bed like a sensible boy."

"But everything to the south and southwest was fine. So I went on down to New Orleans."

"You what?"

"I'd never been to New Orleans."

"Ben, don't you have work to do? I seem to remember—"

"Then I remembered some friends in Tucson, some painters and sculptors. I'd never been to Tucson, so—"

"What about your work, Ben?"

"If the good Lord had meant me to work, he wouldn't have given me wings." Ben was silent and then he spoke quietly. "Why don't I come see you, Adele?"

"Why, Ben?"

"*Why, Ben?* Because I want to."

"Why, Ben?"

"I don't know . . . Because I feel like being with someone real . . . Adele?"

"Yes, Ben."

"You're not saying anything."

"I'm thinking."

"For Christsake."

"We stopped having an affair, Ben, remember that."

"*You* stopped having the affair."

"*You* don't want to get married."

"It's the age difference. I told you. I know it doesn't make any difference now, but what about later on?"

"The difference is when I started thinking about being four years older than you. I'm thirty years old, Ben. Most women my age have had their children—if they're ever going to have them . . . Ben?"

"I don't want to get married."

"It's all right, Ben. But it's no good for you to visit me. It wouldn't be any fun. For either of us. You see, don't you?"

"Sure. How's the rest of your love life?"

"There isn't any, Ben. What about you?"

"No. Nothing permanent."

"That's what I meant to say. Nothing permanent."

"Do you want to hang up?"

"Not really."

"That's nice. That makes me feel better about everything."

"Do you want to tell me about the Caribbean? About flying it? I was jealous of every mile."

"I want to tell you about it, Adele. But sometime when we're together, okay? Maybe we can have dinner when we're both back in Cornwall."

"Ben, dear . . . I don't know. I wanted to tell you this, I thought I might write it to you. If I don't straighten myself out—about you and a lot of other things—if I don't do that by the spring, I don't think I'll come back to Cornwall. I just don't want to be facing the same questions all the time. Just being here and alone, it's like a vacation."

"Shit."

"Ben."

"I said it quietly."

"I shouldn't tell you this, but I will anyway. Last month I borrowed an airplane here and flew down to Cornwall. I told Jonah and Ev it was just that I felt like flying and seeing them and having lunch. But it was really because I hoped to see you. I thought you'd be back in Cornwall then."

"Oh, Jesus, I *could* have been. If I hadn't gone down to New Orleans or somewhere. If I'd just come home."

"But now I know it was awfully good that you weren't there. I . . . I'm feeling better all the time being alone here. Being by myself. But I wanted you to know. That I've wanted to be with you, too."

Ben was silent. Then he said, "I can't think of anything else."

"Me either."

"Keep your weight on your downhill ski, okay?"

"And you go home and work. What you do is so beautiful." And she hung up.

30

When Perry came home from the airport he could see that Laura hadn't done anything to the house since breakfast. The dishes were still out. Coffee had been spilled on the maple countertop and the spill left there. Perry had built all the cabinets and fitted and finished all the work surfaces in the kitchen. It had been his wedding present to Laura. She had not shown much interest in it. Perry thought she might at least have had some appreciation of the work he had put into it, but she hadn't.

Laura attracted men easily, as she had Perry, with her beauty and vivacity. But rapidly, since their marriage a little over a year before, she had become ill-humored around the house and less and less responsive to Perry's energetic courtship of her good favor. Her nonresponsiveness confused Perry, and he became less responsive himself, less spontaneous, guarded around her.

He had come in through the kitchen door and found himself already angry. That she cared so little for the house, that she cared so little for *him,* that she could leave the kitchen a pigsty. He tried to make excuses for her, any excuse which would mitigate his own anger, *but God damn it,* he did his day's work, why couldn't she? *Christ, I spend as much time taking care of this house as she does,* plus *my own work.*

He found her in the living room. She was humming. She sat with her legs tucked beneath her in an overstuffed chair. An afternoon talk show was on television. She was apparently reading a novel *and* listening to the interviews.

"Oh, are you home?" she said without looking up. "Hard day at the office, dear?"

There was a Scotch and soda on the table beside her. The daily *New York Times* lay on the floor. Smoke spiraled up from a cigarette in the fingers of her left hand. A butt-filled ashtray stood on the maple colonial-style end table Perry had made.

"It's snowing," Perry said.

"Isn't that wonderful?" she said, turning a page.

"Good book?"

"It's just a little more interesting than sitting by the window and watching it snow. But you go ahead, if you want."

"Anything in the *Times?*"

"Oh, just about anything you can't find here. Restaurants, theater, movies, music, ballet, galleries, supper clubs, *news.* What do you care, you never read the *Times.*"

"When you lived in New York, before we were married, in, let's say, the whole year before we were married, how many times did you go to a concert? A ballet? What art gallery did you go to, whose work was—"

"You shut up! I went to all those places, I did! Now you just shut up, Perry Sullivan, I'm in a damn fine mood and you can just shut up or *leave me alone."* She exhaled, stubbed out the cigarette, and lit a new one.

Perry had known better than to get too specific about Laura's intellectual life in New York, a life which had become increasingly real to her the longer she was "stuck in this hick town with these hick minds. I wouldn't mind it if they at least *tried* to be inquiring, but they haven't thought about anything since they were in high school."

Perry had said, "As I recall, you finished two years of junior college yourself and that was it."

"And do you think getting an engineering degree makes *you* an intellectual, *Captain?*"

Perry heard his own voice as if it were a radio voice from some aircraft far away. "I see you've had such a busy day you couldn't get to the breakfast dishes."

She continued to read her book. "Yes, it's been a busy day."

Perry turned off the television set.

"Turn that back on," Laura said, without looking up.

Perry left it off.

Laura put down her book and looked at Perry. She smiled her best smile, the one she had given him when he had been a copilot and she had been a stewardess and they had been introduced before a flight. Smiling, she said, "I see you've come home ready to dump on me."

"No, I—"

Continuing to smile, she said, "Let me tell you about this home. It is not, I repeat *not,* my home. It is a house which you bought before you ever met me. You worked hard and refinished and repaired it. You made all this cute colonial furniture, which is repulsive and common."

"I thought you liked all this when I brought you here."

"That was before."

"I see."

"No, you don't. If you loved me you'd get rid of all this beloved junk of yours and fill this house with things that are bright and contemporary. But you won't do that, will you?"

"I put a lot of work into everything here, including the house."

"See, *you* won't compromise, but you expect *me* to compromise. Marriage is all one way with you."

"That's not true."

"What would be even better would be if you sold this house and everything in it and we moved to a modern house, somewhere near New York or in Connecticut. Then we'd be starting marriage *together*. We'd be building a home *together*. Everything here is *yours*. Everything was here before me. Even the towels are all yours."

"You gave them away. You bought all new towels."

"The sheets, the linens, *everything.*"

"You gave it all away and bought new—"

"I mean *before* I got rid of all that. Do you think I want to sleep on the same sheets where you fucked other girls?"

She had wanted to get rid of the bed. He had made the headboard and frame. He felt lucky to still have it. "Christ, it's going to be a lovely evening, isn't it?"

"Yes," Laura said quietly, smiling, "it is. Ralph Willerwood stopped by."

She picked up her glass, held it up in salute to Perry, and then drank. "I offered him a drink. We had a drink together and a nice talk." Laura carefully pulled down the skirt to her knee-length velvet robe. Perry was very conscious of the wide V the collar made, of the exposure of breast and cleavage. Willerwood would have been quite conscious of it also.

"He just dropped by?"

"He wanted to drop off this book. I'd told him I was interested in reading it, and he brought it over for me. Wasn't that nice of him?"

Perry said nothing.

"*I* thought it was *kind. And* thoughtful. You've got such a *nasty* mind, Perry Sullivan."

Perry began practicing a particularly difficult instrument approach in his head. He rang in a fierce crosswind, an engine failure, and an approach on a single engine. It soothed his anger as a massage might soothe muscle tension.

"We *are* going to have a lovely evening. Ralph has friends up from New York and he's invited us to have dinner with them at the inn."

"Us? Why?"

"Because he's a kind man. And lonely, I think. Being new to the community. He wants to meet people with interests similar to his own. He's just here because he's working on something for Barney Raab, you know. He could be anywhere."

"I get that impression."

Laura smiled at Perry. "He's a wonderful gentleman. He invited me to go to the opera with him in Boston next week. You'll be flying that day, so I said I'd be delighted to go with him." She smiled at Perry.

Perry thought, *For Christ's sake, why am I being jealous? Why am I getting so* damn *upset. I should be* glad *my wife can go to the opera when I'm working.* But he wasn't. His anger and now suspicion were inconsistent with his idea of marriage. For months now he had taken his angers at Laura and her presumed failures to be the result of his own inability to adjust entirely to marriage. He took their situation to be usual, the period of adjustment people spoke about. *But, Christ, there's no relief. And the goddamn dishes are all over the kitchen.*

Looking at Laura's partially exposed breasts, his anger somehow changed to sexual desire, and he knew that would make everything all right. *No,* he thought, *it wouldn't. That didn't work any more. Not for . . . almost since the beginning.* Though he had obscured that from himself for a long time. He had thought it was something that would change. It hadn't.

Laura's eyes looked from Perry's to her breasts. And back to Perry. "Don't get any ideas," she said.

"No. No ideas."

"I guess not. You don't get ideas very often, do you? Married people are supposed to want to make love two or three times a week. You barely come after me a couple of times a month."

"You're not the most *receptive* woman I've ever known."

"Don't blame it on me. Big airline captain. You just don't get it *up* very often, do you?"

"Look, Laura, you want me to go at it till you have an orgasm. That takes twenty-five minutes, God damn it! And that's difficult to do, keeping an erection and not coming. It's supposed to be *lovemaking,* not an athletic contest, not an *endurance* contest!"

Laura stood up. Quietly she said, *"You're filthy."* She left the room.

31

Delaney Howard *strode* back to his hangar. He felt good, very good, invigorated. He felt as if his body weighed less and as if he had grown taller. He saw his condition with considerable objectivity: he had work, therefore he had self-respect again. He saw that for some time he had been wandering into an area of depression. He was safely out of that area now.

He went into the almost dark hangar. The fuselage and wings and tail assembly, the tail fin standing up into the darkness, gleamed as if the aircraft were self-illuminated. Six-five Four-seven November was an Aero Commander, a high-winged twin-engine airplane much esteemed by business for executive use and even more esteemed by pilots for its flight characteristics and its versatility. Del Howard had a little more than one hundred and fifty thousand dollars in the aircraft. Part of it was money from various family sources—both his side and Betty's—and part of it was savings and part of it was financed. He had planned to make the interest and principal payments out of charter work while he and Betty and the kids lived off four thousand dollars of other savings. But here it was seven weeks later and he'd already had to go into household money to make his first aircraft loan payment.

He slid back a hangar door. In the new gray light Four-seven November leapt into being as if it were taking flight. Del was thrilled in an almost erotic way by the aircraft and by the opportunity to use it. He was as thrilled by it as he had been by Betty's nudity one warm spring evening in college when she had allowed him to undress her and take her to bed.

With a towbar he pulled the aircraft forward. It rolled down a slight decline in front of the hangar and then slowed and stopped as he turned the nosewheel.

He went through the exterior preflight inspection.

It was while he was standing on an aluminum stepladder checking an engine cowling that a cool voice in his head said *You know you shouldn't make this flight.*

He ignored the voice.

The weather's against you—

Screw it, I've flown in worse. And this airplane carries a terrific load of ice.

—and you're illegal. You're in complete violation of Part One Thirty-Five. The subsection about icing conditions and operating limitations. Where it says you can't fly for hire into known or forecast moderate or even light icing conditions. Not without the required antiicing equipment. And you just haven't got that equipment.

Guys fly in violation of that section all the time. Commercial pilots just like me.

The voice was silent.

This one time. I've got to do it this one time. Then I'll never have to do it again. I'll start getting business. This is the beginning. After this people will know there's another real goddamn pilot on the field.

The two men in the Mercedes watched Delaney Howard go around his airplane unscrewing and rescrewing, peering into apertures, pulling the props through, draining and securing. They both wore overcoats. Gilbert Whittier wore a silk scarf under his collar, Congressman Dougherty a scarf of wool tartan.

"I don't much look forward to this," said Dougherty.

"Neither would I if I were going," said Whittier. "Still, you'd rather be able to tell them you tried to get there than that you didn't try at all. You'd much rather be able to tell them that."

"That's why I'm going."

"Your pilot's waving. I guess he's ready."

The passengers' area was a nicely appointed section of six fat seats that reminded Dougherty pleasantly of a lounge rather than of an airplane. The congressman carried a briefcase and an overnight case. Del placed them in the cabin area and secured them.

"You can make yourself at home in here," Del said, "or you can join me up front, if you'd like."

"I'll come up front. I always like to know what's going on."

"There won't be much to see."

Del got the congressman hitched into the copilot's seat and had him practice fastening and releasing the seat harness.

Dougherty looked at the instrument panel in front of him. "You just look at all these instruments and you don't have to see outside," Dougherty said.

"That's about it."

"It always amazes me. That it's all done with just numbers and needles. There's nothing pictorial here. Not really."

"The numbers make pictures. Very exact pictures."

"Yes. You don't have radar?"

"No. It would be nice. If I had a lot of money. But it's really not necessary. Now, Congressman—"

"You might just call me Lyman, since this is a joint endeavor we're involved in."

"Yes, sir. Lyman it'll be. Now, Lyman, I got to be frank with you and say that much as I'd like that three hundred extra dollars, I have little hope that we'll be makin' a landin' there today. We'll jes go over as ATC clears us along. When we get to the Sky Ridge Lodge area, then we'll see. If things aren't favorable, we hightail it right back here."

"I understand."

Del noted the congressman's tension as the flight began to become a reality.

Shit, maybe it's me who's beginnin' to tighten up, Del thought as he began the "Starting Cold Engine" checklist. In a moment he turned the ignition switch to START. The three propeller blades on the left engine moved, faltered, moved, and then disappeared as the engine coughed from ignition, quibbled inside itself, and then roared steadily, the thrill of the engine vibrations, of its power, traveling through the wing and into the fuselage and rocking the flight deck slightly. Del moved the ignition switch to BOTH and reduced power. The flight deck hummed but barely vibrated. The oil pressure was up.

Del started the other engine. It caught without hesitation. The oil pressure moved up slowly, as had the first oil pressure. The oil was cold and sluggish. By the time he was out on the runway there would be plenty of pressure. He taxied slowly, letting the engines warm longer than usual. Short of the runway there was still a chance they might not go—if a magneto in the engine checks failed to perform properly.

The engines ran up perfectly. The needles of all the engine instruments were in the green arcs. It was time to go. He completed the "Before Takeoff" checklist. He taxied out on the runway.

"Congressman, I've asked for sixteen thousand. That should put us on top for a while. We'll be using oxygen from time to time."

"Lyman," said the congressman.

"Yes. Right. Lyman."

Del had the nosewheel on the white center strip of the runway. His hand moved forward on the engine control pedestal and gave the engines full throttle. The center strip began moving backwards from the end of the runway in brief white dashes that disappeared beneath the nose. Then the white dashes became insistent white streaks and then a rhythmic white line with seemingly no breaks. Del lifted them off.

The congressman looked straight down from his side window at the earth withdrawing beneath them. The earth was snow-covered, but there were areas of brown and black, and as they went higher it all turned a muted brown.

Del saw none of this. He was on instruments. He settled the climb speed at 140 miles per hour.

The congressman said, "I can't see the ground any more."

All he could see was a thin grayish white. No matter where he looked. Except for the wings. The wings were the only material matter he could see outside of the airplane. They looked far too heavy to hold the two of them up in that thin grayish white in which there was nothing else to be seen.

32

George Detwiler was at the Registry of Deeds searching titles on behalf of his employers, Sutcliffe & Lowe, Attorneys at Law, Cornwall, N.H.

Five days a week, from eight-thirty to five, George was a law office clerk. The job paid a hundred dollars a week. He hoped he was learning by experience. Three evenings a week he drove to Boston College, where he took classes. He was a third-year student in law. Most nights he worked till two or three in the morning on his studies. Some mornings he got up at five to continue study. Sometimes during the day he was so tired he could not remember what he had been doing an hour previous. Some nights, driving back from Boston, he almost couldn't see the road through his tiredness.

At seven o'clock each weekday morning he woke his son Randy and made breakfast for both of them as Randy dressed. That was the best part of the day for George, having breakfast with Randy and talking with him.

Some mornings George saw Ceil's face in Randy's, heard an intonation in his voice that was hers. He never mentioned it to Randy. It was as if part of Ceil—some part of her spirit as well as her body—had entered Randy. It was as if a little Ceil were growing up in Randy. George did not know what to make of it. He loved Ceil's presence—the remembrance of her face in Randy's face—but he wanted Randy to be the boy's own lad.

Those breakfasts were just about the only minutes they had together during the week. Two nights a week they had dinner together as well, but that was usually hurried. And three nights a week Randy went next door to a sitter and George did not see him till midnight or one when he got back from class and carried a sleeping Randy home.

By two-thirty George was through with his work at the registry and was ready to drive back to the office. Some flakes of snow were falling, so few that each seemed isolated from all the others. As he drove, the flakes seemed to increase in density, but George thought that was only because his driving speed made the snow seem quicker and of greater intensity than it was. Still, this would be a class night, so he turned to a Boston station and waited for the weather.

It was an important enough story to be carried live and off the hour. "We can't be at all optimistic, as we were yesterday, that Boston will escape a major snowstorm beginning later this afternoon. Snow has already begun in the Monadnock region just ninety miles to our west. And that weak low pressure area to our south, which I thought might move out to sea, has intensified and is making its way north on an inland route—" George turned off the radio.

As a pilot he had not much liked storms, not storms of this magnitude.

But now George found snowstorms to be kindnesses from heaven, gifts beyond his capacity to wish for them. He couldn't go to class. He and Randy would be locked in their own home by the great snowstorm. George could sit with him. Take time making a good dinner. Have a fire in the fireplace, maybe cook a steak there, and popcorn afterwards. There were games that Randy wanted to play with him, and tonight he would have a world of unexpected time to play games with Randy and to be with him.

Best of all about a snowstorm, and being closed in with Randy by the storm, was the feeling George got that nothing bad could happen while the storm went on. The accumulating snow was like accumulating protection for him and the boy. No, nothing bad could happen while it was snowing.

33

"Boston Center, this is Aero Commander Six-five Four-seven November."

"Six-five Four-seven November, this is Boston Center, go ahead."

"Six-five Four-seven November off Cornwall two-four, climbing to maintain sixteen thousand."

"Roger, Four-seven November, squawk ident and report reaching sixteen thousand." Del activated the transponder and the controller's voice said, "Four-seven November, radar contact."

Scanning his instruments, Del said to Dougherty, "He'll flight follow us on radar through his sector and then hand us off to the next sector. Actually, all those guys are sitting in one big dark room back in Nashua, New

Hampshire, and they've got a few hundred radar screens in front of them and they're monitoring every flight in New England. Almost out to Cleveland. And south into New York State."

"Four-seven November, what is your present altitude?"

"Center, Four-seven November is out of eight for sixteen."

"Roger."

The grayness had taken on a white brightness. The brightness was so sharp that Dougherty squinted his eyes. There was nothing to be seen upwards or downwards or forwards or sideways except the wings, and looking at the wings, Dougherty had no sense of motion, no sense of progress.

"Do you know where we are?" he asked.

Del was following his instruments. He glanced at his watch. "I'd say we're just coming up on the Connecticut River. Brattleboro, Vermont, ought to be off to our left."

The bright whiteness burst brighter and then washed over the windscreen, and in that instant Dougherty was looking at pure blue cloudless sky above and gleaming white cloud below. The cloud cover ran unbroken to the horizon, seemed to climb up into the blue of the sky like an endless snowfield.

"Boston Center, Six-five Four-seven November."

"Four-seven November, Boston Center, go ahead."

"Four-seven November is on top at ten, requesting twelve for altitude."

There was a pause and then the controller's voice said, "Roger, Four-seven November. Climb to and maintain twelve thousand, report reaching twelve."

"Roger. Twelve is approved and report reaching. Can you give me the current Albany weather?"

"Ceiling five hundred overcast. Visibility three-quarters of a mile in snow. Wind from two seventy at twenty, gusting to thirty. Barometer two-niner four-three."

Del said, "The sonofabitch must have had it right in front of him."

"What?" said the congressman.

"The Albany weather."

"What does that mean? Him having the Albany weather right there?"

"It means he's got time to worry about us."

"Do you think he's worried?"

Del watched his instruments for a few seconds. "I'd say he's concerned."

"Four-seven November, this is Boston Center."

"Forty-seven November."

[93]

"Four-seven November, Albany traffic is presently being diverted to Montreal, Cleveland, Boston, and Portland."

"Thank you, Center," Del said. And to the congressman, "He didn't have to do that."

"Do what?"

"Fill us in that way. He's really trying to help us."

"What do you think, Del?"

"I think less and less of it."

"Can we poke in there? Can we poke into Sky Ridge like you said? And come back if we can't get in?"

"We can give it a try."

"I think we better give it a try."

"You think it's that important."

The congressman thought about it. "Well, yes, I think it's that important. Some people expected me there. I gave my word I'd be there. But one thing or another . . . and then this bad weather came up. It would have been hopeless to try to drive."

"Man, you sure go about things the hard way."

"I'll make that bonus an even five hundred if you get us in." After a moment the congressman said, "Did you hear me? About the bonus if you get us in?"

Del nodded. "We'll have a look."

The endless snowfield seemed to be rising before them, climbing up to meet them. Dougherty saw Del looking down. Dougherty looked down. Just in the few moments the cloud tops below them had gotten strikingly nearer.

"Boston Center, Forty-seven November."

"Four-seven November, go ahead."

"Four-seven November's at twelve and I'm down to about a thousand feet above the tops. I guess we're goin' to be back in it in a couple of minutes, sir, and I just want to advise you we won't be remaining visual much longer."

Dougherty watched the shining, sunlit surface of the clouds ahead. It was so bright here, so dark down below. He experienced a sudden dread of reentering that white darkness. He shut his mind to the dread and listened to the voices of his pilot and the controller. Both pilot and controller seemed matter-of-fact about their business.

"Four-seven November, advise when you can no longer maintain VFR."

Dougherty was looking at the instrument panel when the illumination in the cabin changed. It had abruptly darkened a shade, as if a slight shadow, perhaps from a cloud, had fallen across the windscreen. Dougherty looked outside. They were in the thin bright whiteness again, some sort of netherworld that was stranger than darkness. Dougherty had that sense of not moving again, except for the insistent sounds and vibrations of the engines.

"Boston, Four-seven November is no longer visual."

"Roger, Four-seven November."

Dougherty saw that Del was looking out at the wings, first on his own side and then on Dougherty's side. Then Del looked back at the panel and quickly studied the engine instruments cluster.

The air around them seemed to be darkening, Dougherty thought. The bright whiteness was no longer bright nor white. They were in a kind of still grayness. The subdued illumination from the instrument lights had become noticeable again in the pale light from outside.

"Six-five Four-seven November, contact Boston Center on one two seven point niner now."

"One twenty-seven point nine. Thank you, sir, and good day."

"What's that about?" Dougherty said, startled.

Del was switching radio frequencies. "We're about halfway to Albany and he's handing us off to the next sector controller."

"Boston Center, Aero Commander Six-five Four-seven November says howdo."

"Six-five Four-seven November, radar contact, the Albany altimeter is two-niner four three."

"Four-seven November."

Dougherty watched Del peer out at the wings again. Dougherty looked out and saw nothing but increased darkness. The space ahead was a blurred and swirling white that seemed to spread and streak by the windscreen. Del turned on the landing lights: *snow.* He flicked the lights off. The air the snow rode looked gray to Dougherty; the quality of the natural light was such that he thought there must be something like a black ceiling somewhere above, but when he looked up he could see nothing, just grayness becoming darker and darker until it was beyond being seen at all—perhaps only a few feet from the airplane.

Dougherty watched Del look out at the wings again. "You looking for something out there?"

"Ice," Del said.

"Six-five Four-seven November, Boston Center."

"Four-seven November."

"Four-seven November, hold on the one-hundred-degree radial of Albany, two zero three degrees Cambridge. Hold east, twelve thousand. Expect further clearance at five-seven."

Del repeated the instructions while he set up his second navigational radio on the Cambridge VOR.

"What does five-seven mean?"

"Fifty-seven minutes. You never use the hour, just the minute of the hour. He says we can expect to get cleared in about six minutes."

"Why's he stopping us?"

"Other traffic, I 'spect. Goin' up or comin' down. Somethin' that might pass too close to us at our altitude if we didn't wait up a bit here."

"I'm not happy here. I confess it."

"Want to head back, Congressman?"

"If I want to, I'll tell you."

While talking, Del was concentrating on the instruments and on making timed turns to different compass headings to stay in a precise holding pattern.

"Boston Center, Forty-seven November."

"Four-seven November, Boston Center."

"Boston, can you give me the Albany temperature?"

"Four-seven November . . . Albany temperature is thirty-three degrees."

"Four-seven November. Thanks." Del said, then added, "Shit."

"Why's that?"

" 'Cause I don't know what it means. Thirty-three degrees could be too warm for ice, but then maybe it could be the Ice Follies a couple of hundred feet up from ground level."

The aircraft was struck and struck again as if by something solid.

"Oh, Christ," Dougherty said.

"Yes," said Del, making a slight correction for course and altitude, "I guess that rattled our teeth all right. I 'spect we're into the front now. It'll be this way for a while."

"My God, is that all it means to you? *This.*"

"That's all."

"Well, that's goddamn reassuring, Del. I mean that."

"Well, I'll tell you what's not so reassuring."

"What is it?"

"We're picking up ice now. See the white line below the leading edge of the wings?"

"Yes."

"See here at the corner of the windscreen?"

"Can you do something about it—the ice?"

Del did not make an immediate reply. When he did, he said, "What I think I'd better do, Mr. Congressman, is give you a short lecture on this airplane. Ice usually forms on the leading edge of a wing and on the props. This airplane does not have deicing boots, which are supposed to pop the ice off the leading edges of the wings. Nor does this airplane have a propeller deicing system. What this airplane *does* have is the capacity to carry a *shitload* of ice. And I mean a *shitload.* Anyway, ice doesn't form on the leading edges of these wings. It forms underneath the leading edge and spreads backwards. I've seen it spread back a foot and a half, two feet. Flying in precip, you get impact ice. That is, the precipitation forms into ice on impact. What happens is, the nose of the airplane goes up, you get into a climbing attitude to compensate for the ice. And you lose speed.

"On most airplanes you'd have to worry about ice forming in the fuel system. But we have what's called a fuel injection system, and I've never heard of it icing up on this model. If there was any indication of icing up like that, I can use carburetor heat. Or I can shut off the door of the ram air intake system. Then the engine'll stay all warm and cozy in its own heat."

"You've got confidence in this airplane, Del."

"Complete."

"And in yourself."

"I wouldn't be here otherwise."

Whack.

"What the shit was—"

Whack-whack-whack.

"What the shit is that?"

"I guess some ice is gettin' thrown off the props."

Whack. Whack. Whack-whack-whack.

"Shit, that's scary."

"You're goddamn right it's scary. Sounds like explosions, doesn't it? Ice hittin' the sides of the fuselage. Prob'ly just outside where we're sittin'."

"Four-seven November, Boston Center."

"Boston, Forty-seven November."

"Four-seven November, you're cleared according to flight plan to De Lancey VOR via direct Albany direct De Lancey, maintain twelve thousand."

"Roger, Boston. Four-seven November cleared direct Albany, direct De Lancey. What've you got for a lower altitude. Can I get down to eight or six?"

"Four-seven November, standby one."

"What do you want to go lower for?" Dougherty said. "I thought pilots prized altitude."

"You're right about that. Except sometimes. Like now. Indications are temperature's warmer down below. Might be warm enough to keep ice from forming. We'll try it. Just a little bit. If there's any ice down below, that's it, my friend. Home we go. Just as fast as we can. We're still not in any trouble with ice, the little bit we have doesn't trouble me. It's the more we might pick up that I'm givin' considerable consideration to."

"Four-seven November, Boston Center."

"Boston, Four-seven November."

"Four-seven November, all altitudes below you are available. Six thousand is minimum. If you want six, I'll have to hand you off to Albany Approach through their terminal area. Advise altitude requested."

"Boston Center, Four-seven November will take six."

Cleared down, Del began the descent. "Congressman, it's goin' to be a little bumpy on the way down, but pay it no mind. It's just the fractious nature of this front we're pentratin'."

The aircraft pitched and lurched. There were loud sounds like metal breaking. *"Oh, Jesus,"* Dougherty said, *"the miracle of modern aircraft."*

"You are so right," Del said. "Boston, Four-seven is through ten for six."

"Roger."

"We're encounterin' moderate chop on the way down."

"I'll make a note of it, sir. Thank you."

"The wing," Dougherty said. "It's gone."

"The fucking wing?" Del said, not taking his eyes off the instruments.

"The ice. That line of ice."

"Praise the Lord," said Del.

34

"Four-seven November, contact Albany Approach one-twenty-five zero at this time. Tower code is zero five hundred."

Del acknowledged and made the necessary changes. "Albany Approach, Six-five Four-seven November is with you, six thousand, and squawking zero five hundred."

"Roger, Four-seven November. Albany altimeter is two-niner four-three. Maintain six thousand and report crossing the VOR."

"Four-seven November."

"Are we right over Albany?"

"Pretty close to it. We're in the airport's control zone. Well, how do you like it here, Congressman? I got an outside temperature of thirty-one degrees and the snow is just *flirtin'* past us and there just ain't no ice astickin' to us."

"Will we get in at Sky Ridge?"

"That's still open to speculation."

"How far away are we from it. How long?"

"Hell, we're *close,* Congressman. Another twenty-odd minutes to De Lancey and then about five minutes to make the approach to Sky Ridge. *If* there's enough visibility to land after the approach."

"Well, you sure are doing a fine job, Del, a *fine* job. You're earning your money. Every cent."

"I hope to earn my money. Always."

The congressman listened as his chartered flight was handed on from Albany Tower's Approach Control to Boston Center's Albany Sector Control and then to Boston's Utica Sector Control. Del changed frequencies. "This is the last ATC frequency change we'll have to make. The man I talk to now is the man I'll be working with down to our approach."

"It seems smoother," Dougherty said. "Not so rough."

"These are like long swells here. It'll get rough enough when we get down into the hills."

"The Catskills? They're mountains, I'd say."

"I'd say, too. Boston Center, Six-five Four-seven November."

"Six-five Four-seven November, Boston Center. Radar contact. The Binghamton altimeter is two-niner two zero."

"Now what the hell?" Del said.

"What?"

"It's not right. That pressure should be higher. The front's supposed to have gone through. The pressure goes up after a front goes through. This pressure is lower."

"Maybe the front hasn't gone through yet. Is that a possibility?" A moment later Dougherty repeated, *"Is that a possibility?"*

"It's a possibility. Something else to consider is that sometimes things are worse behind a front than in it. You get low cloud around mountains. Updrafts that produce snow. They supercool the moisture in the air. Sometimes it's worse than the front."

"Do *you* want to go home, Del?"

"No, damn it. I told you we'd take a look."

"Do you know your Southern accent seems to come and go?"

"That's what they tell me."

"Does that mean anything?"

"It means when I'm nervous and when I'm not."

"Which is which?"

"It's inconsistent. Or so I'm told."

"Now that the air's kind of smooth, I feel okay. Except that it's so goddamn dark out."

"There's a hell of a snowstorm out there, Congressman. I don't plan to stay around for more than one approach. If we don't make it that first time, we're gonna head back. Cornwall and everything else in the neighborhood will probably be closed. We're goin' to have to go all the way to Boston,

[99]

I figure. Before we can set wheels on the ground. Boston is just the earliest we can outrun this thing. To see well enough to get down."

"You don't think we'll get into Sky Ridge."

"I don't think so, no. Not from what I've been hearing on the radio. On the other hand, here we are comin' up on Oak Hill. That's an intersection pretty close to De Lancey. Almost there. So now my professional judgment is, we've come this far, we're not picking up ice, let's give it a shot, things don't work out we'll hightail for home. Or Boston."

"Good. I stopped worrying when we stopped getting bounced around."

"I didn't stop worryin'. I jes slowed it down a bit when we stopped pickin' up ice."

Del figured they damn well wouldn't get in. But if they did, if there was one lucky shot and he made it, there would be five hundred dollars. He thought of the nagging little debts the five hundred dollars would pay off all at once. The people he couldn't quite look at with his head held up. The dry-cleaning man, the office-supplies man, the little grocery store where they charged when they didn't have the cash to go to the A&P or Grand Union. He could make a part payment to the oil man and have the money to make a whole payment for his quarterly life insurance, but not enough to do the house and car insurance which were coming due. He thought of the man who owned the Ford garage. He owed him for auto repairs. And the pharmacy, the druggist. He owed him for the medicines when both kids had gotten sick after New Year's. And that made him think of Brown and Simonetta, the pediatricians—he owed them and . . .

He asked permission to leave the ATC frequency briefly and then he dialed in unicom and called Sky Ridge.

"Aero Commander Six-five Four-seven November, Sky Ridge Lodge. Go ahead, sir."

"Four-seven November is about five minutes out from the De Lancey VOR, and we're mighty interested in your landing conditions."

There was a long silence.

"What the fuck—?" Del said.

"Four-seven November. If it was me, sir, I'd tell you go back where you came from. Over."

"Just tell me the field conditions."

"Roger, Four-seven November. You can't see a thing and what you can see is blowin' to hell and gone. The wind's at thirty-five knots just now, but it gets down to twenty. It's from two-sixty to two-ninety degrees. We got like two feet for a ceiling and a hundred feet forward visibility. You try to land here you're gonna kill yourself."

"Who the hell are you?" Del said.

"I'm the kid they hire to be lineboy. Over."

A new voice came on. "Aircraft talking to Sky Ridge, this is Sky Ridge. Is Congressman Dougherty aboard?"

"Congressman Dougherty is right here," Del said.

"Would you be kind enough to put him on?"

"Hello, Sky Ridge. Lyman Dougherty here."

"Hello, Lyman. We've been waiting for you and we're sure glad you made it. Would've been a terrible storm to drive through, wouldn't it?"

"Yes, Sky Ridge."

"Let me talk to the pilot now. Pilot, are you listening?"

"Listening."

"Conditions are changeable down here, but they can be beat."

"Sky Ridge, are you a pilot?"

"I've got experience."

"He's no fucking pilot," Del said to Dougherty. To the radio Del said, "We'll make one approach."

"Well, now, that might not be enough. May I talk to Lyman Dougherty?"

"All right, I'm here."

"Lyman, we expect you down here."

"Well, we're going to try."

"That'll be just fine."

Del switched frequencies again. "Boston, Four-seven November is back with you."

"Four-seven November, roger." There was silence for a minute. Then, "Four-seven November, Boston Center, we have you as a target coming up on De Lancey VOR."

"Roger, Boston."

"What's that?" Dougherty said.

"It's a little reminder. He wants to know what my intentions are. He knows what the weather conditions are down there and he wants to know what my intentions are." Del watched the instruments and thought. Then he keyed his boom mike and said, "Boston Center, Four-seven November is coming up on De Lancey and we'd like to be cleared down for an approach to Sky Ridge."

"Four-seven November, this is Boston Center. How will you close out your flight plan?"

"I'll close by telephone."

"Roger. Six-five Four-seven November is cleared for an approach to the Sky Ridge Lodge airport. Radar service terminated. Cleared this frequency."

"Four-seven November."

35

Del glanced at the approach plate in his lap, though he had already memorized it. His right hand began setting up for the landing approach. He flipped the fuel boost pump switches on and moved the mixture controls to full rich. He checked the landing gear warning horn and then lowered the gear and watched carefully as the landing gear safe lights came on. He glanced at the hydraulic pressure indicator and saw that it remained normal. Then he began slowing the airplane to his approach speed of a hundred and twenty miles per hour. He wanted the speed because of the turbulence and the possibility of ice.

"It seems awfully quiet," Dougherty said.

"I just reduced power."

"Not just that. I guess I got used to hearing the radio. The controller. Feels like we're kind of alone now."

Del nodded, watching the instruments, making minute corrections— though the aircraft was being so roughly treated by the wind Dougherty was surprised and concerned by the delicacy of the pilot's reactions.

Dougherty saw the lights of the instrument panel glowing as if they had been set in a dark room. Then he realized that the interior of the cabin had become quite dark. They seemed to be losing light as they lost altitude.

Dougherty said, "That line of ice is back on the wing."

"I know." Del depressed the mike button on the yoke. "Sky Ridge, Four-seven November."

"Four-seven November, go."

"We're on approach now. Keep an eye and ear for us. We should be on you or over you in four minutes."

"Okay, and good luck there, Four-seven November."

Whack.

"My God!"

"That must have been a hell of a piece of ice," Del said quietly. "Help keep a lookout ahead, Lyman. We're watching for the runway lights."

The sounds of ice hitting the fuselage had become continuous and sharp. Dougherty felt his arms trembling. He held on to the underside of his seat. "I don't see anything," he said.

"A couple of minutes yet," Del said. A minute and forty-eight seconds, he made it. He had to add a little power to both engines.

The engines were terrifically loud, Dougherty thought. He had a sense of the outside rushing by, but he couldn't see it.

"I still don't see anything."

"It's not time yet, we're still descending."

Descending in mountainous terrain, Del thought. He had a picture of the mountains around the aircraft. He was on a safe line of flight and descent as long as he stayed to that line and maintained the minimum allowed altitudes on the approach. Sky Ridge Lodge was at an altitude of 2,508. Three miles beyond it there was a piece of terrain that rose 2,843 feet. Into the blind sky, Del thought. A missed approach called for an immediate pull up and turn to the right. Then back to De Lancey and hold northeast of the VOR with left turns.

"See anything now?"

"No. Should I?"

Del looked up from the instruments and out ahead. "It should be there right in front of us."

Del pulled back on power and looked at his watch. Eight seconds to go. He lay back on power again, looking, *looking* . . . Then he pushed on full power and began a climbing right turn and retracted the gear. Something threw an amount of ice that was like a protracted thunderclap against the fuselage, and afterwards there was a sound like a human moan from somewhere in the airplane.

"What you say, Sky Ridge? We come anywhere near you?"

"Four-seven November, you got your landing lights on?"

"Affirmative on the landing lights."

"Well, I thought I saw some light up there."

"*I see it!*" Dougherty said. The aircraft was in a climbing bank, with Dougherty's side the low side. Del looked quickly, saw nothing and went back to his instruments. "It was there just as clear as it could be. Like the wind blew everything off it."

The moaning continued.

"You saw the airport?" Del said.

"Clear as could be. The lights, anyway."

"Runway lights?"

"Two rows of lights, just as clear as could be."

Climbing out they were just a little slower than they should have been, Del noted. They had picked up some ice down in the orographic effect, down near the surface where the wind running so quickly over the mountain contours ballooned up and supercooled the moisture in the air, moisture that would attach itself to any cool surface as ice. The ice seemed to be spreading thinly backwards on the underside of the wing. The moaning came from ice built up on some irregular exterior surface like an antenna.

"Clear as could be," Dougherty said. "I sure would like to try it again."

"One shot," Del said. "That's what I said I'd give it. That's what I gave it."

[103]

"Look here, Del, I know that was our agreement. But if we had made that approach just what—ten seconds later? If we had made that approach just a few seconds later you would've seen the airport and we'd be sitting down there now, having a drink, and you'd have earned your bonus for getting me in. Now, what I propose is this. Take one more run at it. I'll give you a hundred dollars for one more run at it. If we don't get in, I won't say another word and you'll have an extra hundred dollars. If we get in, you'll have Whittier's bonus, too. I tell you, I wouldn't even be thinking this way, because, frankly, I didn't think we'd be able to get in. But I *saw* it. Maybe we'll get lucky this next time."

Del thought about it. They were in level flight now, slightly nose-up and carrying slightly more power to compensate for ice, but only slightly changed in both instances. They were coming up on the De Lancey VOR.

"By rights I should hold at the VOR and give center a call and declare a missed approach and get cleared for another shot. But I purely don't want to take the time. I'm just goin' to turn around right here . . . just like this . . . over the VOR . . . and come back some on power . . . And here we are, Congressman, in another instrument approach to Sky Ridge." Del got on the radio. "Sky Ridge, we're atryin' it again." He went through the "Before Landing" cockpit check, watched the landing-gear safe lights come on. Four minutes and twenty-one seconds to go.

A shrill keening, a wailing joined the moaning.

"My God," Dougherty said.

"Ice, more ice," Del said. He looked at the wing. The ice had broadened. As they lost altitude in the approach, the orographic and impact effects were producing adhesive ice at a rate more pronounced than on the first approach.

Just this once, Del thought. He subtly jockeyed and interworked the flight and power controls. He *studied* the aircraft on down.

Thirty seconds to go.

He eased off on power. He decided to sneak down below minimums. He rationalized that he could get down more quickly and more safely if the airport should be briefly visible. What he really wanted, he knew, was to be closer to the ground in order to have a better chance of seeing the airport. He knew what he was doing was dangerous.

Zero seconds to go.

The airport was not in sight.

He slowed up, bled off a little more altitude.

The sky was like night now, black dark all around them. The airport was not in sight.

Del added full power and went through his missed-approach procedure

—to go home. That felt good. But the airplane didn't, and he was suddenly alarmed. The gear would not retract. He looked at the hydraulic pressure. It was normal: ice.

The airplane climbed slowly, the altimeter needle moving hardly at all. Del was uncertain about what altitude he needed for immediate terrain clearance. With full climb power he would not have needed to know. Now he didn't have time to consult a chart. It made no difference. Without climb he couldn't get over what might be immediately in front of him even if he knew it was there.

"Home, James," the congressman said, and sat back, satisfied that the dangerous part of the flight was over.

The sounds of wailing and keening and moaning came from several sources now.

He was flying an aircraft—barely flying an aircraft, Del knew—that was no longer aerodynamically sound, its flying surfaces distorted to something else by build-ups of ice. *One hundred thirty miles per hour* indicated, stall speed probably up around a hundred, nose high and going higher to correct for the ice.

He didn't know how much ice he had on the propeller blades. He wanted to slow the engines and run them up again to try to throw off prop ice. But he thought it might be suicide to cut back one iota of power with that configuration and load of ice.

He looked out at the wing. The ice was perhaps more visible. The engine instruments were steady, the engines unaffected by the cold and icing conditions. The rate of climb had grown sluggish again—the gear would be picking up more and more ice.

The altimeter read not quite four thousand feet and remained on the indication. They were not yet at the VOR and Del could not get another foot of altitude. If he could hold the four thousand it was conceivable that center could radar-vector him around dangerous terrain and . . .

But altitude was slipping off.

Del checked the engine instruments. They were still all right. Airspeed was down to *one hundred twenty-five.* God knows what the stall speed had gone up to.

The aircraft shuddered. Del shoved his yoke forward, pushing the nose of the aircraft down toward the ground. The airspeed raced up, and he carefully brought the aircraft back to nearly level flight. But now he kept the nose tipped down slightly.

Like a dumb student who didn't know any better, he had let the airplane get to the edge of a stall, that attitude where the wings can't lift any more and the aircraft ceases to be flying.

Now he was losing altitude on purpose—to keep flying. If he had tried to maintain level flight the airplane would have tumbled out of the sky like something leaden.

Like something ice-ridden, Del thought. He was turning the aircraft so carefully and gently that the congressman didn't notice.

It was night, night all around, and Del thought he might never get out of that cabin ever. He thought of Betty and of Mark and of Sheryl and his fear and grief were so strong he was briefly unable to see the instruments in front of him.

The aircraft had begun to fall away to the starboard, and he righted it and righted himself.

"Sky Ridge, do you read Four-seven November?"

There was silence. He tried again. There was no reply.

"Sky Ridge, Four-seven November. Any station, Six-five Four-seven November is going to attempt an emergency landing at Sky Ridge Lodge airport. Six-five Four-seven November."

The congressman had drawn back in his seat. He was staring at Del. "No," he said to Del. *"No."*

"Yes," Del said. Then he tried to raise Boston Center, but there was no answer. Their low altitude and the mountainous terrain prevented the signal from getting out.

Del switched over to one-twenty-one point five, the emergency frequency. He repeated the word *Mayday* three times and then gave the aircraft's numbers, approximate position, and intentions.

36

Dr. Glynn's nurse was getting ready to go home. She and Jonah had been in the same high school class twenty years before. She smiled. "Doesn't seem possible, does it?"

"No," Jonah said automatically. And then, "Yes, it does." Because Jonah could account precisely for a lot of hours in those twenty years. They were all neatly, and sometimes not so neatly, annotated in his flight logs. He could look at an entry and see that on a June day in 1964 he had flown a charter to Cincinnati and by association he could remember the rest of that day and the day before and the day after. He now had eight thousand one hundred and sixty hours annotated in his logs.

"Ruth, do you know why Dr. Glynn wants to see me?"

"No. How is it out, Jonah?"

"It's coming down pretty steady. We've had about five inches."

"Anyone saying how much we're supposed to get?"

"I don't know, but Albany's already had about a foot in six hours and it's supposed to go all night."

She tied her coat around her and pulled a ski hat on. "Dr. Glynn won't be long, Jonah, he's just on the telephone. I told him you're here. Say hi to Yvonne for me."

"I will."

Alone in the waiting room Jonah discovered that his hands had become fists. He relaxed them, but the fingers drew tightly against the palms involuntarily. The waiting room was warm—more like a small living room, with old pieces of furniture and a cheerful rug. The light over Ruth's desk and the lamp on it were out. There were pictures of sailing craft and horses on the walls. Jonah felt disquiet spread through him as if it had infused his blood.

"Jonah."

"Doc."

"If you'd step this way."

Jonah followed him down a short hallway, through a door to the right, and into Dr. Glynn's office. Usually Jonah would have gone through the door to the left into the examination room; he had a flight physical there every six months.

Jonah sat down across Dr. Glynn's desk from him. The office was nearly dark. A short fluorescent lamp on his desk illuminated the desk surface and Dr. Glynn vaguely beyond.

"I thank you for coming, Jonah. You haven't mentioned this to your wife?"

"No." Glynn had a soft Welsh accent and his voice was usually charged with encouragement. Jonah was seized now by the man's cautious tone.

"Now, Jonah, your wife came to see me for a routine obstetrical examination yesterday afternoon. On her last visit I was able to detect a fetal heartbeat, as she may have told you. As she also may have told you, the heartbeat, at that time, was something of a surprise. Most usually it is not audible so early. But neither is it extraordinary that it was audible. So we need make nothing of that, I should say—it's entirely possible that Yvonne became pregnant a month earlier than we have supposed. And in that event, the fetal heartbeat became audible right on schedule. I'm inclined to believe the latter—that Yvonne's pregnancy is of a longer duration than we had supposed.

"Now, what I must explain to you is that yesterday the fetal heartbeat was no longer audible."

Jonah felt his own heart beat rapidly. Where he had felt disquiet, he now felt a rush of sorrow. The sorrow was beyond his experience. He felt it would express itself in tears, but it remained unexpressed as the doctor's words continued and surrounded him.

"I am, I am afraid, talking about the possibility, the strong possibility, of an aborted pregnancy—a miscarriage, if you wish. There are some few other signs consistent with this possibility, Jonah. Yvonne complained of some minor cramps, quite minor, in fact, but they might be contractions, such as are present in a miscarriage. She has also had some staining in the past few days. This too is consistent with the possibility of a miscarriage.

"What happens is that for one or several of a very, very many reasons, nature decides to terminate the pregnancy. The fetal life, such as it is, ceases. In so doing, it becomes a foreign object to the woman's body. The body then goes about the work of expelling the no-longer-developing ovum. It does this in a similar fashion to childbirth itself. Through contractions to force the foreign object out.

"I did not want to discuss this with Yvonne because she seemed to me, at least yesterday, to be under some nervous strain already. Would you know what that might be?"

My flying, Jonah thought.

"No," he said to the doctor. Then, "I think she worries about my flying."

"Well, that would be something . . . not susceptible to treatment by me. Anything else?"

"Not that I can think of."

"What I wish you would do is let me know if any of these signs become more pronounced. She might, for instance, complain of a bloody discharge. That in itself could be the expulsion of the ovum. Or her cramps might become more severe. Anything which bothers her in the next few days, I wish you'd let me know.

"As I say, I did not want to distress Yvonne with this speculation. She may have a healthy fetus developing in her. I don't want to add any stress to the stress she may already be experiencing. Stress itself can precipitate a miscarriage."

Jonah said, "What about danger to Yvonne?"

"Yes, I wanted to cover that. The danger to the mother is minimal. Women have normal, if you will, aborted pregnancies often and don't even know they have occurred, didn't even know they were pregnant in some circumstances.

"No, Jonah, not to worry. Your wife is well. I gave her a thorough examination and she is a strong, healthy woman. We must watch her for a few days and then, in two or three or four days, decide whether the miscarriage needs assistance for the ease and protection of the mother."

"You're sure it's gone." Jonah was going to say *the child*. Instead he said, "You're sure the pregnancy is gone."

"No, Jonah, I'm not that certain. I would say that there are seven chances in ten, though, that the pregnancy has been terminated."

37

When Jonah got home, a few minutes after six, Yvonne was not there. *"Christ!"* he said. She was even out in *this*.

Today was supposed to be one of her early days home from school. He turned on a light in the dark kitchen and looked at her calendar to make sure. There was nothing on her calendar. She should have been home by three-thirty.

Then he saw the mail on the kitchen table. So she *had* been home that afternoon. He thought of her shoveling snow, of skiing, of other strenuous things he had asked her not to do for the baby's sake. He thought of the very delicate balance within her between life and death—the very possible miscarriage. Going out in *this* was just *courting* trouble.

There was an already opened letter from Yvonne's mother. It contained a couple of newspaper clippings about ways in which expectant mothers should take care of themselves. There were three bills that came to ninety-six dollars and some cents. The only mail specifically for Jonah was a brown manila envelope containing fifty or sixty revision pages for his Jeppesen manual of instrument-approach plates. Each page contained some slight but important change from previous specifications. The airway manual revisions arrived every few days, and substituting them for the old material they replaced took him about half an hour. Still another Jeppesen manual also required as much attention.

Jonah sat down and began inserting the new material. Getting behind with Jeppesen revisions was like knowingly taking a step into quicksand.

Jonah heard the outside weather crackling against the windowpanes over the sink. He worried about Yvonne and continued to work on the Jepp manual. The silence in the kitchen was as real to him as the sound of the weather against the window.

When the telephone rang and he looked at his watch, he was surprised to find that he had only been home a little while.

It was Yvonne, and she said she was at Betty's.

"Betty who?" Jonah said.

"Betty. Betty Howard's. Del's wife. Jonah dear, please come over."

38

Jonah had never been in the Howards' house before. He parked in the driveway and entered through the kitchen door, passing from the cold air and the stinging dry snow into the yellow light of the old farmhouse kitchen.

Betty Howard put down a knife and some celery she was cutting up, wiped her hands on a paper towel, came over to Jonah, and shook his hand.

"I'll take your coat," she said. "It's good of you to come. Did you hear anything about Del at the airport?"

"No, what—"

"I tried to get you earlier," Yvonne said. She took his hand. "I tried the airport, but you'd gone, they didn't know where."

"Ev shut things up at three. I had to—I had an appointment later, so I just hung around downtown. What about Del?"

"Someone from the airport, your mechanic"—Betty looked at a piece of paper—"Case Broadwell. He called here. To see if Del was home." Jonah nodded. Betty went on. "That's all. Air Traffic Control called to see if his airplane was back in Cornwall. He didn't close his flight plan. They don't know where he is." Betty went back to cutting up vegetables. "I'm making a stew for all of us. A beef stew. The kids love it. I had it cooking this afternoon. I'm just adding some more vegetables. I hope you like stew."

"Jonah?" Yvonne said. "Betty asked you—"

"Oh, yes. Stew is fine." Jonah thought how nearly he had taken the flight, how chickenshit he had felt when he hadn't. Del had called him that, hadn't he? chickenshit? And here he was in the man's house and the man hadn't closed his flight plan.

"Suppose I call over to Boston Center," Jonah said. "Maybe there's someone over there who'll talk to me me."

"Oh, *thank you,* Jonah," Betty said.

Jonah got through to the watch supervisor. " . . . The sector controller cleared him for an approach to Sky Ridge and after a number of minutes, when the controller couldn't raise him and the flight plan hadn't been closed . . . uh, the sector controller initiated action. He called Sky Ridge on the phone and asked if they had an arrival. They said no, he's not on the ground. Next, uh, the sector controller requested that they call him on the radio and get his status. The controller's report says *unable to contact.* The controller's report to the watch supervisor reads *aircraft unreported on approach, no contact.* We figured fuel exhaustion about forty-five minutes ago, at six-thirty. We put out an Alert Notice. All we can say now is the usual—aircraft presumed involved in an accident, operations in progress."

"What sort of operations?" Betty asked.

"ATC alerts the Coast Guard. The Coast Guard heads it up. They have the search helicopters and they have a network to alert all the other responsible agencies. But the helicopters can't do anything in the weather over there. They cleared a search plane into the area, but all he'll be able to do is overfly it and hope to pick up a signal of some sort. A radio transmission or a locater beacon."

"He could have had radio failure," Betty said. "He could even be down somewhere safe where there's no communication because of the storm. I keep thinking hard on that."

She turned back to the cutting board. Then she took the few handfuls of cut-up vegetables and put them in a bright red Dutch oven on top of the stove. It was a very modern piece of design in the old kitchen, with its creaky floor and cracked enamel paint. Steam lifted off the stew and rose into the air in waves. Betty put the cover on the oven and the steam disappeared. She turned down the heat and came over and sat at the kitchen table across from Jonah and Yvonne.

"In the Navy, he'd be aboard ship most of the time, and so most of the time I didn't know when something might be bad. But when we were at South Weymouth, he lived at home, and so I'd know when something might have gone bad. We all had husbands who flew," she said to Jonah, "I mean we just seemed to know each other, the wives of the pilots. Anyway, we all learned right quick when something bad might have happened. We just naturally let each other know. And we'd sort of help out at whoever's house it was. Someone would take the kids, a couple of others would sit it out with the wife. That always happened. Thank God I only had to go through it twice." She looked at her fingers, which she'd been moving hurriedly back and forth as if she were playing a vertical piano. "I used to smoke," she said. "Both times I had someone to call when no one knew what had happened to Del. I had a lot of people to call. People who understood. *Tonight I just didn't know who to call.*"

She looked at Jonah as if she were going to cry, and she shrugged as if apologizing for having called.

Yvonne went over and put her arm around Betty.

Betty continued to look at Jonah. "I just thought and thought and *thought,* here I am in this cold winter place and I don't *know* anyone, I don't know anyone who *understands* about what goes on out there, about times like this . . . Then I thought of Yvonne and Jonah. They understand, I thought. They'll understand."

Christ, yes . . . no, Yvonne doesn't understand at all. Sitting there maybe with the little lost baby in her, and not knowing, and losing the baby because she worried about me, and . . . No, that's not true, Jonah. Just wait a bit. Just think about it at another time.

"What happened the other times?" Jonah said. "Those two other times?"

"He had to make emergency landings. Once because of weather and once because of a mechanical. Word was just slow getting back to us."

"Maybe it's the same this time," Yvonne said.

"I'm going to set the table," Betty said. But she remained in her seat looking at the tabletop, the circular blond-stained table. "This was our first dining-room table," she said. "Right after Del got his wings. Sheryl's ten years old now and Mark is seven," she said. "Jonah, over there in the floor cabinet next to the sink—that's where we keep our liquor. Would you please give me two fingers of bourbon on ice and fix yourself and Yvonne something."

A few minutes after eleven, while she was on her fourth or fifth cup of coffee since dinner, Betty said, "Don't they let you know?"

Jonah said, "ATC? They can't tell you anything if they don't know anything."

"Maybe they lost my number, maybe they don't want to let me know, maybe—"

"Betty," Jonah said, "my friend at ATC promised to call as soon as there's any word. He will."

"But they haven't called."

Jonah heard his own words as he spoke to Betty, and he thought of Dr. Glynn talking to him earlier. Jonah thought it had not been nearly so difficult for Dr. Glynn. "Betty, we have to realize that Del suffered fuel exhaustion hours ago if he was still flying. There's no chance that he's still flying now. ATC didn't have any unidentified targets within a hundred miles of De Lancey VOR during the period when Del was making his approach. They didn't have any unidentifieds after that, either. Nothing appeared on their screens that wasn't identified. They've talked to every likely airport he might have tried to get into. They've talked to every radio facility he might have tried to talk to. All they have is a report of an aircraft in distress which *could* have called from that area. But it was picked up by a TWA flight flying at thirty-six thousand feet. That signal could have come from thousands of square miles . . . The rest of it is, it's a lousy night out there, it was lousy this afternoon, too. That's lousy terrain he was trying to get down into."

Jonah went to the other side of the room and made himself a cup of tea.

[112]

When he came back to the table, in the silence of the phone not ringing, Betty said, "Maybe he got lucky."

Jonah thought, *I don't give him one chance in ten.*

"Jonah?" Betty said.

"If he got lucky, we would have heard from him," Jonah said.

A few minutes before midnight Betty got up and began cleaning away the few cups and dishes still out. As she put the dishes in the dishwasher she went through her mental list of the needs of the house before bed. She had to rinse the dishes before she put them in the dishwasher. *If a dishwasher can't wash dishes, how can you expect an airplane to fly?* The children were asleep. Betty had said to them, "Dad has to stay away overnight. Because of the weather." Now the kitchen was straightened, and Jonah and Yvonne were looking at her. The doors had to be locked and then she could go up to bed.

She said to Yvonne and Jonah, "Would it be a *terrible* imposition to ask y'all t'stay over tonight?"

Yvonne went over and put her arms around Betty and held her. And then the three of them sat at the empty table for a few minutes more. They sat there without saying anything. The hands of the clock stood upright at twelve. At a few minutes after midnight Betty Howard began to cry.

IN
FLIGHT

flight[1], n. 1. act, manner, or power of flying. 2. the distance covered or the course taken . . . 3. a number of beings . . . passing through the air together. 4. a trip by an airplane . . . 5. a scheduled trip on an airline . . . 7. act, principles, or technique of flying an airplane . . . 9. . . . transition . . . 10. a soaring above or transcending ordinary bounds . . .

flight[2], n. 1. act of fleeing . . .

—*The Random House Dictionary of the English Language*

Before getting into weather flying, we should talk about emotions.

— (Captain) Robert N. Buck

39

Perry Sullivan sat in a swivel chair behind a desk in the small office which belonged to New EnglandAir's Cornwall station manager. He looked out through a rain-smeared expanse of glass at a waiting airliner, a Fairchild Hiller FH 227. It was nearly five o'clock of a March afternoon, and with the warm, windy rainstorm it had already gotten as dark as night outside. The 227, which was New EnglandAir Flight One-six-five and belonged to Perry, stood motionless on the ramp, the rotating beacon atop the tail fin sending split red flashes into the darkness. The flashes reflected sharply and brilliantly for an instant off the wet ramp. The black figures of two men loading baggage were substanceless shadows until the light from the beacon caught them and illuminated their shiny yellow slickers. When the wind gusted enough, the high wings of the 227 moved languidly.

Intermittent gusts of fog obscured the baggage loaders and rendered the 227 indistinct. Then the fog ballooned with light from the rotating beacon. It was very pretty to watch. But it was the ground fog that concerned Perry —that and the instrument conditions above it.

There were very brief periods of time during which there was enough forward horizontal visibility for a legal takeoff. There were longer periods when there was no such visibility. The situation varied by the minute, sometimes by the seconds, and the decision whether to go or not to go was Perry's. He had made two approaches before getting in. The third time the entire length of the runway had cleared while he was still above decision height and he had landed with fine visibility. And then just after he had gotten down, his surroundings had become so laden with fog that he'd had to taxi with sole reference to the white taxi stripe on the ground below him. There had been nothing else to see.

At the terminal it had not seemed that bad. He had been able to look across the field to lights in the old wooden building that housed the office of Yancey Flying Service. Then a flood of fog had swept across the field. First the building had disappeared and then the lights within it. He had gone into the station manager's office and called New EnglandAir's dispatcher at La Guardia for the weather there. It was much the same as at Cornwall. Some flights were getting in, most were not. He got a U.S. Weather Bureau briefing from Concord, New Hampshire, and was told that present local conditions in the Cornwall area were expected to persist throughout the evening. No one suggested what a wise decision might be. To go or not to go was entirely a captain's decision. Captain Perry Sullivan's decision.

The fog dissipated for a moment, and there again, across the field, was Yancey Flying Service. Perry thought of young Perry over there, trying to learn to fly an airplane, and he thought of all his old instructors—Ev Goodsom, Falun Aigborg, George Detwiler from time to time, others . . . This terminal building hadn't been built then, the FH 227 hadn't been designed. The building and its light disappeared again in fog.

The only light now on in the New EnglandAir office was from a small, shaded fluorescent lamp on the manager's desk. When the rain spread in slow, thin waves down the plate glass it filled and glowed with red light from the insistent rotating beacon. Perry thought about to go or not to go. He had just had his thirty-fifth birthday. He had four gold rings on his sleeve. He sat in the swivel chair with one foot on the desk and watched Flight One-six-five being loaded out on the ramp. And he watched the gusts of fog and the slow, color-filled, downward progress of the rain on the plate-glass window.

The problem was twofold. There was Laura and there was— He stopped himself. The problem had nothing to do with Laura. The problem was the weather here and the weather in New York. He had ordered extra fuel here. Plenty of fuel to hold in the New York area and then go on to an alternate —Philadelphia or even Washington if necessary.

In the meantime, here he was—home. Just a stop on the route for One-sixty-five, but his residence when he was not flying. He was not flying tomorrow. So if he got One-sixty-five into New York this evening, he could drive home to Cornwall tomorrow morning or even tonight if he felt like it. But Perry'd had a progressively disheartening feeling that Cornwall was less and less his home. His exuberance and enthusiasm upon coming home to his own house had used to be powerful. Now, returning from trips, when he turned his car into the rural lane that led to his house, he grew anxious about what Laura's mood might be and felt himself pervaded with dejection.

Perry's mind went to money. He was making good money now. He could expect to clear over twenty thousand dollars after taxes. But Laura had insisted on a new sports car for herself. Perry had taken a car loan from the bank. Seventy-two dollars a month. The mortgage on the house was two hundred and thirty-eight. Town taxes were another thousand. In January alone Laura had spent nearly five hundred dollars on clothes at "sales" in Boston. Various pieces of insurance came to another six hundred a year . . . When he added it all up, those things and others, he was appalled. He had achieved the level of income he had always aspired to, and yet to get through the year he would have to go into his savings or investments. Laura insisted on redoing the bedroom. She wanted flowing, gossamer curtains, a huge canopied bed, deep carpeting—"It's really for you," she had said, "a husband should feel like he's entering his mistress' bedroom when he enters his wife's bedroom." The statement had baffled Perry. And Laura was insisting upon structurally redoing the bathroom. She wanted a sunken tub, a vanity counter with a theatrical mirror, a . . .

"*Christ!*" Perry had said.

"Why did you get married? You didn't want a wife. You didn't want a *woman*. What *did* you want?"

Perry was too bewildered, in his attempt at honest answers, to find an answer for her.

"See? You don't *know*," Laura had said.

She had been talking—on her own—to an officer of the bank. She had been arranging a new mortgage to pay for the new bathroom and the new bedroom. Perry felt violated by her going to the bank about the mortgage, about redoing the house, his house.

Well, shit. It was half her house. He had put it in both their names. He appreciated that he had lived alone a good time in that house. Maybe he was selfish about it.

But all that goddamn *money* going out.

With all her insistence upon redoing the house to be a woman's house, she refused to occupy herself and her abundance of empty time with some of the more common attentions of the woman at home—she refused to "depress" her life with housework. She had a maid in half a day three days a week. The maid and Laura sat and drank coffee together and Laura listened earnestly to gossip about people she didn't know. When Laura had affectionate words for Perry they often began with "Remember when . . . ?" and went on about something during their courtship. Such shared memories having accrued over a period of only a few months, they did not provide enough material for prolonged conversation. "Now all there is to do is watch television," Laura said. She was passionately jealous of his work, that his time was so occupied. "*You're probably screwing some stews when you're in New York,*" she said violently.

"Hell no, Laura."

"I know you."

"What do you mean by that?"

"Never mind."

"Laura, I swear to you—"

"Captain?" He was jerked back by the voice of his copilot, R. W. Roy. Perry looked away from the rain-smeared window. Roy and the station manager stood in the doorway to the office. Perry stood up. "Christ, with all the goddamn electronic equipment, the satellites, weather radar, I've still got to walk outside and look to see if it's go or no go."

He went outside and looked. The fog lay still, rushed away, and then coursed in again.

He went back into the terminal through the main entrance. Some thirty passengers looked at him. Most of them were standing. In spite of the delay, they expected the flight to be boarding. It was very bright in the terminal waiting room. Perry had a semiconscious thought that he didn't want to go home just then, didn't want to have to be alone with Laura. He said to the station manager, "Tell them Flight One-six-five now loading Gate One and get their asses out there."

40

Taxiing out in the darkness and wandering fog, Perry had glanced left through his windscreen and a trick of light had produced his reflection in the windscreen. He thought of shaving while Laura was trying to brush her teeth. So much intimacy, yet so much contention. As he had been shaving and looking at himself in the mirror, Perry had suddenly recognized that both of them were trying desperately and separately to preserve the self-image of themselves that they had had before marriage. At the same time each of them was holding an unforgiving mirror before the other.

The white taxiway stripe slipped under and under the nose.

Perry looked ahead. He had spent his first twenty-five hours on this route with Tony Bergeron, the line's chief pilot, sitting next to him in the copilot's seat. In the more than one hundred hours since that time, Perry had encountered nothing like this—a situation in which he would be totally dependent upon instruments and his responses to them virtually from liftoff to final approach.

For the first time during the eleven years he had been with the airline Perry was, in spite of the copilot next to him, alone. Perry was pilot-in-command. For the first time he was faced with the work that they say is what a captain is actually paid for: the decision to go or not to go. He still was not committed to go. That decision could not be said to have been irrevocably made until he had, by a combination of speed of aircraft and diminishing length of runway, committed the aircraft to takeoff.

The instruments glowed in the night-darkened cockpit and the rain sluiced across the windscreen. The airliner rocked on its gear and shuddered in heavy winds as it stood halted short of the runway. Perry's copilot was reading off the pre-takeoff checklist and Perry was responding but thinking *What am I doing here?* and remembering all the captains who had always made this go or no-go decision for him before—and then flown him through and out of whatever perils might have resulted from the decision to go.

Perry had always considered fear, or even panic, a possible factor of flight. His "open door" in such a situation was to be his own skill. But now, as captain, pilot-in-command of an aircraft carrying thirty-eight passengers and crew, he was experiencing fear. He felt again his aloneness in the darkness and in the weather. He thought of the passengers waiting in their seats behind him in the aircraft. Reading lights would be on. In his mind Perry saw a fat man with glasses reading a newspaper. He saw a woman with a young child in the seat next to her. The woman was trying to peer out into the darkness. Perry saw that she was nervous. They were flash images. If he decided not to go, the company would not dispute his decision. Still, captains are paid to get flights through, and if he refused a takeoff, it would go on his record. Some time, Perry thought, he might need to refuse a takeoff more than he needed to now.

I am the captain of my ship, he kept thinking. *I am the captain of my ship, the master of my craft . . .*

"Gyro."

"Set," Perry responded.

"Altimeter."

I am . . .

"Set."

The master of my ship.

Perry moved the FH 227 out on the runway and aimed it down the runway centerline. His right hand pushed the throttles forward. The power indicators leapt across their calibrations. The body of the aircraft jarred but did not move forward. Perry had not released the brakes. The power continued to build.

I am the master of . . .

He released the brakes.

My ship.

I am the goddamn master of my ship.

She was heaving now, her speed and mass in conflict with the force of the wind across the runway. Ground fog leapt up. Then there was no end of the runway to look for, there was no runway to be seen at all. But Perry had already gone on instruments.

The copilot called, *"V one, rotate!"*

Committed. There we are, Perry thought, committed.

Cautiously his fingers felt against the tension in the yoke. He brought the yoke back toward him, and then, satisfied, and without pause, further back, firmly and as if in deliberate slow motion.

"V two!"

His right hand left the twin throttles and, palm up, fingers gesturing upwards, he said to the copilot, "Positive rate, gear up."

A hollow bump, a clink. The gear was folding up into its nests in the wings and belly. She was a smoother ship now and flying faster and with more response and, to Perry, with certainty.

"Time off," Perry said, and the copilot, who a moment ago had distrusted this new captain's abilities and who had been afraid, casually retrieved the clipboard on which such entries are made and casually made the entry.

When One-six-five had gotten everything sorted out with Air Traffic Control and was at altitude and set up on autopilot and when Perry was satisfied that there was nothing that potentially might sneak up on him, he looked briefly out at the darkness. There was no reason to; he could see nothing and had expected to see nothing.

He picked up the public address telephone and said, "Welcome aboard, folks. I'm Captain Sullivan and your first officer is R.W. Roy. Your stewardess is Miss Tate. We're at an altitude of ten thousand feet and our flight time to New York will be approximately one hour, though I expect we'll have some delays due to traffic and instrument conditions . . . Uh, New York is rainy and overcast and the temperature there is fifty-two degrees." Perry looked out into the utter blackness. "Immediately below us," he said, "shining beneath the setting sun, is Quabbin Reservoir, all fifteen miles of it." He smiled, thinking that a few of his passengers might actually be taking a look down. "Those lights up ahead belong to the great city of Springfield, Massachusetts. As we go along, I'll point out further significant sights. Thank you," and he clicked off.

He hoped he had amused the nervous woman with the young child, given her some relief and the same to other nervous passengers. He hoped they might think well of their captain. Then, Perry thought, they might think he was crazy, too.

41

"Christ yes, he's dead," Ev said. He looked out at the filthy March late afternoon—not that he could see anything through the fog. He turned so that he was facing back into Yancey Flying Service's waiting room and said to no one in particular, "Del Howard's dead." Falun Aigborg nodded.

"But he *could* be alive," the reporter said. He looked at Jonah.

"I don't think so," Jonah said. "I hope so, but I don't think so."

"Where Delaney Howard probably went down," Ev said, "it's so remote none of the search and rescue people found *anything,* and by God we crisscrossed that area in planes for *days*—"

"I know, but—"

"For days. We had plenty of people out there on snowshoes and snowmobiles, and God knows what all."

"All I said was, he *could* be."

"You mean you need something to fill some space. So you want the goddamned airport manager, with all his years of flying, to say Del Howard might still be alive. Well, I God damn *won't do it.* Del Howard's dead."

Falun was watching the three of them, trying to listen to them. But he found it difficult to stay in the room. He kept drifting, perhaps *flying* to other rooms, other times, other people. He knew that he was drifting, and he seriously tried to keep himself in the present. But recently he had found it very difficult and sometimes impossible to keep himself in the present. It required more energy than he had and more concentration than he was capable of. He was looking at . . . who? Jonah? And he was looking at, in memory, that warm spring night when he and Marion had moved into their unfinished house. They had been living in an apartment in town, the house framed in, roofed, walled, electrified, but unfinished. Then the smell of spring had gotten into the apartment and Falun had said, *C'mon, let's go, let's start living there tonight.* The house lonely up there on the hill then. And not a light to be seen on any of the hills around. Other lights had come later, a long time later. That was all right, he had let it happen, and he had done all right selling off the land, he and Marion had been comfortable and Marion *would be* comfortable. There it was again. The quick terror. Quick and awful. A bird of prey plummeting through his innards. Striking. Seizing. Then gone.

It jarred him into looking at the others now, people he didn't know. In December Dr. Glynn had told him he was probably going to die sometime in the new year. That was when Falun had begun noticing the other people, the people whose names he knew, though often he did not know the people themselves. Claude Dornier. December fifth. First all-metal airplane. Eighty-five. So many since then, so rapidly. Bertrand Russell, the philosopher, ninety-seven. Marie Dionne, the littlest of the Dionne quintuplets, only thirty-five. Falun thought, *I have already had more than twice the taste of life she had, the poor little girl* and the bird struck him again . . . And William T. Piper, someone he had *really* known. Bill Piper had been eighty-nine. Falun remembered standing on runways in Bradford and Lock Haven with Bill Piper, remembered flying the prototype J-2 Piper Cub to a total altitude of five feet, remembered the hours he'd spent in a bleak building in Lock Haven working on the prototype J-3 Piper Cub with Bill and the exalted hours flying the new monoplane . . .

There was the hammer-pounding sound of a multiengine aircraft accelerating out on the runway.

Ev didn't bother to turn around to try to look. "Some damn fool flying in this stuff?"

"New EnglandAir One-sixty-five, I guess," Jonah said.

"That's my damn knowledge flying out there," Ev said. "*Captain* Perry Sullivan, for Christsake. Damn fool."

"Ev, you're so proud it even shows," Jonah said.

"Let's shut this place up," Ev said. "Ain't nothin' else gonna fly tonight. Not here." Ev suddenly said to Jonah, "You made the right decision, Jonah. You know what I'm talking about." Then he went to his office.

"What's he talking about?" the reporter said.

Jonah shrugged.

"Probably," Falun said, "I think probably Ev is talking about a flight Jonah decided not to make." Falun looked at Jonah. "I've always known you were a good pilot, Jonah. That day I learned how very good."

"Thank you, Falun."

"How is your wife, Jonah? I heard there was trouble about the baby."

"I thought it was all over. When Doc Glynn called me in." He sat down next to Falun. "Christ, Falun . . . *I thought it was my fault.* Because Yvonne got nervous about my flying." Falun nodded. "She's all right now. They kept her in strict bed rest in the hospital for a few days, and they say she and the baby are fine now. If she takes it easy." *How can I take it easy,* he heard Yvonne say, *when I worry so when you're flying? If I lose the baby, it will be because of your flying. Do you want the baby or do you want your flying?* Dr. Glynn had said there was no such decision to be made, it was not within Jonah's compass, Yvonne would keep the baby or lose it as the result of a constellation of factors over which Jonah had very little influence and absolutely no control. Jonah said, "Drive you home, Falun."

"No," Ev said, coming back into the room. "I'll drive the old bastard home."

42

Laura Sullivan felt her dinner companion's hand brush the hanging drape of the white linen tablecloth aside and, after a second's hesitation, settle on her thigh while the man, Ralph Willerwood, was saying, " . . . and of course I'd pay the entire way, we could have separate rooms if you wished, but I must describe the *magnificence* of this place, the sheer magnificence. First . . . "

They were sitting side by side at a table in a booth. The table faced out into the restaurant. It was a new restaurant some twenty miles from Cornwall. No one in the restaurant knew Laura or Ralph. The restaurant was dark. Ralph Willerwood was describing to Laura a new ski resort he wanted to take her to. The resort was four hours away. It didn't matter that Laura didn't ski, Ralph emphasized, because "It would be just like going out to dinner—as we're doing now. But we wouldn't have to rush back. We'd just have dinner and stay overnight. There's a lovely little bar for dancing and . . . "

She had spent a pleasant afternoon doing her hair and scenting and powdering herself. She wore what she knew was a most provocative dress, roundly and deeply cut, and thin and clingy. She had chosen underwear that was lacy and diaphanous. Slowly grooming and dressing herself for the evening she had thoroughly excited herself without once thinking of Ralph Willerwood.

Ralph had called for her at six. They'd had a drink. In the kitchen, getting out the drink things, she had felt his hand patting her bottom. Three quick little strokes. She had countered by handing him the icetray to open—a deft little move on her part, she had thought. But that had been the first instance. Later, as they were getting ready to go and Ralph was about to hold her coat for her, the back of his hand had somehow slid up across her breast. So slowly that it had almost lingered. Before she could react he had been standing behind her holding her coat. That had been the second instance.

Now they were having an after-dinner cognac and his hand rested on her thigh. Three times, Laura thought. Three times is too much. She smiled what she thought to be her best smile. "Ralph," she said, "what you're doing is *quite* irritating."

The hand withdrew.

"I think, dear, you better keep both your hands on the table." The smile, she knew, was ravishing. It was the smile she had practiced for when she wanted a man to feel singled out at a party. "It's a dear hand," she said, "but it's so *busy.*"

Ralph smiled at her uncertainly.

"Why don't you have another brandy?" Laura said. "I can always drive. Go ahead. Enjoy yourself."

Ralph ordered a double.

"Now, about this overnight you have in mind," Laura said.

"Yes, Laur. What about it?"

"Have you thought about me?"

"Why, yes, that's all I've thought about. I mean, I—"

"But you haven't, you see. Do you think I just go off and have intercourse because a gentleman offers to take me to dinner?"

"Now, Laur—"

"What about Perry?"

"I didn't think you cared about Perry."

"I care very much. He's my husband. Is it your practice to—to *insinuate* yourself into a married household?"

"No."

"Aren't there plenty of single ladies around?" Laura looked at Ralph and smiled slightly. "Does it have to be a married lady, Ralph?" Looking at his face she sensed that she had excited him. She smiled again, her eyes on his. She took his hand in hers. "Why, yes, it does. It *has* to be a married lady, doesn't it? for *some* reason. How sweet, Ralph." And she kissed his hand lightly with her lips. He began to tremble. Laura laughed.

On the way home she began to cry. She did not know why except that perhaps she had drunk too much wine and that she felt very, very alone. Ralph became worried. He tried to soothe her. She found that his worry felt good. The tears continued, and she turned her head from him and rested her forehead against the cold glass of the passenger window. After a while she stopped crying. By then they were nearly home. Her sobs had become those of a young, tired child.

She said, "I feel so much better, Ralph."

"Yes," he said.

She laughed. "You don't have to be a grouch about it."

"I'm not. I'm glad you feel better, Laur." He pulled into her driveway. "Let me come in for a drink."

"No."

"Just to show you're not angry at me."

"No. Thank you for a pleasant evening, Ralph." She started to open the door.

"God damn!" he said.

"Really," she said, and got out.

She had to find her key. He got out of the car and came and stood by her as she looked. "Laura, please."

The words were said tonelessly. Laura thought she understood from the way in which they were said that Ralph was not going to call her again. Not unless . . . Something.

Then what will I do? she thought. The feeling of absolute aloneness came on her again. No Perry. No one. Not even Ralph Willerwood.

She unlocked the door, went in, turned, and nodded to him slightly. "Just for a minute," she said. She didn't turn the light on. She opened her coat but did not take it off. He wore no coat. She stood with the small of her back against the kitchen counter, her upper torso cocked back slightly, her pelvis thrust slightly forward from her upper body. A girlfriend with whom she had once roomed when she had been a stewardess had taught her the stance and told her that it drove men wild. She had used it on Perry successfully. Ralph came to kiss her. She turned her lips away from his. He kissed her cheek and held her strongly. He pushed his pelvic area against hers. She pushed back.

One second, she thought. *Two seconds. Three.* She moved from him quickly. "Now you have to go. Hurry. Or I won't speak to you again."

"All right." He looked at her and then left.

She locked the door and turned off the outside light. She stood alone in the darkened room and in her own voice screamed in her head—to Perry, to the room, to the house—*What was I to do? What can I do?*

What could I do? what could I do? There is nothing to do. There is never anything to do. I'm always alone . . .

She heard the sad, lonely, tired voice.

It was hours before she took her coat off and went to bed.

43

In fog and darkness, on instrument final approach to La Guardia Runway Three-one, Perry had never been more confident of a landing. Every needle on the instrument panel stood or progressed as it should. His speed and altitude control were perfect. His adjustments to keep the needles where they should be went unfelt in the aircraft—except for the sounds of the engines and some slight vibrations, One-six-five might have been standing still. Perry felt a mastery and an exuberance that were thrilling. This was the sort of approach one might like to extend forever. The aesthetic part of his mind experienced all of that while the professional part of his mind continued as before—cool, dominant, and persevering.

Peripherally Perry became aware that the quality of the darkness outside the flight deck was changing. There seemed to be a difference in the illumination of the panel and then there was an abrupt white brightness above the panel and in the flight deck. Immediately R. W. Roy spoke to the tower and said, "One-sixty-five has the runway in sight."

Perry was now visual on the approach, his fingers on the yoke and power controls now translating what his eyes saw *outside* the aircraft into commands to the flight surfaces and power plants of New EnglandAir One-sixty-five. He eased the aircraft down. The runway lights ceased being still and became oblong blurs rushing backwards as he set the aircraft on the runway. There was no feel of it. Perry grinned. "Are we down?"

"One-six-five, left turn as soon as practical. Please expedite. Contact La Guardia Ground Control one-two-one point seven."

Perry remained in his captain's seat on the flight deck. The maintenance people had not yet come aboard to taxi the aircraft away for cleaning and inspection. He could have left R.W. aboard to wait for them and turn the aircraft over to them, but Perry felt a high from which he did not want to come down. He sat in the darkness and the stillness of the flight deck and thought through the flight again, from his anxiety on the ground in Cornwall to his growing feeling of mastery and sureness as he had climbed out to his absolute sureness and pride as he had brought his flight to its destination. R. W. Roy, who had recently been his colleague and peer as a copilot, had said laconically as he had picked up his flight bag to leave, "Nice flight, Captain." It was the first time in the trips they had flown together that R.W. had called him captain. And it was the first time since he had worn them that Perry felt that the four gold rings on his sleeve belonged. His feelings were immense and exultant and Perry felt like calling Laura and sharing them with her.

But no. The Laura he wanted to call was someone he could hardly remember. He decided not to drive home that night but stay over in the accommodations the company provided.

Perry thought again of the flight. He sat in the darkness and stillness of the flight deck. He didn't want to come down.

44

New EnglandAir kept a number of rooms booked at a hotel in midtown Manhattan for members of its flight crews as needed. On the way in, Perry kept thinking of Fran and Nick Howzer. Fran was a sweetheart from his college days. He had run into the Howzers recently at La Guardia and had been invited to call them the very next time he had to remain overnight in New York unexpectedly.

When Perry got to the hotel room he found that it had a feeling of emptiness and isolation quite beyond the studied neutrality of its furnishings. Perry thought again of calling Fran, but he was hesitant to do so: he barely knew Nick, he hadn't seen either of them in three or four years, and it was already late to be calling, after seven. Perry showered and put on slacks and a jacket and tie. He *ought* to do something about dinner. He finally decided to call the Howzers because they were no part of his life with Laura—they didn't even know her. Fran Howzer said come right over, she and Nick had a guest, dinner was going to be a good one, and the man they had expected to make a fourth at the table had come down with the flu.

Fran and Nick's guest was a pretty young woman from Minneapolis, a cousin of Nick's, who was in New York doing some buying for a department store back home and who was staying with the Howzers for the pleasure of their company.

Dinner was by candlelight. A second bottle of wine had to be opened before they were through the main course. There had been drinks before dinner, and since Perry was not flying the next day, he'd had two Scotch and sodas. He found the dinner joyous. The emotional warmth was almost physical. He was deeply glad that Fran had such a sunny marriage and that such marriages did indeed exist.

After coffee they went back to the living room. Nick set out a silver tray of cordials, brandy, and glasses on the coffee table, and the four of them sat around the table talking and sipping at bright, aromatic liquids that made Perry think of tiny, vibrant flames caught in small, glass torches. So much warmth was suddenly almost unbearable to him.

The guest's name was Sally and she was so cheerful and so generously friendly that Perry began wondering what it would be like to be married to her. For a few seconds he imagined that he *was* married to her and that here they were, all family together. What a perfect family, he thought.

But of course he couldn't be married to Sally because he was married to Laura.

Just as if he had a separate, presently sober part of his mind that had pulled up an invisible chair next to him in order to better hear what he was saying, Perry listened to himself say, "Laura and I are still living together. That is, we're both in the same house. But we're getting a divorce. You see, I fell in love with someone who never existed. I mean, I think I made her up. The Laura that I fell in love with. So, you see, it's not her fault." Perry felt that he was being scrupulously honest, commendably fair, in not laying responsibility on Laura. He described some of the failures of their marriage

—clinically, he felt—and some of Laura's behavior. He was surprised when he found Fran's arms around him and heard her saying, "Oh, poor Perry. Poor Perry." He was astonished to find that he had tears on his cheeks and in his eyes.

The invisible Perry sitting next to him in the invisible chair said, "Sullivan, you're crocked."

Perry had not been crocked since he'd been in college. He liked to drink when there was a party and he liked the happy feelings he got from it. But he so disliked the feelings of spatial and emotional disorientation that came from too much drinking that he had not since college drunk enough to go beyond the little feelings of unexpected euphoria.

But at the Howzers, he decided, he had drunk rather more than he had noticed he was drinking. When he got back to his hotel room he was in orbit somewhere in the night around himself.

The room was still possessed by loneliness. The time was a little after midnight. His emotions were running like air currents across a mountain —up and down with great force—and he felt stimulated beyond his capacity to contain his sudden acquisition of a sense of hope, of the possibilities of newness. He called an old girlfriend in Boston, a girl he had been seeing on and off for several months before he had met Laura and responded so totally to that smile of hers which he had thought was for him alone and to that suggestive body of hers and to those words which were so quick and humorous and then so quick and loving. When the girl asked what in heaven's name he meant calling at that hour, he said that he was lonely and drunk and that he was getting a divorce and that he had to talk to someone and that he had felt the need to talk to her. In a few minutes both he and the girlfriend were crying. Not much, but a little. He told her he would call her again soon, when he could see her, when the divorce had progressed. The response was gratifying. He no longer felt angry or entirely alone. He felt happy and vaguely saddened by his impending divorce. He went to sleep with a sense of liberation and of hope.

45

George Detwiler was trying desperately not to go to sleep. He had the radio on and periodically pounded the floor of the car with his foot and sang out loud when he knew some of the words to a song. The radio was playing rock. He detested rock, but it was a good friend when he was driving home from an evening of law classes at Boston College after a full day's work in the law office in Cornwall and a late night's study before that. His classes during the evening had been in Estate Planning and Federal Income Tax and Jurisprudence. His thoughts were strident and disorderly. He thought of marital deduction trusts and inter-vivos trusts and pounded the floor and sang some of the words of "I'd Like to Get to Know You" along with the radio and thought of Adele Fortune, her smooth slim body, and thought of Ceil, where had she gone, as if she had gone into the sky, and thought of Oliver Wendell Holmes, who just that evening had said, in Jurisprudence, "The common law is not a brooding omnipresence in the sky," and the car skidded a little on the slick road, skidded as he braked coming into a mountainside turn too fast, tree trunks stark and black and glistening wet, snow almost gone from the warmth and the rain, foggy smell of spring in the air, and unrelated business income, and he pounded the floor and sang, not hearing a word of it as he worried about the state bar exam coming up in the summer, the exam upon which his future now depended, and worried whether it was an exclusionary exam, how many new lawyers the brothers of the bar association were going to let into the trade, and in his anger that two or three practicing lawyers might exclude him from the practice of law after the dean and all the faculty of the law school of Boston College had certified him competent to practice law, George's fury was such that he went into another curve too fast and the ass of his bird (for he had the feeling of flight) swished a bit before he got it straightened out and everything settled down, and he wondered that Holmes had said, "The Law, wherein, as in a magic mirror, we see reflected not only our own lives, but the lives of all men that have been!" and where therein was the life of Ceil Detwiler, née Jutras? his wife who had disappeared into the sky, the sky where the law was not a brooding omnipresence, and goddamn Holmes anyway for pointing out what George had been suspecting but wished not to know, that *The life of the law has not been logic: it has been experience,* "For God damn it," George said out loud, pounding the floor with his clutch foot, "I went into the law for *logic,* for *walls* of logic!" and this time the car skidded and turned too far and got away from him and George finally saw Ceil again. She was smiling at him. And in that instant he discovered something terrible: that he wanted to go to her. But he *longed* to stay with Randy too. Why couldn't the *three* of them be together? The radio played "Jesus, If Ever We Needed You" in a harsh rock style, and the car had entirely gotten away from George—it was as if the steering wheel had become disconnected from the steering mechanism.

About to die, he was interested that he could do the one thing he could not do in an airplane. Apply brakes. There are no brakes in an airplane. Not in the air. And, George realized, he had been driving as if he had been flying. He had been driving as if he were in the air and there were no brakes and the simple proposition was, as it always had been professionally, *You have to get through.* He had told his own young pilots, "Problems are there *to be gotten through.* " He came to a stop with the passenger side of the car crushed in, the windows splintered, from shearing against a tree.

He sat for a moment. There was no fire, he was unhurt. The sudden restraint of his seat harness seemed to him the first real thing that had happened to him since he had started studying the night before.

When he began to drive again there was an awkward sound from somewhere around the front right tire, but the car moved perfectly well. He drove home slowly. He got Randy, asleep and in his pajamas, from Mrs. Barnes next door, and put him to bed. Randy did not wake up at all as George carried him from the bed in one house to the bed in the other.

George closed up the house and then had a solid drink of straight whiskey. Then he turned out the living-room lights, went upstairs and got into pajamas, brushed his teeth, and got into bed. For all the time since his near death George's body had acted as if it had been subjected to nothing out of the ordinary. But once he was in bed, and felt the safety of it, and thought of Randy safe and asleep in the next room, George's body began to tremble. He tried to subdue the trembling. He tried to control his body. But he could not. The trembling continued into the dawn, into the light. Then he slept, exhausted.

46

Adele saw herself nude, rising from bed: white sheet, white wall, white against white, so airy. She, the girl, might be taking flight, like something gossamer borne aloft by the simplest breeze . . .

She awoke. She thought of when she had first seen the photograph last fall. She had been sitting next to Ben on the couch in his living room as he lay out the photographs of her on the long teak coffee table. For a few minutes it had been as if Ben had not been there. It had been as if she were alone with the girl in the photographs. The girl was so beautiful, but so vulnerable. She had begun to cry. She had taken Ben's hand and held it against her breast.

Nighttimes now, the airy picture returned, gentle and beautiful, but always woke her. Then she lay awake restless as her mind sought to envelop itself in the serenity of the image it had recalled.

She got up and went to the single window in her small room. She opened it all the way and felt the air touch her body. She breathed carefully. The air was a mixture of chill and warmth and was scented with raw earth, raw wet earth where the snow had melted and the sun had gotten down to the ground and released the scent of renewal.

Adele sat on the side of her bed. She resisted herself for a moment and then picked up a pack of cigarettes and lit one. "Christ," she thought, "I didn't know it till now, but I'm going back to Cornwall." The decision made her more restless.

47

Jonah too could smell the scent of coming spring. The night rain made a *tatting* sound on the roof, and when a breeze caught it the rain splashed against the glass of the bedroom windows. Yvonne slept easily beside him. Jonah thought of the growing infant harbored in her body. He touched Yvonne lightly as she slept and then withdrew his hand before he woke her. The smell of coming spring was a presence in the room. In the soul of him Jonah was dispirited by the coming of spring. It brought him that much closer to having to leave flying. Spring would end and then it would be only two or three or four weeks into summer, when the baby would be born; then he would have to leave flying. Unless Ev made him a part of the business. But Ev would not even talk to him about it. The last time Jonah had mentioned it, a few days before, Ev had just walked away from him. Jonah was beginning to resent the baby—it was because of the baby that he would have to leave flying and find a job where he could make more money. Those instants of resentment of the baby disturbed Jonah. They were *wrong,* and he could not reconcile them with the deep love he already felt for the child. Daytimes now he experienced periods of gloom, an unfamiliar emotion. And nighttimes he was frightened by the potential loss—the loss of flying. Loss of self.

48

Madelon Zur, in Geneva, decided to go back to the house in Connecticut, and then later, at first opportunity, to Cornwall. She had not been to Cornwall since the one visit shortly after she and Rupert had met Ben Cain. Rupert always preferred that Ben visit them rather than that they be guests of Ben's. Madelon thought of being alone in Ben's house with him. She knew he was attracted to her. She wondered what he would do and not do in bed. She rather liked the idea of cuckolding Rupert with Ben. Rupert admired Ben, and Rupert had respect for very few men. He had admiration for women, though of a different sort. She wondered that she had been so silly as to have been entirely faithful to Rupert through their six years of marriage. She had been attracted to other men, but had done nothing about it. Rupert did not hide his attraction to other women and, she thought, did something about his attractions.

After New Year's, Madelon had gone back to Geneva to see to the apartment there. Rupert had had business in New York. Then he was to have returned to Geneva for the late winter/early spring months to see to business in Geneva and London and elsewhere in Europe. But he had not come. He had sent excuses, letters of excuses, and made transoceanic calls of excuses. Other people had sent Madelon news, and even photographs, of Rupert and Doris, the sad merry widow from St. Thomas. They were *a couple* in New York.

Madelon was not hurt by that, she thought; but it made her angry. In fact she was she knew, just a little pleased with having this small excuse to be unfaithful to Rupert. And wasn't it nice that Ben was available, probably a little nervous in bed as Americans seemed to be, but such a nice body, and quite young enough to learn how to be properly attentive to a lady in bed. *Young enough,* Madelon thought, in what she knew to be ripping ill-humor. *Young enough. And what am I?* I am only *twenty-eight!*

49

After Las Vegas Ben had flown to Chicago and Terre Haute and Cleveland and other places where he had friends or a gallery which handled his work or both. He knew he should have been home working. But then he had been lent this ski chalet in northern New Hampshire, and he had been home to Cornwall only long enough to get his ski things. He had the chalet to himself and had been skiing all day every day for almost two weeks. Three different girls had come home with him and spent the night or nights with him during that time. As the airplane flew, he was less than half an hour away from Adele over in Vermont, but she just did not want him to visit her.

He woke at about four in the morning and at first did not know what had awakened him. He was conscious of the smell of it first—the green air of springtime, chill from moving over the snows, and warm from its origin in the southwest. It encouraged him. Like alcohol it gave him confidence in going home and starting work.

Then he heard the sound of it. Water moving in a brook. Moving rapidly. A lot of water. The snow was melting and melting terrifically fast.

He listened to the running of the waters in the brook—the skiing ending —and the fears about confronting his work returned.

DAY
FLIGHTS

How can he fly from his feathers?
. . . .
Heavily he flies.

    —Ted Hughes

Human events display two faces, one of drama and the other of indifference.

    —Antoine de Saint-Exupéry

. . . the hawk comes.

    His wing
Scythes down another day, his motion
Is that of the honed steel-edge, we hear
The crashless fall of stalks of Time.

    —Robert Penn Warren

J

onah was in the hangar. His legs sticking out a door of the airplane, he was on his back with his head below the instrument panel of the Skymaster. With a small flashlight and a probe he was looking for an errant wire which might cause breakup in voice reception on one of the radios. He sat up and got out of the airplane to stretch. He looked out of the hangar at the sharply visible peak of a mountain thirty miles away.

There was a fragrance of moist earth warming in sunshine. On the other side of the field, pines which had been loaded with white snow two weeks before swept away green to hills and high ridges beyond. The I-beams that straddled the upper reaches of the hangar had become disorderly perches for springtime birds, all of them assertively vocal.

Behind him Case Broadwell, the flight service's mechanic, turned up the volume on the radio on his bench.

"*. . . Here aboard the U.S.S. Iwo Jima, at sea in the Pacific and standing by to make the pickup, the mood is expectant, but cautiously optimistic. Mission Control continues to tell us that Apollo 13's splashdown will occur at one-oh-seven Eastern Standard Time . . .*"

Jonah looked at his watch. Ten minutes after eleven A.M.

"I bet those guys are working their asses off," Case said. "How'd you like to be stuck in that thing?"

"I wouldn't," Jonah said.

"One mistake and poof. Shit, they don't even know if the heat shield will work this time. How'd you like to give yourself the possibility of being dead in less than two hours?"

"I wouldn't."

"*. . . All in all, the astronauts have done a remarkable job, a superlative job since the explosion Monday night that canceled their moon-landing flight.*

They have had to operate continuously in the four days since then in emergency conditions. But there has been no question of the astronauts' ability to get headed back toward home since Captain James A. Lovell, Jr., the commander of the flight, radioed yesterday that they were turned around and halfway home. 'Aquarius is coming in,' he radioed. There was applause here aboard the Iwo Jima *when the message was replayed over the public-address system. The critical moments will come just about fourteen minutes before splashdown. This is when the command module begins to encounter earth's atmosphere. At that time there will be nothing more the astronauts can do. Jim Lovell and Fred Haise and Deke Slayton will be simple passengers aboard their own damaged spacecraft.''*

"Christ," said Jonah. "How do you like *them* apples?"

"I'm just mighty glad to be right where I am," Case said.

"Jonah," said Ev's hoarse voice over the intercom from the office across the parking lot, *"come on over, got a student for ya."*

When Jonah came into the office Ev grinned at him. "Jonah, I'd like you to make the acquaintance of Mr. Amory Blane."

The student was twenty-five or a year or two older. He wore jodhpurs and gleaming jodhpur boots. His shirt was a pale blue with white stitching. Around his neck and hanging down his chest was a white silk scarf. Dangling from his left hand was an oldtime aviator's leather helmet with goggles.

The student pursed his lips and studied Jonah. Then he said, "Glad to meet you, sir." He extended his hand.

Jonah shook hands with him. The student looked familiar, as familiar as a neighbor without a name. But Jonah didn't know him at all. He found the unidentifiable familiarity disquieting. "Amory, didn't you say?" Jonah said. *"Amory Blane?"*

"That's right. I'd like you to teach me to fly, sir."

Jonah took an unlit, half-smoked cheroot from his mouth. "Ever had a lesson before?"

"No, sir."

"Well, let's just sit down and talk over some of the fundamentals of flight."

"Oh, hell. I mean, I can read that sort of thing. What I'm interested in is actually *flying*. In an airplane. Flying it myself."

Jonah relit the half-smoked cheroot. "We have to start with this so you'll know what I'm talking about when we're flying."

"If you insist."

Jonah explained the aerodynamics of the wing, the forces that create lift and make it possible for a heavier-than-air machine to climb in air and even glide on it without power. "We'll use the engine to climb with, but when we get as high as we want—"

"How high will that be?"

"We usually train at three thousand feet. All right?"

"I guess."

"At altitude we can cut back on a lot of that power and we'll just stay right up there. If you want to slow up, pull back on the yoke, nose up. If you want to go faster, push forward on the yoke and the nose goes down and we pick up speed. If you want to turn right, turn the yoke to the right and the right aileron will angle down under the right wing and set up drag, and the airplane will turn to the right. Use a little right rudder to help bring the tail around. Most of the time you'll use aileron and rudder together for a nice, coordinated turn. We'll go up and try some straight and level flight and some shallow turns, and see how you do. Okay, sport?"

"Yes. Let's go."

Jonah tapped the cheroot till it was no longer lit and placed it in the ashtray on his desk. "And it better be there when I get back," he said to Ev as he started to leave the office.

"Christ, Jonah, I wouldn't touch that to throw it out."

"That's all I was worried about."

51

The white wings and body of the Cherokee shone in the sun.

"This," said Jonah, laying his hand on a wing, "is an airplane."

"Golly gee, Mr. Jaquith."

"Call me Jonah."

"I'm Amory."

"So you said. Okay, Amory, the first thing we do this time and next time and every time we fly is give this airplane a careful walk-around inspection inside and out. We check the engine to make sure there's oil, we drain the wingtanks to make sure there's no water in the fuel, we shake the wings to make sure they'll stay on, we check the hinges on the tail assembly to make sure the control surfaces won't fall off, we make sure the pitot tube is clean so we get an accurate report of our airspeed, we do a whole *hell* of a lot of things, including we look at the tires for wear, and do you know why we do all these things?"

"Golly gee, no, Mr. Jaquith. To make sure the airplane doesn't fall apart in the air?"

"That's *exactly* right, Amory. I can see you're to be a brilliant student.

[139]

Also to make sure the engine doesn't quit. And we do this every single time we fly, Amory. Every single time."

"Every single time," said Amory.

"Every *single* time. I would like you to develop good habits, Amory. Because we owe it to our passengers and to ourselves to get everybody up and down safely."

"I'm with you," said Amory.

"*Good.* Amory, you and I are going to get along just famously. Now would you tell me what your real name is?"

"Amory Blane."

"Bullshit."

"Look, my family name is Blane. I can't help it if some wise-ass named me after a character in a book."

"Can I see something like a driver's license?"

"Is it required?"

"Not legally."

"Then I'll just ignore the request. You want to teach me flying, or not?"

"Climb in, Amory. Take the left seat. That's the captain's seat. You'll find the weight of command heavy on your shoulders."

"Yes, sir. Where are you going to sit?"

"Oh, I'll be down here on the ground. We always fly students by remote control at first. Too dangerous to go up with them."

"Now you're going to taxi this airplane," Jonah said. "Use the rudder pedals for direction and the throttle for forward motion." Jonah indicated the hand throttle, a knob-ended rod which stood out from the instrument panel. "You can give it a little more power," Jonah said as they failed to move. After they were in motion and Amory had executed a turn from the ramp to a taxiway, Jonah said, "Not bad."

"You're kidding me. There's nothing to this."

"Some people have trouble coordinating the rudder pedals. They keep wanting to use the yoke to turn with, like it was a steering wheel. Or else they use too much power and get racing along. Okay, let's stop short of the runway. Take your power back . . . good . . . and apply your toe brakes. Hey there, Blane, you'll be doing chandelles in no time."

But Amory was looking out at the runway.

"This is where we go through runup. We test the engine and check controls and set the navigation instruments . . . You listening, Amory?"

". . . Sure."

"I'll go through it this first time to show you what we look for." But as he ran the engine up and pointed out the proper readings on the instruments, Jonah noticed that Amory was not paying attention. He was staring out the windscreen, but no longer at the runway. His vision was fixed on something very far away, probably his own death, Jonah thought. A number of students got very scared before their first takeoff. Jonah set the gyro compass to the magnetic compass. "That completes the 'Before Takeoff' checklist," he said.

"This airplane doesn't smell right," Amory said.

"Say again?"

Amory's visual focus had returned to the cabin. "This airplane doesn't smell right."

"It smells like any other airplane. We've been sitting here in the sun and running up the engine and—"

"I tell you, it doesn't smell right."

"As soon as we get up in the air, you won't smell a thing."

"I don't like it."

Jonah did not want the responsibility of *talking* someone into flying—other instructors might do it, but Jonah refused to. He said, quietly and casually, "You don't *have* to fly, you know."

Amory was silent. But he watched Jonah.

Jonah said, "It's no reflection on you. You're *interested,* you came out to investigate. But maybe you just don't really want to fly."

Amory cocked his head at Jonah but said nothing.

"That's nothing against you. Hell, I'm interested in manned spaceflight. But you wouldn't get me into one of those capsules for a million dollars."

Amory remained silent and continued to look at Jonah.

"So, if you don't want to try it, don't. *I* wouldn't."

"I don't know," Amory said.

Jonah saw New EnglandAir One-six-five taxi out from the terminal and hold short of the runway. He picked up the microphone. "If New England-Air is guarding Cornwall unicom, the Cherokee will hold short of Runway Two-zero till you're airborne."

The landing lights on the high wings of the FH 227 flashed on and off, and the airliner moved slowly out on the runway and turned ponderously to face down the runway. There was the whine-turned-to-shriek of the turboprops and then, with a little start, the 227 began moving along the runway. Where it finally became almost small to the eye, the 227 rose gracefully and then swiftly into the air, folding its legs into itself and becoming very little as it climbed higher and higher away from them.

"I always watch that with amazement," Amory said. He was still watching.

"There isn't a pilot who doesn't."

After a moment Amory said, "Go ahead, take me up."

*　　　　*　　　　*

They rose above the runway. Jonah felt the slight but real sensation of the strain of the lift. He made it as gentle as possible. Trees began to look minute. Jonah made his turn. There was the runway again, small now and behind them. They lifted higher, sunlight gleaming into the uptilted windscreen.

Jonah began an easy turn to take them to the practice area, but as the horizon slid around them he felt a tap on his shoulder. Amory was pointing back to the airport. "Take me down."

Jonah nodded. He cut back on power. "Okay. Let me show you what I'm doing as we go in. It's something you'll have to learn anyway. First—"

"Just get me down."

They were flying alongside the airport when there was a voice on the cabin speaker. "Cornwall unicom, this is Cherokee Eight-niner Zero-niner Whiskey."

"Sonofabitch!" said Jonah.

"What is it?" said Amory.

"Hold on."

The clear voice of Ev's secretary came back, "Eight-nine Zero-nine Whiskey, this is Cornwall. Hiya, Ben. Go ahead."

"Zero-niner Whiskey is five miles north. Request winds, active, and local traffic. Hiya, Lucy. Over."

"Winds are southwest at two-four-zero degrees at five to ten. Calm wind runway Two-zero in use. Barometric pressure, three-zero three-one. Jonah's in the pattern."

"Okay, Cornwall. Cherokee Zero-niner Whiskey is on a long straight-in for Two-zero."

Jonah had the mike in his hand. "Zero-niner Whiskey, do you read Fifty Pop?"

"Fifty Pop, how y'doin', Jonah?"

"Hey there, Phantom Ace. Welcome back. Where y'been, Ace?"

"North and south. Here and there. Up and down."

"See you later, Ace?"

"I'm gonna have lunch at the airport and get the garage to send my wagon over. Then I'll have to unload. I'll be around a couple of hours."

Ev's voice came over the speaker. *"Will you jokers get off this frequency?"*

"Ten-four and all that, you old buzzard," Jonah said.

Ben's voice came back, "And, Cornwall, Zero-niner Whiskey is two miles out on a straight-in for Two-zero."

"There he is," Jonah said, looking off his wing and about to turn final.

"Where?"

"There."

"Where?"

"Never mind. You'll learn."

"Who is he?"

"Name's Ben Cain."

"The *artist?*"

"The same."

"I didn't know he lived around here."

"You live around here?" Jonah said.

"Right now I do . . . Jesus. Ben Cain. His own airplane?"

"Yeah."

On the ground, the engine shut down, the two of them standing next to the airplane on the hard concrete of the ramp, Amory said, "What would have happened if you'd had a heart attack up there?"

Jonah grinned apologetically. "You'd be dead, Amory."

Amory, scarf hanging over one shoulder, walked away. Twenty odd feet away he stopped, turned, said "Thanks," turned quickly again, and went off toward the parking area.

"*Jonah!*"

Jonah turned. Case Broadwell was waving at him from in front of the hangar.

"They're down!" Case yelled. "*The astronauts are down safe!*"

52

Out on the ramp Ben was unloading his winter kit from the Cherokee to his station wagon. From behind him, on the other side of the fence where the parking lot was, he heard a mechanical sound which was as familiar to him as a human voice. He turned and watched Adele's maroon Triumph pull up to the fence, her three pairs of skis poking up from a ski rack mounted behind the black canvas car roof. The windshield faced him directly and Ben thought that Adele must see him, must be looking at him. He waved. But nothing happened.

In a moment the car door opened and Adele got out and walked over toward the flight service office.

You could judge the seasons by Adele Fortune's arrivals and departures, Falun thought. Departure—early winter, almost enough snow on the ground up north to ski on. Arrival—snow turning into rushing brooks and, if you bent down to see, green shoots bending up from the wet earth. Falun returned Adele's kiss and hugged her.

"By God, another year and you didn't break a leg," Ev said. He made no move toward her, but Adele went to him and kissed him on the cheek. Ev looked away. "My wife says to bring you home for dinner when you showed up."

"Your wife's name is Charlotte," Adele said.

"I know my wife's goddamn name."

"Later in the week. I'd like to get settled in tonight, get the apartment cleaned up."

"It's been closed all goddamn winter, what the hell do you expect to clean up, for Christsake, Adele?"

"Dust," Adele said. "Winter."

"You see the Phantom Ace out on the ramp?" Ev said.

"No. Not really."

"Not *really?*"

"How's Jonah? Where is he?"

"Jonah's flying. He's okay, I guess. Yvonne almost lost the baby, but *she's* fine now. Now Jonah's not so fine. He's jumpy. Well, not jumpy, no—preoccupied. You coming back to work?"

"Tomorrow. All right?"

"Suits me. You current?"

"I got current this past week."

"All right, so you start tomorrow. Good. Some guy's been calling asking for you."

"Who?"

"How the hell should I know? Been callin' and askin' were you back. Wouldn't leave his name. Just said he wanted to go flyin' with you when you got back."

"Fortune's the name," Adele said flatly, "and flyin's the game. What did he sound like?"

"Christ, Adele—"

"He sounded nice," Lucy the secretary said. "I spoke to him a few times. He's been calling the last week, ten days. He said he thought you'd be back because the weather was warm. He sounded real nice, Adele."

Ben stood in the doorway. He smiled at her. "Hi," Adele said.

"Hi, Adele." He came over and kissed her on the cheek.

She nodded at him and said nothing.

"The goddamn Phantom Ace," Ev said. Ben shook hands with him and then with Falun.

"You've flown a lot this winter," Falun said.

Ben smiled.

"You've flown a lot of places."

"I guess," Ben said.

[144]

"You should make it your profession," Falun said, "you do so much of it."

Ben looked at him but he could not tell the nature of Falun's remark. Falun looked at him steadily.

Falun thought, To be looking down on the Caribbean again. When the miles ahead were endless. And the days and years ahead were endless . . . He found the conversation around him fading out, like radio signals from a distant station. It was because he was thinking about the Caribbean, he realized . . . He saw Adele looking at him, smiling. He thought of looking down on the pale hues of springtime from aloft. He smiled at Adele and stood up. "Adele, how would you like to take an old man flying?"

"If you do the flying."

"I'll do that. But I need someone to make sure I'm paying attention. Ev, how about your old J-3, is it flying?"

"The Cub? The goddamn machine just got relicensed last week. How, I'll never know. That goddamn Case Broadwell's a goddamn airframe and engine genius."

Falun looked at Adele. "*Good.* We can open the window. Let the spring-time *in.*"

Falun had taken the front seat of the J-3, the instructor's seat, and as they slowly climbed out in the old, low-powered yellow airplane, he turned and called to Adele in the seat behind him, over the steady hoarseness of the engine, "The *lift* of the J-3, these long, wide, wonderful wings, it's as if *springtime* is lifting us, isn't it?"

Adele nodded, smiling. Imagine, she thought, *flying with Falun Aigborg.* It was always a wonder to her. He had said to her, a year or so before, "My love of flight is as gay today as when I was a child."

They were at three thousand feet; Falun had opened the window and the air was chill. He was looking down, his eyes squinted against the rush of air, the deep lines at the corner of his eye spreading out like the tail of a comet, Adele thought.

Falun was looking at the new down on the earth. Pale yellows and pale greens, dark rectangles of brown where a farmer had plowed a field. There was still ice on some of the lakes. The bird of pain plunged from some altitude vastly superior to that of the J-3 and struck through him, piercing his innards. His hand tightened on the stick and it was as if they had struck a gust of air, and then the bird and its piercing beak were gone and Falun's hand relaxed . . .

Looking at the earth, he was enveloped with his own *not being here next year.*

He willed it away, as sometimes he was able to will the bird away.

He pulled back on power and applied carburetor heat and set up a long, gentle glide over the springtime earth.

53

"Center, Six-two Alpha Golf, turning. We've got a small line of storms about twenty miles ahead. We'd like to bear to the right . . . okay."

"TWA Seven-one, that's an okay turn, we're direct Kennedy now."

"Scandinavia Four-eight coming back on speed now."

"From Albany south it appears scattered—no sweat getting around them."

54

The rain began as a fine drizzle—like falling mist, Jonah thought. The gray light of the beginning of evening was still bright enough so he and Yvonne could continue to work on their gardens, Yvonne on a border of flowers and herbs around the house, and Jonah on what would be his vegetable garden when he started to replant it in two weeks—the first of May. With a fork, Jonah was tining the ground, working in compost and lime. He sweated and small bugs made the flesh of his face itch. But it was the smell of the earth which occupied him.

A small rabbit came to investigate the woodpile Jonah had begun to saw and stack for the next winter. Yvonne stopped work and watched. Jonah came over and stood beside her. She took his hand. The rabbit's head and body remained absolutely still, but its nose described quick partial rotations. One ear straightened and then leaned towards them. For several seconds the rabbit stayed motionless. Then it turned and bounded from them. Jonah touched Yvonne's stomach. She smiled and said, "I was thinking of the baby, too."

The drizzle had become the warm, mild rain of spring. Yvonne stood still, smiling again, letting the rain run down her face.

"C'mon," Jonah said, "let's go in."

He took the tools to the garage. Yvonne paused in the open doorway to the kitchen and turned to look at the rain and to breathe the fragrance of it. *This is where they trap you,* she thought. *With rain like this. With things that make you happy. As if what you love will never be taken from you.* She reached her hand out to let the rain fall on it.

When Jonah came in, Yvonne was showering. He washed at the sink and got a bottle of beer and then sat down at the kitchen table and began collating a new set of Jeppesen approach plate revisions.

After a while Yvonne came into the kitchen. She was wearing a summer robe and her belly stood out roundly underneath the belt. "I think I'd like a glass of wine tonight," she said. Jonah went to a low cabinet and got out an open half-gallon of red wine. Yvonne sat down. "I'll get dinner in a few minutes. I'm so tired tonight."

"Maybe you shouldn't have worked on the garden. Spading and—"

"*Oh, Jonah* . . . I'm fine now. Dr. Glynn said so. I'm just tired. That's normal about this time." Jonah gave her a glass of wine. "That's awfully good," she said. "Just what I wanted. Listen to the rain. Maybe you won't have to work tomorrow."

"It's just a small low passing through. It'll be clear before we get up tomorrow."

"No day off," she said.

"No day off," Jonah said. "Hey, let me tell you something funny, love." He told her about the student Amory.

Yvonne listened. She laughed when Jonah described the old aviator's costume. "Still," she said when he had finished, "I'm glad he's not going to be a student."

"Why?"

"I'm just glad. I don't like him."

"Oh love, don't be unfair. He's a scared kid. Well, older than a kid. He just tried something he really didn't want to try. Okay?"

"I'm just glad he's not going to be a student."

"Good. Because he's not."

The rain was heavier. Yvonne put her hand on top of Jonah's. "I feel so cozy, Jo. I feel so safe. If I felt like this all the time, I'd never worry about you flying."

Jonah went upstairs and took a shower and afterwards put on a short-sleeved jersey and lightweight slacks, the first summer clothes he had had on this year. From downstairs he could smell chicken frying. He opened a cold beer he had brought up for himself and went back downstairs. In the hallway to the kitchen he paused and went into the baby's room. The wallboard was nailed in now and the room smelled of fresh paint. There was a small bureau Yvonne had refinished. A basket of small toys was in the corner. There was a disassembled cradle. After the baby was born Jonah would set the cradle up in their bedroom. The baby would sleep with them so Yvonne could nurse it in the night.

The telephone rang. Jonah went to the door of the baby's room and looked down the hall and into the kitchen where Yvonne stood with the phone to her ear.

She listened and did not say a word. Jonah felt uneasy.

"I'll come right over," Yvonne said after listening for two or three minutes. She looked vaguely in Jonah's direction, but she could not have seen him. Her face had shiny lines of tears down it.

"Oh, oh . . . Then it wouldn't do any good, my coming over." She looked at the ceiling and Jonah saw the tears running down her face. "The children, could I . . .?"

She shook her head silently and put the receiver down. Then she continued to stand there with her hand on the receiver. Jonah went to her and put his hands on her arms. Her head was bent. Her tears dropped and made little spatters on the linoleum floor.

She looked directly up at Jonah. "That was Betty Howard. They just called her. The New York State police. There's a reservoir called Pep—*Pepacton* Reservoir. It's just three or four miles from the De Lancey VOR."

"Yes," Jonah said.

"There's a river or stream that feeds it. The water comes down a valley —a narrow valley, Betty said. Some of the water that supplies the reservoir. It's not even half a mile wide, that little narrow valley. But the hills on both sides—mountain ridges, she said—they go up to two thousand feet and higher."

Yvonne took the handkerchief Jonah held out to her and wiped her face and blew her nose. Looking directly at Jonah she said, "Some State Fish and Game people were walking up that little river, or whatever it is, and they saw something sticking out of the snow high up on the side of one of those ridges. They went up to look. It was the tail of Del's airplane. Sticking out of the snow. The airplane went right into the side of the ridge. Del and the congressman were still in it. Betty says the bodies were still frozen. They told her—Jonah, they told her the pilot's face was still identifiable. She's being driven down there now to make the identification."

"What about the children?"

"They're staying over with neighbors. Do you know what, Jonah?"

Jonah shook his head.

"They offered to fly Betty down there."

55

Captain Elmo Reed was twenty years Perry's senior in age and at least that many years in seniority as line captain. He and Perry shared a ride in from La Guardia. Reed studied the columns of small print of the stock-market report in a late-afternoon New York paper. He said, "You look dressed for a big night."

"I'm married," Perry said. Now there's an odd reflexive statement, Perry thought.

"I know. But what the shit difference it's got to do with what I just said, I don't know. At your age." Reed repositioned himself. "How's it going, Sullivan? I mean the route, flying captain."

"Fine."

"That's all? Just *fine?*"

"I never have any trouble flying."

"Jesus Christ, I wish I could say the same thing." Reed took the cigar out of his mouth. "Come to think of it, Sullivan, I *did* say the same thing. Just exactly the same thing. When I was your age." Reed studied Perry. "Judging by your haberdashery, you don't look like you're going out to the YMCA social or a poker game neither."

"I'm not."

"I bet you're thinking it's none of my fucking business."

"Not in those exact words."

"Good. I'm glad you've got respect for your elders." He continued to look at Perry. He smiled and smiled and waited.

Perry sighed. "This girl—*woman,* I should say. She was my girl senior year in high school. I'm taking her out to dinner."

"Not married?"

"I don't know."

"For Christsake, Sullivan. What kind of an answer is that?"

"Since I have these free nights in New York, I've been looking up people I used to know in the area, and I tracked her down over in New Jersey, so I called her when I was in last week. She said she'd meet me for dinner. Here in the city."

"Know this girl pretty well, did you?" said Reed.

I knew every inch of her body, Perry thought, above the waist. He nodded. "We were close. We talked a lot."

56

It was almost nine o'clock. George Detwiler sat alone in his living room. Randy had gone to bed early, his young body exhausted from baseball practice. George was trying hard not to have a Scotch and soda or a capsule of Librium. He had rarely had a drink since New Year's, though almost daily he had longed for the hour or two of tranquillity that alcohol might bring him. Librium helped, but George resented its impersonality. There was, at least, something personal about Scotch. It was like being with a friend.

There was only one lamp on in the living room. There was no need for more light. George wasn't reading. He wasn't doing anything. He felt his heart on the verge of tachycardia. He wanted to run. He wanted to smash. He wanted to fly Randy high above the earth in a soundless airplane, some magical sailplane. He wanted to lie down gently with a woman. He *wanted*.

George kept expecting the furniture to move—if only because he stared at it so intensely. He became aware of the soft rain outside, the earth smell in the air—like the fragrance of a woman who had been in the room and gone—and of the stillness in the house, the stagnation of winter still lying heavy all about him.

He wanted to be *moving*. He was desperate for *motion*, for *change*.

He went to the telephone and dialed Adele Fortune's number. He had been calling it for nearly two weeks now and he knew by heart the response he would get: a click, a sound like surf, and then a voice which said, "This is a recording from Cornwall, New Hampshire. I'm sorry, the number you have reached is either not in service or has been changed. If you need assistance, please hang up and dial your operator." But tonight there was no click. The telephone rang five times. George thought he must have misdialed. "Hello?"

"Hello? Adele? Adele Fortune?"

"Yes. Who is this?"

"Adele. This is George Detwiler."

". . . George Det—Oh, *George*. I'm sorry. I'm just back from up north and I guess I haven't got myself settled back in yet."

"Even if you had," George said, "I don't suppose we've ever spoken more than a few words to each other."

"Really?"

"Well, that's not exactly what I meant. I think we always used to talk about flying. When I saw you at the airport—or at parties."

"I count that as talking," Adele said.

"I've been trying to get hold of you."

"Did you call the airport?"

"Airport? No."

"Didn't you call about going flying with me?"

"No."

"You're sure."

"Absolutely. Adele, maybe I'd better call you some other—"

"No, no—I just had something on my mind. Someone who's been trying to get me. But I don't know who. What *do* you want, George?"

"I want to have dinner with you," George said.

George listened to her silence. He was twelve or fifteen years older than she was, he wasn't sure. He had a nine-year-old son. He was still legally married. He should *not* have called Adele. *Not not not . . .*

"We could do that," Adele said. "Have dinner together."

"How would tomorrow night be?"

"Couldn't be better," Adele said. "I'm trying to clean my apartment and I'm going to start work tomorrow. I'll be glad to go out."

"Seven-thirty?"

"Seven-thirty is fine."

"Well, then. Good night."

"Good night, George."

Adele hung up.

George replaced the receiver and stood for a moment. Phantoms of possibility shoved against him. His heart was excited. But he felt no danger in its exultant percussion.

Then George did something he had not expected to do, something he had not even thought about.

He dialed Jonah Jaquith's number. "Jonah? George Detwiler."

"How are you, George?"

"Jonah, I'd like you to take me on as a student. I want you to get me current again. Oh, I doubt that I've forgotten that much about handling an airplane, that'll come back quickly enough. But I never did have much experience in civil aviation. And I'll need help getting back into IFR capability. Just single-engine stuff, Jonah. I'd like to be able to take Randy on trips, do some business flying on my own, things like that."

"What I have to wonder about, George, what *you* have to wonder about if you're going to fly solo—can you pass a third-class physical?"

"I haven't had the bad symptoms in two years. Not the bad ones. Anyway, I won't be flying solo for a while. Can you work me in tomorrow?"

"I'll have to look at my schedule at the office. I'll call you in the morning."

"That'll be fine, Jonah."

57

It was seven in the evening and the midtown Manhattan street was relatively quiet, but inside the bar the din was abrupt and almost physical in its intensity. People were crowded along the length of the bar. In the rear, beyond the bar, the space widened into a room with tables. Perry edged his way toward it. Well-dressed men and women with drinks in their hands glanced at him from their conversations as he made his way through— glanced at him just long enough to measure him in some way or another.

"Sir?" A man in a black suit, white shirt, and black string tie stood in front of Perry. "May I help you, sir?"

"A table for two," Perry said.

"Do you have a reservation, sir?"

"No. No, I don't."

"I'm afraid I haven't a thing just now, sir. Perhaps you'd care to have a drink at the bar."

"I'm waiting for someone."

"Yes, sir. But I'm afraid there won't be a table for hours."

"You have a couple of empty tables," Perry said.

"They're spoken for, sir. Perhaps the party you're waiting for made a reservation?"

"I don't think so."

"Might I have the name?"

"Mrs. Campman," Perry said.

"Ah, Mrs. Campman. Very good, sir. She did indeed call. I have her favorite table for her. If you'll just follow me, sir."

Perry was taken to a corner table. The room was dark, the tables candle-lit. Crystal sconces protruded from oak paneling and provided muted flares of light. "A drink, sir?"

"Scotch on the rocks," Perry said.

"Very good, sir. Mario, a Scotch on the rocks for the gentleman."

When the drink was set in front of him Perry picked it up and looked through the heavy glass to the amber liquid making little swirls around the ice cubes. He tasted the drink carefully and set it down. He looked at the people at the other tables. They all seemed happy and important. Perry was pleased to be among them. It was as if Laura did not exist, as if he were not married.

"Perry."

The voice was very soft, very near. Kit Campman stood in front of the small table. She wore a dress of some pale green material, a light material that emphasized her slim figure and rounded bust. Her hair was dark red. It had been *done,* coiffed, the hair arrangement of a grown-up woman, but the face was nearly the tender and youthful one he had known in high school. She put a hand on his shoulder. "Don't get up," she said, and she slid herself gracefully between the tables and to a seat on the banquette. "I'm sorry to be late. I had to have a drink with a client."

"A client?"

"I'm a stockbroker. I got my license three years ago. The kids were in school all the time, or in sports, or going to something, and husband John's business—well, it wasn't going as well as it might have. He was—he was distracted, he just wasn't paying all the attention to it he might have, and so I came over to the city every day and worked in a brokerage office and studied and here I am. The usual, Mario," she said as the waiter came to her.

Then she looked at Perry. "Oh, my," she said. "I can remember kissing that face of yours . . . Remember that car you had? It used to be so *cold* sitting out there. And I used to get so *hot.* Do you know what we'd be doing if we were teenagers today?"

"What?"

"We'd be screwing," Kit said, lighting a cigarette. She put it out immediately. "I *am* going to give these things up." She put her hand gently to Perry's head and drew his cheek to her lips. "Dear lamb," she said. "Dear Perry. What we missed. And now you're a pilot. And married."

"Sort of," Perry said.

"Sort of a pilot? Sort of married?"

"I'll tell you later."

She raised her martini. "To auld acquaintance. And to further disclosures."

"What about your kids?"

"John Jr. is sixteen. All he thinks about is sports. Gwen is fifteen going on thirty. All she thinks about is boys. When she was fourteen she asked me if she could start the Pill."

"What did you say?"

"What *could* I say? We're an enlightened society, right? *I* was pregnant at nineteen, did you know that? With John Jr. Of course, I *wanted* to be pregnant. Husband John and I were married while I was still a sophomore at Wellesley. He was a grad student then. At Harvard Business. I thought it would be *great* to have a little family of our own right away. He did, too. At least that's what he *said* then. Events proved differently. I'm dry," she said, putting down her empty glass. She inclined her head toward the waiter. Mario was taking an order at another table but he glanced at Kit and nodded.

"Christ," Perry said, "I didn't even think he was *looking* this way."

"He wasn't. He just *intuited* my want. I bring a lot of clients here. It's important to have your own place. Small pond, big frog. This is my small pond."

Mario was standing by their table. "Another for you, sir?"

"No, I"—but Perry saw that his glass was empty—"yes. Another."

"Very good, sir."

"Do you have pictures of the kids?"

"No. No pictures."

She took out a cigarette and handed Perry her lighter. A small gold Dunhill lighter. She leaned forward and held his hand to guide the flame to the cigarette. She took the lighter and put it back in her bag. She inhaled deeply and put the cigarette out. "I *will* give these things up." She picked up her glass, saw that it was empty, and put it down. "Actually, well, yes, I lied. I *do* have a picture. I just don't like to show it because husband John is in it." She got it out of a Florentine wallet from her bag.

"They're good-looking kids," Perry said. "You should be proud." Mario was setting the drinks on the table.

"I am. They never study and they both get straight A's. That's husband John. He gets A for alcoholic. I'm a widow, but my husband's not dead yet. I've stopped staying at home. A woman I work with is in London for two months, and I have the use of her apartment. I stay there a lot now. You were lucky to get me at home the other night. I started staying mostly in town about two weeks ago. Husband John can con anyone. We went for couple counseling. You know what that is?"

"I wanted to do it. I figured Laura and I sure as hell could use it. But I was scared about it. Consulting a shrink—that doesn't look good on a pilot's record—"

"I'll tell you what happened with us—"

"But I went ahead anyway." Perry remembered Laura screaming that *he* was *sick, he* should go on his own. And then begging him not to make her go with him for counseling. She had sobbed, pleaded, diverted him with sexual gifts of herself. But what he remembered most and what had most affected him had been her childlike fear. "I told her we ought to. If we wanted to stay married."

"What did she say?"

"She—I finally gave up on the idea. As I say, I wasn't too hot on it myself. I didn't want it on my record."

"Husband John quit drinking for our sessions. I mean, he quit drinking *cold.* He came on like Mr. Mental Health. The shrink made out that the problems were mostly mine."

"What happened?"

"I told the shrink I wouldn't go to a shrink unless John went to a shrink too. So that was that. We went home and John merrily started drinking again. So when this opportunity came along—my friend's apartment—I started staying over here." She put her hand on Perry's. "It's saving my life."

Mario was standing in front of them. "Mrs. Campman?"

"Yes, please, Mario."

"Sir?"

"No, I'm fine. Thank you."

"I'll just have the one more," Kit said, "and then let's go somewhere fun for dinner."

"What's wrong with right here?"

"Oh, my dear, no one *eats* here."

The waiter poured for Kit, but Perry placed the flat of his hand over his still partially filled wine glass. "Monsieur does not care for the wine?" the waiter asked.

"It's an excellent wine," Kit said.

"I'm sure it is. But I've had enough. I told you I wouldn't be drinking half a bottle, Kit."

"One just takes one's time with it."

"I see."

"Don't you drink wine?"

"Not often. I like a glass or two."

"You're not flying tomorrow."

"No." Perry grinned. "But I'm doing a pretty good job of flying right now. I just don't do much drinking, Kit."

"You get used to it. You build up a greater and greater tolerance."

"You're remarkable, Kit. I'd be under the table."

"I've had a lot of practice, recent years."

"Your husband?"

"You might say I couldn't have done it without him. Wouldn't have, anyway." She studied her wine glass and then looked up at Perry. Her voice was serious. "I often think of you, Perry. Ever since I learned you became a professional pilot. There are a lot of times when I think of myself as a pilot. We're all pilots in life. Getting around storms. Trying not to hit too hard when we come down. Trying not to run into things we can't see. I often think about myself as if I were a pilot. Does that sound corny?"

"Sort of. Yes, it does."

"But I think that seriously."

"Flying isn't like that. It's not so—it's not so *dramatic.* "

Kit sipped at her wine and put the glass down. She made an odd gesture of opening her hands toward Perry. "Do you go out with women often? I mean, when you're away from home?"

"No. Not at all." But he had been feeling so young being with Kit—his past was so *recent* to him. The time of *possibility* was so recent—and so recently cut off. "I'm thinking of getting a divorce, Kit. I've pretty much decided I'm going to."

She looked at him sadly and solemnly. "Are you happy about it?"

Perry thought. "By God, I am."

Kit continued to look at him.

*   *   *

She took him to a piano bar. In the cab she had said, "Kiss me once just like you used to . . . No. With your mouth *open.*" Perry had felt the remembered desire of adolescence—intense and tentative—and the present desire of the man, even and assured. For the rest of the cab trip he and Kit had held hands. He was careful to have his erection subdued by the time he had to get out of the cab. In the bar they held hands again. Kit drank Scotch and soda and Perry had a beer. He liked the music. He closed his eyes and put his head back against the top of the banquette. He was tired. Awfully drowsy. Something. He listened to the music and smelled cigarette smoke and Kit's fragrance and felt her hand on his thigh and his fingers in hers. He was dreaming of high school. He was supposed to be studying, but he was watching clouds out the window and dreaming of flying an airplane up there, flying near the clouds.

"Do you screw the stewardesses? I guess they prefer to be called air hostesses now. Do you screw them?"

"I married one," Perry said without opening his eyes.

"Oh. Yes. But that doesn't answer my question, does it?"

"I guess not." Perry was watching clouds.

"Are they as good as they're supposed to be?"

"No one will ever be as good as I used to dream you'd be. Back when we were in high school." He opened his eyes. "But you know what? I can't remember how I dreamed you'd be. I just remember I used to think about it all the time. Being in bed with you."

She lay her head on his shoulder and held his near arm against her with both hands. "Oh, it feels so good to be with someone friendly," she said.

Kit's borrowed apartment was in the Thirties off Park Avenue. There was a living room and, just off it, a bedroom. The furnishings were those of a woman with some money who had found almost nothing from the twentieth century with which she wished to live. Kit allowed Perry to take her coat and hang it in the hall closet. He stood in the living room and listened to her put ice in a glass in the kitchen. "Nothing for me," Perry said.

She came into the living room with a drink in her hand and said, "Follow me." She took him into the darkened bedroom. Perry heard, in the darkness, her shoes drop to the carpeted floor. It was a strangely sensual sound. She turned on a lamp next to the bed. She was sitting against the cushioned headboard of the bed. "I'm awfully sober," she said. "More sober than you can possibly imagine. Sit by me?"

Perry went over and sat on the edge of the bed. She put her hand on his arm, smiled at him, and turned so that her back was partially toward him. "Unzip me?"

"No," Perry said gently while he thought *Why the hell not?*

She turned back to him. "I'll try to be as good as you dreamed I'd be."

Perry felt like lying down beside her, like holding her. But not to make love. "No," he said. He heard himself say softly, "But thank you."

She looked at him, composed. "Why not?"

Why not? Perry thought. "Because you're married," he said.

She picked up her glass and drank from it. The ice made the only sound in the room.

Perry thought, I wonder who it is that does the drinking in your home, Kit?

She said, "Will you call me? Take this number and call me? When you're back in town sometime?" Perry wrote the number down. "Can I bring the kids to see you with your airplane sometime?"

"Sure. Aren't they old for that?"

She nodded. "Yes. You're right. They're too old for that. I forget sometimes." She swallowed from her drink. She put her hand back on Perry's arm. "We could've had a nice evening."

"We did."

He sat with her for a few more minutes. He found himself looking at her shoes lying askew on the floor. When he looked up she was looking down at her hands on her lap. There were bright lines of tears on her face, but she was silent. He held her against him. For a few seconds her arms tightened and she held him. Then she released him. She bit her lip and smiled at him. "I'm the one who's too old for all this," she said.

Perry kissed her and got up. As he walked through the living room to the door he heard ice clink against glass.

On the way back to the hotel he kept thinking, *Am I that husband? The one who can't be lived with?*

He could have been driving home, but of course he wasn't. For a pilot he was strangely without destination, Perry thought.

58

Adele awoke to brightness and warmth. It was seven-thirty. She had worked till three in the morning vacuuming, washing, packing away ski clothes, getting out warm-weather clothes, ironing . . . Drawers had been left open, boxes pulled out of closets, there was still the refrigerator to do, but thank God the bath was done, and the day was a *spring* day. Over coffee she had a feeling of happiness. She did not understand the source of the happiness until she had the thought that spring had separated her from her past. Without any past Adele to contend with through the day she was free to be happy. It was like flying, but on the ground. Here was spring. Here was an unexpected beginning. "Happy new year, Adele," she said to herself.

<h1 style="text-align:center">59</h1>

Ben too had put his winter gear away, but that was about all he had done —the night before, his first night back—about settling into his house again. The house was immaculate. His maid had come in regularly while he was away. When he'd gotten hungry he'd called Adele to see if she would go out to dinner with him.

"No," she'd said.

"You mean it's the same as it was when I called from Las Vegas?"

"Sort of like that."

Ben had taken some magazines from his accumulated mail and gone out to dinner. When he had come home from dinner he had walked around the outside of his house, inspecting it as if it were a piece of sculpture—as in some ways he had intended it to be, in his design. The house stood alone in a pine and hardwood forest, a private mile-long dirt road leading to it from a secondary town road. The house was built at the edge of and partially cantilevered out over an abandoned soapstone quarry. The quarry was always filled with water. A wooden deck ran the length of the adjoining living room and master bedroom and overhung the water. Ben went out on the deck. The spring night air was chilly and damp. Ben thought of the Caribbean and of standing on the terrace at Rupert and Madelon's, but when he looked down, the water was black and formless as if it had no surface, and when he looked up, there were no stars. Steps had been carved in the side of the quarry and ran down from the deck to the water. Ben remembered a morning last fall when he had been swimming and Adele had sat nude on the bottom step. Then he had taken her up the stairs, gotten out a camera, and begun photographing her. He took pictures of her having coffee, moving in the leaves, getting up from bed after they'd made love, wandering around his studio touching things . . . He thought of all the work waiting for him in his studio. He went back in the house. The living room was big and cold. He built a fire and began playing Dvořák chamber music. Ignoring all the mail stacked on the coffee table, he sat down with a brandy and thought about going into the studio. To look at the work left there— some unfinished, some hardly begun and existing only in his mind—excited him, all the possibilities in that undone work, the potential. But he couldn't bring himself to go to the studio—though a great, great deal of what he loved was in there. Tools, materials, smells, and *the work itself,* he thought. *I love it so, why does it scare me so?* He'd gotten out a volume of Van Gogh's letters to his brother Théo. Across a hundred years Van Gogh breathed the intoxication of creativity and a desperation to work into Ben. Tomorrow, Ben thought, *tomorrow* I will begin to work. The brandy and the music and Van Gogh had made it seem possible that he *could* work.

In the morning the sun was bright and the air so warm Ben took his coffee out on the deck. He decided that before he tried to begin work in the studio he would bring all the accumulated mail out on the deck and go through it while he had more coffee. There were letters from friends, from students who wanted to do papers on him, from galleries wanting to borrow works, from publications wanting to negotiate for one-time reproduction rights, and there was one letter in the familiar textured gray envelope with brown logo and return address that caused Ben anxiety. It was marked *Hold for Addressee.* Ben put it aside. There were no bills. His attorney had taken care of all the mail, like bills, that had required some immediate response.

Finally Ben opened the gray envelope, a letter from his dealer, the gallery in New York. It said what he was afraid it would say, but it was only confirmation of what Ben knew to be simple necessity: ". . . *and so, not having heard from you in all this time, and having had no indication that you will have sufficient work in a finished state by this fall, I have reluctantly withdrawn your name from our listings of fall exhibits. As you know, I had scheduled your show for the full month of October, possibly our best month of the year. Our time and space is intransigently committed to other artists for the remainder of this year and well into next. With some juggling I could give you two or perhaps three weeks in April"*—a whole year away, Ben thought—*"but April, it has been my experience as a dealer, is among the cruelest months. Naturally I am eager to have a show of work by Ben Cain as soon as possible, but you must be appreciative, Ben, that I've already put this show off once and you promised you would have at least* some *work for me to see in February. You cannot be aware of it, because you didn't answer your phone, but I have been calling you regularly since the first of the year. Previous letters were answered by your attorney simply stating that you were away . . . no indication of when you would return . . . left me no option but to cancel . . . hope you can understand . . ."*

Ben felt as if he were flying an airplane in which the engine had just failed.

60

Conrad was on the farm gang. Attridge State Correctional Facility grew as much of its own food as it could. The farm gang was getting the ground ready for planting. The ground was wet, the sun was getting hot, and small, biting bugs were swarming everywhere. Toward midmorning there was a break. Conrad lay in the shade looking up at blue sky and shiny clouds. The air was still. Way above an airplane with long thin wings wheeled and swooped and climbed—a sailplane. There was a soaring school not too many miles away. Since the warm weather Conrad saw one of these silent airplanes once or twice a day.

He thought about being up there, alone, not going anywhere, just free of everything.

He thought of Lou-Ann. Looking at the sailplane he thought, *If these fuckers think I'm going to wait to leave till they say I can, they're crazy.* There wasn't much to keep him in, just some fences, some walk-around guards who didn't even carry guns, real minimum security. Getting out wouldn't be a problem. *Gitting* would be—getting gone, real gone. He thought of Lou-Ann again.

"Hey, Miles," he said to another resting inmate, "what day's today?"

"Friday," Miles said, not moving.

"The shit it is," said a voice beyond Miles. "Today's Satuhdee."

"The shit it is," said Miles quietly.

"The shit it ain't," said the voice. "I do early kitchen on Satuhdee and I damn well did early kitchen *this* mornin'. Out bed at three-thirty A and M."

"Okay, it's Saturday," Miles said. "He's right. It's Saturday."

All *right* then, Conrad thought. Sunday just about here and Lou-Ann comin' visitin'. Didn't he have a thing or two for her to get workin' at *now?*

The sailplane disappeared a long way away. Just like yours truly, Conrad thought. Oh, Dad, just keep that Thursday money comin' in.

61

"Who's the gent sitting out there in the sports car?" Jonah said.

"I don't know," Ev said. "But he booked Adele for a scenic at eleven o'clock. Insisted on Adele."

"He the guy been calling?"

"I'd say that would be a good bet."

The secretary said, "Name's MacMullin, initials D.G." The phone rang and she picked it up. "Yancey Flying Service . . . Jonah, for you."

"Hello," Jonah said.

"Mr. Jaquith?"

"Speaking."

"It's me, your erstwhile student."

"Which one?"

"Amory Blane."

"Oh, yes. Amory Blane."

"I'm sorry about . . . about yesterday. Quitting."

"Forget it."

"I'd like to try again."

Jonah recalled Yvonne's apprehension about the student.

"I thought about trying again all night long," the student said.

"Well, sure, okay. I can fly you at one or at three."

"One."

"See ya," Jonah said. He hung up and made the entry on the appointments calendar. "I'm flying a long day for you today, Ev."

"I hear you, Jonah."

"I don't think you hear well enough."

"I'm working on Mrs. Yancey, God damn it!"

"Ev, one of these days I'm going to tell you to go fuck yourself."

"You *mind* yourself, Jonah!"

"Good morning, gentlemen," Adele said, coming in from the parking lot.

"Yeah, sure," Ev said. "You've got a flight, Adele. Guy's been waiting for you."

"Where?"

"Here he comes now. Guy in the corduroy cap."

Oh, Jesus, Adele thought. *Oh Jesus, Jesus, Jesus.*

She remembered adhesive tape being ripped off her arms, an intravenous needle being torn out, a catheter, D.G. screaming at her, her own screams and her fresh blood on the white hospital sheets, and finally D.G. being pulled away.

Eleven years before.

She had not seen him since. He had spent some years, on and off, in institutions of one sort or another. When he had been allowed to go home he had called her on the phone a couple of times. He had been so docile, even kind.

He came in the screen door and stood just inside, the corduroy cap now in his hands. His hands clenched and unclenched around the cap. His face was both smiling and sorrowful. There was fear in his eyes, the innocent fear of a child. The face was that of the young graduate student she had married. Only the lines in the face were those of a much older man. He was wearing well-pressed yellow deck slacks, worn chukka boots, an immaculate button-down sports shirt, and an old denim jacket. He was like two people wearing the same clothes. Or like a man wearing clothes that belonged to two different people.

"Hello, D.G.," Adele said.

"Hello, Adele." Then he just stood there.

Whatever it is, Adele realized, he must think something's very important to bring him here. "Do you want to have some coffee, D.G.? We could sit down and have some coffee."

"That would be good. That would be awfully good, Adele."

Adele went to the hotplate and poured two cups. "Black?"

"Still black," D.G. said.

"Let's sit outside. It's nice and warm out."

"All right."

At the end of the building there was a picnic table. They sat there.

"How's your mother, D.G.?"

"She's fine. She sends her best to you."

"She knew you were coming?"

"Yes. She didn't want me to."

"Why not?"

D.G. looked away. "She thought it would be destructive for me. To see you. A *blow* is what my mother said."

"Is it? Destructive? A blow?"

"No. I knew it wouldn't be. The doctor—I've been seeing this same doctor five days a week for over six years. About a year ago we started cutting down. Anyway, my doctor says I've come to terms with myself."

"I'm glad to hear that."

"I'm not comfortable yet, but I manage, I cope . . ."

"I'm glad, D.G."

"*I get along without hurting people,*" D.G. said in a rush.

Adele nodded. "That's very good, D.G. You never did *like* to hurt people."

"I know. The doctor found that out right away. That's one of the places we started from. They never did find that out when I was at those other places."

"Are you doing anything?"

"No. Nothing. I get frightened. But I'm looking around. I'm *trying* to find something I can get into. I've got a good business head. I— Oh, I see. How do I get along?" He laughed. "Grandfather left me a lot of money. A lot. It's paid for everything. Just the income from it pays everything. You know I have an appointment with you, Adele? To go flying? Would you believe it? I've never been up in a small plane before."

"Why did you come to see me, D.G.?" Adele said.

"Because I think about you all the time. I wanted to see *you*. I wanted to see *real* Adele—so I could get rid of the Adele in my head. The one who I—*the one who I hurt in the hospital.*"

"I—"

"The Adele I have in my head . . . was a long time ago. I thought it would be helpful to see you now . . . It would help get rid of that part of my life . . . To see that you're really okay."

"I'm really okay. Did your doctor know you were coming?"

"Yes. He thought it was a good idea of mine. But . . ."

"But?"

"But he thought I ought to ask you first. He thought I ought to call you or write you and ask if it was okay. I couldn't, Adele. I was afraid you'd say no." He looked up at the sky. "You don't have to take me flying if you don't want to. I mean, I know that."

"Why do you want to go flying?"

"Not just flying. I want to go flying with you. With you in particular."

"I don't know, D.G. I don't know . . . Why just me? There is a good man here who—"

"I wouldn't trust anyone else. Anyway, Adele, it wouldn't make any difference to me if I went flying with someone else. It's . . . I can't explain it. Not even to myself."

"D.G., I just don't think . . . I'm sorry. I can't bring myself to trust you. Not alone in an airplane."

D.G. nodded. He looked away for what seemed like a long time, and then he looked at Adele and nodded again. His face had become empty.

Adele was alarmed. She had been used to passion in his face, rage and pain and sometimes love, but she had never seen this emptiness.

"How do you feel, D.G.?"

D.G. shrugged. "Disappointed." His eyes were wet, his face less empty. "But I was prepared for . . . I'd prepared myself for . . . the reality of the situation."

Adele said, "D.G., what the hell, I'll take you flying."

At first there was enough to do with the airplane to keep Adele from thinking too much about D.G. seated next to her. But then there was little to do, just steer the airplane and climb and look out for other traffic. Adele thought back to when she'd said to D.G., just a few minutes before: *I'll take you flying.* Now that she was the pilot, alone in the airplane with him, she felt as if she had had nothing to do with what she'd said. If D.G. started ripping things out now . . . if he tried to take the controls . . . She felt herself tensing at the controls. The tension grew greater and greater. She had never felt such tension while flying.

Even though they were riding in a closed aircraft, D.G. felt that it was a boat—a very fragile boat, like a canoe—that might tip at any moment and fling its passengers into the sky. He felt that there was nothing substantial beneath his seat, that he might fall through the underside of the aircraft and hurtle to the ground. The airplane banked and some voice inside him screamed—he thought they were going to fall over.

He looked at Adele. She was intent on flying the plane. It didn't worry her at all.

"That's Mount Monadnock up ahead."

"Adele?"

"Yes, D.G."

"Could I—could I touch the controls?"

"I don't think—all right, D.G. Put your right hand on the yoke. Like you were driving a car one-handed. But lightly. Just use your fingers . . . *Too much,* D.G. That's it . . . You're almost flying this by yourself, D.G."

"Could I do it? Just for a few seconds. Alone? Without your hand on the control?"

Adele put her left hand, her yoke hand, on her lap. It became a fist. She covered it with her right hand. "You're flying the airplane, D.G."

"No, no . . . Yes, all right . . . All right, Adele, *that's enough, please fly it yourself.*"

She took the control back. "You did very well, D.G.," she said quietly.

"Did very well," D.G. said, looking out his window. "Everything looks so thought out down below. Like a crazy quilt. But there's sense to it. Isn't there, Adele? From up here it looks like there's sense to it."

"There's a lot of open space too."

"Yes, I see that. More than you'd imagine." He was silent for a long time. Adele looked at her watch. They had been up for thirty-five minutes.

"The scenic flight's just for half an hour," Adele said.

"That's all right, Adele. I can afford it. I'll pay for the extra time."

"Really, I'd just as soon go down."

"Just a little longer, Adele, please? You know what?"

"No."

"It's so calm up here. I'm surprised. I was afraid at first, but now I'm not at all. You're trembling, Adele. Did you know that? That you're trembling?"

". . . It's a little chilly at this altitude."

"Yes. Do you want my jacket?"

"No."

"Can we fly some more?"

"All right, D.G. Of course we can. Where do you want to go?"

"I don't care, just keep flying."

Adele kept looking at the clock on the panel watching minute after minute go by. D.G. was silent. All he did was look out the window beside him. Adele saw only the back of his head.

When he turned toward her after seventeen minutes he had a small smile. "You can go down now, Adele. I just wanted to know what it was like up here. All these years I've heard about how you had this career as a pilot. I just wanted to know what it was like up here with you. I wanted to learn from *you* what it was like . . . It's wonderful."

When they were near the field and she had called in and pulled back on power as she turned final approach, when they were on the long quiet glide down to the runway, D.G. said, "You're still trembling, Adele."

After D.G. had paid Ev and said he guessed he'd drive home to New York now, Adele walked to his car with him. He turned to her and the words he said came out in a quiet cry—"Let me call you, Adele. In a year? Or two? Let me?"

My Christ, D.G., Adele said in her mind. But she said no word of it out loud. All she could say to him was "Drive carefully, D.G."

The empty look returned to his face. "I will, Adele. And thank you, Adele, thank you."

62

Laura Sullivan stood on the bare stage and looked down at the director, Rodney LeMay. He was so far back in the seats that she could hardly see him. Emogene Walker, the owner of the summer theater, sat beside LeMay. LeMay was just up from New York for a working weekend getting ready for the season that would begin in mid-June. Laura held the script in one hand. The scene was over, but the actor, Hilary somebody, continued to hold her hand. She didn't mind. It felt good, reassuring. It felt as if, through the actor's hand, she were connected to the theater.

Rodney LeMay came down the aisle and stood in front of the proscenium looking up. Laura wondered how much he could see up under her short dress. That was all right, too. It fit the part.

"That was fine," LeMay said, *"super.* You'll need a bit of work on projection, but not to worry, I'll tend to that with you personally. It's a small part, Laura, but important. So lucky, Emogene. Just what we need. A real sex bomb. How clever of you to find her."

"I was looking at summer dresses in Bonwit's in Boston, and I saw this girl, this extraordinary *creature,* and I said to myself, 'That's our Honey for *The Cat's Meow,'* but never *dreaming* we'd have the opportunity to use her. I thought she must be a Bostonian. But then I heard her give her charge address—Cornwall—and you see, *voilà,* here she is."

"Extraordinary luck. You should still be doing professional casting, Emogene." He gazed at Laura. "Just what we need, a sex bomb."

Laura smiled and took her hand from Hilary's. She was wearing a light, low-cut dress she had bought for afternoon wear in the city. Luncheon. Cocktails. A former beau, looking down it, had called it her Lady Bountiful dress.

"Hilary," LeMay said, "I'm so glad you're available for a bit of early work—you are, aren't you?"

"Yes."

"Splendid. Laura is not, of course, a professional actress, though quite competent, quite competent. It won't be too much of a chore for you to coach her? Run through your scenes a few times before we start rehearsals?"

"My pleasure."

"The two of you were super," LeMay said, "just super. How did it feel to you, Hilary?"

"It felt fine," Hilary said. He glanced at Laura's décolletage and smiled at her. She smiled back.

"You want to concentrate on the lines when you work with her," LeMay said. "You know, up on the stage, you probably couldn't appreciate how well she moved. She already uses her body as an instrument."

"Oh, I think I was appreciative."

Laura and Hilary stood in the theater's parking lot. The sun was warm. Shoots of green were appearing where last year's grass lay brown and lifeless.

"When shall we get together?" Hilary said.

Laura took out a cigarette and waited for Hilary to offer to light it. Finally she lit it herself. "Are you someone I should know?" she said.

"What did you have in mind?"

"I'm talking about professionally. Have I seen you?"

"I don't know. Have you?"

"Don't play games."

"That's a fine idea, Laura. You try to remember it."

"I haven't the faintest idea—"

"You're game-playing right now. You game-played with the cigarette.

You've been game-playing since I met you. The little tease and twitch and come-on. That's all right. Just don't expect me to play it with you. Yes, you've probably seen me on TV. I'm the guy who says, 'I will if you will.' "

"Of course. You're terrific."

"Thank you."

"I really am impressed. I think it's going to be fun working together."

"I hope so."

"Look, Hilary, have you got a number?"

"Can't I call *you?*"

"I'd rather you didn't. It might just . . . make things difficult."

"Husband trouble?"

"You could put it that way. Look, I'd just rather keep this . . . I'd just rather not get into this with him right now. He's not going to like the business where you kiss me, and he's not going to like me being alone with you when we practice the scene. I'm just going to have to lead up to it. One way or another."

"That's not my problem. I just asked when we can get together to work."

"My husband's an airline pilot—"

"Really?"

"A captain. He's away three and four days in a row. We'll have plenty of time to get together. Just give me a number where I can reach you."

Hilary wrote out a number. "This is a pay phone at the house where I'm staying till I move out here. You can try to get me after six. And before eight. I go out around seven-thirty usually."

"You do? What do you find to do?"

"Things."

"Around here? What sort of things?"

"Amusing things. But that's really my business, isn't it?"

Laura dropped the cigarette on the ground but didn't bother to put it out. "Is that your car?"

"I have a feeling you're going to put me down because of this car. Now, why do I have that feeling?"

"It's an awfully shabby car. For a well-known actor."

"It's so I can go about unrecognized among the common people," he said, nodding to Laura. "Now you study on being a sex bomb and give me a call between six and seven-thirty sometime."

Hilary got into the car and drove away. He found his muscles were taut, straining against each other. My God, *what a scene* he had played. What a piece of *improvisation.* The intensity of it, the exertion of it, had left him exhilarated. He had been right: he *did* find amusing things to do.

63

Jonah's day had already been occupied by a professional fund raiser at eight o'clock, a lady professor of English at nine, a priest at ten, an ice-cream-stand owner at eleven, and a housewife at noon. Jonah was still out on the ramp when Amory showed up. The student was dressed the same as the day before—jodhpurs, boots, white scarf. Jonah started with him exactly where they had left off the day before. "You just pay attention when I'm trying to teach you something. Okay, Amory? When I get that heart attack I wanta know you can bring me in. Who wants to die in an air crash, right?"

"Yeah. That's what I worry about. Don't *you* ever worry?" Amory looked at Jonah steadily.

"When there's something to worry about. We'll go through the preflight together now."

"If it's all right with you, I'd like to try the preflight on my own. Just show you as much as I can remember."

Jonah nodded and Amory began the walk-around inspection. He borrowed a sumpstick from Jonah and sumped the fuel tanks and checked the fuel for water, contamination, and octane rating. He opened the cowling and pulled the oil dipstick and checked the wires with his fingers. He explained to Jonah everything he examined by eye alone.

"You ever do this before?" Jonah said.

"No, sir."

"You sure?"

"Yeah. Sure."

"You've got an awfully good memory," Jonah said. "You remember more after one lesson than most students remember after five."

During Amory's taxi, Jonah said, "That's not half bad. And you started it up like you'd done it a few times before, too."

"I've got good kinetic memory."

"What is it you do, Amory?"

"I amuse myself."

"Okay. You're in the captain's seat. Put your left hand on the yoke. When I tell you to, gradually apply power with the throttle till it's all the way in. Use your right hand. Then follow me through on the takeoff. Put your feet on the rudder pedals and just *feel* what I'm doing. Same on the yoke. Whatever I do with my controls will happen on yours, they're entirely interlocked, you can't move one set without the other set moving the same way. Okay?"

"Okay."

"Cornwall unicom, Fifty Pop is rolling Runway Two-zero." There were two clicks of acknowledgment on the cabin speaker. "Give me full throttle now," Jonah said.

Amory plunged the throttle forward. The engine became violently loud and the airplane jerked. Amory's hand leaped back from the control. "No sweat," said Jonah, "just too much throttle too fast."

They started to move and then were moving with increasing speed. The far end of the runway began to widen. There was a feeling of hard surface beneath the airplane. Bright shots of sunlight glinted off surfaces to the side as they swept past. The yoke came back toward Amory. The feeling of hard surface beneath the gear disappeared. They rose in the air, and at the same time their forward progress seemed to slow and the sound of the engine seemed to subside and become smoother.

Jonah gave Amory straight and level flight and then level turns. After that he pulled back on power and gave him glides and gliding turns.

"I like this *best*," Amory said loudly. *"Gliding.* That's what I think of as really flying."

"Blane, you might become a pilot."

Jonah gave him some climbs. Amory offered to try a climbing turn.

"Go ahead."

When Amory had finished and leveled off, Jonah said, "I'm not sure you know exactly what you just did, but you just executed a coordinated climbing turn." Jonah broke it down and went through the elements of it and Amory repeated the performance. They had been up for nearly an hour.

"Okay, hotrock. Now let's see if you can do something easy. Take me home."

"Sure thing." Amory peered ahead and to both sides. Then he started a cautious turn, his left hand gripped tight on the yoke as if he were holding the airplane in the air by main force. Jonah reached over and tapped the hand.

"I like to discourage white knuckles," Jonah said. "Relax."

"Oh, sure. *Relax.*"

"You going to keep flying us in a circle?"

"You distracted me. With that white-knuckle crap."

Amory continued the turn—around for a second time—studying ahead. What interested Jonah was that he was studying the horizon rather than the terrain below the way most students would have done.

"All *right,*" Amory said. He leveled off with Mount Monadnock directly

[169]

ahead. Then he started a turn which he ended when Monadnock was directly off his left wing. "The airport should be straight ahead. Somewhere. More or less."

"Now that's just exactly about right, Amory. And I'll tell you, that's pretty good work. Just how did you figure that out?"

"When we took off I watched Monadnock. Off to our right. I figure keep it to the left on the way back and just about the same distance away and eventually I'll see the Cornwall airport."

"Amory, I'll tell you straight out, the students who think ahead enough to find their way back to the airport at the start like this, they're rare. Okay, you see the airport ahead?"

"No."

"Look where I'm pointing."

"I don't see it."

"Yeah, well, that *is* something different. Knowing where it is and *seeing* it *are* different. You have to change the way you see up here. You have to change what you look for. You can't be so literal. What you're really looking for is like a shiny gray Band-Aid up ahead in the green. Okay, start to let down now. I'll talk you through part of the approach and then you follow me through on the landing. First, check that your fuel selector is on both tanks . . . Good . . . Mixture, rich . . . Fuel pump on . . ."

When they got out of the airplane Amory's shirt was dark with sweat.

"That was *terrific,*" Amory said. "*That was terrific.* Jesus Christ, that was *wonderful.*"

"Hotrock, you're on the ground now."

"The hell I am. That is some high. I'm still *up there,* man."

Jonah grinned. "You think you want another lesson sometime?"

"Christ, yes. Tomorrow." He looked worried. "Tomorrow *okay?*"

"Same time," Jonah said. "Let's get you a logbook. And I'd like you to get a couple of primary instruction books. If you don't want to buy them, I can lend you—"

"Hell, Jonah, I'll buy a whole fuckin' library! Wasn't that *terrific?* That was *terrific.* I tell you *that was wonderful!*"

64

The rest of Jonah's afternoon was occupied with still other regular week-end students. At two o'clock a doctor. At three o'clock a woman who could only take lessons on Saturdays when her husband was home to babysit. At four a businessman who always came over after his golf game. At five a car with streamers flying from it drove out on the ramp where Jonah was waiting by the Skymaster. A young couple got out of the back seat of the car. The man wore a suit and tie, the woman a tailored dress and jacket. The driver wore a white tuxedo jacket and the young woman with him wore a pale-rose party dress. The driver was grinning, a little drunk. His girl-friend alternately laughed and cried as she hugged the young woman in the tailored dress. Jonah and the driver put some store-new luggage in the Skymaster's cargo compartment. Then the honeymoon couple got in the back seat of the Skymaster and Jonah flew them to Kennedy International to make an early evening connection with a flight to Paris.

Jonah got back to the airport after seven. In the air some last white light had been visible at the edge of the horizon. On the ground there was only night. Jonah hangared the Skymaster and got home a few minutes after eight.

Yvonne was at her small dropleaf desk. She was surrounded by lined papers—student tablet papers—filled with entries and figures. She kissed Jonah and held her arm around his neck for a few seconds as he bent to her. "I thought you'd be back about six."

"I had that honeymoon flight to Kennedy."

"I forgot. I called the airport. Ev wasn't there. No one knew where you were. I got awfully worried again. Till I remembered. Tired?"

"You know it."

"There're some things I've got to talk to you about."

"Okay. Let me get a beer."

When Jonah came back Yvonne had seated herself on the couch. She had a sheaf of lined papers on her lap. Her hands were folded. Jonah sat in the easy chair opposite. "The memorial service is Tuesday," Yvonne said.

"For Del?"

"They can't get the . . . the remains back here till Monday."

"What time?"

"Eleven. Eleven in the morning."

Jonah nodded. "I'll cancel the students for the morning."

"Afternoon too, Jonah. Till three, anyway. Just be available? For Betty's sake?"

"I'll see what Ev says."

"I'll see what Ev says."

"All *right*, Yvonne."

"You work seven days a week as it is. Though of course you don't call it work."

"It's work. I get about a quarter of the year off, remember that. Every day there's no flying, that's a day off for me, just remember that."

"Except that you're teaching ground school or—"

"Ground school is extra money for us. That doesn't come under salary."

"—or you're out there for some reason or another. Ev needs you for something or other. Or you're on a charter flight and you get stuck somewhere—"

"Jesus Christ, Yvonne, of course I get stuck. I can't control the weather."

"Don't get angry, Jonah. Listen to me. My voice is calm. I have to go over all these things. I have to do all of them together just once."

"Okay. Okay, love."

"You do *not* get *one quarter of the year* off. You always say that, but you don't. You work seven days a week when the weather is flyable. When it's not flyable you mostly do other things for Ev."

"Because he tells me to."

"Well, he doesn't *pay* you that much. You *do* realize that, Jonah, don't you? He doesn't pay you *nearly* enough."

"All right."

"Not for all the hours you put in. But I know what it is."

"What is it?"

"It's your way of paying him to let you fly. It's as if you were some sort of student still paying off flight time by sweeping up. And don't tell me you don't sweep up the office. I've *seen* you do it."

"So the floor's dirty and there's a broom handy."

"Darling Jonah, I'm not putting you down. I married a pilot and I'm worried sick about you living to be a father. But that's my problem, right? My problem. But there's something that isn't my problem alone." She held up the papers. "I get my last check in June. The baby is due in July. In June we'll still be saving money—between what you earn and what I earn and what we spend. In July, Jonah, we'll start losing four hundred dollars a month. You make four hundred dollars less than our fixed expenses. It's here. Do you believe me?"

"I believe you."

"I didn't count in what the expenses will be because of the baby. I don't know what they'll be. People will give us a lot of things to start with. And lend us things. But there're bound to be new expenses. Things we don't know about."

"I know. I think about all this. It scares me."

"What do you—"

"I'm *working* on it."

"You've been 'working on it' since New Year's, Jo."

"I talked to Ev just today."

"Ev doesn't give a shit about you or me or anybody but Ev."

She said it so calmly that Jonah was startled. "He says he's got to talk to Mrs. Yancey."

"Jonah, how long has Ev been telling you he was going to talk to Mrs. Yancey?"

". . . You're right. A long time. A long time."

"And he hasn't done it."

"No, he hasn't."

Yvonne got up and came over to Jonah. He stood up and they placed their arms around each other. "You know I don't want you to fly, but you know that's not what we're talking about now."

"I know."

"There're some jobs in the newspaper you might look at."

"Factory jobs."

Yvonne shrugged. "Jonah, I'm going over to Betty's tonight. To help her plan Tuesday. You could come. I'm sure you'd be welcome."

"I think I'm going to do something else. Try to, anyway."

"What?"

"Work on our money problem."

65

"Shall we have a drink here before we go out?" Adele said when George Detwiler came to pick her up.

George sat in her living room while she made drinks in the kitchen. Adele lived on a comfortable side street of bulging two- and three-story wooden houses. The street was tree-lined and close to the state university extension campus. On the living-room walls there were a number of carefully framed pictures—oils, watercolors, photographs. The photographs were chiefly of people—some of them well known. None of them were of Adele. The largest picture was a black-and-white ink drawing touched with points of color. In one corner there was the notation *Artist's Proof* in ink; in the other corner, the signature *Ben Cain*. In pencil there was the inscription *To Adele, with love, Ben.* The furniture was Scandinavian with heavily textured upholstery —and rather uncomfortable, George thought. He picked up an empty ornate goblet.

"I collect glass," Adele said, bringing George a Scotch and soda. "That's Sandwich glass. I collect old books, too. If they don't cost too much. By old I mean nineteen-forty and before. I find them at flea markets. I have some grammars from the nineteenth century." She waited for him to say something, and when he didn't she said, "Did you have any trouble finding the house?"

"No. It's right where you said it would be."

"Yes. Right . . . The people downstairs own it. He's retired. I have the second floor. Kitchen, living room, bath, bedroom, three closets. A young couple have the third floor. They're both graduate students . . . George, I keep having to do all the talking, have you noticed? You keep looking around."

George put his empty glass down. "Adele, I haven't been alone with a woman—I mean on a date—since—since I don't know when. Since I met Ceil, I guess. But this isn't like that. I can remember now just what it was like to be on my first date when I was thirteen years old."

"Would you like another drink?"

"Yes, I would. What's that you're drinking?"

"Campari and soda? Would you like one?"

"No, thanks. Just Scotch."

When Adele came back, George was walking around. He took the glass from her without looking at it or drinking from it. "Another thing." He stopped walking and looked at her. "I went to the Raabs' New Year's Eve party—I wasn't planning to go, but I went because I hoped you'd be there."

"I have a question, then. But I don't know if I should ask—"

"Ask."

"Had you been thinking about me for a long time?"

"No. No, I hadn't. I was reading the class notes in my college alumni magazine. That afternoon. New Year's Eve afternoon. I was reading these class notes. You know, Charlie Smith has just been made executive vice-president of dum-de-dum company, and Frank Brown has just been named under secretary of state for such-and-such, and John Jones reports he's just back from Japan, where he ran the biggest fishing fleet in the Pacific for five years, and, you know, things like that. Where everyone had got to. And here I was clerking in a law office and studying to complete third-year law."

"That was when you thought about me?"

"I took a nap and had an erotic dream about you."

"Oh."

"I'm sorry. I didn't think it would offend you."

"I'm not offended. People just usually aren't that direct." Adele laughed. She heard her own nervousness in the laugh. "On a scale of one to ten, how did I rate with your other erotic dreams?"

"You're the only one I've had."

Adele looked at her glass. She sipped from it. She put it down. "I can't believe that."

"I just don't remember good dreams. Not any more. I remember nightmares. But not good dreams. With that exception." He stood up. "We ought to go to dinner now. I made reservations at the Cornwall Inn. I haven't been there in a long time. I hope you're not bored with it?"

"I haven't been there since last fall."

"With Ben Cain? I'm sorry," George said quickly. "None of my business."

"That's right. But why did you say Ben?"

George indicated the picture. "It says 'with love.' "

"Do you think we could get a table by a window on the pond side? I love to watch the ducks. Do you know why? You couldn't guess. I like to watch them do their full stall landings."

"Do ducks make full stall landings? That's funny, I never noticed that. Pigeons, yes, but not ducks."

66

"I *do* like it here," Adele said.

Ben Cain was sitting alone at a table on the far side of the room. He was reading a book by the light from a candle in the hurricane lamp on his table. He was drinking coffee and a brandy, and George was studying him. "Does Ben Cain make you nervous?"

"No. I could wish he weren't here just now, but no, his being here doesn't make me nervous."

"Maybe he didn't see us come in."

"Maybe." George finished his second drink and signaled for a third. Adele still had her first in front of her. "I'm enjoying this," George said. He looked across the room. "Now there's an attractive couple."

"Perry and Laura Sullivan," Adele said.

"Yes." He continued to look at them.

"Are you studying them?" Adele said.

"Why, yes, I think I am." The waiter placed George's new drink in front of him. George looked up. "Thank you," he said. "We'll order now." After the waiter had gone again, George sat with his chin in his hand, one finger touching his lips. He was again looking across the room at Perry and Laura. "They *are* an attractive-looking couple, aren't they?" he said.

"Yes. They're both physically good looking."

"She laughs a lot," George said. "Then she looks to see who's watching her."

"I hadn't noticed. But I haven't been looking."

"He frowns a lot. You'd think with such an attractive young woman he wouldn't frown so much."

"Maybe he's worried."

"Just made captain and just married for a year."

"Maybe it's a bad night," Adele said.

"Shouldn't be, now should it?"

"We don't know."

"I didn't mean it that way. I meant, given their circumstances—youth, beauty, accomplishment, good income, recent marriage—all that, they just ought not to have a bad evening. It oughtn't to be dealt to them."

"To use your image, maybe it's just the luck of the draw."

"It's a fucked-up deal, if you ask me. Excuse me. Maybe tomorrow will be all aces." George swallowed some of his drink. "Perry Sullivan, *Captain* Sullivan," George said, "I even gave him a couple of lessons. A long time ago. After dinner, Adele, maybe we could stop by and say hello, buy them a drink."

"That's thoughtful of you," Adele said.

"Well, hello, hello," George said. Ben Cain was standing by their table.

"Good evening, Adele, George."

"Ben," Adele said.

George started to get up. "Don't, George," Ben said.

"All right. I've just been admiring a work of yours."

"Good of you to say so."

"I've never seen an original. Just in reproduction. In magazines."

"Haven't seen you at all, George. Not in a while."

"What's the book?" George said. He took it from Ben's hand, looked at the gold print on the black spine. "Hefty volume," George said. "Feels like a law book. *The Letters of Vincent van Gogh,* volume two. I wouldn't have thought there was enough light to read here. Just candles. Have you read volume one?"

"Yes, but not here." He took the book back. "I just wanted to say hello."

"Well, I'm glad you came by, Ben. From all the way across the room. Always nice to see a familiar face." George frowned as he saw Perry and Laura leave. He stood up and offered his hand. "I am glad to see familiar faces. Haven't done much of that in a while. I'm enjoying it."

"Ben," Adele said, "I hope your work's going well."

"I just got back, Adele."

"I know. I hope it *will* go well."

"Thank you, I'll let you know if it does."

"Do that. I mean it. I'll be glad to hear."

Ben shook his head. "Adele, you just confuse the hell out of me."

67

Jonah drove the long, dark, narrow way through the trees to Ben's house. Jonah had the sensation that—in the three or four minutes between the town road and the house—he had lost human contact. It made him chilly.

Jonah parked. He could see no light from the house. When Jonah had called Ben after eight, Ben had just been going out to dinner. Ben had promised to be back as close to ten as he could. The house was—except for one high, turretlike interruption—long and low, constructed from soapstone cut from the quarry and local pine. It had always looked to Jonah like an elongated science-fiction log cabin. The use of old materials in new forms and contexts was Ben's style. The house had been widely reproduced in architectural magazines. Jonah walked around the outside. A great, two-story gentle curve of translucent plastic flared dully with light from within. Ben's studio. There was an outside door to it, a wide oak door set in a large overhead door for the access of big materials. Jonah banged on it.

"Yo!"

It was Ben's voice, hardly audible from within. Jonah went in.

Ben was seated on a tall, paint-spattered stool, his heels on a rung. Only a floor lamp near the great plastic curve provided any light. Jonah stopped. Large presences loomed out of the darkness, barely touched by the light, the bulks of them hidden in the darkness. Jonah felt a visceral tightening, a swift eruption of adrenaline, as if he had come into some ancient forbidden place and the presences in the darkness were the likenesses of the gods of the place. He said as much to Ben.

"I feel like it's a forbidden place myself," Ben said.

Ben wore a button-down shirt, a tweed jacket, and a tie, and and his loafers were well-shined. The handles of some woodworking tools on a table next to Ben were sweat-stained. Elsewhere an acetylene torch lay next to a mask and some twisted metal. Tools and pieces of material had been left all about the studio like army units involved in separate but interrelated skirmishes. Three canvases, lined side by side, had been marked with symbols that stimulated some vague feeling of dread in Jonah. He asked Ben about the symbols.

"I made them up," Ben said. "It took me years."

"Christ," Jonah said.

"They're not right yet," Ben said.

Jonah pointed into the darkness. "What are those up there?"

"Pieces I never finished."

"Why not?"

Ben said nothing.

"You know, Ben, your stuff is *scary?*"

Ben laughed. "You're telling me."

"Does anyone else say that?"

"Most everybody."

"Don't you think it's scary?"

"It tries to get into people's fears."

"Well, shit, you got into mine and I don't even know art."

"You just know what you like, right?"

"I didn't say I liked it, Ben."

Ben laughed.

"You know who ought to see this?"

"Who?"

"George Detwiler."

"No kidding. Why?"

"He's into stuff like this, someone told me. Phenomenology. This stuff looks like phenomenons to me. Funny thing, Ben."

"What?"

"You sitting there. All dressed up. I mean, you're dressed for someplace else. You don't look like you belong in here."

"Jonah, I don't feel like I belong in here."

"Shit, Ben, I didn't mean—"

"You can't imagine what it took me to come in here tonight."

"I guess not. I wouldn't think it'd be any problem."

Ben laughed again. "Most of the time I don't think it'd be any problem either. Just when I try to do it. That's when the problem looms up."

"I wanted to talk to you, Ben."

"Money."

"Right. I have a good idea of the figures now."

"Let's have a beer."

"That sounds good."

Ben came back with six beers in a large bowl of ice. He gave one to Jonah and took one himself and sat down on the stool again. Ben opened a beer and threw the cap in the direction of an open oil drum in the corner. "How much do we need?" Ben said.

"Depends. Ev won't say a word about my buying in. If you and I set up on our own, I figure thirty thousand. Thirty thousand cash. We ought to be able to get a bank loan for the rest."

"How much more will that be?"

"Another fifty thousand. Minimum. That'll give us a single engine for instruction and short charter, and a used twin, say an Apache, for regular charter. There's insurance and I've got to have a guaranteed salary, and we'll need an A and P for maintenance, and . . . Well, I think we can buy Del Howard's old hangar. I haven't asked, of course, but—"

"Ev Goodsom is going to try to buy that hangar."

"How do you know?"

"Because that's what I'd do if I had the only flight service on the field and I wanted to keep competition off."

"Betty Howard's gotten to be friends with Yvonne."

"That won't count for shit once the lawyers start talking."

"I don't know."

"We can save *some* money," Ben said, "using my Cherokee for charter and advanced training. Like IFR. Or somebody going for a commercial. I just don't want primary students banging the hell out of it."

Jonah listed other initial and fixed expenses.

"All right," Ben said. "I'm not even sure we can do it for fifty thousand. Much less get a bank loan. There's a guy I'm doing some designing for. Part of a new building in Manhattan. I'll get about thirty thousand out of it. I don't know how much'll be left after taxes, even if it's invested in the flight service. I'll have to ask my tax people about it. This guy, his name is Rupert Zur. He's a pilot, too. On the side. His business is export-import. Anyway, I might be able to interest him in putting up some money. But I tell you, Jonah, I'd feel a lot more secure buying into Ev's operation. It's already established. The equipment's there. The business is there."

"I know. But Ev . . . He just won't talk to me about it, Ben."

"Did you tell him you might start your own operation?"

"I hinted at it."

"What was his reaction?"

"He got mad as hell. But that was when Del Howard was just opening his operation. I don't think Ev was overly concerned about me."

"Well, he can be concerned about you now. Who else has he got to fly for him anyway? Adele?"

"Adele's good."

"I know. But she's seasonal. And she's not interested in carrying the kind of work load you do."

"He could bring someone in from the outside."

"Not for the money he's paying you."

"He could bring in some kid. Somebody hungry. He'd work for what I'm working for. Maybe less. I've thought all this through, Ben."

"Yeah, but someone new, a kid as you say, wouldn't have your experience."

"Neither did I when I started working for Ev."

"If Ev got worried, how much do you think it would cost to buy in?"

"I can't see him letting anyone in for less than fifteen, maybe twenty-five thousand dollars. And that wouldn't be equal partners."

"What're his profits a year? Do you have any idea?"

"Including everything, and that includes fuel sales to general aviation as well as the airlines— Do you know he gets ten dollars just to hook up the hose to two flights a day minimum? Plus two hundred gallons minimum each time, and that's at five cents a gallon profit. *Overweight,* he gets five cents a gallon to *defuel.* And the oil company pays for the equipment and maintenance. So putting everything together I'd guess there's maybe a hundred thousand dollars a year. That's the whole pot, though. I don't know how he and Mrs. Yancey split the pot."

"And you don't know who else is in it with them, either."

"Like who? Falun sold out to Ev years ago. When he quit being active commercially."

"I'm not talking about Falun."

"Who then?"

"I don't know, Jonah. But Ev isn't a *bad* guy, you know. There's got to be some *person* or some *reason* why he won't let you in."

When Jonah went home Ben went to his bedroom and bath and got ready for bed. He turned off the lamp by his bed but remained standing in the darkness. When his eyes adjusted he looked out through the sliding glass doors of his bedroom but could still see no sky. He remembered lying in bed in the motel outside of Palm Beach and looking into the blue twilight sky and watching the stars appear as he waited to sleep through the night before he set out across the Caribbean. He thought about that for a long time, and about what he had been thinking about as he lay in that motel bed.

Then he took his robe and got a couple of blankets from the bathroom linen closet and went to the studio. He spread the blankets on the daybed there and lay down under them. He closed his eyes and remembered lying on this same daybed back in November and looking down on the ONC charts of the Caribbean, the odd shapes of islands spread distantly about the long, empty white sea. He thought of statute miles, number of minutes, gallons of fuel . . . Now he opened his eyes and looked up and around at the unfinished work that stood darker than the darkness in the studio.

68

"You've never had trouble sleeping, Ev," Charlotte Goodsom said to her husband.

"I have trouble sleeping now. Go to bed, Charlotte."

"Maybe you ought to see a doctor."

"Doc Glynn'll just tell me I'm sixty years old and people sixty don't sleep as well as they used to. It's a well-known goddamn fact the older you get, the less sleep you manage."

"But you don't give it a chance. You just stay up."

"I like staying up. It gives me something to do."

"Ev. Why don't you just get into bed and *read?* You used to love to read in bed."

"I can't concentrate, Charlotte."

"You can concentrate on that? On television?"

"That's just it. I don't need to concentrate on it."

"No, I guess not. You concentrate on the beer instead. You drank a *six*-pack last night, Ev. Just between the news and—"

"Go to bed, Charlotte."

The room was dark except for the face of the television set and a small lamp next to Charlotte's piano. She kissed him on the cheek and he held his arm around her briefly. "I'll leave your lamp on for you."

"No need," Ev said. "It'll just keep you awake."

"No, it won't. I'll leave it on for you."

Ev opened a beer. After it—and a few more—he might be part of the way to sleep. The announcer looked at Ev. The sonofabitch never sees me, Ev thought. Stares straight at me and never sees me.

"*. . . President Nixon, in Hawaii today, hailed the astronauts and told them their aborted mission was not a failure. Mr. Nixon had this to say . . .*"

A news film began. "*Captain Lovell, it is my proud honor, on behalf of a grateful and proud nation, to welcome you and your colleagues back to the United States of America . . . And on this occasion I am very proud to speak, not just for two hundred million Americans, but for people around this world . . .*"

Ev remembered when he and Yancey, in an open biplane on skis, had located the lost climbers on Mount Washington. Their pictures, his and Yancey's, had been in some big-city newspapers and President Hoover had sent them a wire of congratulations from the White House.

"*I recall, Captain, that when I spoke to you on the phone, you said that you regretted that you were unable to complete your mission . . . I hereby declare that this was a successful mission—a great mission on behalf of your country . . .*"

Ev laughed. I voted for you, you sonofabitch, but even I didn't recognize your miraculous powers. Now if you were to declare to the television cameras that the last flight of Lyman Dougherty and Delaney Howard was a *successful* flight, would the good congressman and his pilot be with us today?

Well, shit, Ev thought, the great thing was that the astronauts *had* gotten back.

"Finally, your mission served your country. It served to remind us all of our proud heritage of a nation. To remind us that in this age of technicians and scientific marvels that the individual still counts. That in a crisis the character of a man, or of men, will make the difference . . ."

You're goddamn fucking-A right, Ev thought. Sixty years old and the individual still counts—damn right I do.

Ev had gotten through his fortieth birthday and his fiftieth birthday without much thinking about them. Those were the birthdays when the sense of mortality was supposed to come down on you hard. But it was this sixtieth birthday, just weeks before, that had done in the spirit of him, left him alarmed by the huge amount of time that had gone by as he had wandered around in his body and done nothing to hold on to the time better . . . until now there was almost none of it left. That was why he wouldn't go to bed. Because it wasted time, it threw away living.

No, he knew it wasn't just his sixtieth birthday that had done in his spirit, it was Falun, too.

"As we look at what you have done, we realize that greatness comes not simply in triumph but in adversity. It has been said that adversity introduces the man to himself."

Yes, Ev thought, and the sonofabitch I'm meeting is a sonofabitch I don't like. Christ, yes, surrounded by adversity. Age on every side of me and pushing in. And along with that, that fucking Jonah shoving as hard as he can.

Ev became aware of another voice, other film. A small building. Smoke. People lying on a floor. Some gazing up. Some not gazing, not moving. *". . . There is no evidence that these Vietnamese hold any sympathy for the Vietcong. But, as these bullet holes in the walls testify, they are being executed as if they had been giving support to the Vietcong. Sidney Kraft, Takeo, Cambodia."*

The station returned to the anchorman in the studio. There was a pause while the anchorman waited to make sure the clip had concluded. In the silence the anchorman looked at the camera/Ev. *The sonofabitch doesn't give a shit,* Ev thought.

The television was off, the room was quiet. Ev had turned out the lamp and sat in the silent darkness, the last beer open in his hand. In the darkness he could look at images of his own choosing. He was looking at Yancey. Reel after reel of his mind's film of Yancey. There was Yancey in a C-3 Stearman, drunk, staggering down the runway on glare ice. Then he had that B-6 Ryan. He used to fly newspapers to White River Junction. Then he'd go on to Canada and bring booze back. He was working for a gang then, a syndicate gang. That was at first, during Prohibition. Out of Schenectady. Then, after his Schenectady dealings, Yancey had gone on his own in some scheme that Ev still couldn't figure. The sonofabitch flew alcohol *north*. Shit, Ev thought, everyone else was hauling it south and Yancey dreams up a scheme to take it north. To Canada. Ev remembered it with pleasure; the big Boeing 95, the 550-horsepower Pratt and Whitney Hornet, could carry one *hell* of a load. Old Yancey. Took pure grain alcohol north and brought back sweepstakes tickets and that's how he got paid, with sweeps tickets which he sold. He used to have a three A.M. takeoff from someplace in the sticks, great big goddamn drum of alcohol in the Boeing. Kept the Boeing in some barn out in the sticks with a little rough runway nearby and it'd be zero degrees outside and at two A.M. he'd build a fire under the engine with a plumber's pot to get the engine warmed up, the oil loosened up, for his three A.M. takeoff, and then, said Yancey, grinning hugely at Ev, "In comes the gendarmes, twelve or fifteen of them, sheriffs, feds, rifles, pistols." "What happened?" Ev remembers himself saying, and grinning now in the dark remembering Yancey saying, "I told 'em I was in the dusting business." "And what did they say to that?" "Well, shit, Everett, I'm *here*, ain't I? You don't see me in no fuckin' pen-eye-ten-tury, do you?"

Yancey dead years later. Straight into a mountainside on a cloudless, windless day, his engine running full tilt. He was going to pick up some blood for someone.

Was that best? Ev wondered. Have it happen sudden and quick. A helluva lot better than waiting around for it, getting scared more shitless every minute, Ev thought. Helluva lot better than waiting around for it every minute. But even that wasn't the worst. The worst was the anger he felt at himself for feeling sorry for himself and afraid.

69

"You enjoyed the evening, didn't you?" Perry said. "You laughed a lot at the inn." He was in bed. Laura had just come in from the bathroom. Her nightgown was sheer and the backlighting accented the lines of her figure. In spite of what he had said, he was not sure that it had been so good an evening. Something had been wrong about his suggesting that they go to the new restaurant that had opened about twenty miles from Cornwall and that he had been told was quite romantic. Something had been wrong about his asking how her interview at the playhouse had gone and whether she was being considered for a play and what kind of part she'd tried out for. After a second drink, and surrounded by the pleasant mood of the inn, he had almost asked her once again to go flying with him, but at least he had, for once, avoided that mistake. Watching her body through the nightgown, he felt his physical desire for her overwhelm his emotional uneasiness; he decided that it was a good thing, it might be a start—lovemaking might release both of them from their reticence with each other.

"The dinner wasn't worth what you spent on it," Laura said. "They overcharge at the inn."

"It was your choice, I thought, Laura. I thought you wanted to go there."

"There really isn't a choice around here, Perry. You know that. You *ought* to know that, you've lived here long enough. No choice at all. One place is as bad as the next. And that man *staring* at me, that what's-his-name—George Detwiler." She looked in a mirror and pulled sharply at her hair with a brush.

"He wasn't staring, Laura. There was just a minute there—"

"I never saw anything so rude."

"George wasn't rude, Laura."

She turned from her mirror. "That's it, Perry. That's it. Go right ahead. *Defend* anyone I criticize."

"I wasn't defending George, I just said—"

"How they ever let *you* be a captain, I don't know. I suppose your copilot has to do all your thinking for you."

"Laura? Just a few minutes ago I was thinking about making love to you."

"You were? Isn't that *thoughtful* of you, Perry. And you *did* think of it all by yourself, Perry, I know I didn't help you at all."

Perry felt as if his anger were a runaway engine in him.

"Perry, I'm going to get into bed. And I'm going to go to sleep. And if you touch me I'll walk out of this house."

After a while in the darkness, Laura asleep from the drinks she'd had, the room silent except for her deep breathing, Perry felt a cool calm spread through him. Laura was in Las Vegas, Reno, Santo Domingo, somewhere, getting a divorce, and Perry was alone here in the house. Captain Sullivan was getting ready for his next trip, about to go away on work, about to meet a number of attractive and pleasant young women. He went to sleep almost untroubled.

70

George parked in front of Adele's house. For the life of him, George thought, it was just like a Saturday-night date when he was in college. There was even a group of slightly boisterous students walking by on the other side of the street. George said, "I feel like I'm waking up. I swear to God I feel like I'm waking up."

"Were you tired, George?" Adele said. "You didn't act it."

"No. That's not what I mean. It's like what I felt when I could first fly an airplane all by myself. The trouble was, I didn't have anything I could *do* with the feeling. I mean, it was there, the feeling that I was on top of everything, I was full of the *energy* of it—but I didn't have anything to do with all the excitement I felt when I wasn't flying. Do you know what I mean?"

"Yes. But I haven't had that feeling for a long time." Adele stopped. "No, I'm wrong. I had an even better feeling than that this morning."

"I can't remember when I had it last," George said.

"George, would you like to come up for a drink? or coffee?"

"Both."

George stopped again at the Ben Cain. The lines of ink made sort of a fish. George had dismissed the picture before. He'd thought the picture was arbitrary, like most contemporary art. Some random black lines, some spots of color. The fish disappeared as he looked at it. The points of color seemed to lie at different depths. They changed color—almost—as he looked from one to another. He began to see vastness and motion.

"George?" Adele set a drink and two cups of coffee on the table in front of the couch.

"I was just looking at this and . . ." He shook his head.

"If you look at it long enough, things happen in it. Different things for different people."

"What happens for you?"

Adele was quiet and then drank some coffee before she spoke. "Mine is based on something personal."

George sat on the couch. He drank some coffee and then some Scotch. "You said you had a good feeling this morning, a special feeling, but—?"

"I had a visit from my ex-husband. Later in the day."

George waited.

"He's called D.G. He used to be institutionalized from time to time. Now he goes to see a doctor. They've gotten him that far. He's been seeing this one doctor for several years. I hadn't seen him for ten, eleven years."

"What did it feel like?"

"I'm just thinking about that."

"Why did he suddenly come to see you?"

"He wanted me to take him flying."

George nodded.

[185]

"That makes sense to you?"

"Yes."

"Why?"

"I don't know. But it doesn't seem nonsensical to me. It seems logical on his part. I don't know why."

"That's not much of an answer."

"Sometimes I wake up at night and I know there's something I have to do to safeguard the world. I don't know what it is and I know it's crazy for me to think there's *anything* I can do to safeguard the world. Then I realize that what I'm dealing with: I have this feeling of danger, and what I really want to do is safeguard my son, my young son, Randy. And so I go into his room and I pull the covers up on him and I kiss him." George drank some coffee and some Scotch.

"Do you think that's what D.G. was doing?"

"Maybe he just came to see if you were all right, how you're getting along. What did you feel about him?"

Adele was quiet for a long time. "I've just been coming to that. All day I've been thinking about what it was that I felt."

George didn't say anything.

"While I was flying him I was scared, about what he might do, if he was still crazy, and I trembled. He saw it. But after he left, I began shaking, actually *shaking.* Now I've figured out what it was. I was shaking because I felt like I'd *survived.* As if being married to him had been a bad automobile accident in which I could have been killed. But I walked away from it. And when I found I was okay, after all this time, and realized how close I'd come, I started shaking."

"How do you feel now?"

"All evening long I've been feeling calm. You feel like you're waking up. I feel like I'm ready to rest."

George finished his drink.

Adele walked with him to the door.

"Thank you for a good evening, George."

"Have a good rest, Adele."

71

The day was brightly sunlit, the sky cloudless, the earth hazeless, the clarity of the detail of the surface of the earth extraordinary. On the unicom frequency there was so much talk from light aircraft aloft in the uniquely benevolent New England skies that Jonah had turned down the volume on the cabin speaker in Cherokee Five-zero Papa. The Cherokee's nose lifted acutely toward the sky, its wings spread as if in benediction over the earth, its forward motion so slight that the airplane seemed to be immobile high in the air. Then the nose fell swiftly, the engine's steady throbbing was reasserted, and from within the cabin, the horizon settled back into its place and seemed to become becalmed, as if it had never moved unnaturally at all.

"That," Jonah said to Amory, "was a power-off stall. Have you got it?"

Amory was staring somewhere out beyond the airplane. His hands made twisting motions in his lap.

"Did you understand it, Amory?"

"I think."

"Want me to go through it again?"

"No."

"All right, your turn."

"Me?"

"Take the controls."

"No."

"Amory, do you realize that every landing is a stall? It's how you get the airplane to stop flying."

Amory continued to look straight ahead.

Jonah said, "Amory, take the controls and fly the airplane. You're not *paying me* to fly the airplane, you're paying me to teach you. Now take the controls and keep us straight and level."

Hesitantly Amory put the fingers of his left hand on the yoke, his feet on the rudder pedals.

"You get a stall when?" Jonah said.

"When the airplane loses lift."

"It usually happens when the airplane is at some extreme angle and when the airspeed is very low. The extreme angle is the difference between someone walking on flat ground and someone trying to scale a mountainside."

"You slip, you fall."

"But in an airplane, you slip, you recover. You push the nose down and that gives you enough airspeed to pull the nose up again and keep flying. You convert altitude into speed and speed keeps you flying."

"I understand all that. But what if you put the nose down and you just keep going *down?*"

"It doesn't happen."

"The *shit* it doesn't, man. What about all those accidents, airplanes stalling out and crashing?"

"They were too close to the ground. The pilots didn't have the altitude to recover. That's why we practice at three thousand feet."

"It felt like we were going to keep going down."

"I know. But I started the maneuver at three thousand feet. Here, I'll do it again—"

"Oh, shit."

"We're at three thousand feet, see?"

"Yeah."

"Okay, my controls. We're at three thousand feet. I pull back on power . . . and I bring the nose slowly up . . . airspeed is falling off . . ." The weight of their bodies seemed to be against the backs of their seats, the seatbacks tipped parallel to the earth. "And keep bringing the yoke back . . ." They could see nothing but sky ahead, they were aiming at the *top* of the sky. "Until there's no resistance in the yoke . . . and *there*—" The nose fell without resistance, the surface of the earth replaced the sky in an instant and seemed to hurl itself up at them.

The engine became smoothly loud, the nose came up. Jonah eased back on power. It was quiet, and they were straight and level again.

"Look at the altimeter," Jonah said. "What does it say?"

"Three thousand feet."

"On the goddamn button. We didn't lose a foot of altitude, did we?"

"No."

"As soon as you feel the stall, just push the nose down and give yourself full power. Your controls."

"Okay. My controls."

"After you do it a few times you can see that everything happens very slowly. It stops being frightening. It starts being fun."

"I can wait on that kind of fun."

"You can't wait very long. Not if you're going to learn to land this sonofagun."

"I'll wait."

"Hell, Amory. Those coordination exercises I gave you, the S-turns and the turns around a point, they're a helluva lot more difficult than a goddamn stall. And you did those like you'd been brought up on them."

"Don't manipulate me. Don't try it."

"Amory, just go through one stall for me."

"No. Let's go home."

"Why not?"

"Because, *God damn it,* I don't feel *lucky* today. I feel like maybe something's waiting to *get* me. I'll do a fucking stall for you next time, *okay?*"

On the ground Jonah said, "You did a nice job again bringing us back. In fact, everything you did up there was a nice job."

"Except not doing the stall."

"Forget it."

"You pushed me."

"You're a bright student, Amory. Some of the things you do with the airplane you do well. I figured a kick in the ass, maybe you'd do a few other things."

"I don't like kicks in the ass."

"You're paying me to teach you to fly, and I don't like to see my students wasting their money."

"Jonah, don't you ever think that one of these days an airplane *isn't* going to do what you expect it to do?"

Amory wiped his sweating face with his white silk scarf and walked away.

72

On alternate Sundays wives and sweethearts and immediate family members were allowed to visit inmates at Attridge State Correctional Facility. Visitors were allowed to bring picnic lunches, which were inspected on their way in. In cold weather these were shared in the main dining hall at long, crowded, wooden tables. In warm weather the inmates and their visitors were allowed to spread out over several fields around the facility's main buildings—they were able to spread out into privacy.

Lou-Ann had brought a basket lunch. She and Conrad sat under a tree. "Just like a picnic in a state park," Conrad said. "You can't even see a fence." He lay back. "'Cept I don't have to *see* them to *see* them. What we got for lunch?"

Lou-Ann said, "There's cold fried chicken and biscuits and coleslaw the way you like it, with raisins, and if you reach down into the jug of orange juice you'll find a plastic pouch jes all filled with vodka."

"Lou-Ann, you're somethin'. But I think, just as discreetly as I can, I'm gonna dump that happy juice out."

"But *why,* Con?"

"I go back feelin' good, sure as hell they're gonna find out why. No, I don't want to give them no excuses to move me out of here."

"Oh. I'm sorry, Con."

"Now don't take on, Lou-Ann. I thank you for it, and I mean it. But you and I'll share a few jolts and some real extra-good laughs someplace else. *Soon,* if you help."

"You know I will, Con."

"Didn't you tell me my daddy's birdman's gonna have a baby?"

"Mr. Jaquith?"

"The same."

"He's not your daddy's—"

"Never mind. His wife's gonna have a baby."

"Yes, she is."

"When?"

"Soon."

"How soon?"

"Lord, I don't know, Con."

"Well, you jes make it your business to find out."

A guard stopped and looked at them from several yards away. "You ought to eat your lunch, Whittier," the guard called.

"That's right, Mr. Vallencourt, you can't live on love here, can you?"

"Not with the food as bad as it is."

Some shouts came from across the field. Some kids and some inmates had started a softball game. The guard moved on.

"Now you listen, Lou-Ann. About two weeks after Mrs. Jaquith gets home with the baby, listen, I'll make it exact: the *second* Thursday after Jaquith's wife gets home with the baby, you jes get up here with a car. Now I'm gonna tell you specific things about the car and where to park it and what to bring. The car has got to be legal. Can you do that?"

"Sure, Con. My cousin—"

"I don't care. Your license legal?"

"Yes, Con, I jes had the state examination when my birthday—"

"Can you get a pistol?"

"Well, Con, I guess I could. I guess I could figure out how to. That cousin of mine, over in Jaffrey? I think he's got two or three."

"Wherever you get it, it's got to be that it's just between you and the person you get it from."

"All right, Con."

"Have you ever shot a pistol, Lou-Ann?"

"Oh, a coupla times. With my cousin. I didn't like the noise."

"Could you aim a pistol at a mother and her baby?"

"I s'pose I could. Why should I?"

"Could you do it for a good long time?"

"How long's 'a good long time'?"

"Six, seven, eight hours."

"How'm I s'posed to go to the bathroom?"

"I don't care. Go in your pants, if you have to. Take the baby with you."

"Gee, Con—"

"You want me out of here?"

"Well, you know I do, Con."

73

"Hilary?"

Hilary was standing at the pay phone in the hall of the house where he roomed. "Beautiful sunset, isn't it? That's why they had to call me to the phone. I was out admiring the sunset."

"Hilary, I've only got—"

"Did you notice it, Laura?"

"I'll look at it after I hang up."

"Good. How's it going, Laura? What's on your mind?"

"If you want to rehearse, I could do it anytime Tuesday afternoon."

"My time isn't as free as yours, Laura."

"Well, Hilary, my time isn't so free either. Tuesday afternoon, take it or leave it."

"I'll leave it. So long, Laur—"

"Just a minute."

"I'm missing the sunset, Laura. I'm missing the best part of it."

"Tuesday afternoon is—"

"The sun's almost down. I don't want to miss the credits."

"Hilary! I've got *another party* to consider, remember?"

"You mentioned him. A pilot. Did I mention that I'm a pilot, too? Big deal."

"Couldn't you make it Tuesday afternoon just this once? Then we can set up another time—at *your* convenience."

"No. I can't make it Tuesday afternoon. Prior commitment. Suggest another time."

"Wednesday afternoon."

"Afternoons are out this week."

"The other party just drove up. I'll call you back when I can."

Hilary hung up. Smiling, he went back to his room. As an actor he was maturing. He'd seen that on the screen in his mind just now. Good, dominating performance. Now if only some director or producer could *see* how he could deliver any reality they wanted to the audience, the way he could deliver any audience, the way he could deliver Laura.

In his room he lay down on his bed and watched the screen in his mind. He saw strong, knowing fingers—his own. They moved without hesitation, moved with command and vitality, moved to the engine controls and . . .

FLIGHT FOLLOWING

Sometimes a pilot has to take a firm grip on his emotions . . . This isn't always easy . . . What we have to do is be big grown-up people and keep everything under control.

— (Captain) Robert N. Buck

74

In the silence of his studio Ben thought lustful thoughts of women he had known and women he imagined. His body was so sexually taut he could feel his heartbeat in his groin.

"God damn work!" he yelled and kicked out at a sawhorse with his work boot. The sawhorse clipped the corner of a workbench and spun against the wall.

Then there was silence again.

It was the loneliness of the work that did it—brought on the great carnal lust. The loneliness and the *anxiety,* Ben thought—the fear of making mistakes.

He thought of the women he could call. There was a nurse in Montreal, an editor in New York, a gallery owner in Boston, an actress in New York. There was a stewardess in Boston who would probably drive over if he could get her on the phone. He saw her undressing. It was simple recall.

He walked out of the studio and stood in the center of the living room. He found he was listening to the silence of his house. If he did not move there was not a sound to be heard. The silence back in the studio had a different quality—the silence back there was vibrant, accusatory, insistent.

He thought of Doris, Doris the sea, and her warm bedroom by the Caribbean, her cool breast in the sunlight, her mouth, the airplane so high and distant over the sea being sucked down, its single engine beating . . .

Ben looked around the living room. It was quiet and stable, like a room where the owners were away.

He and the nurse from Montreal had made love in front of the fireplace. It had been very late on a January night. The heat from the embers and burning logs had been searing, and they'd had to change position often, like sunbathers. Montreal would be fun to go to. Now.

He slid aside a glass panel and went out on the deck. Warm gray air, humid and still, enclosed him. He looked at the sky. A front was spreading over Cornwall, an indefinite grayness which did not yet block out the heat from the sun.

Ben wondered if he ought to make a run for Montreal. It was clear up north, he knew that—the front was spreading slowly southwest to northeast . . . He could pack and be in Montreal in two, two and a half hours . . . His heart beat now with the expectation of it, the ease and comfort of being away from his studio, even if only alone in a hotel room in Montreal, or anywhere.

He hesitated and then went back to the studio.

"Fuck it!" he said out loud, looking at the pieces of work, the interrelations of scraps of paper and rusted pieces of metal and painted quilts of canvas . . .

Shit, the thing to do is to start.

It was like when he had been unable to begin the flight plan for his flight across the Caribbean to St. Thomas. Now he started with a detail. When the telephone rang, he did not realize that two hours had passed. He was working with oil and canvas, but his mind's eye was hours ahead relating carved wood to it.

The telephone rang, a staccato and infuriating interruption of the cocoon of silence.

Ben breathed out. As if he had been holding his breath.

"Is that you, Ben?"

"Yes."

The voice laughed. The sound of the laughter alternated between the guttural and the soprano. "Are you sure, Benjamin? Are you entirely sure it is you? You sound unsure."

"Madelon."

"Yes, yes. Madelon of the skies. I have a surprise for you."

"What?"

"Myself. I am about to descend upon you. Will you have me?"

"Of course. What about Rupert?"

"Rupert is somewhere, I do not know where. Probably Los Angeles. But I am in Burlington in the state of Vermont, where I have just cleared customs, coming back from Montreal—"

"I was just thinking about Montreal."

"And I was just thinking about *you,* you see? There is this *horrid* weather coming and I said to myself, 'Madelon, I do not very much think that you shall make it back to the Danbury airport this afternoon. But there is

Cornwall just a little flying time away, and dear Ben has a house there and I am sure he will offer you a warm bed.' Will you offer me a warm bed, dear Ben?"

"Of course."

"Then expect me at your airport in . . . Let me see, I should like to get some coffee . . . What shall we say, an hour?"

75

By the time Ben went to the airport the air had turned chilly. He went into the flight service office. Ev was stalking about chewing on a cigar. Jonah was selectively removing forms from a file drawer. Adele was seated next to a student explaining the VOR compass rose to him.

"How y'doin', Ben?" Jonah said. "Gonna do a little aviatin'?"

"Waiting for a friend."

Adele looked up. "Hi, Ben."

"Hi, Adele."

Adele went back to work with the student.

Jonah went to a window and looked out and up at the soft gray ceiling. There were alternate ribs of gray-blue and gray-white, like ocean swells seen upside down. The swells ran from horizon to horizon. "Your friend coming from the north or the south?" Jonah said.

"North. I hear it's closing into the south."

"That's what they tell me. Close us up here in a couple of hours."

"Temperature must've dropped ten degrees," Ev said. "Christ, here it is May and it feels like winter comin' on."

"Looks like it, too," Ben said.

Ev had a look at the cloud ceiling. "I'll tell you this, I used to come out of clouds upside down more'n I did right side up."

George Detwiler shut the door behind himself. "That sounds like me today," George said.

"Trouble?" Ev said. "I thought everything was going okay."

"The first couple of sessions were fine," George said. "Just a matter of reacquainting myself with an airplane. No sweat."

"No sweat for George," Jonah said. "But he treats the Cherokee like a fighter. Everything's got to be done *hot.* Still, he's okay visually."

"We tried some simulated IFR today," George said. "Instrument flying just didn't come back to me. I was all over everywhere. I don't know why."

"It'll come," Jonah said.

"Oh, sure, yes. Hell, yes. I'll hack it. No sweat."

Ben said, "Ev, what's goin' to happen to Delaney Howard's hangar?"

"Happen to it? Stay right where it is, I would *think.* Lest some act of the Almighty moves it." He stopped. "Why? You want to *buy* it, Ben?" Ev looked at Jonah and back at Ben. "You been thinkin' of settin' up your own operation here, Ben? Your own flying service?"

Adele looked up at Ben.

"Ev, I been thinkin' about settin' up a fuckin' airline."

"For Christsake, Ben, keep it civil, can't you?" Ev chewed on his cigar. "The Phantom Ace," he said.

"Don't you forget it."

"You want to learn how to *lose* money, Ben, you come see me. I'll tell you about running a flying service."

"I'll do that, Ev. First chance I get."

Ev looked out the window. "Christ, here comes another eagle." Amory came in. Ev said, "You two know each other?"

Ben looked at Amory's costume. "No, but I think I saw this guy in *Dawn Patrol* or *Wings* or something. Amory, right?"

"Yeah. You've heard of me, huh?"

"I recognized your disguise. Ben Cain," Ben said. They shook hands.

Amory smiled at Jonah and said, "No flyin' today, huh, coach?"

"Why not?"

"Well, just look at that stuff."

"I don't see anything."

"All that *gray.* "

"We're not going to fly in that gray. We're going to fly in the practice area. You're goin' to show me some stalls, remember?"

"Jesus, coach, it looks *close* out there."

"Yeah. You let me worry about that. First off, though, we got some paperwork to do."

"Like what?"

"Some papers for you to fill out."

"Again, like what?"

"Your student ticket."

"What's that for?"

"So you can solo. One of these days."

"Not today."

"No, Amory, not today. Definitely not today. You haven't even given me a stall yet. And this here is an application for an FCC license. License to operate a radio station."

"Me?"

"What do you think we use when we're flying? Okay, just fill these things out—name, age, sex, stuff like that. Then sign 'em."

[198]

"Sign 'em."

"Sure."

"When we get back. Let's leave the paperwork till we get back."

"I don't care when you do it."

"Fine. When we get back."

"Also, you'll need a third-class medical. Dr. Glynn's our local flight surgeon. He'll give you the exam. You need a valid medical before your student certificate is valid. You ready to go flying?"

Amory nodded.

"When's your friend getting here?" Adele said to Ben as her student put his notes away.

"Should be soon," Ben said.

Jonah and Amory were leaving the office. "Have fun, boys," Adele said to them.

Jonah and Amory walked across the ramp toward a waiting Cherokee. "I'm sure as hell not looking forward to doing a stall," Amory said.

"I know."

"I'm really not."

"I know."

Amory stopped short of climbing up on the wing to slide into the cabin. "I could walk away now," he said to Jonah.

"Sure."

"All right. Shit, I'll get it over fast, one way or another."

He climbed in. Jonah followed and pulled the door tight.

76

Amory turned the Cherokee onto the runway.

"You didn't check for traffic," Jonah said.

"Yes, I did." Amory lined the airplane up with the runway stripe and then gave the engine full throttle.

"You didn't call unicom," Jonah said. "Your mind on something else?"

"Getting this fucking thing over with."

Jonah picked up the microphone and said, "And Cornwall unicom, Fifty Pop is rolling Two-zero." He replaced the mike and glanced over at Amory. The airplane was hurrying now, and Amory had kept it lined up well with the runway stripe. The intensity of the student's concentration pleased Jonah. The airplane swung briefly to the left and then moved steadily down the stripe and got airborne. Amory kept the airplane moving straight out from the runway. He took altitude smoothly and steadily without too much or too little angle to his climb. Jonah's body relaxed against his seat.

"Good show, eh?" Amory said. He said it grimly, peering ahead and at his instruments.

Jonah said, "Doin' fine." They were just through four hundred feet from the runway level. Jonah looked out to the side, off to the ground and then to the horizon, admiring their easy course through the air.

While Jonah looked off outside, Amory abruptly reached his right hand to the throttle and pulled it all the way back. The engine hushed to near soundlessness, and even as Jonah reacted, the student pulled the nose up swiftly—

—into a stall, Jonah thought, *one hell of a stall and too close to the ground for recovery.* He shoved the yoke and the throttle forward. The noise of the engine was huge, amplified in the sudden silence that had been the beginning of the falling. Jonah saw the earth coming up as if a huge magnifying glass had been placed between the nose of the airplane and the tops of the trees. The magnification increased rapidly. He pulled back on the yoke and felt opposing forces with his fingers.

They were straight and level, the terrain two hundred feet below— hillsides, forest, and fields—steady. Jonah pulled into a steeper-than-usual climb to clear the rising terrain. *"Jesus H. Christ,"* Jonah said quietly.

"There's your fucking stall," Amory said.

"Jesus H. Christ," Jonah said. "You're lucky you're flying such a forgiving airplane."

"We're both lucky, right?"

"What a fucking dumb thing to do, Amory!"

"You wanted a stall."

"We practice stalls at *three thousand feet."* Jonah's anger had gotten into his muscles. He wanted to strike out at Amory. He continued to fly the airplane and to fly himself as well, his mind steadying his emotions.

"Fifty Papa, you read Cornwall?"

"Affirm, Cornwall, this is Fifty Pop. Go ahead."

"You okay, Jonah? Case just came in and said you lost a whole bundle of altitude on takeoff."

"We're okay, Ev."

"What happened, Jonah?"

"Nothing. Just demonstrating an emergency during takeoff." Jonah looked over at Amory. "Everything's fine, Ev. We're proceeding to the practice area." He replaced the mike.

"We're going to keep flying?" Amory said.

"You're paying for an hour, you might as well use it. Take the controls." Jonah eased his body against the back of his seat again. "Now give me a nice, slow, *coordinated* climbing turn to the left and take us over to the practice area. You're going to practice stalls. Power-off stalls, power-on stalls, stalls from turns."

On the ground Amory said, "I felt like I did all those stalls well. Did I?"

"Yeah," Jonah said. "All but the first one."

"That was just a mistake. Because I was *scared.* I wanted to get it over with."

"You damn near got it over with permanently."

Amory looked at his watch. "Oh, Jesus," he said, "I'm late."

Jonah watched him hurry away. Then he thought: He didn't fill out the goddamn papers.

He walked back to the office. He felt as if something were askew, as if he were on instruments and he suspected that the instruments were lying to him in some subtle way. He was terribly uneasy—a residue of fear left over from that low-level stall, Jonah thought. But he was not used to there being a residue of that sort.

77

Ben looked at the office clock. Over an hour since she had called. There must have been some delay in Madelon's getting off from Burlington. An hour and twenty minutes. He found himself looking at his watch when he had just told himself not to look at his watch for a while. An hour and twenty-five minutes. An hour and twenty-seven minutes.

"Cornwall unicom, this is Cessna Six-six One-one X-ray."

Ben recognized Madelon's voice by its intonations. The electronics through which the voice came had left the voice almost depersonified.

"Your friend?" Adele said. Ben nodded. Adele keyed the office mike and said, "Cessna Six-six One-one X-ray, Cornwall, go ahead."

"Yes, Cornwall. I am over your VOR now. Please give me your numbers."

"One-one X-ray, wind is south southwest at fifteen miles, indicating Runway Two-zero. We have no local traffic reported."

"Thank you, Cornwall."

Over the VOR? Odd, Ben thought. The VOR was south of the field. Burlington was to the north. Why would Madelon have flown over the field and on to the VOR? No sense to it. Not with the field open visually. Where could she be coming from? The *south?*

Ben went outside. To the south he saw a hurrying dart, heard mechanism far away. Closer it was like a tiny dart beneath a soft gray umbrella. Then she was downwind, and he could see the airplane slowing, the gear coming down—she did everything so smoothly and so quickly—and she wheeled the 310 in a steep and graceful bank. What had Jonah said? Flying a 310 was like standing on the edge of a knife. Speed was everything, and without it you stalled. Madelon was on base leg now, and she seemed to have the airplane almost stopped in the air. Turning final she was so very close to the ground, and she stood the aircraft up on a wing again as she came around and lined up with the runway. Ben thought for an instant that she was underpowered, too low, much too slow, would never make the runway, never recover from a stall at that low altitude, and then she was down, settled on the runway numbers with hardly any roll left in the aircraft.

Adele had come outside. "Your friend," she said.

Ben nodded.

"That was one hell of a landing," Adele said.

Ben nodded again.

The 310 taxied to the gas pumps and shut down, the engines quitting in obedient solemnity. Ben walked out to the airplane.

The door split open from the fuselage, and Madelon slid out and stood on the wing. She wore pants and a top of some light, bright blue material that accentuated the body beneath it. She waved at Ben and then leaned back into the cockpit and pulled out a shoulder bag—a casual, well-tailored bag, suede perhaps, Ben thought, by Hermès or Pucci, two or three hundred dollars, the merest detail of wealth. She put the strap over her shoulder and took Ben's hand to step down from the wing, her body just brushing against his.

"*Ben,* Ben *dear,*" Madelon said, smiling at him. She embraced him closely, an instant more to the embrace than Ben had anticipated. It gave him a heady sense of well-being. She put her arm through his. "I spoke to them on unicom about the airplane. Now where is your car?"

"No other baggage?" Ben said.

Madelon stopped, looked down herself, smiled at Ben, and said, "Why, Ben dear, do I need anything else?"

Adele watched Ben and his friend leave. Now why should I feel this way? she thought. Why should I feel as if he's leaving *me?*

78

"It's as if Del and I were never here," Betty Howard said to Yvonne.

Yvonne looked around the empty bedroom. Bare wooden floor, flowered wallpaper that had faded and yellowed—not an item or article in the room.

"Now, you look here, Yvie, you see any marks on the floor?"

"No," Yvonne said.

"No," Betty said, "you don't. There's not a *sign* that our furniture was ever in this room."

Betty looked around and then walked out of the room. Yvonne followed her. They went from room to room, opening closets, looking inside, closing them again, making sure all were empty, that the movers had taken everything. They went into the kitchen. A large thermos, open, stood on a counter. "Don't forget your thermos, honey," Betty said to Yvonne.

"There's no more coffee," Yvonne said.

"That's all right. I've saved us somethin' that's gonna do a lot more pure good than coffee." She went to a cupboard and got down an unopened bottle of bourbon.

Yvonne shook her head. She touched her stomach. "It'll just make me queasy."

Betty took the bottle and a plastic cup and sat on the floor. She was wearing jeans and a sweatshirt that had USS WASP imprinted on it. A wasp with a nasty-looking stinger hovered on her front. "I'm sorry there's no place else to sit, Yvie."

Yvonne eased herself to the floor carefully, smiled at her success, and leaned against the door of a cabinet. Betty poured herself some bourbon. "*My*, that's good," she said. "No," she contradicted herself, "no, it isn't." She drank some more. "I don't know why I always say 'My, that's good.' It's not good at all. I've *disliked* the taste of it and all of its relatives for as long as I can remember." She emptied the cup. "*Phew-eee.* I don't believe there's been time, but I feel better already. I think I *do.*"

She lit a cigarette. "Oh, my hands," she said, looking at them, "they are *so* ugly. All little scabs and red and wrinkles. I'll have to learn to hide them. I'll wear gloves, way I did when I was about *six* years old. I remember when I was *so* pretty. I can say that now. Because I'm not pretty any more. I think I started not being pretty when Del started carrier duty. I thought it would be so *glamorous,* bein' an *officer's* wife, a *career* officer, a pilot . . . Thank you kindly, I will," she said to her cup and poured more bourbon into it. "Del, he was already an upperclassman at Annapolis when we met. And goin' on to flight school, he hoped. It was Christmas time his last year and

I was jes a tiny little freshman girl. But I was pretty. Del thought I was *real* pretty. He already had his private pilot's license. He took me flyin' in a J-3 Piper Cub. It was jes so thrillin' with that handsome man. The first time I'd ever been in an airplane. He took me over my home. I looked down and there was everybody, Ma and Pa and my two sisters and some neighbors, they were down there wavin' up at us jes as clear as day—and I waved back, though of course they couldn't see me, so Del waggled the wings . . ."

She flicked the ash of her cigarette on the floor and then looked at how her fingers shook. She got up and put the cigarette in the sink and turned on the faucet. Yvonne heard the cigarette hiss.

Betty came back and sat down. She was facing Yvonne, almost looking at her, but her eyes were closed. Lines of tears ran down her cheeks. She held her face up. "That was in Dyersberg. Dyersberg, Tennessee. Dyersberg's where I was born and growed up and where my folks are and a lot of kin and good friends, too." The tears continued, but Betty had opened her eyes. "I was goin' to wait to go back till the children finished the school year here. But for what? What good would it do? I jes can't stand it in this house any more—"

"It's right for you to go back," Yvonne said.

"I have to go back. Del would say I'm bein' weak. Well, *let* him. He's not the one here alone with the children." She closed her eyes, made a fist in her lap, and said to herself, "Now, darlin', the children will be home soon, *the children will be home soon.*" The now-closed lids of her eyes seemed to squeeze the tears out.

Betty opened her eyes and poured some bourbon into the cup and screwed the cap back on the bottle firmly. "Can you believe that this horrible little house meant so much to Del and me? It was like our lives together were finally starting. But it's jes the opposite. Can you believe I'm not yet thirty?"

Betty got up and went over and got down on her knees by Yvonne and put her arms around Yvonne. "Oh, Yvie, honey, don't cry for me."

"I'm not crying for you alone. It's selfish, but I'm crying for me and," she said, touching herself, "for this little baby."

79

"Now, Cousin Lou-Ann Ralson, what's a little girl like you want with a big, *bad* thing like a pistol?" They were in Frank's house, in his private room, and the door was shut.

"There's nothin' *bad* about a gun, ain't that true, Frank?" Lou-Ann said and giggled. "Ain't that what all the slogans say?"

"I'm in full agreement with that, Lou-Ann." He held up his hand. "And come to think of it, I prob'ly *don't* want to know what you want with a gun. That *mean* friend of yours, the rich kid, over to Cornwall, the one doin' time in Attridge."

"Conrad? What about him, Frank?"

"Maybe he's thinkin' on gettin' the hell out of Attridge. But he don't need a gun for that, now do he?"

Lou-Ann shrugged. "Didn't say it had anythin' to do with Conrad. I just asked you, as my friend and cousin, I just asked you for the loan of a gun."

"'Course, if young Conrad walks out of Attridge, that's not so much good in itself. Where's he gonna go? What's he gonna live on? I suspicion Conrad's studied on that one real hard. Yes, sir, *real* hard. And here you are, my pretty little cousin, askin' for the loan of a small-size shooter. What's he gonna do? Hold up his daddy's bank?"

Lou-Ann shrugged.

"No, I ain't gonna do it, Lou-Ann."

"Ain't gonna do what, Frank?"

"Loan you a gun a mine. That kid hasn't got the smarts to hold up a bank. Next thing you know, they find out his little pistol belongs to me. Then it's *my* ass."

"Frank! You and Lou-Ann come on in here to lunch. It's fixed special." The voice came from another room, beyond a closed door.

"You shut up in there, April!"

"It'll burn."

"Turn the fuckin' thing off."

"It'll get cold!"

Frank got up, went to the door, and opened it. "I don't care if it turns to shit. Now leave us be." He slammed the door and came back to Lou-Ann. He sat down and smiled. "No, I won't do it. I won't lend you a gun. But I'll tell you what I *will* do."

"What's that, Frank?"

"I'll get you a gun."

"That's fine of you, Frank. It doesn't have to be one of yours."

"It damn well won't be one of mine. Nor one I've got anything to do with."

"That's good, Frank, that's real good."

"It'll cost you a hunerd bucks."

"I haven't got it, Frank."

"Get it from your rich friend."

"He hasn't got it neither. What you think he's in Attridge for?"

"For bein' dumb. Passin' bad checks in his own hometown, I call that not the swiftest thing I ever heard tell of."

"Well, you're dumb, Frank. *That* was the smart part about it. Con figgered, hometown, his father a respected member of the community and all, he figgered his *daddy* would cover those checks."

"But his daddy fucked him."

"Yes, he did. I guess Con thought better of his daddy than that."

Frank laughed. When he finished he said, "A hunerd bucks. One pistola."

"I can buy one downtown for what? Thirty, forty?"

"Go buy it."

"You know I can't."

"I know. 'Course you can't. That's why you're just gonna have to pay me—or someone else—a hunerd dollars for a gun that no one's got any connection to. Someone else'll charge you a hunerd and fifty, maybe more. Like you say, I'm your friend and cousin, so a hunerd'll be enough for me."

"I'll get it."

"Good. Now I don't want to hear you've gone and sold your body for it or anythin' like that, not my pretty little cousin."

"No. Con wouldn't like it if I did. He'd be furious. No, I'll get the money some other way."

"You're a good kid, Lou-Ann. I guess I never figured you for this kind of guts. I mean it." He put his arm around her shoulders, enclosed her, pulled her against him. "I could get you the gun for free, you know?"

"Con wouldn't like it."

"You understand what I just said?"

"Yes. And I tol' you, *Con* wouldn't like it."

He took his arm away. "Well, I guess you just haven't got any appreciation. I guess that gun's gonna cost you a hunerd and fifty."

"All right," she said.

"And you make some excuse to April. 'Cause you're not stayin'. You understand?"

"I understand."

"You call when you have that hunerd and fifty."

80

"You still there, Jonah?" Ev's voice was loud and harsh over the telephone.

"Where the hell would I be, Ev? The field's not shut down yet. I'm not flying, so I'm in the office."

"Why don't you get your ass over here? I'll buy you a beer. I want to talk to you."

"Where is 'over here'?"

"Where the hell *would* it be, Jonah?"

Jonah walked across the field to the new terminal building. *I bet he finally saw Mrs. Yancey,* Jonah thought. And he thought he knew why, too: *Ev got a little antsy there talking to Ben, all those cracks of Ev's about the flight service losing money. Why would he say that except he's worried about Ben starting up his own operation and me flying for him? So Ev finally talked with Mrs. Yancey.* Jonah felt as if it were Christmas Eve and he'd peeked under the tree and there was a box that was the right size and shape to hold exactly what he longed for, the opportunity to keep flying and make the income he needed doing it.

The airport bar was almost empty. The only waitress on duty was looking at a magazine. Ev sat in a corner, his large head and heavy shoulders bent studiously over a beer. He looked odd seated against the banquette, the open white shirt against the black plastic leather, gold-colored studs in the plastic like stars in some phony night around him. Jonah sat down opposite him —in a captain's chair. The airport bar and restaurant were done in nautical details, everything clean, inoffensive, and imitation.

"Hilda!" Ev called. "Bring Jonah a beer. Bring me one, too." He drank off what was left in his glass mug and pushed the empty mug away. "The flying business, Jonah. Christ, what do you know about it?"

"I—"

"What, except how to take off and land? And go from here to there?"

"A little more than that, Ev."

"Like what, for Christsake? And don't give me that fucking speech of yours again. About students."

"It's the answer to the whole flying business, Ev."

"My business's goin' along."

"Yeah. Sure it is, Ev. Same as always, right?"

"Right."

"And showin' absolutely no growth. You got the same dollar income now you had five years ago, I bet. Only the dollar's not worth as much. And your expenses are goin' up."

"You can damn well say *that* again." The waitress set a mug of beer in front of each of them. Ev lifted his and tipped it back. He put it on the table sharply. "Goddamn well say that again."

"You haven't got the volume you could have. There're people out there —they're just *waiting* for the opportunity to spend their money on flying, but they don't know it. If I had part of the business, hell, I'd be out talking to Rotary and Kiwanis and Lions, I'd even go to high schools, and don't forget the colleges—"

Jonah stopped. Ev was looking out the window, maybe not even listening to him. Jonah looked out the window. There wasn't an airplane to watch. He drank some of his beer. "Ev, if you don't grow you're going to be *out* of business. Now that's simple truth."

"What the hell do *you* know, Jonah?" Ev said, still looking out the window.

"I know one thing for sure, and so does just about every other fixed-base operator, everyone but that great old-timer Ev Goodsom, who's just gonna do himself right out of business by stayin' so oldtime."

"Oldtime, shit."

"Flying students are the answer to the whole flying business where we're concerned, Ev."

"We. We?"

"Look, Ev. It's a perfect cycle. A student comes out. A businessman, a doctor—*everybody* wants to fly. So he takes instruction. Pretty soon he wants an airplane of his own. So he buys one, new, used—"

"I don't want to be a dealer."

"Then he pays you to give him more instruction, he wants new ratings. He's got the airplane and he flies around a lot and now he wants his commercial, just to prove he can do it or to sharpen his skills. Then he wants his instrument ticket. Pretty soon he brings his wife out, just for an orientation course, and pretty soon *she's* working on her license and then *her* commercial and her IFR and this guy is paying you for all these lessons, and then they both want a faster airplane, or a twin, you sell 'em another one, and meantime you're taking care of their airplane for them, all that maintenance. And they're talking to other people, they communicate their excitement about flying, and pretty soon you got more students than you know what to do with, and every one of them that sticks with it wants to buy his own airplane and—"

"Where're these students now? They're not beating down the door that I can see."

"Of course they aren't. What're you doing to attract them? You haven't got, for instance, a fully equipped IFR trainer—"

"A fully equipped IFR trainer. You know how much money you're talking, Jonah?"

"I know."

"Fully equipped IFR trainer. Shit. Forty years ago, you had an airplane and some gas, you were in business. Virgil Yancey, he came in passenger-hopping once. I just walked out of the crowd and said I'd like a ride, and after that I said I sure would like to know how to fly myself. He just said, 'I'll teach you to fly it for thirty dollars an hour.' Thirty dollars an hour was a good price in those days. He had me soloing in two hours. I'll tell you this, Jonah—you won't like it, but I'll tell you it all the same. You don't teach people to fly any more, instructors don't. You don't teach people how to fly any more—not the art, it's a science now, not an art." He finished his beer. "Hilda, two more!"

Jonah's mug was still half-filled, but he didn't say anything. He's looped, Jonah thought. Crocked. You wouldn't think he'd had the time. Ben was there when? Two, three hours ago? So Ev gets all shook up and—

"Your blessed students, they fly mechanically. Oh, I don't blame you, Jonah. It's the Federal Aviation Agency. What the FAA wants isn't flying, it's mechanical . . ." Ev studied space as the beer was set down. Still studying space he said, "The whole FAA setup now . . . is to blame someone else, not the FAA. It's to cover the FAA, not the poor guy who's flying. You know what, Jonah?"

"No. What?"

"They haven't pinned a pilot violation on me in forty years. Not once in forty years . . . Fuckin' civil goddamn servants. You know what? The FAA today is strictly a civil-service job. They're not out to help anybody like they used to."

"I don't know, Ev, they—"

"After all, they haven't speeded up the air, have they? Christ no, they haven't. You know what, Jonah? One of your students came to me the other day and asked me what a control zone is. You know what I told him?"

"No."

"I told him it was a place to keep the hell out of."

"Ev—"

He drank down more beer. Jonah finished his own.

Ev waved at Jonah's untouched second beer. "Drink up, Jonah, drink up." He said it quietly, sadly, Jonah thought. Ev drank more, emptied the mug. "Hilda! One more." He wiped his lips, looked out at the darkening field. The runway lights were on. "Forty years ago, all you needed was an airplane and some gas . . . After barnstorming was dead, you made your money passenger-hopping . . . So all you needed was an airplane and some gas . . . Then, when me and Virgil and Falun got going, then you needed insurance and other equipment and a place to put it. *Shit,* it's not just the FAA that runs you now, it's the goddamn insurance companies, too. *They tell you who can fly your own airplanes.* And you want into this fucking business."

"I want in, Ev."

"Forty years ago—"

"I know about forty years ago. You just told me."

"You don't know what it was like back then."

"You haven't talked to Mrs. Yancey, have you? Not at all."

Ev was silent for a long time.

"I can't say I have."

Jonah got up and walked out. He heard Ev say quietly, "Hilda, bring me another beer."

81

As Ben and Madelon had driven from the airport to Ben's house, the sky had flooded and crowded in with lower, darker clouds. In the drive through the forest Ben had turned on the headlights. When they got out, the air was cold. Madelon put her arms around herself and looked up at the low, gray sky. "I believe," she said, "even the birds will not be flying tonight."

Ben pointed away to the hills to the west. The hills disappeared in cloud. To the southwest the sky had become dark with rain. "It's going to be wet," Ben said.

"Remember, you promised me a warm bed," Madelon said.

The house was drab with gray light, sullen with the chill of the weather. Ben turned on lamps at either end of the couch. The areas around the lamps bloomed with light and color, and the rest of the room remained near dark. Ben built a fire. As he bent to it, Madelon touched the back of his neck with her fingers. "That is nice, Ben. I love to have a fire." She moved away and sat on the couch. Ben's physical sensitivity to Madelon was such that, in the car, his body had intuited Madelon's, he had felt her presence as if it were a thermal aura.

"Would you like something to drink?" he said.

"When I last visited here, you gave me a lovely amontillado. Have you any of that?"

Ben brought her a tulip-shaped glass partially filled with sherry. She took it and smiled, raised it to the light and nodded. "Are you not drinking yourself, Ben?"

Ben went back to the bar. He looked at the bottles as if each were an option of behavior. Finally he poured himself some straight Scotch.

He went over and sat on the couch. He was exquisitely aware of how Madelon's arms and legs lay against the couch, her body beneath her thin clothes. He drank some Scotch. It was warm and harsh and diverting.

"You have such a lovely home, Ben. It must give you great pleasure." He drank some more Scotch. She watched him and smiled as if he were doing something that pleased her. "You are so *silent,* Ben," she said, mocking him. "What has become of you?"

"I was working," he said. "I suppose I'm not back from it yet."

"And how does your work go?"

"*Mezza-mezza.* Sometimes it goes, sometimes it doesn't."

"And how does your work for Rupert go?"

Ben shrugged. "That's up to Rupert to decide. What he's asked me to do, I've finished. I sent it to him last week."

"Where?"

"The Zurich address."

"Well, he may be there, he may not. Rupert was last that I am aware in Los Angeles."

"Los Angeles?"

"I believe he has become interested in cinema. In film. It has become a study of his." She smiled at him. "Your glass is empty and I think . . . yes, I think your hands are nervous. Get yourself a drink and come back and sit with me. I want to ask you a question."

Ben went to get the drink. He heard her voice behind him, heard her smiles as she talked to him. "Once, Ben dear, last fall, when you were visiting us, and we were saying goodbye . . . I was in my robe, I remember, my white terrycloth robe. In Connecticut, do you remember? Rupert had gone off to New York and the gardener was going to drive you to the Danbury airport for you to fly home. You were dressed and I just had on my robe and you came to give an affectionate goodbye to your hostess, to kiss me on the cheek and embrace me as friends, but do you remember? You held me just something longer." Ben was standing looking down at her. She smiled up at him and took his hand and seated him on the couch, very near to her now. "Your lips stayed on my cheek, oh nothing very long, but just a little bit more than a friend. Sometimes I can still feel your arms around me, do you know that? When we are together . . . you look at me. It is very flattering. Am I wrong? What I am saying?"

"I didn't know you noticed."

"Once, when we were dancing, that same weekend last fall, you had to leave me. Because your penis was becoming erect."

Ben laughed. "I didn't know you noticed."

"But I did. It was so complimentary. Do you know that I was dancing close to you on purpose? I wanted you to be attracted to me. Because I am so very much attracted to you. When you held me that little bit longer when we said goodbye, it was also because I hoped you would. I stayed in your arms."

Ben sighed. "We have such an erotic past. I didn't realize we had such an erotic past."

"But you agree?"

"Yes."

"I excite you."

"Yes."

"You would like to go to bed with me."

Ben looked at her and nodded.

"Then, dear Ben, I make the suggestion that we go to bed together. Now." She smiled at him.

Her abundant cheerfulness, Ben thought, was somehow at odds with the content of her proposal.

"You look so very serious, Ben." She continued to smile at him. "We are strongly attracted to each other. I only say let us act on that attraction. It is not so serious."

". . . I'm only thinking about—I'm Rupert's friend."

"Yes, of course you are. But only Rupert's friend will do. He has very few, you know. Except for female friends. It's perfectly all right, dear Ben, Rupert has a spectacular friend of his own. A lady. He is seen everywhere with her. The movie star Jeanie Tyler. Now, Ben, be a good friend to me and come along and fuck me."

"Jesus, Madelon."

"What have we here? Some silly, little-boy loyalty to Rupert?"

Ben sighed. "I don't know," he said. His mind was in conflict with itself and with his body.

"I am going to have you, Ben. One way or another. I think you will make a mistake if we do not do this together. You may as well have your pleasure. You will pay for it, you know, anyway."

"Christ, Madelon, *you* know I want you."

"But you won't do it . . . No?" She took a sip of sherry and replaced the glass on the coffee table. There seemed to Ben to be as much sherry still in the glass as when he had poured it.

"For accuracy," Madelon said, "I should, as they say in the theater, 'walk through it.' That is what Miss Tyler would say. 'Walk through it.' Let us see. We were sitting on the couch as we are now. You kissed me . . . Ah, *that* must be motivated. You are a man of impeccable honor. Why then would you kiss your friend's wife? We were alone and . . . I told you of Rupert's affair. You kissed me to console me. But our kiss became passionate." She looked at Ben. Then she leaned to him and kissed him. She opened her mouth and Ben responded to that and she moved her tongue around in his mouth. He held her and then let her go. "Poor Ben," she said. "Such restraint. That is at least something, that you kissed me back." She stayed near him, her arm around his neck, her hand on his shoulder, her body touching him. "So. Our kiss became passionate. Utterly passionate. Then your hand went to my breast." She placed his hand on her breast, caressed herself with it. Ben stood up.

"Madelon—"

"Shsh, Ben, I am thinking. All of this is *most* important." She held her own hand to her breast, stroked herself with her fingers. Ben sat down on the hearth and watched. From the altitude of the alcohol in him he now looked down and watched. He was safely out of it, quit of the storm, and now he could watch the scenery, the lovely scenery, and drink Scotch to maintain his altitude. There he was so high above it all. He drank some more Scotch.

"There was more kissing," Madelon said, "more tender fondling. The heat was in us. Did we undress here or in the bedroom? I think here. At least we began here. You lifted off my top, *so.*" She smiled at Ben as she lay the top aside. She laughed. "You stared at my nude breasts. You bent and kissed my nipples. You took them in your mouth. Alternately. I held your head while you did that. We hardly spoke. We didn't speak. Except each other's names. Yes, we would do that. Say each other's names. I'm really doing very well, don't you think, Ben? You may join me anytime, you know. Still no?" She shrugged her bare shoulders. She finished her sherry. She held out the glass. "May I have another? I should like to reflect on what we are going to do next." Ben did not get up. "No? You'll allow me to get it myself?" Bare-breasted she went to the bar and poured herself a sherry.

Then she sat by Ben on the hearth. "You poured us each a drink and we sat a little apart trying to control ourselves. I believe I must have unbuttoned your shirt by now. Yes, of course. I pulled it out . . . In fact, you have no shirt on now. I like to feel flesh against flesh. We are both undressed above the waist now. Let me see . . . I put my drink down and put my head in your lap . . ." She did as she described. "Yes. And you see what happened? Exactly what is happening." Ben stood and went to the bar and got more Scotch. From that higher and higher altitude he watched as Madelon continued just as if he were still beside her.

"You sit me up and kiss me. My hands, my lips, my breasts. Your head goes lower. You push my pants down. *So.* Your lips kiss my stomach. Your hand goes inside my pants. So. My hand responds, I embrace your member through your trousers. I stand and you pull my pants down. So." Ben watched her remove her pants. She was wearing panties still. "We go to the bedroom," she said. Ben followed her, feeling as if his legs were a long way away from him, wondering what interesting thing this woman might do next.

"Here, by the bed, you kneel and slip my little panties down. You kiss my very private parts. You stand. I kneel and undress you." Ben watched her from across the room. She was kneeling by the bed. "I make you lie down on the bed. We do not remove the covers. I kiss your private parts." She was kneeling on the bed. "Then we embrace." She lay full length on the bed. "Then—then we fondle . . . Then I think we do it like this . . ." She lay on her back. Then she sat up. "Yes. You were quite good, Ben, quite

[213]

satisfying. I think I cried a little tiny bit. Yes, the merest tear or two. In remorse or in joy? Who knows?" She put on her panties. "Of course, we stayed in bed." She walked into the living room and began to dress. "We made love once again before getting up and having dinner. It was that marvelous *boeuf bourguignon* that you make that you always keep frozen for unexpected guests. As when Rupert and I first visited you." She picked up her top and stretched herself into it. "We made love upon going to bed for the night. You were a man among men. You had me once more, I believe. In the morning. Upon awakening. You had me sideways, I believe. That is the morning position. Besides, we hadn't tried it yet." She sat down and drank a sip of sherry. "Really, Ben, we had a *marvelous* time."

82

When he got to New York Perry would call Laura and lie to her that Operations had suddenly placed him on standby and he would have to remain in New York over the weekend. He already felt anxious and guilty about lying to her. After the telephone call he would take a cab to Don and Jessica McCallies' apartment in Manhattan. He had met the McCallies on vacation in the Caribbean a couple of years before. Afterwards, while he was still a bachelor, he had spent a lot of his New York time with them. Then he had met Laura and he and she had begun their jetspeed romance. Don and Jessica had not much cared for Laura—their usual spontaneity turned to courtesy where she was concerned—and Perry had not seen them in a year. When Perry had spoken to Jessica on the phone a few days earlier she had been saddened for the pain Perry must be going through getting his divorce, but she had been delighted that he was "unloading that *steward-ess.*" Of course, he must come to dinner Friday when he was through flying, spend the weekend. First, though, before all that, he had to get One-sixty-five to La Guardia.

There was nothing to be seen beyond the windscreen of the flight deck. One-sixty-five was on autopilot. Perry was sitting back in his seat, one leg cocked up, the twin yokes before himself and his copilot moving slowly and slightly in dull and robot harmony. Perry monitored the instruments, foresaw the flight ahead, and listened to the compound of transmissions from Air Traffic Control, some subsystem in his mind alert and sensitive to the numbers *165,* but otherwise not entirely attentive to the transmissions between ATC and other flights. His attention had drifted partially to himself. Sitting up there in all that grayness, with no detail of anywhere within eyesight except for the instruments, Perry noted of himself, in a sort of

clinical observation, that what he was living in New York was a fantasy—
a very pleasant one, but unreal nonetheless; and that what he was doing in
Cornwall was usually involved in *getting away from it,* denying its reality;
and that the only real time he had any more was right here, on the flight
deck, doing his work. He even had his instruments and ATC to confirm and
insist upon the reality. The little flights of fancy in New York were pleasant,
all right, but he was most comfortable and most totally himself—of a
oneness—here on the flight deck, working. He startled his copilot then by
laughing—laughing at the thought that the only real part of his life was
here, where he could presently see nothing.

"What's funny?" R. W. Roy asked.

"Oh shit, R.W., nothing's funny. Go back to sleep."

At ATC's instruction he flew a holding pattern over Stamford, Connecticut—though there was nothing to distinguish Stamford's grayness from
Cornwall's or that in between—and then following subsequent instructions,
he had let down on a pathway in his mind, which he obtained from his
instruments, to La Guardia, which was nonexistent except for the reaction
of an occasional needle and a voice from the ground that purported to
originate from the airport. After a while the grayness seemed to thin and
then to disintegrate, and there was the real world below, as if it had been
there all the time.

Passively saluted by lights on either side of him, he set One-sixty-five
down, the runway slightly slick and a little shiny from rain, and then he
guided the air machine along the ground to its appointed company gate,
shut it down, and went inside the terminal and called Laura Sullivan, a
former love, and told her that on company instructions he would be remaining in New York for the weekend. He and Mrs. Sullivan seemed to be jointly
relieved at this news.

The McCallies felt that Perry would probably want a quiet evening alone
with them. They had dinner by candlelight. Perry found, as he pursued
what he had come to think of as *Sullivan's Divorce,* that he ran into an awful
lot of candlelight. He wondered if by its softness it was meant to spare him
the hardness of reality. By midnight he and the McCallies were happily and
mildly intoxicated together. "Yes," Perry said, "Las Vegas. I think Laura
is going out in about a week. The lawyers are talking about it now." After
the McCallies went to bed, Perry lay awake on the living-room couch and
thought sadly of Laura alone in Las Vegas. But she had brought it on
herself. He went to sleep content.

Saturday night he and the McCallies went out to dinner with another
couple—the Tuttles—and then on to a party. During cocktails Perry went

out for a few minutes and, from a pay phone, called the girl in Minneapolis, Sally, the girl the Howzers had introduced him to, Nick Howzer's cousin. She was happy to hear from him. "You must be very lonely," she said.

"Yes," Perry admitted. "I'd like to get out and see you."

"I wish you would."

"When things get more settled."

At dinner Florence Tuttle suddenly said to Perry, "Didn't you marry a girl named Laura, a stewardess?"

"Yes," Perry said.

"I thought so," Florence Tuttle said. "I was a stew for a while. I flew with her once or twice."

Jessica McCallie said, "They're getting a divorce."

"Is that good or bad?" Florence Tuttle said.

"Good," Perry said.

At the party he was introduced to a single girl who illustrated children's books. She had shiny blond hair that she wore in two long braids. Perry took her home, had a drink with her, told her he would call her—probably as soon as the lawyers worked everything out—kissed her good night on the cheek, and rode back to the McCallies' in a cab. *Two* girls, he thought. In one evening. The one in Minneapolis and the one here. And he wasn't even divorced yet. Things had not been anywhere near so simple when he himself had been single. Poor Laura, so lonely for her in Las Vegas.

On the McCallies' couch he slept well until late in the night when a realistic and unslumbering part of his mind reminded him that, no matter what, in a few days he would have to go back to Cornwall and be with Laura.

83

There was nothing on television. After Perry's call, Laura had gone to *TV Guide* and looked at the listings for the evening. There was just nothing she wanted to see. The house was getting dark. She turned on some lights. She made herself a Scotch and soda. Back in the living room she reopened a novel. She had tried to get into reading it twice, and now, the third time, she found herself putting it down again. She looked at the blank television screen. "You dimwit," she said to it. She felt like going out to dinner. She felt like *being taken out* to dinner. At the same instant she suddenly thought of all the stews in New York who would be glad to get up against a captain, rub their steaming little bodies against Perry. She thought of three or four stews who would be glad to do it just out of spite to her, Laura, because their own boyfriends had paid more than passing attention to her. She found herself *furious* at Perry—as if he were about to give them the opportunity to laugh at her.

She picked up *TV Guide* and looked in it again. Surely there was *something* she could watch. But there was nothing. She looked at her empty glass. There was a distant mechanical thump and sigh from the basement of the house as the heat came on. She went to the telephone and dialed the number she had for the actor Hilary—something she had decided several times not to do.

Someone said they would get him, and when he came to the phone she said, "Look, my husband just called from New York. He's got standby duty down there. I thought this might be a good opportunity for us to get together here and rehearse."

"I don't know," Hilary said.

"Well?"

"I don't know. I wasn't planning on it. I'll have to think about it."

"Think about it?" Laura said.

"Yes, *think* about it. Can I call you back?"

"All right, but I'm not going to wait around all evening." She hung up.

In his room Hilary lay on the bed and thought about those wonderful round boobs of hers. He saw his hand go into the top of her dress, scoop underneath one of those wonderful round boobs. He felt his own desire, thought of calling her right away. No, he thought, better wait, don't let her see any eagerness, let her get hot for him. For a while he played with the film in his mind . . . *airplane controls and Laura's naked round boobs and his hands on them both, controls and boobs, and* . . . He let the time go by, playing and replaying.

"Don't you think it's late?" Laura said when Hilary called back. Her voice sounded cool to her. But she had become impatient and unable to concentrate as she had waited for the telephone to ring. "When I said come over, I did *not* mean call up at nine and come over some time later." She put out a cigarette. "Anyway, you're not coming over here at this hour."

"Let me tell you what I had in mind."

"I think I'll say goodbye now, Hilary—"

"No, no, this is *serious,* Laura. It's about our parts."

"I'm still here."

"All right. Here's what we *ought* to do. Professionally. We ought to get together and discuss *concepts*. We ought to discuss our conceptions of our characters. Who they are. How they interact. We ought to do that *before* we begin to rehearse, *before* we start on our lines."

"That sounds sensible."

"All right then—"

"But not tonight."

"We could at least get started tonight, Laura. You said before that—"

"I said what I said *before.* This is now and you're late, Hilary, just plain *late.*"

"Tomorrow evening then."

"Tomorrow during the day, Hilary. Morning or afternoon?"

"Laura, you know what? I think you're *punishing* me. I think you're sitting there administering *punishment* to me."

"Morning or afternoon, Hilary?"

"I can't. Morning or afternoon."

"Too bad. Call me when—"

"I *can't,* Laura. I'm sorry, I *really* can't. I have to—I'm busy. But I could tomorrow evening."

"Hilary, tell me something. Why did you wait so late to call me back?"

"I . . . Oh. Well . . . Laura, you still there?"

"Of course I'm still here. But I won't be much longer."

"Now don't rush away. Don't. It was because . . . Oh, all right, I'll tell you . . ."

"Well, go ahead, tell me what?"

"My *character* wouldn't allow it."

"Your *what?*"

"My character. This is serious. The character I play just wouldn't respond to the character you play by coming right over or calling right back."

"I really don't know whether to believe you or not, Hilary."

"You better believe me. Our characters depend on it. If you don't believe in my character, your character won't come off. Believe me. You'll just look phony, phony, phony on stage. You better start believing in my character now."

"You make it difficult . . . All right. Tomorrow evening. But Hilary. About getting into our characters?"

"Yes?"

"They meet at the country-club bar. That's their first scene."

"Right."

"It's a dance. He's wearing a summer tuxedo."

"She's wearing a very low-cut dress."

"I suppose she could be. The directions just specify the tuxedo. Though she *might* be wearing a low-cut dress."

"You do a low-cut dress a lot of justice."

"Thank you. Now, Hilary, what I have in mind. About getting into our characters, discussing concepts—"

"Yes, Laura."

"I'll put on a low-cut dress and I'll pick you up in my sports car. In return, you will put on your tuxedo and take me to dinner at the Tallyho, which is our most fashionable nightspot and where there is dancing."

"I couldn't afford that, Laura."

"On your residuals? I know what residuals are, and I know you must still be getting them for that commercial and—"

"You're right. But that money is allocated. It's going into something else."

"Too bad, Hilary."

"Look, Laura, I even have to work—till the theater starts paying."

"I'm terribly sorry to hear that. Call me when you have a morning or afternoon free."

"All right, Laura. But drinks only. I can only afford drinks. I'll put on the tuxedo and all that, but I can only afford drinks."

"Nine o'clock tomorrow evening. I'll be wearing a little white sports car. And a low-cut dress, sir."

She hung up and laughed. Men were so easily handled once they were sexually interested. Laura felt keyed up and relaxed at the same time. And the situation was *perfect*. She could go anywhere with Hilary, do almost anything, for they were in a play together and they were only preparing their parts. Even Perry couldn't object to that.

84

On Friday evenings George Detwiler got back from Boston early, as early as ten o'clock. He parked the car and went next door to pick up Randy. Randy was allowed to stay up and watch television till George got home on Friday evenings, but this Friday evening he had fallen asleep in front of the television set. George walked and carried him back to their own house, got his boots off him, and put him to bed in his clothes. George kissed him and then, briefly, stood over him, his hand on his sleeping son's shoulder.

George went downstairs and then outside and across his front yard to the mailbox. It was the only journey he made any more which could consistently awaken his emotions. One never knew what omen or what piece of luck—good or bad—the mailbox might contain. Walking back to the house and looking through the few pieces of mail in the half-light cast from the front door, George found an envelope in which, perhaps, there lay significant news of his future.

Inside the house he saved that particular envelope until last. When he opened it, he did indeed find auspicious word about himself. In his ebullience he went to the phone and called Adele.

"What I was thinking of was, could we have dinner again?"

"I think so, George. When would you like?"

"Tomorrow evening?"

"Well, yes . . . I'm free."

"I was thinking, could we do it here? You see, my son Randy—I don't like to be away from him. When I don't have to be. If being with a youngster won't bother you?"

"Not at all."

"It's that . . . I like sharing things with Randy. When I have the opportunity. And I'd like you to meet him."

"What time, George?"

"Six. We can have a drink while I'm fixing dinner. I'll cook outside. You know, just a steak."

"*Just* a steak. Have you bought a steak recently, George?"

"Actually, no." George laughed. "Because of the price. But never mind. We'll just have a steak, a very expensive steak."

"Would you like me to bring a salad?"

"I can take care of everything."

"I'd like to."

"All right, do that. Bring a salad."

"Six o'clock."

"Yes. Thanks, Adele. Good night."

85

Madelon was sitting in an armchair, her legs curled, a novel in her lap. "This is really very good," she said to Ben. Ben was sorting small pieces of old glass—busywork. There had been no question of Madelon or anyone flying out of Cornwall, and she had refused to go to a motel. She had had her way about having Ben's standby *boeuf bourguignon* for dinner. They had had a bottle of wine and some pleasant conversation about flying and people they knew who flew and about books they had read recently and art they had seen recently. In their continued nearness to each other, Ben's desire for Madelon had almost overcome him, but he had dulled the desire with a superfluity of wine. Madelon put the book down. "Quite good," she said, "but I do need some sleep. Do you mind if I sleep in your bed, Ben? Forgive me, but I do remember the bed in your guest room. Most uncomfortable." She got up and kissed him on the forehead. "*Such restraint,* dear Ben." She smiled. But then she said to him quietly, "Do join me if you want. It is, after all, your bed."

She went to his bedroom. He heard her in the bathroom. He thought he heard her get into his bed.

He went to the kitchen table and sat at it and drank straight Scotch until he felt demanding tiredness take hold of him. Then he went to his studio, surprised at how his feet made mistakes getting there, lay down on the daybed from which in his mind he had overflown the Caribbean, and went to sleep, dragged down . . .

In the morning he took Madelon to the airport, and on his way home he remembered that he had dreamed or that during the night it had happened that Madelon had come to the daybed in his studio and sat beside him and touched her fingers to his hair and said to him *Too much restraint, too much restraint, I really would have liked to fuck with you, dear Ben, dear Ben,* though he wasn't sure.

86

Amory still wore the white scarf and carried the helmet and goggles. When other people—students, pilots, passengers, anyone happening by— stared at him, he grinned and stared back at them. Sometimes he clicked the heels of his boots and bowed. This early Saturday morning—seven-thirty—he also affected a cigarette holder. It was elegant, Jonah thought, an elegant detail, black with a circle of ivory at its tip. Amory kept it between his teeth, elegantly, to the side of his mouth. But there was no cigarette in it.

Amory and Jonah were alone in the office—too early for anyone else. Amory had said the only time he could take a lesson now was when he could be through well before nine. "Got yourself a job?" Jonah had said to Amory. Amory had shrugged.

He didn't take the cigarette holder out of his mouth until he was seated at the controls of the airplane. When they were on the taxiway, Amory suddenly applied the brakes without reducing power. The Cherokee stood in the middle of the taxiway trembling, vibrating with power against its brake-enforced stillness. "I don't know about landing this thing," Amory said.

"I know. We'll just keep working at it."

"Till I get it right."

"Of course."

"You wouldn't solo me till I get it right, would you?"

"Of course not." Amory nodded, reassured, Jonah thought. "C'mon,

[221]

sport, let's get moving." But Amory didn't release the brakes. Jonah reached over and reduced power.

"Did a plane ever get away from you?" Amory said. "Did you ever lose control?" He was looking straight ahead.

"No. Not really." Jonah could not say to himself why, but the question made him uneasy.

At eight hundred feet above the airport, Amory guided the airplane parallel to the runway below, opposite to the direction of their takeoff. Halfway down the runway he slowed the airplane to its landing approach speed.

"Good work," Jonah said.

At the downwind termination of the runway, Amory cut power and began a smooth, gentle glide. Jonah saw him smile as the glide took hold and as he held it. Then he banked too tightly as he turned base, the first turn toward the runway.

"Gently," Jonah said. "Gently. Easy now . . . Are you too high or too low?"

"Hell, I'm just right."

Jonah was silent. They were too low. Maybe Amory would correct himself. Amory suddenly applied full power, retained altitude, and wrenched the Cherokee around in a low-level steep turn till the runway was straight in front of them. Then, erratically, he got the wings level again.

"That's no way to turn final," Jonah said, restraining himself from taking the controls. "That's a good way to stall in. Have you ever heard of a high-speed stall? Have you ever heard of a cross-control stall?"

"Roger."

"Make those turns gentle."

"Roger."

"Coordinate the turns."

"*Roger.*"

The leading edge of the runway danced in front, jumped high to the right, then skidded low to the left and then jumped high again to the left.

"Easy now," Jonah said, his hands in his lap. "Don't overcorrect. Light on the controls now. Watch the far end of the runway, not this end. Keep her straight and level . . . Now ease back on the yoke slowly till you feel the stall coming."

"*Roger.*"

They stood a little high off the runway but Jonah let the student continue the maneuver. Suddenly, the nose high, the wings about to stall out, with no altitude to recover, Jonah saw in his mind the Cherokee plummet into the concrete of the runway, himself and the student killed. But in the instant before the imagining became reality, Jonah applied full power and pushed the yoke forward. There was a roar and they were level. Then he cut the power again. "Okay, it's yours. Land it. You pulled back too fast on the controls."

There was no answer.

"It's yours, I said." There was still no answer. The runway was moving backwards beneath them. *"C'mon,"* Jonah said. Then they were over the far end of the runway. Jonah said, "Take her around again. And this time show me a landing."

There was silence and then the student said, "I don't want to. You land it."

Jonah applied full power and established a climb. "Take the controls."

"Next time."

"Take the controls. Christ, Amory, you know how to climb."

Amory put his left hand on the yoke, then his right hand on the throttle. He carefully maneuvered the airplane back into the landing pattern. When they had turned base and then turned final approach to the runway, he said, "You take it."

"I'll talk you through it."

"Next week."

Jonah looked at him. "Okay, sport. Next week it is."

Jonah took the controls and landed them.

After landing, Amory put the cigarette holder in his mouth, took the controls, and taxied them in. When they were shut down and out of the airplane he started to walk away again without saying anything.

"Not this time," Jonah said. "Come into the office."

Jonah sat at his desk for a minute, two minutes, but Amory had not followed. Jonah decided that he had perhaps seen the last of the student. Jonah was thinking about his vision of the Cherokee plowing into the runway. He was not used to imaginings of that sort.

Amory came in.

Jonah said, "Here are those forms to fill out. Student ticket. Communications license. Amory, I have decided to quote to you from the federal aviation regulations. My text is taken from Part Sixty-one, Subsection forty-eight, a bit of gospel which has to do with applications, certificates, and falsification. I quote the word, Amory. 'No person may make or cause to be made any fraudulent or intentionally false statement on any application for a certificate or rating under this part . . .' "

"Coach, I dig. I really think I do. *Coach,* do you really find it so strange to have a student named Amory? If you'd like it better," Amory said, rolling the cigarette holder in his mouth, "you could call me something like Sam or Bill or *whatever* pleases *you.*" He said the words *around* the cigarette holder. It changed his speech and inflection, made his words clipped and intense, rather Eastern and upper class. He took the cigarette holder out of his mouth. "What if I don't fill them out?"

"It's no skin off my ass," Jonah said. His hands were in his lap. He looked at the student. "Did you get your third-class medical?"

Amory paused. Then he reached into a rear pocket of the jodhpurs and his hand came back with a piece of paper the size of a driving license. He flipped it on Jonah's desk. Jonah didn't pick it up. "You didn't think I'd get it, did you, coach?" He grinned at Jonah.

Jonah pushed across the other applications. The student shrugged. He picked up the papers and a ballpoint pen and went to sit in a writing chair. He bent over the papers.

Ev came in. *"Christ, have I got a head!"*

"I'm all out of sympathy," Jonah said. He went over to a blackboard, picked up some chalk, and wrote:

> *nor did he scape*
> *By all his engines, but was headlong sent*
> *With his industrious crew to build in hell.*

He stepped away and turned to Ev. "The moving finger, Ev," and Jonah prodded the air with his middle finger, raising the finger to Ev.

"Christ, Jonah, I told you I'm sick." He looked at the words.

"Milton," Jonah said, going to the chair behind his desk and leaning back in it.

"You're not the only college fucking graduate flies an airplane."

The student was looking up. "Milton. Milton?" He looked at Jonah.

Jonah looked back. His words came out tonelessly. "You didn't know you were in the fucking groves of academe, did you, sport?"

Ev was still peering at the words on the blackboard. "That's interesting, Jonah. A very interesting citation. Do you note that it includes you? It says *with his industrious crew.* That's you, isn't it?"

"No. The day the baby's born, that's the day I quit."

"Shit, Jonah. I thought a lot last night. I've been remiss. I know I have. If you can believe it, and I'll say it straight out, sitting there and drinking beer and thinking about it, I'm afraid of Mrs. Yancey. I just came to realize that. I'm a little afraid of her. That's why I haven't gone to see her. I will. Now."

"Right now," Jonah said.

"I don't mean *now.* Christ, with *my* head. But I'll do it, Jonah."

Jonah made a spitting noise to one side.

The student came over and put the papers on Jonah's desk and walked out.

Jonah picked up the papers. The name written in, where the true legal name under penalty of law was required, was *Hilary Blane.*

87

Adele felt all evening as if she and George Detwiler's house were conspiring together. She thought *the house wanted her.* Coming down from the bathroom upstairs, going into the kitchen alone while George and Randy had been outside cooking in the twilight, she had felt her absence in the house. Later, when they had sat in Randy's bedroom and taken turns reading to him from *Tom Sawyer,* the sensation of conspiracy had come to her again. But it's not in my nature to be a *conspirator,* she had thought.

When they went back downstairs there was only one lamp lit in the living room. There had been no light at all upstairs once Randy's light had been turned off. "I keep the rooms dark," George said. "It makes me more comfortable. Most people feel more comfortable in the light. I must confess I feel very uncomfortable in the light sometimes. Since Beirut. One of the things I remember there was white, white light. I feel . . . *protected* in the dark. We have some wine to finish here, if you'd like."

"Yes."

George poured for each of them. "Since Beirut," he said, sitting again, "I haven't thought about the future much at all." He laughed. "Oh, I *contracted* with the future when I took up law studies . . . But I didn't take the contract very seriously, I suppose. I was more interested in the study itself than in what it might lead to. Now it's led to something—a possibility, anyway—and I wanted to tell you about it. Because it has to do with my future."

Adele nodded.

"My old university has an employment placement bureau, and a couple of months ago I wrote them and gave them my situation and qualifications. Former military pilot qualified in heavy and light aircraft, single and multi-engine, piston, turboprop, and pure jet, especially qualified in high-performance single-engine jets, no longer flying because of a medical incident, presently subject to no medical restraint. I said I expected to graduate from law school in late spring and I asked if they might know of a position where this marriage of law and aviation expertise might be useful.

"It turned out I couldn't have written at a better time, Saunders-McConnell Aircraft was looking *specifically* for someone like me. And the man doing the looking is my old classmate Cornelius McConnell. He turns out to be Saunders-McConnell's vice-president in charge of special projects, and he'd written the university placement bureau and asked if their computer had anyone stored inside it who was qualified both in the cockpit and in lawbooks."

George poured himself another glass of wine. "I spoke to Corny McConnell this morning—I got a letter from him yesterday. Assuming I graduate, he wants me to come out to this place of his—it's an estate of his, I guess, or his company's, has its own private strip—Burning Cabin, it's called. I even found it on a sectional. Anyway, he wants me to come out there, out in western Pennsylvania, and spend a weekend and talk about my possible future with Saunders-McConnell."

"That's *super,* George. You'll go. Of course you'll go."

"Oh, yes." George seemed distracted. He seemed to chew on his wine as he thought. "It would be much better if I could fly in. And I'd like to take Randy. Make a flight together."

"It's a lovely idea. Why don't you do it?"

"I can't afford the rental of an airplane for all that time." He stood up. "And even if I could, Adele, I'm not sure I could even pass a third-class physical. Not with my medical background. Doc Glynn says it's sure to be reviewed and time-consuming no matter how normal his findings may be."

Adele looked at George. "So you need a free airplane and a free pilot to go along and make it legal."

"It doesn't have to be free. I'd pay all the expenses. But yes, it galls me, but yes—I'd need another pilot with me. You're looking at me . . . *oddly,* Adele."

"I'm thinking an odd thought," she said without smiling. "Ben." She picked up her glass but then didn't drink from it. "He has the airplane and the license. And he could learn a great deal from you on a flight like that."

"But?"

"It would be taking him away from his work. Ben is easily persuaded away from his work."

"He's grown up, he can make his own decisions. He can always turn me down. The contact, you know, might be valuable to him. Big companies buy art now, they commission art . . ."

"You're perfectly right, George, Ben should make his own decision."

"What about . . . Would he be bothered that I'm seeing you?"

Adele laughed. "Ben would just have to decide that, too."

"It's *possible,*" George said, laughing, "the *flight* is possible." He put on music, brought out some favorite books of photographs and paintings and drawings of flight, went up to look in on Randy once, brought out some more wine, his mood lighter and lighter, Adele thought, like something ground-bound taking flight. She sat feeling the conspiracy around her, enjoying it, the house wanting her. The conspiracy felt warm. Warm and hazy. That was the wine, the haziness. Maybe the warmth, too. She saw George yawn. Not the first time. He had tried to hide it several times. "I better go," she said. "You're tired."

"I'm sorry. Yes, I am. My schedule— Till exams are over, anyway. It catches up with me. The job and the driving and classes and study."

"And Randy. You make time for him. I see that."

"I try to."

In the hallway George faced her and took her hands. Then he put his arms around her, slowly, tentatively. Adele was not sure whether she kissed him or allowed herself to be kissed. She *did* know she *held* him.

She had worn a straight, simple, sleeveless dress. Yellow. A little dressy for a backyard cookout, but she had wanted to wear it. It had made her feel good. In her apartment she took it off, hung it up, and went into the bathroom and began combing out her hair. It was not something she had thought about doing. It was something she found herself doing. The warmth and the haziness were gone. She wiped hair from her comb and alternated the comb and brush, looking at herself in the bathroom mirror. *Look, I'd like to do something for you, but I don't know what to do.* She studied the mirror. *Tell me what you want me to do for you.*

88

It was nearly nine in the evening and Yvonne was doing the Lamaze technique exercises for natural childbirth, Jonah timing her and instructing her with reminders as he would at her bedside and in the delivery room. Jonah sat on the side of the bed and watched the stop hand on his pilot's watch. "The contraction is building," he said, "building, it's peaking, it's over . . ." Yvonne's breathing went from a quick pant to a long inhalation and long exhalation. "Finished," Jonah said.

Yvonne let her arms and legs lie at ease on the bed. "It's *so* relaxing," she said. She looked at Jonah, smiled, and took his hand. "I'm glad you're doing this with me." Her fingers became firmer on his hand. "I know you're a little afraid of it. I know you'd rather not do it. I mean later, being in the delivery room with me."

"That was just at the beginning. I was worried about *me,* not you. I wondered how I'd react. I know, they don't call it pain in class, but that's what I was worried about, how I'd be in the delivery room with you in pain."

"And now?"

"I still worry. But not as much."

"Aren't you scared for me at all?"

"I worry. God knows I worry sometimes. But no, I'm not scared for you. You'll handle it. You and the doctor."

"That's the way you are about flying, isn't it? You're not scared, you'll handle it."

"I guess. I get scared sometimes, flying. When something sudden happens, something unexpected. The same way I do when the car starts to skid on ice. Things like that. But it's just for an instant. Till I get things under control. I think I'm good enough not to lose it, control, not for more than a very little bit."

"I know, Jonah. I know you're that good. But I never trusted flying. Never. Even though I knew you did it. Then I was pregnant and I started worrying. Then—then Del Howard and I got scared. *Scared.*" She held his hand to her. "I'm not asking anything, I'm just telling you."

"Del scared the shit out of me, too."

"Except that you wouldn't make that flight. Falun told me that. Falun said if I couldn't stop worrying about you flying, I could worry less. Because you'd refused that flight. He said you'd refuse all the rest like them. He was very proud of you."

"I didn't know he'd said anything to you."

"At least I'm not worrying any *more* than I was. The fear didn't get bigger as the baby got bigger." Yvonne smiled at him. "Jonah dear."

"Yes, Yvonne dear."

"Would you do something for the baby?"

"What did you have in mind?"

"The baby would like some strawberry ice cream."

"You're kidding. Strawberry ice cream in the middle of the night. It's a cliché. It's an old wives' tale. *No one* believes in it any more."

"It's not the middle of the night, Jonah dear. It's just ten after nine. The ice-cream place on the square is still open."

When Jonah got home with the ice cream he said, "I think I just saw that student again. *Hilary.* And that's the third time today. Up till today I'd never seen him *anywhere* except the airport."

"Much less known his real name," Yvonne said.

"Much less—*if* it *is* his real name." They sat at the kitchen table and ate ice cream. "First I had that early appointment with him this morning. He was wearing the jodhpurs and scarf, that usual outfit of his. Then it turned drizzly and everything got canceled, everything on my calendar, and I called home—"

"And I asked you to stop at Street's on the way home and pick up the TV, it was all repaired—"

"That's when I saw him the second time. Or thought I saw him. Outside the department store. I was walking to the car in the parking lot out back, carrying the portable, and it was drizzling, and that's when I thought I saw him. I even put the portable down and I stood still and watched. It *looked* like Hilary. But there was the drizzle and he was about a hundred feet away and the light wasn't any too good where he was working. If it was Hilary, he was working on the store's loading platform. He was dressed in fatigues and he was hustling flattened cardboard cartons out of the store and into a truck."

"Didn't you go over? You could have said hello."

"I don't know, I felt like I might be intruding on him. Like, what he does when he's not flying is his private business, if that's the way he wants it. And since he never talked about what he does . . ."

"If he's loading boxes at Street's, I guess we can forget my theory that he's a playboy of some sort."

"Wait," Jonah said. "When I was getting the ice cream just now, across the square, this sports car squealed to a stop over there, in front of the Tallyho. And there was Hilary again. In a white tuxedo jacket this time, black tie, it looked like—the works. He was getting out of the sports car. Now the doorman over there, he was holding the car door for the driver. A young woman in a summer dress. She got out and took Hilary's arm—"

"If it was Hilary."

"Right. *If* it was Hilary. The young woman was Laura Sullivan."

"Oh, dear."

"Now we don't know that there's anything to say *Oh, dear* about, do we?"

"No. No, we don't . . . I wish, though—oh, Lord, I wish you didn't have to give him lessons." Yvonne shrugged. "I know. I said that before."

Jonah stayed awake in the darkness of the bedroom that night, worries and dreams and claims upon him juxtaposing themselves within his mind. When he slept it was as if he were still awake—there was no rest, no transition . . . He was flying with the student Hilary. The student refused to take control. Jonah took the controls. The airplane trembled and then plunged. *"My God, you've lost it!"* the student screamed. And then Jonah himself was screaming *Yvonne, my God, you've lost it!* but then he saw that he had done it, he himself had lost the baby, people were *yelling* at him *My God, you've lost it,* but it was the baby they were talking about, not control of the airplane, but it was his flying that had done it, lost the baby, either before or after it was born, but it was his flying that had killed it.

Jonah awoke without believing he had slept—it had been something other than sleep. His heart was pounding in him. He was sweating. He knew it had been something like a dream, but it had been real enough, real enough . . . It had been like a warning, he thought. Like Yvonne almost miscarrying, that was a warning.

6

SUMMER
FLIGHTS

If a pilot uses logical thought processes and keeps his
emotions under control he will be able to handle tough
problems. And if he trains himself to think the proper
way, he probably will not get into bad situations in the
first place.

— (Captain) Robert N. Buck

The sky's a membrane.

—Paul Malamud
From The New Yorker

The sky is dead.

—Elizabeth Bishop

89

Jonah stood out on the ramp watching the changing light of the late June dawn. He was waiting for Hilary. Quarter of seven and the air was already warm and Hilary was fifteen minutes late. The sunlight, blocked by the hills around the field, was not yet down on the runways. The field was in shadow, but the hills that Jonah faced had turned bright in the direct rays of the sun. The aircraft on the field, the lightplanes tied down in two long rows, stood motionless, black silhouettes against the bright hills.

It was going to be a hot day. By midmorning the air over the hills would be turbulent with the effect of temperature exchanges between the ground and the air over it. The turbulence would be enough to make students, flying at lower altitudes, queasy. The forecast was for building summer disturbances with the prospect that, by midafternoon, flight for light aircraft would be hazardous when thunderstorms, in concentration and in advance of a front, moved across New England rapidly. A tornado watch had been predicted for parts of Massachusetts and southern Vermont and New Hampshire.

But now the air was still. There was a heavy gentleness to it. Jonah was thinking about soloing Hilary. He had been doing a good job on landings and takeoffs and the emergencies Jonah had thrown at him.

"Just like downtown," Jonah had said after one landing.

But Hilary had reacted badly. Whether by intent or out of worry that if he continued to do a good job Jonah would solo him, Hilary had fouled up the next landings. The lesson after that, Hilary had started off well. He had made nice landings and been enthusiastic. Jonah had been silent, waiting to see if Hilary could maintain the consistency.

But then Hilary had said, "Just like downtown again, huh?"

"Right."

Hilary had tightened up on the controls, begun overcontrolling. Jonah had sat back and let Hilary try to work himself out of it. Hilary was going to have to land the airplane alone sometime, and Jonah figured he had better learn how to deal with himself as well as with the airplane.

When they had gotten back on the ground at the end of the hour Jonah had said, "I liked the way you kept at it there after you began screwing up."

"Thanks for all the help you gave me. Silent bastard." They were walking back toward the flight service office. "You don't like my clothes, do you?" Hilary had suddenly said. "You don't approve of them." He was, as usual, wearing the helmet and jodhpurs and white scarf and boots. "You always look at them. My clothes."

"Do I?"

"With distaste."

Jonah was cautious with his reply. Hilary had been picking small arguments with him ever since his student license—his government permission to fly an airplane by himself with his instructor's endorsement—had arrived about three weeks before. Hilary, Jonah thought, just did not want that endorsement. "The way you dress is none of my business," Jonah said.

"If you don't like it, you don't have to fly me."

Jonah was walking away. "That decision is yours."

Hilary had caught him and stopped him. The cigarette holder was back in his mouth. "I just wanted it to be a little extra fun. You know, dashing. Like the old days."

"All I know about the old days is what I read." And what Ev tells me, Jonah had thought.

"What's wrong with having a little fun?"

"The fun is supposed to be in flying the airplane," Jonah said. "I just don't think you're having much fun flying the airplane. In fact, I don't think you're having any fun at all. I don't think you want to solo—and that's okay, too."

Hilary had ignored that. "Okay, coach. You tell me how to dress next time I come out. What'll it be? Tweed jacket? Business suit? You name it, huh?" That had been the last thing he had said. Then he had walked away. He had made this appointment by telephone with the secretary.

The light was bright on the cement of the ramp now. The sun would be burning out the mist that had remained in low places. It would burn hotter and hotter during the rest of the morning, bringing the big boilers, the thunderstorms, to early boil.

Ten after seven and Hilary still hadn't arrived.

Jonah thought he could understand something of Hilary's fear—for Jonah could at will recall the fear and horror he had felt in the dream when he had lost control of the airplane.

For a few hours of flight after the dream, Jonah had experienced a cautionary emotion he was not used to. Not fear, not even worry, but a tendency to suspect things, and even his own manipulation, of going amiss —before there was any sign of anything going amiss. But that had disappeared. It was a curiosity now. As was the intensity of the horror he had experienced in the dream.

If the baby were born healthy, and if Yvonne had no difficulty in giving birth to it, there was nothing else Jonah wanted except to keep flying.

Keeping flying was up to Ben now. Up to Ben's money to back him in their own flight service.

Jonah walked back to the office. Hilary wasn't going to show.

Everything was up to Ben now. Ben and his money.

90

When the telephone rang it was the first man-made sound Ben had heard from outside his house in two days of attempts to work. He had been standing in the studio looking out at the distant blue and the gleaming white build-ups. Ominous build-ups, Ben had been thinking. You usually don't get build-ups like that till midafternoon, not in New England, and here it was just after ten in the morning. It was a hot day, a very hot day. The silence in the house and the heat were such that Ben thought he could hear the heat.

Then the telephone had rung. The sound had seemed huge, ominous like the clouds, after all that silence and aloneness.

Ben put down his coffee mug and answered the phone.

"Ben."

"Yes."

"Rupert here."

Christ, Ben thought. He looked out at the clouds. "How you doin', Rupert?"

"I am well, Ben. And yourself?" He had not waited for the reply. "I find you at home. Good. Will you be at home in an hour, Ben?"

"As far as I know."

"Please be at home. I am at the Boston airport—flying myself—and I thought I will divert my flight home just enough to stop off and see my good friend Ben. Will that be all right with you, Ben, my good friend?"

"Yes, Rupert. Fine. I'll pick you up—"

"No. No, no. I will not hear of it. Unnecessary. I shall taxi out from your airport."

"That's not necessary, Rupert, I can—"

"Oh, I prefer the taxi, Ben."

"Will you have lunch here?"

"I will not be remaining that long," Rupert had said.

Ben turned on the VHF monitor he had built from a kit when he had started flying. When Rupert called Cornwall unicom for landing information Ben heard him. He heard Rupert ask that a cab be ordered for him. Rupert getting closer and closer. "Shit," Ben said.

Since Madelon's visit Ben had avoided thinking about what she might or might not tell Rupert. It was beyond his ability to speculate about, just as it was beyond his ability to speculate about Madelon herself. But with Rupert's approach, Ben felt an uneasiness that was growing stronger. He felt like getting out of his house, avoiding Rupert altogether, getting into his airplane and flying . . .

"*Shit.*" There he was—in his mind—in his airplane again. *Shit.* The lengths we go to, Ben thought, to get away from ourselves—and anyone else who happens along. Ben thought of Andrea del Sarto, called "The Faultless Painter," whom Browning had had say *I, painting from myself and to myself,/Know what I do, am unmoved by men's blame/Or their praise either.* Unmoved by men's blame or their praise either. I will be unmoved, Ben thought. He felt his own agitation, felt the nature of it. Somehow his fear of Rupert was the same thing as his fear of failing in his work. It would come to the same thing, whatever that was. *I will not move,* Ben thought, standing still in his studio, waiting for Rupert.

When, through the open windows of his studio, Ben heard the car off in the pine woods, he was standing at a worktable looking down at the open pages of a book and reading about the life of Saint Philip Neri. Something to do. It had been del Sarto's frescoes of the life of Saint Philip which had given del Sarto his soubriquet. A car door thumped shut outside.

Ben felt quieted by his research. He touched the book as if to close it, then left it open and went through his house to the door that faced the driveway. Through the screen door Ben saw Rupert standing by the cab. Rupert was facing the screen door, but he did not take a step toward it. The light outside was bleaching white, more like the Caribbean than New Hampshire. Ben went to the screen door and held it open.

"My good friend Ben," Rupert said. He looked at Ben carefully, as if trying to memorize him—or remember something about him which he did not see. "Somehow, some way, I expected you to be a better friend, Ben."

"Better than what?"

Rupert came forward then. His hands were clasped behind him and they remained so as he walked past Ben and into the house.

Ben followed him. Rupert seemed certain of purpose.

"This house always intrigued me," Rupert said. On the edge of the large, open living room he stopped. "Now I do not know." He nodded, looking around. "Now I do not know. Perhaps it was all just a contrivance."

Rupert went to the long couch, looked at it, looked at the long coffee table. He went to the bar and looked at the room from there. Then he went to the hearth and looked at the area of the hearth near the fireplace.

"If you're studying the architecture—" Ben started to say.

"I am not studying the architecture," Rupert said. He went across the room and on into Ben's bedroom.

"Rupert, I think you better just get the hell out of here."

But Rupert said nothing.

Ben went to the doorway of his bedroom and looked at Rupert looking around the room, looking at the bed, looking up at the ceiling. There was a set to Rupert's face, an absence of identifiable emotion.

"Out," Ben said. "This is not a public part of the house."

Rupert turned to him. "Do you object to strangers in your bedroom, Ben?"

Then Rupert walked by Ben to the living room, but did not stop there. He went on toward the door, stopping in the foyer. The taxi was parked out there behind him in the white sunlight, dark woods behind it, soft dark shadowed light here inside where Rupert stood. Ben studied it as if it were a problem in painting.

Rupert said, "First she tells me she has slept with you. I am not pleased, but then I am not either terribly bothered by it. People express their warmth for each other sometimes in this fashion. Madelon is not a slut, I will not concern myself. Then she tells me no, you would not do it, she undressed for you but even then you would not do it . . . What is wrong, Ben? Is she not good enough for you? Is my wife not good enough for you?" Rupert stared at Ben.

Ben said, "I can't think that's a serious question."

"Really, Ben. In any event, we had best conclude our relationships, both business and pleasure. My attorneys will contact you. I believe there is a clause in our agreement which reads that either party may withdraw from the agreement upon payment of some small penalty fee. A check in that amount will be in the mail this week. I cancel the agreement, Ben. I cancel all the money you would have made. I cancel you, Ben."

91

"Clipper Seven-niner. Can we make a right turn to that heading? If we make a left turn we'll go into one hell of a storm."

"New EnglandAir One-six-five. We're in pretty good shape here. We're still threading our way through, but there're storms all around . . . Thank you kindly, we're leaving six thousand now for eleven."

"Boston Center, Whiskey Fox, and we're going to need all the help we can get to get around this line of build-ups east of Albany."

"Air Canada Five-zero-zero would like to deviate as far to the east as you can let us—to avoid this line of build-ups . . . Oh, thirty miles, if you can . . ."

"Heavy, heavy rain for fifty miles, right on our road. Can you give me a deviation? . . . Okay, thank you, it looks real hairy here . . ."

"Eight-sixty-seven, direct Riverhead, and are you painting any build-ups between our position and Cornwall? . . . Okay, all clear, and thank you."

"Here's your ident . . . Here's your ident . . ."

"American Four-five-four. Our radar is showing more of this stuff up ahead. It looks like the only way we're gonna get out of this stuff is to go over it . . . Okay, out of sixteen for twenty-two."

"A good line of build-ups here. Another hour it's really going to be solid up here . . . Uh, coming up on Cornwall."

92

Jonah stepped down from the Skymaster and felt the heat of the cement through his shoes. He was just back from flying a businessman to Montreal on a charter. Returning, he'd had to fly rather east to avoid thunderstorm activity, and he'd had to work his way around a couple of thunderstorms even then. The heat and humidity on the ground was terrific. It was almost midafternoon and Jonah had not had lunch—he hadn't wanted to take the time in Montreal. Not with all that thunderstorm activity moving toward his line of flight and building up at all quadrants.

Jonah saw Ben's station wagon parked at the fence. Ben hadn't been flying since his long winter rambles. Jonah looked at the isolated build-ups, like scouts, nearing Cornwall. Crazy day for Ben to start aviating again.

Jonah thought it was an unlikely group he found talking together in the office. Adele Fortune, George Detwiler, and Ben Cain. Ev was seated at his secretary's desk paying no attention to anyone.

Ben was saying, "I'll tell you, George, I wouldn't mind a flight right now. I wouldn't at all. Let me think about it."

"Plenty of time to think. It's about three weeks away. You might do yourself some good, Ben. Maybe they'd be interested in the work of an artist who flies."

"I said I'd think about it."

"The hospitality will be pleasant. I'm sure. There's tennis. You're a tennis player, aren't you?"

Ben thought of playing tennis, of lying by a swimming pool, of having drinks and conversation with new people and not thinking at all about work for a few days. He thought about flying—he was pretty good at it in his little airplane, given its capabilities and limitations. Yes, that was true, but not entirely, he thought immediately—not until he got his instrument ticket; he swore to himself that he would get into concentrated work on that before the summer was over.

"He is," Adele said. "He's not bad at it, either."

"The man we'd be visiting, Corny McConnell, was once nationally ranked."

Ben had discovered he wasn't jealous. He felt nothing about that relationship, Adele's and George's. Now that George had been away from flying for these three or four years, Ben wondered if maybe he himself might not be the better pilot now, better at it than George.

Jonah said, "Christ, George, did I forget I was going to give you time this afternoon?"

The telephone rang and Ev picked it up.

"No. I just stopped in to see Adele."

Ben said, "Jonah, can—"

"Jonah," Ev said, "blood run."

"Where?"

"Manchester. Police car'll meet you on the runway."

Jonah looked at Ben as he started out the door. Ben said, "Wanted to see you about something, but it can wait."

Jonah didn't preflight. He started the engines of the Skymaster without consulting the checklist, and he made his instrument and cockpit adjustments and did his runups as he taxied. He heard Ev's voice on unicom warning off any traffic that might be approaching for a landing. The wind was picking up and brief gusts were erratic, coming from almost any direction, but the mass of it was moving from the west. Jonah made a quick study of the sky for traffic at the approach end of Runway Three-one and then swung the Skymaster from the taxiway and out onto the runway without pause. He pushed his power controls forward and straightened the aircraft to the runway as power turned to speed. Peripherally he saw small, tornado-like flights of loose dirt swirling at the edge of the runway. Flying into the gathering wind, the Skymaster rose upon gusty waves of air.

Jonah turned and flew almost due east, twenty-six miles to Manchester's Grenier Field. He stayed low, just touching three thousand feet, to avoid wasting time in climb and descent. The terrain, with few houses or roads below, was turning deep green from spreading cloud cover. At the horizon ahead the deep green faded in haze to yellow, and Manchester appeared to be a very large and widely spread village, the airport a nearer community. The runway before him was quite clear, quite sharp, the numbers at its approach end still an oddity to him. Jonah always found the numbers painted on the surface of the world an oddity. And runways never looked as if they belonged either. On a taxiway he saw the flashing cartop lights of a police cruiser. They reminded him of Conrad Whittier and Lou-Ann Ralsan in the light from the rotating beacons of the police car in Poughkeep-sie that cold night at the beginning of the year. He was making a rapid letdown, doing a lot of things quickly, but the airplane was responding without fault. The tower had cleared him right in and authorized him to stop on the runway.

He came in hot and steeply and then dumped the flaps and set the aircraft down hard and ungracefully, spoiling all its lift as soon as he could. He used the brakes hard and left some good rubber on the cement of the runway. When he came to a stop the police car was off his left wing and a man in uniform hurried toward him, a sealed cardboard box cradled in his arms. The canisters of blood would be inside cushioned with balled-up newspaper.

Jonah opened his door, took the box, secured it with cargo belts in the copilot's seat, and signed for it. He pulled the door tight, pushed the power controls all forward again, and took off.

The flight over had taken him ten minutes. The flight back seemed to be against some huge, taut rubber band stretched across his path. The closer he got to Cornwall the more resistance he met and the slower his progress was. With the field distantly in sight, the air became fitfully violent.

It was like New Year's all over again, Jonah thought. As bad as that and worse. New Year's Eve was something he had known he could handle. That wind and turbulence, except for takeoff, had been mainly in the air, in the sky. What made this worse was that he would have to land in it.

If it hadn't been a blood run he wouldn't be flying in it at all; he certainly wouldn't try landing in it, he'd go somewhere else and wait till the approaching storm had passed away from the area. But he had to get the blood down on the ground at Cornwall.

It's just a landing, he told himself. The aircraft pitched. He rode with it.

I didn't come anywhere near losing it, Jonah thought, nor should I have. The air was cool now, but there was sweat holding his shirt to his skin. He called Cornwall and told them he had the field in sight.

There were several horizons and they were mostly bright and cheerful, yellow with the sunlight of a summer afternoon. But the light around them was queer, as if it were not sunlight at all, but some other illumination. What would have been a single horizon was interrupted by storm activity. To the west the front was textbook visible: a band of high cumulus stretching south to north, brilliant shiny white at their rolling and anviled peaks, clear blue sky above them, and thick blackness beneath them. Ahead of Jonah a gray curtain was moving toward the Cornwall runways. A rain shower. Above the rain shower there was a diffuse cloud, possibly cumulus. There was no telling what violence might be in it. Or around it. Jonah was low now, pattern altitude, eight hundred feet above the rough, tree-covered terrain. Dirt or sand lifted off a road like a flag unfurling. Jonah was carrying a great deal of power to maintain his forward progress. His altitude varied often and abruptly within a vertical of a hundred feet. The gray curtain had turned to black and was about five miles from the airport.

"Two-two Charlie, you read Cornwall?"

"I'm with you, Adele."

"Jonah, we've got winds at twenty-five knots now. Gusting higher."

Jonah did not reply. His mind was busy with the theoretical mathematics of the landing.

"Two-two Charlie?"

"I'm here, Adele. Understand winds at twenty-five with gusts."

"Affirmative, Jonah. Winds are west southwest at twenty-five knots, now gusting to forty. Barometer two-niner six-zero and falling. Will you be landing, Jonah?"

"That's affirmative."

"The wind is quartering Runway Three-one. It's a hell of a crosswind, Jonah."

"I understand. No sweat. I'm on a straight-in final for Three-one right now. About a mile out."

"Roger, no sweat." She clicked the microphone twice.

Jonah was looking down a runway that had turned sullen and gray and dark. Give it power, you damn fool, he told himself. *Go away!*

He held his descent. The aircraft was tumbling now. The pitches upwards and rolls sideways kept the stall-warning horn in broken cry. You're nearly out of altitude for recovery from a stall, Jonah said to himself.

He kept the airplane coming to the runway.

[241]

Relax, he said to himself. Relax. He forced his hand on the yoke to open its fingers, his hand on the power controls to lighten its grip. Relax, he said, you are not going to fly this airplane by *holding on to it.* Relax and fly it . . .

He knew he should apply power and climb and make a one-eighty degree turn and climb some more and go some place safe for a landing.

About a hundred feet up from the trees now, pitching and rolling badly, and not even over the deck yet. That was when it caught him. The wind lifted his left wing till the wings were vertical to the ground, and the aircraft was blown perfectly sideways and toward the ground with no effect from power or controls, Jonah a helpless passenger within hearing himself say, *"Oh, Christ, you've lost it!"*

Ben, Adele, and George had gone out to the ramp to see Jonah in. Or to see him climb out and go away. Ev had stayed inside with the radio. Rain had begun just in the moment they'd come outside. The fat, wet isolated *warning* drops which were in seconds superseded by gusts of hard, cold rain.

Jonah's airplane, still in the sky, floated at them, driven by invisible power, its wings vertical to the ground, its belly pushed by the giant wind, some flying phantasm, not at all like an airplane, not standing in the sky like that, but other-worldly, like no airplane they'd ever seen before, not standing like that and so low to the ground . . . Adele screamed.

From within him, George, who knew from seeing it what had to happen, heard a moan.

Ben disbelieved. It seemed as if there were all the time in the world. He looked at it, studied it, the black silhouette, that *apparition* in the air, moving toward them, growing in size to nearly the size of an airplane. A voice was screaming, *"Do something! Do something!"* Ben heard it and did not realize it was his own voice.

As if hearing the command, the airplane turned in their direction, slowly pivoted on the axis of its vertical wings until the nose was pointed at them. It stood that way as if it were peering at them sideways.

"Run!" George yelled, and just as instantly the high wing snapped down to level, the low wing sweeping up, the airplane swooped at them, driven down by wind, the engines loud and harsh even in the wind, and then the airplane lifted away from them, climbed away and turned with its tail to the wind, using the wind to hurtle itself away.

There was no sound on the ramp but that of the wind in the air and the rain on the concrete. There was nothing to see of the airplane in the sky. It was gone.

In the office Ev looked at George and Ben and Adele and was afraid. He had not been able to see what they had just seen. But the remainder of something terrible was in their faces.

"Is Jonah—?"

Then they heard his voice from the radio. "Cornwall, Two-two Charlie. I think I'll just go over to Nashua and set down there for a while. Everything looks real peaceful over there to the east. Real peaceful. You want to get the state police to drive the blood back?"

93

"Think you earned your pay today, Captain?" Captain King Kahn said to Perry Sullivan.

"Busy day," Perry said, seated in the captain's seat, the left-hand seat, and repacking his flight bag. Last time he had flown with Kahn, Perry had been the copilot. All *this* day Kahn, the very senior captain, had sat in the right seat and acted as Perry's copilot—taking orders, offering no criticism. Kahn had been giving him a line check. A little odd just four months after the chief pilot had checked him out, but Perry had decided not to sweat it. Some time in the next few minutes Kahn would tell him whether his performance had been satisfactory or unsatisfactory. Perry kept quiet and continued to repack his bag.

They were still on the flight deck of the FH 227. The aircraft stood abreast of a company gate at La Guardia, the passengers disembarked, the last flight of the day for Perry complete and only an hour and a half late. He had been dodging weather all day, working center hard, taking doglegs around the weather he could see, sometimes penetrating it, sometimes climbing above it to the calm bright air above the clouds, that white glare up there, and then back down in—when it had to be—sliding down into whiteness that turned gray as sunlight could not follow their descent and then on down further into dirty grayness and the startling shocks of turbulence. Over and over, most of the day, the pattern of changes in light and visibility sometimes repeating itself in just a few minutes. Up, down, around . . . Until a few minutes ago, when he had taken them out of a low cloud deck, down into another kind of dirty grayness, the wet air that hovered over the endless dirty buildings and streets around La Guardia. It was like a stereopticon picture come into focus. They had been in the blur of cloud. Then the cloud itself had become visible streamers whipping by the windscreen and there ahead—something blurred, but substantial. And then it had become sharply and intricately focused. Over the water to Runway Three-one it was, as always, like an approach to a stationary aircraft carrier. They had touched down without a jolt.

In all that weather he had not given the passengers a bad time, Perry thought. Not a *bad* time. He had been judicious in chosing a balance between time-consuming weather avoidance and, on the opposite side, accepting some of the turbulence of the weather in order to fly as direct and schedule-oriented a path as possible. King Kahn had sat beside him, following Perry's commands, making general small talk, occasionally asking specific questions about the reasoning behind Perry's decisions.

There was nothing else for Perry to do on the flight deck. Kahn would tell him sat or unsat. A jet took off, climbing steeply, folding its gear into its belly, an oily black exhaust briefly visible from its engines. Perry thought the exhaust made it look somehow primitive.

"You did a good job for me, Perry," Kahn said.

Perry nodded. "I'm glad to hear it."

"You feel okay about all of this."

"About all of what?"

"Flying in weather."

"Sure."

"Some people get surprised. They go along for years flying in weather in light aircraft, and no sweat. They fly for years copilot on an airline, and again, no sweat. Then they get a command of their own and they're not only flying in weather, but they've got a lot of souls on board behind them. They begin to sweat. It happens slowly, but they know it's happening. Like the symptoms of a disease. You don't recognize what I'm talking about."

"No."

"No, I didn't think so. You like the route?"

"Yes, I do."

"Familiarity hasn't bred contempt?"

"There's always something new on this route. The weather sees to that." Kahn had stood up.

"What about the people who begin to worry—" Perry asked, "the ones who begin to sweat?"

"Pretty soon the sweat shows. Someone picks it up. Usually it all comes out in the first few months of captaincy." Kahn put his jacket on. "How's your wife?"

"Fine."

"Miss flying? The handsome captains? The glamour of cleaning up after everyone?"

"Not so much. I think she misses New York, though."

"Well, yes, that's a problem. Taking a young woman out of New York after she's gone to all the trouble to get there. Laura from a small town?"

"Yes. Being a stew was her way out, I guess. Flying was."

"Well, I'm glad you like the route, Perry. I think it's going to be yours for a while. Say hello at home for me."

94

Jonah rode in the Skymaster more as its passenger than as its pilot.

The weather behind the front, once it had passed, was soft. Sunlight suffused it. The air was mild and warm, the heat of the afternoon swept away. In the sky the air was cool and stable. The Skymaster was as if it had been on the ground. The seat beneath Jonah was rock firm. A lonely straggler of a thunderstorm stood isolated against the blue sky to the south, its anvil beginning to disperse. There were some streaks of cirrus, but mostly the sky was blue and calm.

He had *lost* it. There had been all those seconds, hundreds of years of seconds, when he had had no control over his own airplane. He had sat in it powerless and had expected to die. How he had righted it, how the ineffective controls had suddenly taken effect, he didn't know.

Jonah had had moments of trouble before. A blown cylinder. A tire burst on landing. A loss of power on takeoff. Instrument and radio failures while he was flying with no outside visual reference . . . But it was the *quality* of this moment that lingered and terrified him. The *passivity* he had experienced, the helplessness.

He found it *disturbing* that he could sit in this airplane now, in complete confidence, but be terrified of the recurrence of that moment, be terrified of even the *possibility* of the recurrence of that moment. A professional pilot cannot fly only in stable air, in clear weather.

On the ground Jonah called Ben, and Ben asked him to come out to his house before he went home. Jonah looked at his watch and was surprised, very surprised, to find that it was only a few minutes after five.

"Christ, you don't know what you *looked* like," Ben said.

"I know what it felt like," Jonah said.

"What did it feel like?"

"Like nothing. Like nothing at all. I couldn't make anything happen. I couldn't do anything. Nothing."

They were drinking beer and sitting on the deck of Ben's house above the water. "Looks calm enough now," Ben said. The blue sky had softened and gotten a little yellow. Friendly clouds were moving in.

"It *is* calm."

"Does something like that," Ben said, "what happened this afternoon, does it stay with you?"

"No," Jonah said quickly.

"I mean, doesn't it still scare you?"

"It scared the shit out of me when it happened."

Ben sighed. Jonah wouldn't talk about it. "When's the baby due?"

"Three weeks, maybe less."

Ben wanted to tell Jonah about the drawings he had made for the child's room. It had been the only work he had done for the sheer exuberance of it in months. But Ben decided not to tell Jonah about the drawings. He didn't want to bid for Jonah's good will in advance.

Ben said, "I've got some shitty news for you, Jonah. It seems unfair after what you've been through today already."

"That's nothing. I'm here, aren't I?"

They each opened a second bottle of beer.

"I just thought I ought to tell you right off. Rupert Zur—the guy I was doing the designs for?"

"Sure. I met him today. At the airport. Jolly little man."

"Yeah, jolly. He came over here to see me to tell me he was firing me. There was upwards of thirty thousand dollars in our contract. That was the money that was going to finance our flight service."

Jonah looked down from watching the soft yellow clouds. He looked at the decking beneath his feet. He was silent for a long moment. "No flying service, huh?"

"There's no money. Every cent I've made went into this house. And the airplane. I haven't got three thousand dollars in the bank. I'm dependent on what my dealer sells for me to get through each month."

"No flying service." He drank some beer and looked back up at the sky.

"You're welcome to my Cherokee," Ben said. "If you think we could get started with just the Cherokee."

"No way." Jonah thought about it. "No way. Look at Del Howard and his Aero Commander and . . . Ah, the hell with it." He stood up. "Ben, I'm going home. It's been a long day and I'm going home."

95

Ben wasn't sure what Jonah's attitude toward him was when he left. He went back and sat on the deck a while longer, drinking beer and watching the sky darken; then he got another beer from the refrigerator and came out again and watched the sky. He remembered, for the nth time, lying on the bed in the motel room outside of Palm Beach and watching the blue sky darken to dark blue, the hard white lights of the stars coming out. That memory kept returning. That night just before his long flight over the Caribbean. To Madelon and Rupert's, he thought. Rupert, that bastard. Who the hell *were* those people fucking with his life?

In anger Ben went to his studio. He looked at the slowly advancing work. So goddamn little progress. And no freshness, nothing exciting.

I have got to get *away* from this *shit,* he thought.

He went over to the phone and looked up George Detwiler's number and called it. George was a long time answering.

"I was just cooking dinner," George said. "What have you got to tell me, Ben?"

"Let's go. Let's fly. I'll make your flight with you."

"That's fine, Ben. That's just fine of you. I'll pay all the expenses and—"

"We ought to get together and go over this thing."

"Sure. Whenever you say."

"Tomorrow evening—oh, I forgot. You go to classes."

"Didn't you know I graduated?"

"I guess not."

"Top two percent. No more night school. Classes in the daytime now. Studying for the state bar exam. Left my job clerking, I'm all on my own now. That's why it's so important for me to see this guy Corny McConnell. That's why I want to show him I'm still a pilot *as well as* a lawyer."

"Well, okay, George. Tomorrow evening. Why don't you come over here about—"

"Ben, I'm sorry. I've got to ask you another favor. Would you mind coming over here? Randy goes to bed and, hell, I could get a sitter if you want me to, but I'd rather be here, you know, in the same house with him."

Ben remembered Ceil's disappearance. That had been four years ago when he'd first moved here. He'd never known Ceil, just heard about her, met George after he wasn't flying any more, a stubborn-looking, silent man then. A man filled with anger, Ben had thought.

"Okay, George, I'll come over there."

"I'll pick up the charts," George said. "One other thing. I ought to familiarize myself with your airplane. I should set up some time with Jonah in it."

Ben felt himself angered. *Fly my airplane? Without me there?* No one had done that. No one.

Okay, Ben said to himself, do *you* want to go out there and give him time in it yourself?

"You do that, George."

Ben hung up.

He felt as if he had become disoriented. His destination was in the studio, but he was once again flying *from* it. It was as if he had missed a rendezvous with himself.

96

George was seated in an armchair on the other side of the small living room from Adele. He seemed to have selected the chair for its neutrality. Adele was sitting on the couch. She wondered if she had selected it for its *availability*, the extra seats by her.

George said, "I think it was this afternoon that put me in mind of it. No, that *clarified* it for me. Seeing Jonah there in all that wildness. *Wildness.* Nearly dying. I realized I'm living as if I'm dying. I mean, I'm still living as if Ceil might come back. I'm still living as if I couldn't have a family again, a whole family."

Adele looked at George and then at her snifter of brandy. She smiled. She was amazed at how young she felt, how kittenish, and how self-conscious. As when she was young and on a date and wanted a boy to kiss her and knew he wanted to kiss her too.

"That wildness," George said. "What Jonah was subject to. That's what *my* life has been subject to. That's what I've been fighting and studying and trying to understand. *Arbitrariness,* that's what I'm talking about. Once it happens to you it becomes the obsession of your life."

In spite of George's talk of wildness and arbitrariness, Adele found herself imbued with serenity. Randy was in bed in his room upstairs. Adele felt affection for the boy. The world, for her, became calm when she was within their home, Randy and George's, close to their relationship.

George got up and came over and sat near her, though not beside her. "I just wanted you to think about marriage. I've begun to think about it a lot. Just think about it. I guess, what I want to know is, is marriage to me something you could think about? Now that I've brought it up? Or would you just rather—"

But Adele had nodded at him when he had asked her if she could think about being married to him.

She stood up and went to him. When he held her, she felt warm and safe. And calm.

Adele had images of D.G. pulling the intravenous needles out of her after the miscarriage. Images of Ben and his tenderness. The hurt when he would not marry her, in spite of her love for him, her passion for him . . . But when George held her, those images went away.

97

The still evening was warm and fragrant with the renewal caused by the rains of the storm line. Laura Sullivan had looked out into the night air and thought the air itself must be green, it smelled so green.

They sat on the floor, she and Hilary Blane. On a low table behind them there was a lamp, the only light on in the room. Hilary had said she ought to get used to darkness in front of her when she worked. Not that you couldn't see the audience from the stage, but so much darkness out there beyond the footlights sometimes threw people, disoriented them.

They each had a copy of the play, underlined and notated now, but the scripts lay open pages-downwards as Hilary coaxed and coached Laura through the lines she was still trying to commit to memory. When Laura drew on a cigarette, the end of it glowed in the semidarkness and created an aura of orange light about itself. The ashtray behind her was filled with cigarettes, her own. She could no longer smell the night air. Hilary kept the cigarette holder—a prop central to his character in the play—always in his mouth or hand, but he did not light the cigarette in it.

"Was that all right?" Laura said.

"You're getting near to it. But you still have to spend a lot of your energy trying to remember your lines. Your character isn't developing a relationship with my character yet. You're not responding to *me,* you're just trying to remember all your lines."

"Well, I'm *trying* to respond to you, I *am.* It's all new to me. I don't know how *she* responds yet, the character."

"It should be you responding, Laura."

"I'll fix us a drink. We've worked hard enough. It's all right now, isn't it?"

"Yeah. Sure. Maybe it'll loosen you up. Then we'll try some more."

She got up and went off to the kitchen. Jesus, talk about response, Hilary thought, watching the motion of her body in her tight pants as she left the room. Talk about response, I've been responding to the little bitch all evening. And this wasn't the first such evening, either, he reminded himself. He'd been getting hot for her every time he'd been with her, five or six evenings over the past two weeks.

In mid-June rehearsals at the playhouse had begun, and he had been able to leave his job at the department store and the room in the boardinghouse and move out to a cabin at the playhouse—which he shared with two other actors. He was in rehearsal for one play now, and when that opened, in less than two weeks, he would be playing that play at night and rehearsing, during the day, the play that both he and Laura were in.

Laura came back in with the drinks and a bowl of crackers and nuts. Hilary decided that—because of the way in which she had dressed herself —she was being deliberately provocative. A slim white shirt was tucked into the pants. The shirt had a V neck and Laura had left the button at the bottom of the V unfastened. Underneath she wore a white bra—a fancy one, Hilary saw, very fancy. It lifted her and revealed her. The bra seemed to be presenting Laura's breasts to him. Hilary felt inflamed and nervous with sexual tension and desire.

He gulped down some of his drink and chewed some of the crackers. What was *most* irritating was simply that Laura pretended not to notice her own provocation. And Hilary knew that was a lie.

He said to her, "Do you realize that in ten days you'll be in *real* rehearsal?"

"I know. It makes me nervous. I don't want to look like a fool. I keep being afraid I won't know my lines."

"Don't worry about your lines, you're learning them, they're coming."

"But I'm scared I won't remember them. I'm scared I'll forget *everything* opening night."

They were seated cross-legged almost knee to knee next to each other. He took her hand between both of his, resting the package on Laura's thigh. "Everyone has that fear," Hilary said, looking at her with seriousness and compassion. He projected the compassion into her eyes. "Even pros. Like me."

"Like you?"

"I even thought I'd forget that one line *I will if you will* once the cameras were on me and all the technicians waiting and the agency people and all that money. I was scared I'd forget even that one damn line." He let her hand go. Must not let her make an issue of that little intimacy. "So you see," Hilary said. He took a swallow of his drink and watched her. She was watching him. "No, you'll know your lines all right. The problem, the basic underlying problem that no one will face, even a lot of actors—except for the great actors like Olivier and Brando and women like Woodward and Hepburn—the *biggest* thing is just the simple problem of *knowing* your character, having *confidence* in your character, so that whatever you do onstage or in front of a camera, *whatever* you do, you know it's *right* for that character. Why do you think everyone picked up on my line, on *I will if you will?*"

Laura smiled. "It's sexy. It's a big come-on."

"Sure it is. But if your grocer said it to you, or the guy who fixes your car, would it be such a hot thing then? No, it wouldn't. Because those guys don't have the confidence. When I said *I will if you will,* everyone knew that he *would* and that he expected the girl to, too. I *projected* that confidence into every TV screen in America. And you know how I did it? By knowing my character and my relationship to the character of the girl I was working with. I could have *hiccuped* and the vast majority of television viewers would have gotten the message. Because I knew my character."

"You're telling me I have to know my character."

"Exactly. That's fundamental."

Hilary was silent. Enough said for just now, let the silence speak to her for a little while.

He put his drink down and got up. He put his hands in his hip pockets and looking up at the ceiling walked in and out of the darkness. He had seen a director do this once and it had been a hell of a piece of drama—how to make your point, deliver a lecture, and keep yourself a dramatic focal point.

"What you have to do is learn to work with *me* freely. After that everything else will come easily. You won't even think about remembering your lines. The lines will come spontaneously. You'll just *look* at me, wherever I am on stage, whatever I'm doing, you'll just *look* at me, and whatever you're supposed to say will come out of you."

"I'd love that. I'd really love it. I wouldn't be scared. I could just have fun . . . and be an *actress*. Could I be an actress? Do you think I could, Hilary?"

"Sure you could. You've got all the equipment. Voice, looks, intelligence. Your voice is great, Laura. You could recite the Magna Carta and make it sound interesting. What you don't have is . . ."

"Well, what?"

"Confidence in your body."

Without pause she looked down her shirt, then quickly up, her hands, fingers spread, touching her rib cage. "I've always thought I did. I always thought I had a good body."

"Oh, sure, you do. But you don't have *confidence* in it. Your body is an instrument, Laura. When you're an actor or an actress, your body is an instrument and has to be treated as such. You'll get out on that stage and you'll just be self-conscious. What you need to do is turn your body into your servant. Your servant as an actress. Make it be the character."

Laura thought about it. "I understand. I understand what you're saying. It makes sense. But . . . I just don't know how to go about it. After all, you've had all that training. Ballet and gymnastics and mime and—"

"You don't need all that and you haven't got time for it. Why don't you freshen our drinks and think about what I said?"

Laura got up and smiled at Hilary as she did so, seeing him look down her shirt. "I'm not *entirely* without confidence in my body," she said. "Not when I can get looks like that."

"Just think about what I said."

"I am. But there was so much. I don't know what to concentrate on."

"All of it."

"I'll try."

When she left the room this time, she seemed somewhat subdued, Hilary thought.

Sitting alone, he became aware of a photograph of a man he took to be Perry Sullivan. Sullivan and an older man were standing in front of a New EnglandAir FH 227. Both men wore uniforms and visored caps. Both men had wings on the left breasts of their jackets, and both men had four gold rings on their sleeves. The men were shaking hands. The photograph was in color, and the sky behind the two men was blue and benevolent and seemed to be bearing witness to the occasion like a colleague. It occurred to Hilary that Perry Sullivan was the kind of guy he wanted to be. He remembered being back in that cold room on New Year's Eve, the ginned-up girl next to him, the rumble of aircraft in the night sky he couldn't see, his resolve to become a pilot. He had been scared, he admitted that to himself, scared of soloing, scared of *flying,* for Godsake. But he had the resolve now and the confidence. The drink was doing it and Laura's slow submission, if that was what it was, and his working every day at what he wanted to work at, instead of at some dumb hick department store . . . Whatever it was, he knew he could solo now. He had the confidence finally.

Laura came back in. She silently handed him his drink and sat next to him again. She had some of her drink, then put it down on the table. "I'm listening," she said.

"To *really* work together freely, we ought to get a sense of each other's physical presences. I mean, I've been in classes where, when a girl and I were preparing to do a scene together for the class, when we were rehearsing alone together we'd get undressed and rehearse that way."

"I couldn't do that," Laura said.

"I didn't say you could," Hilary said. It was all coming so freely, so spontaneously, like a problem in improvisation that he was suddenly doing without having to think about it. "No, I didn't say you could. I said that was your problem. You couldn't be free."

Laura lit a cigarette and thought about that. She looked at Hilary. "No, I couldn't."

Hilary shrugged. "For an actor, that's like being an orchestra and throwing away the string section." He looked at her.

Laura looked back, not at all the pompous little beauty queen, Hilary thought. He saw something plain and—God help him for noting a professional detail right now—something *effective,* a young girl's face emerging out of all that grownup, show-off woman, some kid looking at him.

"You're getting it," Hilary said quietly. "Just the way you're looking at me now, you're letting the person underneath the clothes emerge. Doesn't it feel good?"

Laura nodded. She drank and nodded again. *For Christ's sake, she was crying.*

She sniffled and turned her head as if tossing the sniffle away.

"It's not something a married woman should do."

"Your husband doesn't have to know. As to the rest, all it's going to do is help turn you into an actress."

She studied him steadily. The younger woman studied him, the girl. "And you think I could be an actress?"

He kept his voice very low, almost inaudible. "I think you could be an actress."

Laura said, "All right." She sounded unhappy. She looked down at her hands. "But just halfway."

"All right. That's a start."

She would not look at him. "Take off *your* shirt," she said. "Not that it matters," she said, still looking at the space between her Indian-crossed legs.

"It matters," Hilary said. "We need to know each other." He took off his shirt.

He put the shirt aside and Laura watched him. Then, looking away, she reached behind herself and pulled her shirt out of her pants. She straightened her body, pulled her shirt out in front, unbuttoned it, took it off, and put it aside. She paused, some sort of thought occupying her so that her eyes saw nothing outside herself, and then she bent forward and reached behind herself and unhooked her bra and slid it down her arms and left it beside her on the rug.

Hilary swallowed and thought of rules for voice control and said, as if he had been conducting a class in emotionlessness, "Let's do the bar scene. Where they meet. You know those lines. We'll say our lines and do what's in our minds."

She nodded.

As they went through the scene he reached out occasionally and touched her breasts, her legs. Ran his hand down the side of her, tipped her head back and touched her lips with his.

"They're sitting at the bar," Hilary said as they went through the scene the second time. "Doesn't she want to put her hand on his penis?"

She turned abruptly away.

"He's straddling a bar stool. They're *immensely* attracted to each other. His mind touches her with his hands, like I'm doing. That's what he's doing in his mind. He does it with his mouth." He leaned forward and cupped one of her breasts, and for the first time put his lips to it, put the nipple in his mouth. His other hand felt her backbone straighten, pull back, but she did not push him away. He sat back. "Doesn't she want to reach out and touch his penis? Feel it underneath his pants?"

Laura looked down at her own hands and said, "I don't know."

"Well—"

Laura stood up. "That's enough. That's enough playacting for tonight. I'll think about what you told me. I'll study it. But that's enough."

She had her shirt on now. "Put your shirt on. Go ahead. Quickly. *Quickly,* I said."

Hilary dressed quickly.

98

Driving home Adele still felt George's arms around her and the good sensations of warmth and serenity she had felt in his house. He had not yet tried to go to bed with her. She wondered whether that was a matter of caution or of some formal sense of courtesy on his part. She had not stayed on after his question and the one embrace. She had felt it best that the evening not go on after that.

She found herself parked in front of her house and still sitting there. She had wanted to marry Ben. That was true, profoundly true. But Ben did not want to make a commitment. Stupid Ben. But she *had* wanted to marry Ben, and not so very long ago. All last winter she had hoped he would call and say he couldn't abide being without her and that he wanted to marry her and live with her. Was that fair to George? That so recently she had so deeply wanted to marry Ben?

She got out of the car and went to the front door of the house. She'd gotten out her key, but the door was not locked. That was all right— sometimes the owners of the house, who had the apartment on the first floor, didn't lock up the entranceway until later in the evening. But the owners were not home. Neither was the faculty couple on the top floor. All away on vacation. It was dark on the stairs. Had she forgotten to leave a light on? Had the bulb blown out? She went up and let herself into her apartment —had she not left any lights on there either? She reached to the switch inside the door, turned it on, and pulled the door closed behind her. The switch controlled a lamp across the room by a chair.

A voice said, "Hello, Adele."

She knew the voice, and hearing it now, alone in the house, terrified her.

She turned and there was D.G. seated in the chair next to the lamp. He looked at her, and Adele knew by the look of him that he was upset, agitated. It was something like the look he'd had when he had come to the hospital room and ripped the IV needles out of her. After the miscarriage. The miscarriage of their baby, hers and D.G.'s, after D.G. had pushed her down the rocky seashore bank.

She might have moved to the door then. Just two paces away. She might have gotten it open and she might have been able to outrace D.G. to the front door and out on the street. Where she could call for help. She might have been able to, but she wasn't sure. And she wasn't sure whether he might have some weapon as well. She thought it was safer to see first what his mood was, what he might want. Maybe he was okay. Maybe.

"Where's the child, Adele?"

"What child?"

"Our child."

"We don't have a child, D.G."

"Where is the child, Adele? I'm not leaving here till you tell me. I've looked all through your apartment and I can't find the child anywhere. I've looked in your bags and in all the drawers and everywhere I can think of . . . Now, Adele, I know the child is here. Just tell me where."

"There is no child, D.G. The child doesn't exist. I had a miscarriage, remember?"

"Nonsense. There was no miscarriage. That was just a story people made up. When they sent me away. The child, Adele."

"The child does not exist, D.G. You pushed me down, remember? You came to the hospital and—and *attacked* me, remember?"

"None of those things happened. Don't lie, Adele. People have been lying to me for years now. My mother, *my own mother,* just yesterday, *she* started telling me those lies all over again. How I was supposed to have pushed you down some hill and you hit rocks or something. How I was supposed to have gone to the hospital and done bad things to you. But I know that's not true. Not true at all. If I'd done anything like that, I'd *remember.* Anyone would. No, Adele, no more lies to me. My own mother sat there and told me what a horrible person I am, and she made the mistake of bringing up those lies—among many, many lies, a whole lifetime of lies— she brought up those lies about you and the miscarriage and the hospital . . . And, Adele, I just said to her, 'That's enough. I've had enough of your lies, all your lies. I'm sick of them. I'm going to shove the lies right in your face. I'm going to Adele and I'm going to get the child and bring the child back. Then we will have had enough of your lies,' I said to Mother."

Adele thought: But she would have called. She would have called me. And then she thought: but I've been out all day. D.G.'s mother doesn't know I work at the airport, she wouldn't know who to call there . . . Maybe his doctor would remember where I work . . . But there had been no call.

The telephone rang.

"I suspect that's Mother," D.G. said. "Just don't answer it, please. It would make me extremely angry if you answered it, you understand that, Adele."

Adele counted fifteen rings before the telephone became silent.

"Now, I can understand your reluctance to give up the child. After all, you've kept the child from me for eleven years, you don't suddenly want to change the situation. But the situation must be changed, Adele. Now. Immediately. Do you remember this?"

When she saw the knife she knew she would have to run. It was the silver carving knife D.G.'s mother had used to carve the Thanksgiving turkey, the Christmas roast. D.G. had been looking at it when—just before he had pushed Adele down the bank. D.G. now held it, blade pointing straight up, for her to see.

"The child is—is at a sitter's house. We'll have to go there."

"No, the child is not at any sitter's house. First of all, you *never* take the child out. *That's* why no one ever saw the child. Second, if the child *had* been at a sitter's house, you would have picked the child up on your way home."

"No . . . No, I wouldn't—I mean, I didn't. The child is sleeping there overnight. I knew I'd be late and I—I didn't want to interrupt the child's sleep."

"I have no faith in you, Adele. None whatsoever." He looked at the blade of the knife.

"Do you remember the day we went flying?"

"Yes. That was nice." He continued to look at the blade. "Do you know what I think? This is something I haven't told anyone. Not even the doctors. But I've suspected this for a long time—a very, very long time. I know where you've hidden the baby, Adele. I know where you've hidden the baby *all* these years." He stood up.

"Where?"

"In you. Isn't that true? Never mind, you wouldn't tell me the truth anyway. All these years and you wouldn't let that baby come out. Well, Adele, I brought this knife so I could let that baby out. The baby will like that. Then the baby will come home with me and everyone will *know* you didn't have a miscarriage and that all those other things my mother says are lies, too."

He moved toward her.

"D.G., do you remember when we went flying?" Adele barely got the words out. She felt them constricted in her throat, constricted by terror.

D.G. paused and looked at her. "Yes, I do, Adele. I said so. I said it was nice."

"Do you remember what you said then?" She spoke hurriedly, but tried to make her voice even. "You said it was so calm up there."

"Why yes, it was, Adele. It was very calm."

"You looked down, remember? You looked down on the earth. And you said—you said from up there it made sense. It looked like the earth made sense."

"Yes, I think I did."

"This doesn't make any sense, D.G."

He looked at her and the terror she felt was like the stab of a knife. He said, "I don't care, Adele." He looked at her and his eyes were sad, almost gentle. He shook his head slightly, slowly and sadly. "I don't care."

My God, Adele thought, *he's sane.* In this moment he knows what he's doing. She had never thought that he'd known what he was doing when he'd pushed her down the bank or come to the hospital. But he knew what he was doing now.

She stepped back and reached behind her. Her hand could not find the doorknob. She pressed her body back, felt the doorknob against it. D.G. was about six feet from her, a simple long reach with the knife. She turned and pulled the door open. She felt the knife, she thought she felt the knife, but no, he had not stabbed her, not yet—she was in the dark hall, going down the dark, carpeted steps, her body knowing the stairway, her feet knowing the steps and risers—

"Adele!"

She heard the scream. It sounded like a child calling for its mother. And then she heard the thuds behind her and another scream, no word in this scream, but she was on the ground floor and out the door, and the streetlight and the openness around her lessened the terror—even on the porch she was able to turn, knowing she was safe.

She went back in and turned on the hall light. D.G. lay against the side of the hallway, his legs drawn up as if to protect himself, his body bent in the fetal position as if to keep warm and to sleep. She saw the blood first, a great deal of it pooling beneath him, running, spreading, before she saw the knife handle stemming out from his abdomen.

D.G. was crying very softly, very privately, to himself.

She went quickly back to her apartment and called an ambulance.

There were two neighbors from across the street in the hallway when she came down. When they saw her they stood back as if they were intruders.

D.G. looked wonderfully calm, Adele thought. She knelt by him. He was dead.

99

The morning air was warm and sunlight turned the green leaves glowing. Laura felt the air and the sunlight on her body as, in a thin nightgown, she walked in the country privacy just behind the house. She was barefoot, and she sipped black coffee from a fine china cup that belonged to a set she reserved for entertaining only. She imagined that the cup was a crystal goblet and that her nightgown was a transparent ball gown. She looked down to see herself beneath the gown, the beauty of her breasts, the nipples dark and erect. The other women at this sunlit ball were jealous of her beauty, and every man coveted her.

Laura could not think when she had felt so good, felt so much *herself* . . .

Why she had ever given up that other life, she didn't know. The handsome pilots—well, many of them were good-looking, anyway, even if most of them were married—the businessmen who were always attentive and admiring and would spend money on you and take you places if you let them, the many different cities, the fun with the other girls . . .

When she had had her little flirtation with Ralph Willerwood she had felt guilty afterwards, had not felt good about it at all. But *Hilary* . . . It's not really being unfaithful, she thought, I'm learning how to be free to express myself. She felt so *happy.*

She went into the kitchen, put the cup carefully down, and called the playhouse. Someone went looking for Hilary. In a few minutes he was on the phone.

"It's not ten o'clock yet," Laura said. "I hope I'm not interrupting anything. You haven't started rehearsal yet?"

"No, just about to."

"I wanted to thank you for last night."

"Thank me? I thought you were pissed off. You told me to leave, remember? You said do it *quickly.*"

"I'm *learning,* Hilary. You're teaching me and I'm *learning.* But it's all new. You can't expect me to understand everything all at once."

"Well . . . All right then. All right."

"I feel so *good.* After last night. I don't feel scared anymore. It's going to be *fun.* I'm *full* of confidence. I think I love you—I mean, love you *for* it. For giving me the confidence."

"Well, thanks, Laura, thanks for telling me."

"I'll call you when we can get together. In two or three days, I think."

*　　　　*　　　　*

After he had replaced the receiver, Hilary stood by the phone. He felt exuberance and confidence he hadn't felt since—since the early days of the *I will if you will* commercial, when producers and directors and casting directors had, for a brief few weeks, been interested in him.

He could still feel her breasts in his hands, the smoothness and warmth of her skin, the touch of her lips. Christ, he could do *anything*. He called the airport and got Jonah.

"You don't sound too good," he said to Jonah.

Jonah was silent for a few seconds. "We've had a couple of uh . . . well, a tragedy last night. Nothing to do with the airport. You'll probably read about it in the paper." Very far off, as if he were talking to someone else, Hilary thought he heard Jonah say, tiredly, ". . . and a near thing and a disappointment."

"I'm sorry to hear that, Jonah. I really am. You have all my sympathy . . . But, *Jesus, I feel great.* I tell you, I'm ready to solo. If you're ready to solo me."

"You been drinking, sport?"

"I'm high. I'm damn high. But I haven't been drinking. Or smoking or any of that other shit. What do you say?"

"I've got an hour between one and two tomorrow."

"Nothing today?"

"Not a thing. Not with weather like this."

"Tomorrow's fine."

In rehearsal, the director said to Hilary, "Come down, Hil, you're too up. Way too up."

100

Yvonne and Jonah sat in Dr. Glynn's office across the desk from him. It was late afternoon and Jonah felt tired, the tiredness of someone who didn't care, who had given up, who had been beaten—he didn't know. He kept thinking, I just feel *low*—that poor sonofabitch last night. None of us last very long, do we?

But he had always thought that he would last—as long as he could fly an airplane, he would last.

"Yvonne is in splendid condition, splendid," Dr. Glynn said. "No signs of anything from the past to worry about. You both should be very pleased." Yvonne took Jonah's hand and smiled at him. "The cervix is now at two fingers, and that is a significant change from two weeks ago, when it was one finger. I would say that the baby would like to make its entrance into the world in the next few days. Within the next week." He smiled.

"Every indication is that we are through the difficult time, everyone is healthy, and you may as well get on with delivering that baby. You've been taking the Lamaze classes, so you know about the water breaking, the onset of contractions, bloody show . . . Know it rather better than I do myself at this point, I suspect. Do call in when you have anything to report."

"Thank you, Doctor, I will," Yvonne said, standing.

"And now, Yvonne, if I may borrow your husband for a few moments, *I* have a question for him. Something of a personal nature—to do with flying."

"That's right. You were in the RAF, weren't you? . . . Doctor, you're not going to talk about me? Just assure me of that."

"Yvonne, I assure you of that. You have my word of honor."

"Well, then . . . Thank you, Doctor. Jonah, I'll wait in the car."

When the door was closed Dr. Glynn reseated himself. "Sit down, Jonah. I want to talk to you for a moment as *your* doctor. Your flight surgeon, if you will."

Jonah sat down.

"Jonah, you've been coming in with your wife regularly now the past few weeks. I must say your appearance isn't very good. Any symptoms, any physical symptoms?"

"No."

"I thought not. Now I will tell you what I surmise, what I hazard, and you may do with it what you will. I surmise you are under a good deal of emotional stress. I do not know its origins, I do not know its causes, and, in any event, I am not qualified as a psychiatrist. I remember, during the war, the worst thing I ever saw. And I remember the look of other people who saw it—"

"What was that, Doc? the worst thing you saw?"

Dr. Glynn took off his glasses. "I suppose it was the context which made it so terrible. A perfectly beautiful day, clear, blue sky, chaps coming home, runway before them, safe, you know . . ." He swiveled in his chair and was looking away from Jonah toward the lines of sunlight in the Venetian blinds behind him. "I was flying a Wellington. I liked them. Canvas-covered, geodetic construction. The Wellington was a good ship, most responsive; you could even sideslip a Wellington. This was in Italy. Late afternoon takeoff from my own base to go over to an American base. To air-test a Wellington. Bright, sunlit late afternoon, almost cloudless, like joyhopping at home, ended in worst thing I'd ever seen. Probably because of the peace of the sky. Let me see. My Wellington was directed into a returning file of American B-24's, and I recall that when I touched down I was glad of the day and even glad to be flying, but the chap in the tower told me clearly, just as I touched down on the grass, chap said, 'Keep that goddamn cloth bomber rolling"—so hardpressed were they, Jonah, to land the returning B-24's. Got myself off the runway and out of interference and I faced the approach end of the runway till such time as I might taxi back, take off, and return home. Clear blue sky, sunlit, watching the aircraft land, in file, one after the other. Then a B-24, downwind, stopped flying and spun into the ground. A moment from arrival. On a bright, sunlit afternoon. American crew. All perished . . ."

He turned back to Jonah but did not seem to be looking at Jonah until he put his glasses back on. "I remember the look of other people who saw it. I remember the look of people who had to fly and who . . . let us say, people who were losing their confidence. People who were fighting great emotional beasts within themselves . . . If you recognize anything of what I'm saying, Jonah, I would be glad to talk with you. As your physician, as your flight surgeon, as a fellow who was once a pilot himself—as a friend."

"You flew again?"

"Oh, yes. Had to, didn't we?"

"Thank you . . . Thank you, Llewellyn."

"You *will* bear it in mind. What I've said?"

"Yes."

"Now go home with that splendid wife of yours and have a whiskey soda and practice all those breathing techniques."

IOI

For the first time in her life Adele was drinking alone.

Not that she hadn't ever had a drink alone—but that had been all it had ever been, a drink. When she had gotten to her room after a terribly cold day of skiing she might have a shot of straight whiskey to begin warming herself before she took a shower. After a long time on instruments or after a particularly demanding flight she might come home to her apartment and have the single drink of straight whiskey.

But now she was drinking alone, rather steadily. She had come back to her apartment in midafternoon. She had made a statement for the police, spent some time on the phone with D.G.'s mother several times during the day and of course last night had "seen to things at your end" as D.G.'s mother, who could not be bothered to come up herself, had asked her to do. She had seen to the legal requirements relative to the interstate shipment of a deceased human being. She had identified D.G. *three* times, for some reason. They had slid him out of a wall and pulled a cover back and asked her who he was. She had almost screamed the second and third times.

She had been drinking bourbon and water since about four o'clock in the afternoon. It was now eight and she was just about even, just about balanced inside herself. George had called, but she had not been able to talk to him for long. She'd been overtaken by terrible nausea and had to hang up and go to the bathroom and throw up. Just as if George was going to get killed for loving her. Just as if D.G.'s death were her doing and George would get done too, and soon, for loving her. She had called George back and they had talked for a few minutes; then she'd said she was going to bed. But instead she had gone back to drinking.

She made another drink, a very strong one, half water and half bourbon, and this one soothed her, she could feel the calmness in her. If only D.G. could have stayed in the air, Adele thought. That moment in the aircraft, he had been away from his whole life then, away and calm. The moment haunted her. That day with me, she thought, if only D.G. could have stayed in the air. He would have had that moment of calm forever. But he had had to come down. If he could have just stayed in the air, Adele thought, seeing herself rise into the air, the airplane lifting her, the bright white clouds and even the blue sky coming down at her as she held the airplane in a powerful climb and rose away from the earth, not seeing the earth at all, but rising toward the cool, pure blue sky . . .

When she went to bed then, she continued to rise. She passed above the clouds. The sky darkened and then turned black. She climbed toward the stars and was, for a few minutes in that flight, calm, until her dreams began.

102

When Jonah drove to the airport in the morning, the ground-lying mists in the low places were already burning off. The air was sweet, the sky bright. A field of knee-high corn looked glossy. There was the smell of pine when he left the main road for the narrower road to the airport. A cheerful day, a hopeful day; but Jonah was marking it as probably one of the last days in which he would be a full-time professional pilot. He had called Barney Raab the night before and asked him if he could see him, briefly, first thing in the morning. The airport road went by Barney's electronics plant, a low modern building with a lot of long, narrow glass windows, like marching soldiers in a phalanx. And, Jonah thought, if I'm *lucky* I'll become one of those soldiers. He slammed his car door, but then was afraid that maybe he couldn't *get* another kind of job and that no matter what he did he had, through his own self-indulgence—the years of flying just because he loved it—condemned the baby, this new life, to the edges of poverty, and if not quite that, to a sort of social deprivation in which his own child would never, as a child and as a youngster and as an adolescent, enjoy the same opportunities as his friends.

Jonah and Barney chatted a bit, and then Jonah asked for a job.

"Jonah, we don't have a company pilot," Barney said. "You know that. If I needed one, I'd come to you first off."

"I'm not asking for a job as a pilot. I'm asking for a job."

Barney showed no reaction save for a few seconds of silence. "Jonah, the only position we're looking to fill right now is vice-president in charge of production—and I don't think you're equipped for that. Oh, of course, there's always stuff on the assembly line, but—"

"I'm looking for anything, Barney. As long as I can learn a new trade and move up as I master it. If I could start out just soldering transistors, or whatever you do, and have the opportunity to move on to—"

"Jonah, you through with flying? Is that what you're talking about?"

"Barney, this is the simple thing. You take all the hours I put in flying for Ev, working in the office, sitting around on my ass in the office when the weather's down, you take all that, and like Yvonne says, I don't make as much per hour as one of Barney Raab's janitors."

"But, Christ, you love it. The flying part of it."

"It doesn't make me enough money, Barney. I just need a bigger pay-check. No matter what I do."

"What do you need, two-fifty? Three hundred? Could you settle for less to start with?"

"Barney, I make a hundred and fifty dollars a week."

"What about a percentage of the lessons? Don't you get—"

"There is no *what about.* I make one-fifty a week, period. Whether I work eight hours a day or fifteen."

Barney sighed and looked out the window. He continued to look out the window as he said, "Jonah, make a date with my personnel man. He'll find out what you can do. Then we'll see. We'll find you something."

"Thanks," Jonah said, and stood up. He was going to shake Barney's hand, but Barney had swung around and was looking out the window.

"Shit," Barney said.

103

There was Mrs. Yancey's house.

Jonah passed it so often, but never regarded it. Virgil Yancey had had the house built back when he and Falun and Ev had started Yancey Flying Service, back when there had been only a grass runway here. Yancey had built the house with rumrunning money, people said, had started the flight service, his share of it, with rumrunning money, people said. Virgil Yancey. The hero. One of the most innovative single-engine pilots who ever lived, people said.

And it was that man's widow who could let him in or keep him out of Yancey Flying Service. It was *her* decision whether he could continue to fly professionally and make a living for himself and Yvonne and the baby. But, Jonah realized, he had never thought of asking Mrs. Yancey directly to let him in—as if to do so he would have had to push aside the ghost of Virgil Yancey.

Well, for Christsake, Virgil Yancey was dead. His only active partner, Everett Goodsom, had done nothing for Jonah. Jonah felt unsure of himself—it was not his kind of thing at all—but he decided to call Mrs. Yancey. One of his motives for doing so surprised him—the unborn child, because of whom he would struggle with whatever he had to struggle in order to remain Jonah Jaquith, the father he wanted for his soon-to-be-born child.

When Jonah got to the airport and parked his car, he went to the outdoor telephone booth and looked up Mrs. Yancey's number and called her. "This is Jonah Jaquith, Mrs. Yancey."

"Why, Jonah Jaquith. You're well, I trust."

"Yes, ma'am, and you?"

"And your pretty wife. I hear she's expecting very soon now."

"Yes, ma'am."

"Well now, Jonah, I know you didn't call to pass the time of day with me. What is it you want?"

"Mrs. Yancey, I'd like to call on you. This afternoon, if I might."

"Jonah, I can't imagine what you'd want to call on an old lady like me for." Her voice fell to flatness. "I can't."

"Mrs. Yancey, there's something I have to ask you about."

"Is it about Virgil?"

"No, ma'am, it isn't."

"I will *not* discuss Virgil. There have been *so* many people after me all these years. Writers from New York. Newspaper people there at the beginning. Someone from television called just the other day. They wanted me to talk about how Virgil was a hero, the way he died. Wouldn't do it."

"No, ma'am. I want to ask you about something else."

She was silent for a number of seconds, and then she said, "Jonah Jaquith, I can't imagine what you want to ask *me* about, but I'll be here this afternoon. Any time it suits you to come by, I'll be here. I am always here."

106

Hilary saw his instructor waiting out by the airplane. Jonah standing out there. Preoccupied.

Hilary was late. A lateness of his own designing. He could have been on time, but he had found reasons, occupations, things to be done at the playhouse—so that he was late.

He had come down. If he could have just stayed up. If Jonah had just let him fly yesterday before he came down. He had been so *up* after that evening with Laura and her call yesterday morning. He could have handled *anything* then, including flying an airplane by himself, with no one there to help him out if he made a mistake. There had been no self-doubt, none of that stuff. Then Jonah couldn't make time for him. Then the director had started pulling him down. Then he had felt as if just the minutes of the day going by had been bringing him down. *If I could have just stayed up . . .*

He did three landings niftily, just as he knew he would. He could have allowed himself to screw up, but he didn't. Not even when Jonah threw emergencies at him. He *wanted* to screw up, the fear in him wanted to screw up, and he wanted to give in to the fear, part of him did, but his pride in what he could now do, take off and land an airplane by himself, was just a little bit greater than the desperate fear for bodily survival that tried to grab hold of him and pull him down even further.

The engine running, the prop turning, the airplane braked on the taxiway just short of runway Two-zero, Jonah popped open the door, slid out, and hopped off the wing. Holding the door against the prop wash Jonah said, "Okay, Hilary old sport, go kill yourself if you want to," and then slammed the door tight and walked away. So quick, Hilary thought. And here he sat alone. Supposed to fly an airplane by himself. And bring it back safely to earth. With him as its pilot and with *him* as its mortal passenger.

He sat alone with the sound of the engine, the feel of the airplane around him, the mechanical thrills running through it. The silence since Jonah had left, the sense of aloneness was severe. So much could go wrong. He was sweating and his fingers shook.

"But *if* you can fly an airplane, you'll be grown up, in charge. That's what you told yourself." He heard his thoughts back in his room that cold New Year's Eve night. *You will be* in control. *In control of every aspect of your life. That's what being a pilot is. There will be nothing you'll be afraid of any*

*more if you're a pilot. How could there be? Pilots are not afraid . . . That's
what being a pilot is, being in control . . .*

He let the toebrakes go. His upper arms were trembling now.

"Check the instruments, you goddamn fool." He looked them over. "The
oil is low, isn't the oil low? Forget it, you going to stop now?" He had a
feeling of sickness, maybe he wasn't well enough—but he had allowed the
airplane to move out on the runway. He pushed the throttle in slightly, got
the prop spinning fast enough to turn the airplane. "Line it up, line it up,"
he said to himself, all his words aloud, as if he were his own instructor,
guiding himself through, preventing mistakes. "You fucker, you forgot to
check for traffic!" He waited for the impact of an airplane settling on his.
But there was only the sound of his own engine, light blue sky ahead,
terrible heat . . . The airplane was moving in a very slow taxi down the
centerline of the runway.

Hilary put the power all the way on. "Keep it straight with the rudders.
Left rudder to compensate for torque, too much, c'mon, you fucker, keep
it lined up!" There were some bounces, some unexpected bounces, and the
runway stripe wove back and forth and then the bounces disappeared and
the centerline straightened out and he was easing back on the yoke and he
felt himself being *lifted* into the air and it thrilled him so that he cried out.

"Steady now, steady. Keep the climb, keep the airspeed right on eighty-
five. You forgot to look at the *airspeed* before you took off. *Dumb,
dumb* . . ." The airplane *felt* lighter, *rose* more quickly—and Hilary became
mindful of the empty seat next to him.

At precisely eight hundred feet above the field he pulled back power,
maintained the altitude, and swung the nose neatly across the horizon and
back into the landing pattern. It was quiet and cool now. He shook, but not
with fear. *He was flying an airplane.*

Setting up for the landing approach, he pulled back on power. It felt as
if the airplane were dropping away beneath him. He checked the altimeter,
but he was almost at the precise altitude he should be. He checked for traffic.
Nothing around. He turned base, started down the incline, *"Too steep, too
steep,"* it felt awfully fast, but his approach speed was nearly what it should
be, and he pulled back on the angle a little till the airspeed fell off, but then
it fell off too much, red light of the stall-warner blinked on and off and he
felt the aircraft begin to sink away from him softly and he pushed the nose
down, picked up speed, turned sharply into final approach and aimed down
the runway, trying to look at the far end of the runway the way Jonah had
said, but hardly able to keep his eyes away from the near end, holding the
airplane *off, off,* but wanting to get it *down,* and then he *hit,* a hard jolt,
is the landing gear still there, is it? but the airplane moving docilely forward
and he put full power on again, Jonah had said go around three times, yes,

but only if he signals to—Hilary looked out the window, couldn't see Jonah, concentrated on the takeoff, all that power getting ready to pull him into the sky again—

"Cornwall unicom, this is—"

The voice from the cabin speaker was so startling that Hilary jumped, his shoulders started up. He was amazed to see he was still going down the runway without deviation.

Three times around, Jonah had said.

Hilary lifted the nose and found he was flying again, looking at nothing but soft blue sky and taking himself there. *In control.*

Hilary jumped down from the wing and surprised himself by hugging Jonah. "I did it!" he said. "I can goddamn well do it. I can do *anything!*"

In the office Ev and Adele congratulated Hilary.

Jonah signed his logbook and endorsed his student certificate for solo flight. "Theoretically you can go flying by yourself any time you want to now. But I tell you when. And it's local flight only. I haven't endorsed you for cross-country flight." He handed the certificate to Hilary. "You realize this does not permit you to carry a passenger."

Hilary nodded, leaving, going to his car. He had done it. He had done it himself. He was alive. He could do anything.

105

Mrs. Yancey poured tea from an old china teapot. She had put the preparation of the tea between herself and Jonah's attempt to talk with her. They were seated in what she had told him had been Virgil Yancey's den. A helmeted and scarfed Virgil Yancey grinned down at them. Yancey was standing in front of a huge radial engine. There was nothing but sky above the man and the blunt thrusting nose of the airplane behind him. Jonah accepted the cup of tea and a slice of raisin toast.

"Not the usual fare of a flying man, I know," said Mrs. Yancey. "Virgil himself preferred bourbon, but *I* prefer not to serve it."

"I appreciate your fixing all this, but it wasn't necessary."

"Nonsense. Now I suppose I must hear you out, Jonah. I don't want to. I don't like to discuss business. Not at all. But go ahead, go ahead."

"What I was trying to get at, Mrs. Yancey, is that Yancey Flying Service isn't a manufacturing company. It's a *service.* And, as far as I can see, I'm just about the only one providing it."

"Yes. Yes, I know, Jonah. I know you're doing most of the flying."

"I'm *carrying* Yancey Flying Service, Mrs. Yancey."

"Yes, yes . . ." She sighed. "I'm sure you're right, Jonah. But then, you're only doing what you're being paid for, isn't that right?"

"No. I'm not being paid enough for what I'm doing. Not nearly."

"I'm sorry to hear that, Jonah. Perhaps if you spoke to Ev—"

"I did. Ev says it's all up to you."

"Ah."

She looked at him, and then Jonah saw, as she quickly looked away, that she appeared quite frail suddenly and as if something had frightened her. She was looking at the picture of Virgil Yancey.

"What was it Everett said is all up to me?" She was still looking at the picture.

"I'd like to be part of the business. I'd like to make decisions in how it's run and take my pay in a share of the profits. Believe me, Mrs. Yancey, Ev is doing nothing with that business and it could be growing, you have no idea—"

"Ev said it was my decision?"

"Yes, ma'am."

"Then the answer has to be no." She stood up.

"But, Mrs. Yancey—"

"I have no choice. I'm sure Everett Goodsom will confirm that I have no choice."

"Mrs. Yancey—"

She had gone to the door with quickness and held it open now, the late afternoon sun and the outside air a rush of heat and brightness in the little dark hallway.

"Now I must excuse myself. I am most tired, Jonah."

"Mrs. Yancey, after all the work I've done for you, I think—"

"I am most tired, Jonah."

She stared at him with her age, the child's vulnerable eyes in the lined skin, and Jonah allowed himself to be cut off, sent outside. *Bitch,* he thought. Goddamn old *bitch.*

She had not been truthful with Jonah and it troubled Mrs. Yancey badly. But what would it cost her if she *were* truthful? She had no savings. All she had was the income from Yancey Flying Service.

Mrs. Yancey stood inside the door she had just closed on Jonah. She was trembling. Fingers, hands, arms, shoulders—all trembling. She remained there in the hallway and looked into the living room—the living room in which she took such pride. Where she had done so much entertaining, entertaining for *Yancey,* entertaining men like Jonah who cared only about flying and cared nothing about the furniture on which they sat, the pictures that hung on the walls, the sounds which might be produced from the piano

. . . But she had loved those men, she had to admit, loved them for Yancey's sake. Even when they spilled their drinks on the Persian rug or overwhelmed the house with the smell of their cigars so that it took a week of open windows before the stench was gone . . .

The living room. There were dust covers on the furniture now. Even on the piano. Heavy white clothes. It's like my life, she thought, dust covers on most of it now . . . waiting for a mover. The curtains were drawn, and the covered furniture also looked to her like round white ghosts asleep in the darkness. Mounds of somnolent white ghosts. Ghosts of what? She shrugged. Sometimes they were like living things to her, resting, asleep, after a wonderful party.

She went to remove the tea service from Yancey's den and looked at the picture of Yancey at the 1948 Cooper Cup races. That huge radial engine and four-bladed propeller behind him. His old cloth helmet rolled in a ball in his huge hand, the enormous grin on his face. A year before he died. His mouth was grinning, Mrs. Yancey thought, but she could see plainly that his eyes were not smiling. He had almost killed himself later that day, too. She looked at the eyes, trying once again to estimate how much alcohol was in him when the picture had been taken. Around the house she had been able to tell by his behavior. But she had not gone out to the Cooper Cup Races that year, hadn't been with him the day the picture had been taken.

She thought of Yancey and Ev and Falun Aigborg and Jonah. All they care about is flying, those men. Let them get into an airplane and get into the air and they worried about nothing.

Though, finally, that had not been true for Yancey. And if she understood him, probably never had been true for him. Yancey had been afraid of flying. She was sure of it. As his fear grew his appetite for alcohol grew with it. Or vice versa. It made no difference. He finally had killed himself. He was a hero for dying the way he did. Taking off in fine visibility—bright, clear, summer weather—to fetch blood from Boston for a child. He had run into Mount Monadnock head on. *Impacted* was the word the accident investigators had used. But she had known as he stood in the doorway, about to go, so *angry* and so helpless—she had known he was thinking of doing away with himself. It would be another time, not the first. She had tired of begging him not to fly when he was filled with alcohol, when he had been yelling at her and at the world . . .

No, Jonah *wasn't* like that at all. Flying was not *all* he cared about. He so obviously loved his wife and was so filled with love waiting to be given to the baby. She wondered if Jonah had had time to get home yet. She couldn't remember what time he had left, but it was getting on dusk now; there was blue on everything outside the windows.

She looked up Jonah's number, but did not dial.

She was thinking about what had happened. Not why it had happened
—she could never satisfy herself about that—but just what had happened.
Yancey had gotten so he wasn't much good for anything. He kept thinking
that she was even *saying* that to him, but no, it had always been him saying
it to himself; she had loved him too much to have ever said that, even when
he had gotten not much good for anything. Not even flying. Not commercial
flying, anyway, where there were passengers or students involved and Ev
wouldn't let him do it. Oh, he always flew. But he was boozed. So he'd gone
to racing. Huge new ships every year or two. Selling pieces of his major
interest in the business to Ev, nobody knowing where *Ev,* for heaven's sake,
got the money, except that he had it, to pay for buying most of Virgil's
interest in the business. Got it, she had learned years later, borrowing
money over and over from the bank—living in hock, Ev had once said, like
an animal living inside bars.

. . . But, Virgil. I will put all of that away, she thought. I will cover it
with dust covers and not disturb it again. After *this.* If they'll let me.

She dialed Jonah's number. To tell him the truth.

106

When Perry got home at eleven the house was as dark as the night around
it. On the phone the night before, Laura had said that she was going to be
out for the evening this evening. She had forgotten to leave a light on for
him. Or for herself, for that matter.

Perry liked coming into the silence of the place. It was friendlier that way,
friendlier than with Laura in it. Still, he was also somewhat annoyed at her
for not being there. I wish I could make up my mind about her, what I really
feel about her, Perry thought, but it was not a thought he paid much
attention to, it was gone as quickly as it had come to him. It was a thought
he had often.

Laura had said that she was going to a play at the playhouse this evening
and that she had been asked to stay afterwards for a cast party. She had
not suggested that he come out there and join her for the party. That was
what was annoying him.

She would probably come home high. She did a lot more drinking than
he remembered her doing before they were married. The trouble with her
being high was that her happiness could so quickly turn to anger, to bitter-
ness, and most recently to fury at the *isolation he* had imposed on *her.*

Inside the house he turned on a light in the kitchen, one in the hallway,
and two lamps in the living room. As the room appeared around him he

thought *There,* now I'm home. But he did not go on into the bedroom. He was surprised to find that, standing there on the living-room rug, he had not put his suitcase down. His flight bag was on the floor beside him. Still he didn't put the suitcase down. As he held on to it he felt he was holding on to something else as well.

When he heard Laura's car approaching and saw the lights illuminate the front living-room windows he was sitting in the living room. He had his uniform jacket on—the four gold rings still very bright from their newness —and had not even loosened his tie; this puzzled him. Usually he showered and changed when he got home. When it was this late, he just put on pajamas. He had gotten himself a beer, but he hadn't drunk much of it. He looked at his watch. Ten after one. What had he been thinking about? He didn't know. Not exactly. There had been so many things. Girls he had met in New York, his line check with King Kahn, the pleasantness of being with happily married couples, some orange groves he had once seen in Florida, the fireside at a ski lodge where he and a girlfriend had once stayed, a New Year's Eve party he had given in this house just before he met Laura . . .

The first thing she did was slam the door to the kitchen. Then she came straight to the living room. She moved to the center of the room and looked at him. He could not make out her expression. Anger, yes. Strong anger. But with it—contempt? hatred?

"What—*what* have you been telling people?"

"What?"

"That we're getting a *divorce.* Have you been telling people that we're getting a divorce?"

"Telling who?"

"Florence Tuttle called me this afternoon. To commiserate. To tell me how sorry she was. That things hadn't worked out for us." She lit a cigarette and stared at Perry.

Oh, God, Perry was thinking. The Tuttles were the other couple he had gone out to dinner with and to the Saturday-night party with when he had just recently stayed with the McCallies. The Tuttle woman had said she *thought* she had known Laura—she had been a stew with her sometime.

"You've been telling people that we're getting a *divorce! Haven't* you? It wasn't the first time Flo had heard it. You've been telling people we're getting a divorce!"

He wanted to say, Aren't we? but checked himself. For no reason he could think of he found he was afraid to break with Laura. "No, of course we're not," he said.

"Why did you *say* it? Why did you *tell* people that?"

If he made any motion at all he thought she would strike him, claw him, try to tear him apart.

"I'm a good wife. I am! I am!"

Perry stood up slowly.

"You told people we're *getting a divorce!*"

"I didn't mean it. I just said it."

"You're *crazy.*" She went into the bedroom.

He stood there. He looked at the suitcase.

He *had* meant it. About the divorce. It was, at any rate, what he wanted. God, yes, I'm crazy, Perry thought. I've got to be crazy or something like it to be married to Laura.

He was still looking at the suitcase. He thought of picking it up and walking out. But then he left it where it was, only looked at it, and then looked away. It was like entering the first turbulence of a front. *I'm entering the reality of divorce,* Perry thought. He listened to what she had said, what they had said, once again. He was still standing in the living room. He felt as if he had not been in this room for weeks or months. Now he saw it, saw the room. He was really in it. He picked up the suitcase and the flight bag and walked out.

She caught him as he was putting the bags in his car.

"What do you mean by leaving me? What do you mean?" she screamed at him. He was very glad they didn't have neighbors.

He let the Saab's lid fall shut. It sounded like a grunt in the darkness.

"I'll take it from you!" She pointed at the house. "I'll take *all* this from you."

"But you don't want it. You don't want to live here."

"But you love it, and that's why I'll take it from you. You're not going to leave me. When *I* decide to leave, *that's* when this marriage will be over."

"I'm leaving, Laura."

She smiled at him. "No, no, you're not. Because if you do, believe me, it will cost you everything you love, all of this that you've worked so hard for so many years, as you keep telling me. All the work you've put in here being an electrician and a carpenter and all that, all that work. Are you going to let me have that? Just so you can get a divorce from me?"

"What are you going to do with it?"

She smiled at him. "Sell it."

"I'll buy it from you, Laura. I'll buy your share."

"No, you won't. Because I'm going to get the whole thing. If you leave me."

"I *am* leaving you, Laura," he said quietly. "Just now I don't even feel angry at you. Whatever the lawyers work out . . . we'll see what that is."

"You can't leave me!"

She took him by his shoulders and tried to shake him. When he didn't move, she slapped him as hard as she could.

He nodded at her and got into the car.

She came to the window. "I'll tell you something," she said, her voice low now, intense, but not screaming. "I have someone else. And you're not going to be very happy about it when you hear who it is."

He started the car.

"Don't you drive away from me! You hear me out! I'm holding on to this car till you hear me out. Unless you want to drag me down the road. The judge will like that." He didn't put the car in gear. "The person who is going to have me—and this house, if he wants, this house with all your work in it . . . the person . . . he's a pilot."

"What's his name?"

"Oh, no, no, my darling. Why would I give you information like that? No, no. But I'll tell you what I've decided to do. I've decided to go flying with him. He asked me just this afternoon. I think I'll go flying with him. Do you realize you and I have never gone flying together?"

"You never wanted to."

"That is *a lie!*"

"You always had excuses."

"There was always a *reason.* Can't you understand! The whole world's schedule can't fit yours!"

"So long, Laura. Happy landings."

"You bastard! You bastard!"

But she had let go of the car.

He backed it away from the house and turned it as he had thousands of times. This time maybe not coming back. Except to get clothes. The inside of the Saab had always reminded him of the inside of a four-seat lightplane. The dashboard looked a little like an instrument panel, and the emergency brake was between the seats the way the flap handle in a lightplane often was. The size of the interior was just that of a lightplane. As his hand went up to change gears he saw the gold rings on his sleeve again. Captain, my captain, he thought, smiling in his own company. Yes, indeed, I am the captain of my ship . . .

He was sorry he had said *Happy landings* to her. Sorry he had said it in the way he had said it . . . He felt miserable driving away. But it was because he was leaving what he had worked so hard on—the house—not because he was leaving Laura. Happy landings to us all, he thought.

[273]

107

Adele watched Zero-nine Whiskey, Ben's Cherokee, lift off Runway Two-zero and begin a steep climb. She would have known that George was doing the flying even if she hadn't seen Ben give him the left-hand seat. Since he had begun flying Zero-nine Whiskey a few days before, George had overdone everything with it, been precipitous in all his maneuvers, taking off steeply and landing steeply, fast and hot. It seemed more as if he were trying to dominate the lightplane rather than fly it.

Ben was in the right-hand seat and Randy Detwiler was in the back seat. They were going to western Pennsylvania to spend the weekend with George's friend from college, Cornelius McConnell, the aircraft-company vice-president.

The Cherokee became a nick in the sky and then dissolved in the milky blue as Adele watched. Some huge weather system was moving in, something that was supposed to be hot and stagnant and oppressive. It had been lying over the Midwest and now was moving slowly into the east, its hindside still out in the Midwest. She had seen the satellite picture on the morning news. They were gone, both of them, Ben and George, and she felt some odd relief; it made her feel better inside herself. Since D.G.'s death she had felt dirty, contaminated, and as if she could contaminate others. After that first night when she had drunk so much, she had partially come out of the horror. Even the stain at the bottom of the stairs, which was D.G.'s, did not horrify her so much when she passed it, coming down from her apartment or going back to it. She had, in fact, she thought, gained some objectivity about herself and George and Ben. She had seen George's *need* —and *that* had been what she had reacted to emotionally. He had *needed* her, and that had made her feel loved and secure, and so she had supposed she loved George. And maybe she did—but it was his need for her that she most loved, loved better than George himself, and that just wasn't right. And then what she had wanted most in those early morning hours after D.G.'s death, as she'd sat by her window and cried a little and saw the sky begin to lighten and turn blue, what she had wanted *most* then, and again on that afternoon when she had come home and started drinking, was simply to call Ben and go to his house and lie down next to him and have him hold her. It was plain, really. *I love Ben and that's it.* But she would not allow herself to go to him. It would just be Ben having everything his own way.

She walked out on the field. Forty-nine Pop, the other Cherokee trainer, was sitting there with its door open, key in the ignition. She didn't even think about it—she locked the door and started up and taxied out short of the runway. She went through the runup procedures without much noticing. She ran the engine up, but a few seconds later she couldn't tell herself what the gauges had indicated in the runup. She didn't much care. She checked for traffic, more or less, and moved out on the runway. Her long fingers took the knob of the throttle and gently advanced it to full power. She lifted off and climbed rather steeply, but didn't much notice that either. She continued the steep climb. She made procedure turns out of the pattern and maintained the climb. She climbed and climbed. The air began to get cooler. She was at six thousand feet. She hadn't realized that she had climbed so high. The coolness of the air was soothing. She no longer felt so dirty. She continued the slow, steep climb.

108

"Jonah, where *the Christ* have you been!"

Jonah ignored Ev and went to his own desk. He sat at it and began to go through papers. The secretary was writing out bills with a pen.

"Jonah, you hear me? I want an explanation. You realize you failed to show up for two students? Not to mention a charter. You don't call in—now Adele's off somewhere in Four-nine Pop and *she* left a student here and I can't even raise her on the radio. What the fuck's *going on* with you people?"

Jonah continued the slow examination of the contents of his desk.

"Jonah, I'm speaking to you. *Where the Christ have you been?*"

"Looking for work."

"You've *got* work, God damn it. You missed two students and a charter!"

"I'm looking for work that'll pay me a salary I can live on. Me and Yvonne and the baby."

"Well, I've been thinking about that."

"Good, Ev, it'll give you something to do with yourself. Not that I haven't got a suggestion for you. Go fuck yourself, Ev, that's my suggestion for you."

"You asshole, you watch your language!"

"I think, gentlemen, I'll go to the little girls' room," the secretary said and stood up.

"Pardon, Lucy," Jonah said. "I was just thinking out loud."

She left the room and Jonah looked at Ev, the two of them alone.

"Now what *is* this shit, Jonah? You gave me till the baby is born."

"You thought I'd stick with it anyway, didn't you? You thought I couldn't bear to leave flying. You figured you'd offer me a ten-dollar raise or something like that, didn't you? And you figured I'd be glad to take it and keep flying? Didn't you!"

Ev was silent. Finally he said, "I considered a number of possibilities, Jonah."

Jonah grinned at him. "You did. *You* considered the possibilities."

Ev started to speak and then stopped.

"You *own* this fucking operation, Ev."

Ev looked away. "Me and Geraldine Yancey."

"No. *You* own it, Ev. Mrs. Yancey has a part interest in it. A very small part interest. I think it's about ten percent."

"Where did you get *that* idea?"

"From Mrs. Yancey."

"You talked to Mrs. Yancey?"

"I damn well did. You kept promising to do it, promising to do it . . . So I did it myself. What I should've done to begin with."

"I don't know if I can explain this."

"Probably not. Don't try." Jonah laughed. "You *shit.* You poor, miserable *shit.* That's what you are, Ev. A turd on the road. A turd on the road of life. And I happened to step on it and come up stinking. I do wax poetic, do I not, Ev? But there you are. The *scientific* evaluation of you is the same. Upon close analysis you come up a shit."

"You watch—"

"Not only a shit, but a liar—"

"*Jonah*—"

"A *longtime* liar, Ev. All this time you've been living off *my* sweat—"

"And my money, you asshole. My money that I had to scrounge and suffer for, the nights I spent wondering whether I'd be foreclosed or not when a loan payment was due. And sweating myself pissless wondering if the *weather* was going to be *flyable* the next day. So *I* could earn a few bucks and hold the bank off one more day. *You* walk in here and you just have fun flying the airplanes, like there was no other worry in the world—"

"I know there are other worries in the world now, Ev."

"Do you? Like meeting payrolls and insurance payments and town taxes and paying for new equipment and keeping the everlasting goddamned bank loans going? Do you? Do you know how many days a year there's no flying here, do you?"

"About twenty-five percent."

"Goddamn right. Almost a hundred days a year when even the airlines cancel sometimes during the day. I sit here on those days—sometimes you go home—"

"Usually I'm sitting right here with you, Ev."

"I *sit* here on those days and all I can think about is how quickly the money—the money can—can *dissipate,* when it's not being used, all this equipment . . ."

Jonah said, quietly, "What money, Ev?"

Ev looked at him angrily. "Who the shit cares?"

"All the money you've stockpiled?"

"It's there to keep the goddamn banks and insurance companies and every other fucking leach off my ass!"

Jonah sighed and sat back and toyed with a Jeppesen plotter he had found in his desk. "Okay, we've got that settled," he said, looking at the lines and numbers on the plotter. "You've got the money. You've got the operation."

Ev went over to the window and paid attention to the sky.

"There's a big system moving in," he said.

"Cut the shit," Jonah said. They were both speaking quietly now.

"No, this is really something."

"I know. I've been following it."

"I remember the last time we got one of these. A couple of good people ended up in the woods. Fuel starvation. Couldn't get down and ran out of fuel and went down. Suckers' weather . . ."

"Cut the shit, Ev." There was no rancor in his words.

"I started to say before, I *think* I started to say before . . . it's hard, Jonah." Ev was looking out at the sky. "I give you part of the business, I give up part of myself. Part of me just dies right there. I understand that. I *understand* what I feel. But I won't do it. You have no right to come in here and ask for part of something you didn't make, didn't put the struggle into, didn't—"

"I did all those things, Ev. For—what is it? . . . Seventeen years now. You're right, Ev. When I started I was young and gay. All I wanted to do was fly. So *I* paid for my flying, even though you paid me a salary every week, *I* paid for my flying. Isn't that so?"

Ev was studying the sky.

"Dr. Glynn tells me the baby's going to be born this week. I told you I'd work for you till then. Till the baby's born. And I will. But I had to take off today to get started on finding other work. I didn't want to give up either. On my life. But I did. I finally convinced myself flying really isn't all my life. Even if it is."

Ev was silent.

Jonah went over to the secretary's appointment calendar. He looked at it. He said, "I'll be in tomorrow when I'm supposed to be. I've got some students and a charter and a scenic. I'll take care of it all. You don't have to pay me for today. I don't expect you to."

Ev was still silent and looking at the milking-over sky when Jonah left to go home.

109

Ben and George and Randy had gotten to Burning Cabin (marked *private* on the airchart) Friday and it was now Monday morning. They had planned to have been off and on their way back to Cornwall early on Sunday afternoon, but Cornwall, like most of the airports in New England, had been simply unapproachable. As it still was.

Ben lay by the swimming pool, content to be where he was, glad for an excuse not to leave. He had gotten the weather that morning when he'd gotten up at eight, and he had gotten it again at ten, though the man who had given him the briefing to begin with had said there might not be any change for twenty-four hours. But George couldn't accept that—the constancy of the weather system and its slowness to move at all. George was back inside talking to the flight service station or maybe U.S. Weather Bureau Aviation Weather. Ben himself had spoken to both. Randy jumped into the water, paddled to the center, swam back, and got out again.

If you had to be weathered in, Burning Cabin was the sort of place to do it in, Ben thought. Though the weather around Burning Cabin was fine. They were in western Pennsylvania, south and east of Youngstown, Ohio. The sky was clear, the air still, gentle with summer, and buzzing. It was the weather to the east that was terrible. Not that anyone on the ground who wasn't a pilot or a meterologist would have thought so. It would seem just hot and hazy and humid. Nothing dramatic going on. A peaceful air mass—peaceful, passive, and deadly, like quicksand.

If George didn't come back and announce that the sky had parted, like the Red Sea, all the way to Cornwall, Ben was going to go in and ask the kitchen for one of the remarkable rum punches they produced there. And then he was going to come back and lie by the pool and think about the young lady who had shared his bed for two nights. A lawyer, who had questioned George rather severely, Ben thought, she had known Ben's work well and that had served as if they had already had a long personal acquaintance. They had stayed up late that first night, alone, drinking and dancing in the music library, and then they had gone to bed. She was gone now, as was Corny McConnell, their host, and the other visitors—a U.S. senator, an Air Force general, a magazine publisher, a Texas oil man and his wife, some others, mostly men, though there were a few brilliantly beautiful and mostly talkless women . . . The senator had arrived by helicopter, the general in a prop-driven Air Force trainer he piloted himself. The rest had come by car. The white Cherokee was tied down alone out on the long grass runway that was really an extension of the golf course. It was difficult to tell where the golf course ended and anything else began. There was not an untended blade of grass on the whole estate, and there were two hundred acres here, Ben had been told. There was a lodge and a few outbuildings near it, and no other building from horizon to horizon. Nor any burnt cabin.

Ben turned over. "Randy, how'd you like to stay here forever?"

Randy thought about it. "No, I guess not."

"Well, come to think about it," Ben said, "I can see your point."

There hadn't been much for Randy to do, no one anywhere near his age to be with. Ben had tried to play tennis with him a couple of times, but it wasn't a game Randy was comfortable with. He had taken him on a couple of walks and that had been better. Julia, the lawyer, had tried to entertain him, but Randy had seemed embarrassed by the woman's attention. George had spent all of his time in conversation or examination. There had been no time that had been entirely social for George, Ben had thought. Even when he was having drinks with the senator or the general or the oil man or his old classmate Corny McConnell and talking about baseball or bird-hunting, he was being examined, Ben thought, measured.

George came out to the pool. Not dressed for the pool, Ben noted. There was going to be a disagreement—George had no intentions of going swimming. "I called Cornwall and spoke to Ev," George said.

"I spoke to Ev, too," Ben said. "An hour ago. He said the *airlines* have canceled. I told you that."

"But there've been some holes, Ev said."

"I know about holes. You do too. Sucker holes. Open one minute, close on you before you know it."

"So we make an instrument approach."

"George, it's been four years since you've flown instruments."

"Well, you're instrument-rated, aren't you?"

"No."

"Why not?"

"*Why not?* What the hell kind of—I'm not instrument-rated, George, because I never took the concentrated time to go through the ground course."

"I can make an instrument approach, that's no sweat."

"You'll be illegal."

"I didn't say I was going to, just if I had to. Just if we were letting down visually and the hole closed up on us."

"George, why have the airlines canceled? George, they haven't got the visibility there for even an instrument approach."

"The airlines have to come in a lot faster than the Cherokee. They don't have as much time to look around. Now, Ev says there've been five minutes at a time, several times, when he thinks a visual approach could have been made."

"He *thinks.*"

"Do you think you know more about that field than Ev does? Christsake, Ben, he's *been there* for more than thirty years."

"I say we stay."

"I say we go."

"What's your all-fired hurry to get out of here, George? You're not on a mission."

"I don't want to overstay our welcome. I don't want to be here when Corny gets back this evening."

"He said stay as long as we want. He knows flying. He knows what that weather is like back east."

"We already stayed over one day. Fine. But this is the second day. Did you get the extended area forecast for twenty-four hours from now?"

"Yes."

"Okay, then. You know there's a lot of heavy weather moving in here tomorrow. Nothing for a lightplane to be flying in. I say let's get out of here now while at least we can get out of here. We run into something we can't handle over east, we set down and wait it out there. I'll pay the expenses."

"Corny told me at breakfast not to push our luck. He said stay here."

"He was talking to you, and it doesn't matter for you. You're not trying to land a job with him."

"I just don't see it, George."

"Well, God damn it, what kind of a pilot are you, anyway?"

Ben had an impulse to hit George. It was an idea he was not accustomed to. He looked away and said, "I say no, George. It's my airplane."

"I say yes. I'm senior pilot here. When you get into legalities, Ben, just remember as long as you and I are flying, I'm pilot-in-command. How many hours have you got, Ben? A few hundred. I've got over four thousand. Now, I've got some experience, Ben, and I say there's no sweat to this."

"All because of Corny."

Ben thought about Corny McConnell. The sloppy, grinning face, school-boy face, the class prankster, softened out with a little fat below the chin, around the cheeks. And the eyes that didn't go with the sloppy grin at all. The eyes that looked out from above the joke, the grin, the good-fellowship, and seemed to be focusing inside your own head, intense, humorless. Have you ever thought of flight as suitable subject matter for you, Ben? I've thought about it, Ben had said, but it's too personal, too elusive, I can't make anything out of it, nothing that's true to me. That's too bad, Corny had said, at Saunders-McConnell we've recently been commissioning works of art having to do with flight. It's too bad you don't do that sort of thing —and Corny McConnell had walked away.

"All because of Corny?" George said. "Yes. That's fairly put. Corny and the job. Where else could a new lawyer my age start so well? Where else could I use my aviation *and* law knowledge? But if I'm sitting here when Corny gets back this evening he's just going to think old George Detwiler is ineffectual, he can't even take a little old lightplane away in broad daylight. Bit of hazy weather back east just plain robs him of all his confidence. Well, that's not true, Ben. I don't want Corny to see it that way."

"Let's ask Randy, then. Randy can cast the tie-breaking vote."

"Why Randy? He's not a pilot, he's only—"

"Randy's the third member of this flight crew. He helped us navigate out here and he's going to help us navigate back. Whatdya say, Randy? Go or no-go?"

"Well . . ." Randy looked down at his splayed-out legs, his bare toes. "Well, I've got to go along with Dad. I mean, he ought to know what he's talking about, Ben. I believe what he says. Let's just go."

Ben lay back and looked up at the clear blue, cloudless sky. He listened to the insects buzzing. He said, "We fly a little south of east. We flightplan to Philadelphia."

"That's the long way around, Ben."

"We're VFR all the way, from what I understand. Five to ten miles' visibility. North of that track it's marginal VFR. When we get to Philadelphia we sit down, have a cup of coffee, find out what's going on. We'll decide then whether we go up to Cornwall."

"Hell, what is it, two hours to Philadelphia? For another two hours we can always go up and just *look* at Cornwall. It's—"

"I'll call in the flight plan."

"Jesus Christ, Ben. Wasting all that time and fuel to Philadelphia, that's a *shame*. We'll even be flying away from our destination. You know, going south from Cornwall."

"Philly is our destination. George, understand this. You may be senior and legally pilot-in-command, but this is my leg, the whole flight back, and *I'm* pilot-in-command."

"Yes, sir, Captain, sir," George said. And grinned.

Wipe that asshole grin off your face, Ben thought. "I'm going to file. We can be off in half an hour, I guess."

110

Laura was wearing brief white shorts and a thin white jersey. She looked altogether spectacular, Hilary thought, and he could not get his mind, and sometimes his eyes, away from the inside of her legs up where the smooth, tanned flesh slipped into the white shorts. He had blown lines twice. "You seem *distracted,* dear Hilary," Rodney LeMay, the director, had said to him. Wheras Laura was going through her lines without hesitation. "You bring a certain *coolness* to the part, Laura dear, a coolness I had not thought *specific* to the character. But I like it. I like it very much. Keep it in."

When they broke for lunch, Laura came over and stood in front of Hilary —very close to him. He felt as if she were nude, her physical presence was so intense. He started to walk away. "I think you're annoyed at me," Laura said.

"You might say that," Hilary said. "Here I put a lot of hard work in with you, getting you ready for this, and three days before rehearsals start, you bug out on me."

"I just didn't want you coming to the house."

"Oh, thank you very much, ma'am."

"Don't take it personally, Hilary, you wouldn't know what you're talking about. I just can't take the chance of compromising myself in that house just now. Don't pout, I think you'll find things are changing in a way you'll like. Particularly if I've been noticing an admiring glance every now and then?"

Hilary smiled. He had forgotten for a moment that *he* was in control, that he could do anything.

"You remember saying that you're a pilot and you'd take me flying sometime?"

"I think I mentioned I might do that."

"Well, today's the day."

"I don't know, Laura . . ."

"Why not?"

"Well, we have rehearsal, for one thing."

"After rehearsal. Rehearsal's over at four today."

"I just don't know."

She cocked her head. "Now what can it be that this pilot doesn't want to take this lady flying?" She looked at him steadily and Hilary felt the coolness that the director had been talking about. It was an animal coolness, the coolness of the predator, of the bird in flight searching the ground for life. "We don't have to take long, if it's the money that bothers you."

"Yes," he said quickly. "It's the money."

"Well, Hilary, all we have to do is go up and come down. That shouldn't cost very much."

"No, it wouldn't."

"You *can* take an airplane off and land it again?" she said and laughed.

"Of course."

"Of course you can. That's what pilots do. Fly around. And afterwards, Hilary, I think you may get something you very much want."

She looked directly at him and smiled. He thought he saw her move her legs apart fractionally. Still, in spite of the smile that focused on him so brilliantly, and in spite of the fractional turning of the inside of the thigh toward him. it was the coolness of her presentation which he felt, a cool challenge.

Well, shit yes he could take off an airplane and land it again.

"I'll see what I can do," he said. "I'll have to see if I can get a plane."

Jonah said, on the phone, "Just not the day for it, Hilary. Nothing's coming in or out."

"But it's bright sunshine—"

"Look at the horizon."

"It's just a little hazy."

"That *little haze* gets black when you're in it."

He didn't believe Jonah was telling him the truth. He believed that, for some reason, Jonah just didn't want him to fly that day. "I did a good job for you the other day. You said so. When I soloed."

"Fine job, Hilary. But that's got nothing to do with this."

"Maybe it'll lift off."

"I doubt it. This stuff has been sitting here for over a day and it's probably going to be here for two or three days more. That's what it did when it was out in the Midwest."

Two or three days, Hilary thought. Jesus Christ. Laura just wouldn't believe him if he told her they couldn't go flying for two or three days, that this bright sunlight and still air was dangerous to go flying in. Hell, he could see a couple of miles . . . "Hey, I'll check back later, Jonah."

"Okay, but don't give yourself any hope. This stuff is just sitting here and it's not going to move. Not for a while. Anyway, I won't be here. You just caught me. See you," Jonah said and hung up.

So that was it. Jonah just didn't want to hang around. That was just as well, anyway. He'd have to get Laura into the airplane without anyone from the flying service seeing. Because he wasn't supposed to carry a passenger. Well, hell, students did it all the time. Some did. Illegal, yes, but he heard about it. A student was bragging about it one day . . . He could get Laura in at the end of the runway. She could meet him over at the restaurant, get aboard from there, nowhere near the flying service. No one would even see her. And if someone did and made a fuss, he'd hack that later. What could they do, take his student ticket away? So what. He wasn't so sure he was that crazy about flying anyway. And if they took his student ticket, that would be their doing, not his.

He looked at the bright sunshine. Hazy, yes, but when he looked up he could see blue sky, sort of like smoke hanging up there against it, but the sky turned the smoke blue. There wasn't any of that stuff as low as the pattern of the airport, for Godsake. Bright sunlight, still air. Christ, he could hack *that*. No sweat. He was in control. He could *do* bloody *anything*. He thought of Laura's sweet little body, of the flesh of the inside of her thighs under his hand, and he went to tell her that maybe he could get an airplane later that afternoon.

III

All the way over the sky had been almost cloudless above the line that Ben was flying from Burning Cabin to Philadelphia. But just ten miles north of their track, the blue sky was blurred by white haze. The haze hung down and overspread the terrain, obscuring the terrain as if the world were disappearing up that way.

Seventy-five hundred feet below the Cherokee, it appeared that buildings were, like people, beginning to gather together. "Coming up on Philadelphia, Randy," George said, turning in the copilot's seat and indicating their position on the air chart.

All the aspiring buildings looked so low, so artificial, Ben thought, with all the green unbuilt world around them. But the green was fading somewhat. "Getting haze down below even here," Ben said.

"City stuff," George said. "It's always there."

"Could be," Ben said. From their altitude there was no detail of human activity. The city looked motionless.

"Traffic one o'clock," George said.

"I've got them."

A V of three jet fighters in formation, fast-climbing, three winged black spikes silhouetted against the white haze and thrusting up toward the blue. "Air Guard, probably," George said. "You wouldn't find regular Air Force around here usually."

Ben wondered what George might be thinking. It was the first military traffic they had seen in their flight together. Ben didn't turn his head, but his eyes glanced to George. George was looking off there in the distance, the formation having turned and continued its climb, rushing away from them and disappearing.

Ben looked down at the clean division of the city. "Schuylkill River," he said. "We're coming up on the Delaware, Randy."

"What was the last big river we crossed, Randy, you remember?"

"The Susquehanna," Randy said.

"*Right,*" George said. "I thought we were landing Philadelphia."

"I don't want the hassle of traffic there in this haze."

"I'm hungry," Randy said.

"There isn't anything," George said.

"There's a little airport up ahead, the Flying W. Ever hear of it?"

"Airline pilot started it? Keeps horses or something?"

"Combination dude ranch and airport. Kind of an airman's motel. Food's a heck of a lot better than most airports."

"We could just push on," George said.

You're not thinking, George, Ben wanted to say. You're not thinking at all. Is that what happens when you're away from it for just four years? Even though you spent your life at it before that.

But because of Randy he didn't tell George out loud that George wasn't thinking. He just tapped the fuel indicators with his index finger. "Two, two and a half hours left. If it was CAVU we could do just that, push on. Stop off anywhere for gas. I want full tanks and a lot of information before I even *think* about pushing anywhere."

"And lunch," Randy said.

"And lunch," Ben said.

Ben stood outside the wire fence and watched the children and young mothers at the pool within. There was almost no sound, no activity on the runways behind him. But within the fence there was concentrated noise—shrieking and shouting—and motion. Ben didn't expect to go anywhere. In a few minutes he expected to be lying by the pool.

After they had landed and he had watched the tanks filled, Ben had gotten on the Flying W's hotline to weather briefing. There just wasn't any appreciable flying visibility up around Cornwall—none, in fact, in most of the northeast.

But George had insisted on checking again after lunch.

Ben had come outside to walk around. Randy had come along. "In a few minutes, my man," Ben said, "we will be in that water."

"That's all right with me," Randy said.

In spite of the look of shade everywhere, the temperature was high, the air sullen with humidity.

In getting as far as the Flying W they had penetrated the amorphous overhang of haze that the weather briefer had said was everywhere in the Northeast. The quality of the light on the ground was exotic. It gave everything the appearance that outdoor "night" scenes had in old black-and-white movies when they shot the scenes in daylight through special filters. The source of luminosity seemed to be in the ground rather than in the sky.

Ben saw a lightplane turn a long wide base in its approach to landing. His own landing had not, at touchdown, been the piece of art he had wanted to embarrass George with. George's own landing, back at Burning Cabin, had been a hard one. He had manhandled the airplane, as if forcing it onto the ground. Ben had kept his mouth shut. That was all the flying of his airplane that George was going to do anyway. The return trip was Ben's. As long as they were splitting the flying, Ben had thought that George ought to be in the left-hand seat for the landing at Burning Cabin—for whatever impression it might make. That was the idea of flying down to Burning Cabin in the first place—the impression it might make for George.

Ben watched George stride toward him. George had a slight smile and was nodding at Ben. Ben felt his own face tighten.

"It looks okay," George said, "it looks like we can do it."

"The point is we don't *have* to do it, George. This isn't a mission."

George ignored him. "Ev says the sky keeps opening up around the field. He says about every ten or fifteen minutes there's a good hole somewhere around, and it looks to him as if we could get in—"

"It *looks* to him."

George was smiling, affecting a concerned politeness. "The point is we can give it a look, we can *try* to get in. The same storm system that's going to clobber Burning Cabin tomorrow is going to lay this place down, too. They're saying the way the haze is spreading south, this place may be IFR by later this afternoon. At least we can get out. If we can't land in Cornwall, Pittsfield, Poughkeepsie, and Albany are VFR."

"You'd rather spend the night in *Pittsfield* than here?"

"Pittsfield's just a hop away from Cornwall, Ben. Half an hour in the Cherokee? If the weather lets up just intermittently we can be over in Cornwall in minutes. Here we're over two hours away." He smiled at Ben.

The man's goddamn condescension. "What's so important about getting back, George?"

"I just want to be in my house, Ben. If I can. Now let me ask you. What's so important about *not* going back? What do you want to stick around here for? For one thing, it costs money."

Ben didn't remind George that George had said he'd pay the expenses for staying over someplace if Ben decided they shouldn't continue the flight north.

"What do you say, Randy?" Ben said.

Randy was watching some kids jumping into the water. "I sure would like to get home," he said, still watching the kids.

Ben saw what he took to be an enthralling loneliness in Randy. None of this had been any fun for him.

"I guess that leaves it up to you, Ben," George said and smiled at Ben. "It's your airplane."

Shit, Ben thought.

112

When they reached eight hundred feet above the terrain and were quitting the Flying W traffic pattern, it was like thin smoke in the air, too delicate to be seen brushing by the windscreen, but becoming denser the further ahead Ben looked. As they climbed the sky changed from gray to yellowish gray. "We might as well corkscrew up right here and get on top," George said. "Plenty of visibility right here."

Five miles, Ben thought. Maybe five miles. "If we make a circular climb, fifty percent of the time we're going to be flying in an illegal direction."

"Straight ahead you're going to lose a lot of visibility."

"If I have to I'll make a one-eighty and go back to the Flying W."

George was silent.

Ben dialed in Philadelphia Departure Control and told them where he was and where he was going. There was just too much fast-moving traffic around, airline traffic going to and coming from Philadelphia, and too little visibility. He gave them identifying turns and they confirmed him as a target.

"Cherokee Eight-nine Zero-nine Whiskey, traffic is a TWA 707 at eleven o'clock four miles."

"Negative contact."

"Zero-niner Whiskey, traffic is a light twin at your three o'clock position, three miles."

"Negative."

George couldn't see it either.

"Zero-niner Whiskey, traffic is a New EnglandAir 727, ten o'clock at five miles."

"Negative."

"Zero-nine Whiskey, you have a target at twelve o'clock, three miles, fast-moving."

Ben and George leaned forward, as if that might help, stared, saw nothing. "Negative," Ben said, waiting to see the fast-mover hurtle from the bright whiteness ahead directly at them.

"This isn't any three miles' visibility," Ben said. He was sweating and his fingers had gotten achingly tight on the yoke. He relaxed them.

"They're calling it three miles on the ground. Visual flight rules. We're legal."

The hell we are, the hell we are, Ben thought. He was steering around real clouds now, masses of whiteness with real definition, real peripheries, and he was too close. You were supposed to be two thousand feet away from them horizontally. But he couldn't *get* two thousand feet away from them. They were too close together. You were supposed to be two thousand feet away from them to allow a jetliner emerging from clouds, after a fast-moving direct flight through on instruments, time to see you and avoid a midair. The Cherokee couldn't do anything about avoiding a midair like that, it couldn't maneuver quickly enough.

Ben felt his breathing speeded up and realized his hand on the yoke had tightened again. He loosened the hold on the yoke and forced himself to breathe slowly. There was nothing he could do about his soaking sweat.

Looking down, streamers of haze seemed to be hurrying beneath them in the opposite direction. But the streamers were standing still, Ben knew. It was the speed of the Cherokee that gave that illusion. Looking ahead to the mounding clouds the Cherokee seemed hardly to be moving at all, nor the clouds.

The white mounds were all around them and rose too steeply for Ben to avoid penetration. The ground was gone now. It appeared greenly for a few seconds, turned dark, and then was gone, obscured by white. The airspeed was down to eighty and the climb was going to put him in cloud in a few seconds. "I'm starting a one-eighty. We're going back."

Ben tried to move the yoke forward. But it held steady.

"Look," George said. He motioned up. The sky was blue now. "We're almost out of this stuff."

The controls stayed in the climb position. The airspeed was falling off. Ben pushed forward, but the control did not move.

"George, for Christsake!"

George had both hands on the copilot's yoke in front of him and was keeping the airplane in its climb.

"We're almost over it." The nose was pointed up at the blue and George was looking only at that

Ben started to push hard at the controls. But then he stopped. He didn't know how much opposite strain the control cables could take. He was sure they were going into the cloud and it was senseless to go into instrument conditions fighting with each other for control.

Such a reasonable summation, part of his mind said. So reasonable to give up the controls. But very shortly it may not make any difference at all. Because the airspeed was falling off now badly, going down toward stall speed. Could either of them recover from a stall blind, in cloud?

Ben had practiced it. But that was with Jonah sitting beside him. Or Adele. While he wore a device that restricted his vision to the instruments. But Jonah or Adele could see an outside world. There had been no real danger.

This was real danger. Airspeed seventy indicated.

They were in a long upsloping trough. Cloud a few feet beneath them, a few feet off each wing. Walls of cloud on each side rising vertically. Ben felt terrified, helpless. He had a feeling of suffocation. They could not climb as steeply as the trough ascended. The stall warning light was flashing on and off. The air had become insubstantial. They could not maintain this attitude with so little airspeed. In a few seconds they would cease climbing. For a second there would be a feeling of nothingness, of no lift, and then they would pitch into the cloud beneath, into blindness.

Ben jabbed at the red stall warning light.

George nodded. But his eyes remained on the blue sky ahead.

They were at nine thousand two hundred. The airspeed was at sixty-six and slipping. The stall warning light glowed steady red, the stall warner made a steady whining buzz . . .

There was a trembling, a flutter. That would be the beginning of the stall, Ben thought. Might be. It ceased. Maybe just unstable air near the clouds. The fluttering came back and then a bump. Ben looked at the airspeed. It indicated sixty-three. They should stall out now.

Ben *wanted* to put his hands on the controls, but held back, kept them in his lap, afraid to distract George in any way. The one thing he could do was to study the instruments, be ready to do what he knew he could do if he had to, if George would let him—make one hell of an attempt to recover from the stall on instruments alone. He shoved the terror aside, willed himself to think nothing but instruments.

The controls and airplane pitched forward. The engine, at full throttle, took on a huge loudness like a steady explosion. The little white wings of the airplane-indicator in the artificial horizon settled just above the horizon line. The airspeed rose swiftly, the altimeter slowed down, they were no longer gaining feet with the rapidity of a steep ascent.

Ben looked outside. They were on top of glaring white cloud. It was cool, almost cold in the cabin. The sky was clear blue everywhere from shining white horizon of cloud to dome above. They were flying straight in a very gentle climb.

The airplane felt sturdy in the air again, as if the air had thickened. Ben could feel sturdiness and buoyancy. Or maybe it's me, he thought. Maybe that's what I'm feeling inside.

"You want to take it?" George said.

Ben kept his hands loosely in his lap. They wanted to batter George. He said nothing. Probably Randy, in the seat just behind, had had no idea of what was going on. What Ben wanted to say to George would probably frighten Randy, certainly anger him. Ben looked back. Randy was reading a comic book.

"Your controls, Ben," George said quietly, apologetically.

What I was really afraid of was that I might be flying with a crazy man, Ben thought. I let him have his way because I thought he might be crazy and *that's* crazy, giving in to a crazy man.

"I knew we could climb out of there."

"The stall warner said no, probably not."

"I knew we could," George said firmly.

Ben did not want to argue with George, with his possible insanity, in the air.

"Your controls, Ben," George said quietly.

Ben put his hands lightly on the controls. "My controls," he said, and continued their gentle climb.

113

Jonah looked at the bewildering light. It hung like transparent yellow veils everywhere. When he looked far enough into the distance, he could no longer see through the accumulation of veils, all he could see was yellow light.

It wasn't only the light. He had a feeling of bewilderment inside himself as well. He was home. It was early afternoon and he was home.

He was getting tense, too. He recognized that. He supposed it was Yvonne's activity that was stimulating the tension. She was vacuuming the house. He had asked her not to—he was worried about the strain—but she had made fun of him, of his worry, and then, when he had tried to insist, she had become briefly angry and he had let up, apologized, and gone out to the backyard. He hadn't wanted her to undergo the strain of her own anger.

He looked at the light and listened to the sound of the vacuuming from within the house; he felt the heat and tried to think of all the projects and pieces of work he had, for so long, hoped to get to one day. But as he remembered them, he found that none of them interested him. The baby's room was done. That had been the main thing, his big work and big pleasure. The garden was in. It was growing and weeded. The tomatoes were turning from green to red, tiny glossy peppers were growing from white buds, zucchini and cucumbers were almost mature. There were pumpkins coming along. For the baby's first Halloween. Jonah had thought often of the infant's eyes looking at the wavering firelit eyes of the jack-o'-lantern.

He felt useless. He had no work, no gainful employment, and there was nothing left to do, nothing that interested him.

Yvonne paused in her cleaning and wiped the light dampness from her forehead. That was a bit unusual. She never seemed to perspire. She saw Jonah standing still in the backyard, still as still water, she thought. It was eerie out there today, she thought. Bright light, but eerie. Poor Jonah, dear Jonah. He was so troubled. He had gone and quit flying. She had never thought he would. And, she realized, she hadn't really wanted him to. It was her fear, her terrible fright, that had wanted him to quit flying. And still wanted it. For the baby, she told herself. It's protection for the baby.

She wondered if the little things she had been feeling were really the baby coming. Little pains. Not very often, maybe every half-hour or so, and they were so very little she wasn't sure that they could rightfully be called *pains*. She had been checking for some discharge, something pink or reddish, but there had been none of that.

Yvonne laughed at herself. She was becoming impatient, quite impatient with this baby not coming. She turned on the vacuum and went back to work.

114

In the pure, cool air of eleven thousand five- hundred feet, the engine of the Cherokee maintained a steady chordal labor. Ben looked at the outside air temperature. Sixty-six degrees. On the ground it was in the nineties. They had long since lost all sight of the ground and Ben didn't like that at all.

"No problem," George had said. "If we have to go down in it, I'll take it." He sounded cheerful. The old fighter pilot.

"You really think you can," Ben had said.

"No problem."

"It's been four years, George."

"No problem."

"Anyway, if we go down in, that'll mean we've lost the engine, right?"

"Right."

"George, I really don't think much of what we're doing."

"You trust your airplane, don't you?"

A hell of a question, Ben had thought, at ten thousand feet and climbing, as they had been then, all above solid cloud cover.

"Yes," Ben had said.

"Then let's just fly over to the Cornwall VOR. If it's solid there, we'll go someplace else."

Now Ben said, "George, we're climbing."

"I know."

"You looking at what I'm looking at? You *seeing* what I'm seeing?"

"It's difficult to judge, Ben. There's nothing to judge it against."

The brilliant white snowfield stretched horizon to horizon now.

"I can judge it against the altimeter, George. I have to keep climbing to stay a thousand feet above it. George, the tops are climbing. Everything in front of us is higher, and we're going to have to go higher to stay clear of them."

"Let's just see," George said.

"Sure, *Colonel.*"

Ben looked at the vertical rate of ascent indicator. He was climbing at one hundred feet a minute. Not much. No. Not steep. But a thousand feet every ten minutes, and that with full power. The airplane climbed terribly slowly in the thin air. They were over twelve thousand now. Ben looked at his fingernails. He'd been doing that ever since they got out of ten for eleven-five. Looking for a tint of bluishness, a sign of hypoxia. They said that ten thousand, in the daytime, was where some people began showing signs of hypoxia, of oxygen deprivation. They'd been above ten for almost two hours. Ten thousand was marginal. Twelve thousand was the critical altitude. The body just couldn't get the oxygen out of the air so easily at twelve thousand. Because of the lack of pressure. Hyperventilation was another symptom. Breathing fast. Ben thought he might be breathing fast, but so what? He was a little scared, that in itself would make him hyperventilate.

They were at twelve.

"We're going to have to go to thirteen-five," Ben said.

George nodded.

Well, if it doesn't worry George, maybe it shouldn't worry me, Ben thought.

They would have to go to thirteen thousand five hundred feet to be at a legal altitude for the direction in which they were flying.

The Cherokee was climbing even more slowly now, the gleaming round surfaces of the cloud deck below seeming to rise up more quickly beneath them. Ben checked his power settings, thinking to increase the climb. There wasn't any more throttle to go to.

They were now quite illegal if anyone cared, Ben thought. They were not maintaining a thousand feet above the cloud deck below. An airline captain Ben had spent an evening with had said, "You don't know how many near misses there are. No one does. No one outside of the airlines and ATC. Look, just the other day, I was climbing out of Washington. Solid cloud between eighteen hundred feet and six thousand, and then pure daylight and CAVU on top. But it's all IFR in between. So I poke out at six and there's this bastard in a lightplane maybe three hundred feet away. I mean, he's just *skimming* the tops of the clouds."

"Didn't ATC give him to you as a target?"

"No. They don't show up sometimes."

So that, Ben thought, if something is climbing up at us right now, Boston Center may not even have us as a target.

I'm going to give Boston Center a call, Ben thought.

He was conscious of the sweat on his body. He thought his breathing was quick—he knew his heart was quick. But he knew he was uneasy, very uneasy now, anxious, and that accounted for the fast rate of both his heart and his breathing.

His fingertips tingled. He realized he still had hold of the throttle. He let go of it, let go of the yoke with his other hand, and exercised his fingers. The tingling went away. The air was so smooth and the airplane so well trimmed, it flew on its steady slow climb with no more than slight corrections by the rudder pedals.

Out of thirteen now and going for thirteen five. They said you lost judgment, lost objectivity when you got hypoxic. Well, he was still monitoring the altimeter, the directional gyro, the gyro compass, the VOR needle okay . . . Ben took the controls back. He'd exercised the tingling out of his fingers. He looked at his nails. Not blue. Pale? He couldn't tell. Not blue, anyway. Just sort of whitish, but it was hard to tell. He hadn't ever studied his fingernails the way he was now. He couldn't remember what to compare them to.

Thirteen five. He should level off now. But the cloud deck continued, he thought, to push up underneath, and Ben left the power where it was and continued the climb.

He wasn't so worried any more. The anxiety had left him. The airplane was flying right, all the instruments were where they should be.

They said you get feeling euphoric. That's one of the signs of hypoxia. It can be. Euphoria. Apprehension is, too. Hell, I'm not euphoric, Ben thought. I'm managing this flight pretty well. In spite of George. Down there somewhere is what? He hadn't been paying attention. "Where are we?" Ben said to George, after a while.

George had the airchart in his lap. He looked at it for a while. "About here," George said, moving his finger about half an inch.

About forty miles south and west of Cornwall. Ben picked up the microphone and keyed it. "Cornwall, this is . . . this is Cherokee Eight-niner Zero-niner Whiskey. This is . . . Zero-nine Whiskey," Ben said, and replaced the microphone. Ben looked at where George's finger had indicated on the chart. About forty miles south and west of Cornwall. Another twenty minutes, probably less. Ben looked at his watch. He was surprised to see that two and a half hours had gone by. It should have been a two-hour flight. But there had been all that climbing. All that very slow climbing once they were through eight thousand.

He looked at the fuel indicators. Left tank. Right tank.

They were down further than he'd noticed . . . expected. He'd been leaning the mixture to save fuel . . . Ben looked over at the mixture control. He must have forgotten to lean it. Or had changed it. Maybe when they were in that steep climb back . . . Anyway, it was full rich, almost. They were burning up fuel at an exorbitant rate. He pulled the mixture control out. The engine coughed, stopped.

Ben listened to the silence. There was no sound of the engine. That was strange and frightening.

He knew what he was supposed to do. He did all the emergency things he had been taught to do. He switched tanks and he put the mixture to full rich and he turned on the fuel boost pump and . . . there was something else he was supposed to do, but he couldn't think of it.

Anyway, the engine had started.

George was sitting there staring at the panel, his eyebrows raised as if something had startled him. Ben laughed and looked in the back seat. Randy was asleep. He looked down. Jesus Christ, he thought, the undercarriage must be sticking into the cloud. They were at fifteen thousand and they just couldn't climb any more as fast as the deck was rising beneath them.

Well, George, tough shit. Ben began a slow, one-hundred-and-eighty-degree turn to the opposite direction.

George didn't say anything. He was looking out at the cloud deck too, as if he'd just seen it. He kept looking at it.

Ben made a powered descent, and he didn't stay as far above the cloud as he was legally expected to do.

He changed course to due west. Somewhere over there was where he would try to let down for Pittsfield or Poughkeepsie or Albany, he didn't know which yet, he couldn't make up his mind.

115

Ev was standing at an open window in his office, looking out at the far end of the field, seeing nothing but a belly of light, hearing nothing, nothing at all. It was as if nothing had ever moved here or ever would.

He had thought, a few minutes before, that he had heard Ben Cain's numbers on the radio, calling in. But the sound had broken up and he had only heard it that once. He had *thought* he had heard the brief transmission end with *"this . . . Zero-niner Whis . . ."* But there was nothing out there now, no sound of an airplane. He turned back to the room.

Falun, seated against the wall in one of the student's chairs, was staring at him. Staring directly at him. But you couldn't say he was seeing me, Ev thought. Falun often stared at people these days. But apparently he often didn't see them. Falun would be staring at someone but *looking* at something else, someone or something in his own mind.

Falun had called about an hour before and asked if Ev weren't too busy would he come and get Falun and bring him to the airport.

"There's nothing flying," Ev had said.

"I wouldn't think so."

"It's the strangest goddamn light I've ever seen."

"I've seen it. But never this bright."

"You're right. I've been trying to think of what it reminds me of. It's like a mist. A mist of light."

"All you have to do is look at the horizon. What do you see? Nothing."

"But you still want to come down here, Falun? Like I said, nothing's going on."

"Yes. I'd like to be at the airport for a while. I find it very pleasant there. You understand that, Ev."

"Yes. Of course I do, God damn it, Falun. I'll be right out."

When they'd gotten back to the airport together, Falun had gone over to the fence and stood there for a while looking out at the field. Maybe not *seeing* it, Ev thought, but looking at it. Then he had come into the office and gone to that chair. He had asked Ev for a pen and a writing pad, but so far he had written nothing.

Now Falun's eyes seemed to focus on Ev. There was a slight physical change to Falun. His body had been still and now there was a subtle animation to it.

"What kind of baby will Yvonne have, do you think, Ev?"

"Now how the hell should I know that, Falun? How in the hell?"

"What do you guess?"

"It's fifty-fifty, they tell me. A boy or a girl. Though nowadays you can't even be sure of that."

"I believe I read somewhere that there is just a slightly higher percentage of female babies born. More females than males."

"God knows they're everywhere."

"It would make it so much easier if I knew."

"Make what easier?"

"What I want to write."

"Sorry, Falun, I can't help."

Falun was silent. Ev couldn't tell where he was looking, what he might be seeing. He went over and sat by him, the two men alone in this room that they had shared for so long. A room that had once been a shack, a shack that had been enlarged and added onto and now was a small building of several rooms. "Look at it," Ev said, "it's got goddamn wall-to-wall carpeting, for Christ's sake."

Falun nodded. "I could never trust that man, do you know? I could never entirely trust him."

They were even thinking about the same things, Ev thought. They had known each other so long that happened sometimes. "Yancey?"

"Yes, yes, Virgil Yancey. I could not ever bring myself to trust him entirely. Did I ever say that to you before, Ev?"

"No, never, Falun." Falun was silent. Ev said, "But I can't remember your ever very much talking about anyone. I mean, talking them down."

Then Falun was silent for a long time. "It's none of my business," Falun eventually said. "I mean that in the literal sense. This place is no longer my business. But you and I have always trusted each other."

"Yes, Falun."

"I can say, Ev, that I even love you."

"*Christ,* Falun." Ev breathed out deeply. Very quietly he said, "All right. I can say the same."

"What I want to talk about, just for a moment, is Jonah. With your permission. This is not my business any more."

"All right, Falun."

"He should be part of this. It's his turn."

"I thought you'd understand better than anyone, Falun."

"I do. I think so. I think I do. You let him into your business, you give up part of yourself. It's like growing older faster. It's like getting closer to death."

Ev looked away.

"Of course that isn't true. And what if it is? What you come to is that this is not the important thing."

"You mean flying? The business? *What,* for Christ's sake, Falun?"

"All of it."

"Then you tell me what in Christ's sake *is* so important?"

"I don't know exactly. That's what I was trying to write here." He looked down at the blank pad of paper.

Ev got up. Falun lit a cigarette. "Just the thing for you," Ev said.

"It doesn't make any difference now."

I know, for Christsake, I know, don't you think I know? Ev wanted to say. Out loud he said, "It's hot, Falun, you know that? It's goddamn hot."

"Yes, Ev."

"Why don't you and I have a beer? Why don't you and I drink a beer together?"

"That would be fine, Ev. What a good idea. Except that, you know, I'd rather stay here. I really don't feel like going over to the restaurant."

"No, Falun, that's exactly what I thought. I thought I'd run down the road and get us a couple of bottles of something good. What would you like? Dutch? German? Danish? American?"

"You decide, Ev. I will enjoy drinking a beer with you. I will, very much."

"What the hell. I'll get a couple of bottles of each."

116

Flying a course south of west and following the slope of the cloud tops downwards, Ben leveled at ten thousand five hundred. He felt as if his body had compacted, as if it had been in some formless, substanceless state and now it had come back together again into a physical presence. That was it. He had the feeling of the *presence* of himself and he thought maybe that had been missing. But he *hadn't* been hypoxic. He'd been flying all that time. He hadn't passed out.

He looked down and found that the cloud deck had fallen away quite a bit. He pulled back on power and set up a long glide. It looked like he could get all the way down to eight five. There were gray-black holes in the clouds now. Sometimes he could see very small white squares below in the darkness. Houses. Down there, of course, it wouldn't be dark.

He figured he was pretty close to Pittsfield. He had chosen Pittsfield because it was the nearest field to the west and was almost equidistant from Poughkeepsie and Albany.

"Pittsfield unicom, this is Cherokee Eight-niner Zero-niner Whiskey." He had to call twice and wait.

"Yes. Cherokee Zero-niner Whiskey. Pittsfield."

"Zero-niner Whiskey requesting your winds, active, and local traffic."

"Zero-niner Whiskey, Pittsfield is closed to all traffic."

"Now he can't do that," George said. "Unless they have an emergency down there."

"I know," Ben said.

George took the microphone from him. For an instant Ben was angry, but then he decided it was just as well. The clouds were thinning and he concentrated on finding a way down. There wasn't all that much fuel time left. An hour, conservatively. But they were just about right over Pittsfield.

George said, "Pittsfield, Zero-niner Whiskey. Have you got visual landing conditions?"

"Negative, Zero-niner Whiskey."

"What about instruments? Are you up to IFR minimums?"

"Shit, George, neither of us is fit to—"

"Cherokee Eight-niner Zero-niner Whiskey. This is Pittsfield. Pittsfield is closed to all traffic. We are below VFR minimums. Our ADF is down for repairs. We have no instrument approach facilities presently operative. I say again, our instrument approach facilities are down. Did you read that?"

"Affirmative, Pittsfield."

"Zero-niner Whiskey, are you familiar with the field here?"

Ben nodded. "That's affirmative, Pittsfield," George said.

"Well, Zero-niner Whiskey, I'm sittin' here in the office and I can't see the trees on the other side of the runway."

Ben said, "Tell him we understand and we'll go elsewhere. Ask him if he has any suggestions." George did it.

"Zero-niner Whiskey. It's a mess, you know that? Nothing's flying. Not light stuff. To the best of my information, which is now about half an hour old, the only place open to VFR traffic is Albany. They're reporting intermittent VFR conditions. Anyway, they're landing 'em there. Otherwise you've got to go north to Montreal or west to Cleveland or south to Philadelphia. Boston isn't landing anything."

George was silent. "Thank him," Ben said. George did so.

The Pittsfield voice came back once more. "Good luck to you fellows."

Ben had a feeling they weren't going to make it. It was now simple arithmetic. They hadn't the fuel to go anyplace else except Albany. That would be easy, plenty of fuel to get to Albany. But if Albany shut down, they hadn't the fuel to go anywhere else.

It wasn't a panic voice in his mind that said to him so plainly that they weren't going to make it. It wasn't a nervous, easily frightened voice. It was a simple voice. You've extended yourself too far. You've made too many errors and they've compounded each other. You never should have left the

Flying W. You never should have tried to outclimb the clouds. You never should have spent so much time, so much fuel . . .

They weren't that far from Albany. Thirty-four miles. Call it fifteen minutes.

Ben switched over to the Albany VOR and set up a course indicated by the needle pointing to the navigational facility. "Their VOR is right at the airport," he said to George. Then he called the Albany Flight Service Station and amended his flight plan from Cornwall as destination to Albany. Fifteen minutes away. If he had their present position correct. Albany was giving VFR conditions. Three miles' horizontal visibility. Twelve hundred feet vertical visibility. Haze.

"No problem," George said.

Time to let down, Ben thought. He pulled back on power and they descended. And then they were in it. Six thousand five hundred and there was no forward visibility. The sky ahead looked black. Ben could not judge how far *ahead* was, could not judge where the penetrable grayness near the airplane became impenetrable blackness. He said to himself three hundred yards and knew he had no way of knowing.

The odd thing was he could see straight down. The terrain even had some color to it. Faint yellows and greens. But mostly smoky black. Whisps of cloud approached the airplane slowly and then whipped past beneath them.

He looked ahead at the blackness. "They can call it what they want to, but this isn't any three miles' visibility," Ben said. Then he noticed that George had his right hand lightly on the yoke in front of him. His head hardly moved, but his eyes were scanning the blackness with seriousness. There was a slight sweat on George's face.

"Keep the watch," Ben said, "I'm mostly on instruments."

"I know," George said.

Ben hadn't realized it, the transition to instruments had been so unconscious.

"Keep letting down," George said.

"I am." Ben took the Jeppesen manual and opened it in his lap and found the instrument approach plate for Albany. He was okay on instruments here. He could always fly the airplane by visual reference straight down to the ground. But an instrument approach was something else. You make a mistake there, things go bad rapidly . . . You stall in and kill yourself. All three of you.

He changed frequencies. "Albany Approach Control, this is Cherokee Eight-niner Zero-niner Whiskey."

"Cherokee Eight-niner Zero-niner Whiskey, this is Albany Approach Control. Go ahead."

[299]

"Zero-niner Whiskey is about fifteen miles southeast, landing Albany. We're encountering poor visibility in this haze and we'd appreciate vectors."

"Cherokee Eight-niner Zero-niner Whiskey, Albany Approach Control, roger. What is your heading, altitude, and flight conditions?"

"Albany Approach Control, Zero-niner Whiskey is on a heading of three-three-zero degrees. Altitude three thousand nine hundred and descending to three thousand five hundred. I can see straight down, but I can't see much straight ahead."

"Eight-niner Zero-niner Whiskey, for radar identification turn right heading three-six-zero degrees for thirty seconds, then resume heading three-three-zero degrees. Weather measured twelve hundred broken, visibility three miles haze, wind light and variable, altimeter three-zero-zero-one, broken variable to scattered."

Ben tried to retain the numbers, understand the information, and monitor and control all the numbers on the panel in front of him, but it was as if his intellect refused him, rebelled and turned numb in its rigors of concentration, and the best that Ben could do was hold on to his flight instructions. "Zero-niner Whiskey is turning right to three-six-zero degrees."

Ben leveled and banked and watched the numbers on the gyro compass slide by. His eyes went quickly to the altimeter to maintain his altitude and then to the airspeed, the gyro, the artificial horizon, the altimeter, and around the circle again. He was entirely on instruments now and he had never done that before except in practice.

"You're sliding by it," George said.

He was passing zero degrees. He leveled and pushed opposite rudder. Brought the nose down, up, got it level and the flight straight finally and *Shit, I forgot to start timing.* He glanced at the clock. He keyed the microphone and said, "Zero-niner Whiskey is steady on three-six-zero degrees."

"Roger."

Ben kept the scan of the instruments, glanced again at the clock. *Shit where did I start the timing, what number?* He decided to let the second hand go another fifteen seconds. When the second hand touched the chosen number, Ben lowered the left wing and touched the left rudder and waited until he got his original heading back. Then he leveled and flew it. "Zero-niner Whiskey is back on a heading of three-three-zero."

"Roger, Eight-niner Zero-niner Whiskey, radar contact eleven miles southeast of Albany Airport. Descend and maintain three thousand five hundred and proceed to the VOR direct."

"Albany, Zero-niner Whiskey is level at three thousand five hundred now."

"Roger."

Ben watched the numbers and the VOR needle stay where they should be.

"Eight-niner Zero-niner Whiskey, make a three-six-zero degree turn to the right due to arriving and departing traffic at Albany."

Ben initiated the turn and the numbers were already getting away from him, the numbers saying he was going up, going down, picking up speed, losing speed, climbing, slowing . . . He had the microphone in his right hand and wanted to tell Albany he was doing what they had told him, but he suddenly found he could not speak and fly the instruments at the same time.

"Fly the turn," George said. "I'll take care of the communications for you." He took the microphone from Ben. "Albany Approach Control, Cherokee Eight-niner Zero-niner Whiskey is making a standard rate three-six-zero degree turn to the right."

"Roger, Zero-niner Whiskey, maintain altitude, maintain turn."

There was radio silence. The numbers slid by on the gyro compass. Ben saw he was maintaining his altitude. He was doing things smoothly now. After that instant when it had begun to get away from him, a number of things, small things, going askew, and then going askew rapidly and his concentration not up to it.

The radio silence continued. "We must be their only traffic for landing," George said. "Right now, anyway."

"Zero-niner Whiskey, resume heading. Report crossing field."

George repeated the instructions as Ben leveled and set up a new course to the VOR. From moment to moment Ben looked down. The downward visibility had become almost as dense as the forward visibility. He scanned the instruments and flew the airplane with more and more ease. His concentration encompassed more, his control not so strained; his thinking was getting ahead of the instruments, anticipating. He looked quickly down again. It was like a negative down below. All black and near black with a dull, silverish band crossing their flight path on the ground. "Coming up on the Hudson," Ben said.

"Stay on the instruments," George said. "Keep your concentration where it should be."

That shit George, Ben thought. He looked down at the approach plate, the instrument flight route into Albany, that lay in his lap. When he had practiced approaches with Jonah he had been able to study the appropriate approach plate in advance and memorize it. Now the information was hard to grasp. He made some minor corrections, settled the instruments back to where they should be. Fly outbound and turn left heading to three-two-six, the approach plate said. Check instruments, okay, they're right. *But fly three-two-six for how long? At what altitude? Fly outbound from the VOR how long before turning to three-two-six?* The information was all in front of him, but he couldn't find it.

"You're diving," George said.

Yes, he'd gotten well nosedown. He got it back. What was I going to do? Yes. Albany elevation. It was right there in front of him. But he couldn't find it.

"Watch your instruments," George said. "You're all over the place."

The big mistake was much further back than the Flying W. When he didn't go after his instrument rating. And when he didn't tell George to go fuck himself at the Flying W.

There it was. *Apt. Elev. 288'.* There it was, right where it should be on the plate. So he could come in, should come in at . . . There was so much to do now, so much to figure, and he just couldn't *do* it.

Well, really, it didn't make any difference. This wasn't going to be an instrument approach. He took the microphone from George. "Albany Approach, Zero-niner Whiskey. Say again your visibility."

"Zero-niner Whiskey, Albany weather twelve hundred broken, visibility three miles in haze."

Ben stared ahead at the blackness, looked down at the near blackness. "Are you saying you're visual, Albany?"

"That's a dumb thing to ask," George said. "Why don't you *announce* we're IFR?"

"That's affirmative, Zero-niner Whiskey. Visual flight rules are in effect for landing Albany." There was a long pause. "Zero-niner Whiskey, we have you directly over the field now."

Ben looked at the VOR needle. It lay way over on one side. The accompanying indicator changed from TO to FROM. "That's affirmative, Albany. We just crossed the VOR." He looked straight down. "I don't have the field in sight."

"Say again. Can you see the field, Zero-niner Whiskey?"

"Negative. I cannot see the field."

"Zero-niner Whiskey, do you wish to request a surveillance approach?"

"Affirmative," Ben said. "Zero-niner Whiskey requests surveillance approach."

"Roger, Zero-niner Whiskey. Are you instrument-rated?"

Ben paused. There were legal considerations now. They could take his license, he thought. He was flying in IFR conditions without an IFR rating. He wasn't sure if he could handle an IFR approach, but maybe he ought to lie anyway.

George took the microphone from him. "Albany Approach. Zero-niner Whiskey. Affirmative on instrument-rated." He handed the microphone to

Ben. "You take care of this." He put his left hand on the throttle, right hand on the yoke. Ben was conscious that they were both sweating and both smelling of it. "My controls now, Ben." He said it firmly. "My controls, Ben." Ben continued his outbound flight, his management of the instruments.

"Eight-niner Zero-niner Whiskey, roger, fly a heading of zero-six-zero degrees, descend and maintain three thousand, this will be a surveillance approach to Runway One-nine."

"I'm the pilot-in-command here, Ben. I'm senior and I'm responsible. I'm instrument-rated and you're not."

"Not in four years you're not instrument-rated."

"Zero-niner Whiskey, do you read Albany?"

"*My controls,* Ben, I've got it."

"Your controls," Ben said, a surge of fury at George pumping through him. "Albany Approach, Zero-niner Whiskey. Zero-six-zero degrees, descend and maintain three thousand." Ben was amazed how the numbers had stayed with him. George nodded and turned to the heading, lowering the nose. And in the midst of Ben's fury the plain voice asked him if he weren't, anyway, also a little relieved that George was going to make the approach.

He thought about it. A great deal of thought. All in an instant. It could have been that way. But it wasn't.

Ben keyed the microphone and said, "Zero-niner Whiskey is level at three thousand."

"Roger. Zero-niner Whiskey is three miles northeast, turn left heading zero-one-zero, descend and maintain two thousand one hundred."

Ben repeated the instructions and George jammed the nose down. He took off some power and dove the airplane. The vertical descent was up at nine hundred feet a minute. Ben felt it in his ears. Randy made a complaint. George didn't respond. The forward darkness lightened and then took on a yellow cast. "Zero-niner Whiskey's at two thousand one hundred."

"Cherokee Eight-niner Zero-niner Whiskey, recommended altitudes will be furnished each mile on final approach except the last mile."

"Zero-niner Whiskey," Ben said. George continued to fly the zero-one-zero course. Ben thought ahead to the descent to minimums and final approach. "Albany, say again your altimeter, please." George nodded.

"Albany altimeter three-zero-zero-one."

"Three-zero-zero-one, thank you." Ben made a minute adjustment of the altimeter.

"Seven miles northeast of airport," the controller's voice said, "turn left heading two-seven-zero." Ben watched the instruments and repeated the instructions back to the controller.

[303]

"Report when able to proceed visually to the airport."

"Roger, report when in sight, Zero-niner Whiskey."

"Turn left heading two-seven-zero."

Ben said the words back. The controller sounded assured. George was doing things smoothly enough. But they were slipping off course . . .

"Turn left heading one-nine-zero. Prepare to descend in one and one-half miles. Published minimum descent altitude is eight-two-zero."

"Turning left one-nine-zero."

"Six miles from runway. Begin descent to your minimum descent altitude."

"Say it," George said. He was horsing with the controls now, overcontrolling. But getting the needles back where they should be.

"Eight hundred and twenty feet," Ben said. "I'll let you know." Into the microphone he said, "Zero-niner Whiskey beginning descent."

"Five miles from runway. On course. Altitude should be one thousand eight hundred."

They were under it. "Zero-niner Whiskey," Ben said.

"Four miles from runway, altitude should be one thousand five hundred."

Somehow they weren't at it yet. "Zero-niner Whiskey," Ben said.

"Zero-niner Whiskey, three miles from runway, slightly left of course, turn right heading one-nine-five, altitude should be one thousand two hundred."

"Turning right one-nine-five." George pursued the numbers, went by them, made a severe correction to bring them back and had to correct again.

"Two miles from runway on course. Altitude should be nine hundred."

It almost was. Ben looked down. The world was yellow, all soft with yellow light. But he could see it. He looked forward. In front there was still nothing. Nearly nothing. But the air was bright. There were blurred shapes in it. "George, we've got downward visibility."

"Look for the runway. Let me know when you've got it."

"Zero-niner Whiskey, one mile from runway."

George was pushing down to a lower and lower altitude.

"You're at seven hundred, George."

"Nothing yet?" George said.

"Not a damn thing." Ben looked down. A field. Trees. Nice quiet stuff. All yellow in sunlight.

"Zero-niner Whiskey, you should have the field in sight about now."

"Nothing?" George said.

"Nothing."

"Zero-niner Whiskey. Over missed-approach point. If runway approach/ runway lights are not in sight, execute missed approach."

George continued the downward flight. They were at six hundred feet, three hundred below where they were supposed to be.

"George, they told us to pull up. God damn it!"

The yellow air darkened abruptly, took on a regularity, a darkness which grew gray and extended out into the light. Like the focusing of a camera, the blur became defined, white numbers 1 9 in front of them and the approach lights harsh red below them. "We're visual," Ben said. They were down to nearly three hundred feet above the terrain. "Albany Approach, we've got the runway in sight."

"Eight-niner Zero-niner Whiskey, clear to land, contact Ground Control one-two-one seven when clear of runway."

It seemed to Ben a terse acknowledgment.

They touched down, lifted one wheel, and then settled, slowed to little forward progress by the reunion with earth.

"One-two-one seven. Thank you, sir. Thank you very much, Zero-niner Whiskey."

"Your controls," George said.

Ben looked over at him. But George was looking away from him, out the window, the back of his head to Ben. His hands were in his lap. Ben noticed the lines in them. No one was handling the airplane. Ben took the controls and followed directions to the general aviation facility. While he was following the lineman's signals to the tiedown position, the radio spoke again. "Zero-niner Whiskey, the Flight Service Station requests you contact them on the hotline from Page." And so there it was, Ben thought, they'd have his license. The FAA would have his license.

Now how could he be concerned about something like that when a little while ago he was worrying about getting killed, being *dead?*

The righteousness of his fury appalled Ben. None of it was worth so much anger. The license wasn't.

When they were out he opened the baggage compartment and got his bag. He watched the filling of the tanks. He wanted to see how much fuel had been left. George said, "I think we'll go inside."

"You stay right here," Ben said. That was all he said and he was surprised he had said that.

For some reason George stayed. Why? He hadn't all day gone along with what Ben had said.

Because he's had his way, Ben thought. Got where he wanted to go. At least he got the chance to try to go there. Got as close as he could and now he doesn't care. Shit on him, he almost killed his son, much less me.

The tanks held twenty-five gallons each. They put twenty-two gallons in one tank and twenty in the other. Eight gallons was less than an hour's flying time. If you had to do any climbing. Like on a missed approach. Each approach took about fifteen minutes. No sweat if you knew for sure that on one of your shots you'd get the visibility to get in. But George and he had both sweated. *George* had been sweating.

Ben walked toward Page Airways. The architecture annoyed him, affected modern. He was aware of George hurrying up beside him.

"I'll call them," George said.

Ben was silent, kept walking.

"I'll take the responsibility," George said.

"The fuck you will. It's my airplane."

"I was the one who was in violation," George said.

"You're goddamn right."

"Don't make a . . . a *gesture,* Ben. It's not worth it. I can't fly any more. You can. Don't throw away your license."

Ben stopped. "Get this, George. It's my airplane." He walked.

In the building George made no effort to get to the hotline before Ben did.

"It's foolish," George said. "You're throwing away your license."

"It was my airplane, George. You forgot that every mile we flew." He picked up the receiver.

"Flight Service, McIver speaking," Ben heard.

"This is Eight-nine Zero-nine Whiskey. You wanted me to call."

"Oh, yes. Just a minute, sir . . . Okay. We just wanted to make sure you were down."

"We're down."

"Your destination was Cornwall?"

"That's right."

"Okay. That was your flight plan and then they told us you were coming in here. Thanks for calling."

Ben smiled. That's all? "Thank you," he said.

117

Jonah was so *full* of it, Hilary thought. He looked around the field. He could see up and down and sideways. He imagined an airplane at pattern altitude and in his imagination he could see it clearly, a neat black silhouette against the yellow sky.

He heard himself laugh. Setting this flight up was like a caper movie. Timing, and who was where, and place, and all that . . .

There wasn't anyone around. An old man in the office, looked asleep. Falun Aigborg, he'd been told, days before, but he thought Aigborg had been dead for years. Besides, the man didn't look like he could physically drive a donkey cart, much less fly an airplane.

It was still and there was no traffic around. He'd have the sky at the airport to himself. He felt awfully good. Competent. In control. He had had two good shots of vodka—vodka so his breath wouldn't stink—and that had taken the tremblies out of him, the little squiggles of apprehension . . . He was going to fly the airplane now and fuck Laura later, have a good fuck with her finally. He felt invigorated, his body alive and pleasant, a neat place for his mind to be, and his mind felt contented, in control. The world was a happy place in which to be, and he wondered why he had ever thought that it wasn't.

Fifty Pop, the airplane in which he had trained and soloed, stood out on the ramp, its door cracked open to prevent trapped heat from crazing its Perspex windscreen. He had been out there already and seen the key in the ignition. The key was always in the ignition of Fifty Pop. He looked at his watch. Just like in a caper movie. Four fifty-five. At five o'clock he would walk out on the ramp and climb in Fifty Pop and start it up. He'd make a somewhat hasty taxi across the field to the ramp outside the terminal. Laura would come out through the gate over there, he'd push the door open, and she'd climb in. He'd rest his hand briefly on her bare brown thigh for luck, and then they'd go swinging off into the wild blue yonder together. Once around the pattern. No big deal. He'd done it before. He'd been afraid of it then, but *then* he hadn't been a pilot. Afraid of it now a little, but it was only once around. Shit, he'd already done it three times around alone before. And God knows how many times with Jonah before that.

118

They had gotten a cab at Page Airways. George and Randy had gotten into the back and Ben into the front, beside the driver, even though it wasn't necessary. But he couldn't abide to be close enough to George to speak to him. Not in front of Randy. Not in any case.

George had said to the driver, "The Ten Eyck." George knew everything and took over everything. Even where to stay in Albany.

It seemed to Ben an awfully long ride in. His impression was of streets that had never risen higher than two or three stories of wood houses. It was like what he thought of as America before he was born.

The yellow light was everywhere. On the ground it even seemed cheerful. Looking up you could see blue behind the yellow. It was difficult to imagine that that same bright-hued air was black two thousand feet up.

George tried to talk to Ben, to start conversations. Ben looked at the horizons. The bright, nonexistent horizons. Where the sky settled into the earth and left no vestige of the earth out there.

Some little meanness, some very great anger, in Ben would not allow him to reply to George. Ben began to feel he was angry at himself as well.

At the Ten Eyck Ben got out of the cab with his bag and, without thinking about anything but his anger, walked away, leaving George to pay the fare. At the desk he checked in for himself and then heard George, behind him, inquiring about a liquor store. Then George joined him at the desk. "Ben, I'm going to get us a good bottle of Scotch. Come over and have a drink with me."

"I feel like a good, long shower, George."

"After that."

"I'll see."

George looked away and then back at Ben. "Ben, I'm not getting the bottle for me. I mean, not alone. We ought to have a drink together."

"I'll see."

In his room Ben sat on the bedside. He heard the air conditioning, but hardly felt it. He was still hot and sweating. He called down for a double martini on the rocks and then said make it two, tasting the astringent coldness of it in his mouth with some delicate, expectant tongue in his mind, and with some goddamn long deep need in him to get alone with some gin for a few minutes.

He wanted to shower most of all, but lay on the hot textured bedspread and waited for the drinks and tried to think of pleasant things. He thought of the nude body of Madelon. If he had it to do again, he'd sure as hell go to bed with her this time. He thought of Adele. Nude. Vaporizing into the air, disappearing into her surroundings, light as thought . . . Christ, the love he felt for her, but thinking about her wasn't pleasant at all because she wanted him to make up his whole mind forever about his life and marry her . . .

The telephone rang. "Ben, I'm in room six-twenty-two. I've got the Scotch. Why don't you come and have that drink with me?"

"George . . . I'll come over in a while, George."

Ben lay back. The light was soft and he almost rested. But then a picture of the flight came to him, the Cherokee up there above the clouds, and his heart speeded and its pulse deepened.

There was a knock on the door. Room service. Ben signed and tipped and then realized he was in his underwear and a shirt. He drank the soothing coldness of the martini, felt it spread through him, turning vaguely warm. He finished the martini and showered.

He left the steamy, antiseptic-smelling bathroom and went back into the bedroom. He lay down and felt calm.

George called again. Ben said he'd come by in a few minutes. He drank the second martini and dressed in clean clothes. He took a long, safe time. He could feel the calmness within himself. It was like a great gentle sky descending on him.

Ben went down the hall to George's room and knocked. He could feel the wetness of the shower in the hair around his ears. He felt quiet and would say nothing. Have a drink with George. George opened the door. *"You sonofabitch!"* Ben yelled at George.

Randy looked over quickly from the television set.

"What is it?" George said.

"Randy, maybe you ought to go read in the lobby for a while."

"I'll make the decisions for Randy," George said.

"Yeah, you sure as hell did."

"Okay, Randy, we'll meet you in the lobby."

Randy looked at Ben with anger, but left.

When the door was closed, Ben said, *"You sonofabitch, Detwiler. Who the hell do you think you are?"*

"You tell me, Ben. That's what you want to do."

"You almost killed your son today. That's who *you* are."

"You *shut up,* Ben! *Don't you talk to me like that."*

Ben stood closer to George, leaned at him. "You almost killed your son, George. You almost killed all three of us. But I figured almost killing Randy might *concern* you."

"Ben, you haven't even *learned* yet what I've *forgotten* about flying."

Ben spoke quietly. "Exactly, George. You've forgotten it. You can't do it any more. Not safely."

The flesh of George's face paled. For a few seconds he looked as if he might hit Ben. Then he turned and went to a window and looked at the rebuilding city around them. Ben saw the clenched fists at his sides.

"I don't know what you were proving up there, George. Trying to prove. Trying to be the big fighter pilot again? Putting me down because of Adele? I don't know, George. But that's it. You're not flying with me again. When you're ready to go back to Cornwall, rent a car, Colonel."

George turned from the window. "Big fighter pilot," he said. "Big fighter pilot," he repeated, and nodded.

"That was a cheap shot, George. You know it. I apologize."

"Big fighter pilot. I'm glad you said it. That's really something to think about. That's really something for me to think about. I mean that." He looked at his chest. "I haven't got wings any more, have I?"

Ben was silent.

"Or colonel's insignia. Though I guess sometimes I act like I do. Like today. You were right to bring up Randy. I make too many decisions for him. I dragged him along down there. I didn't ask him if he wanted to go. I do all the decision-making in that house. My house. You know I've entirely ignored that Randy has the right to make decisions?"

Oh, Christ, Ben thought, I've gone and . . . and what? Maligned a good man? Well, he wasn't a good man today.

"You ready to have a drink with me, Ben?"

"Sure."

"I've got Scotch and ice. And tap water."

"Yeah. All three."

George said, "You want long water or short water?"

"Make it long."

George went to the bathroom and turned on a faucet and came back with Ben's drink. He held his own drink, Scotch and ice, and looked at it. "My hand feels like shaking," he said. "But it doesn't. I don't know why that's so. Physiologically. Why it doesn't shake when it wants to. Or maybe I should say *psychologically.* What you said about Randy is true. I could have caused his death today. I'm kind of . . . Inside myself I feel . . . It sort of feels like . . ." He looked at Ben. "Ben, I'm standing here. And I'd like to *scream.* Don't worry, I won't. But I'm standing here and I'd like to scream." He spoke with terrible quiet. "I am so *angry,* you can't imagine. I feel like I'm angry at you. For saying what you did. But that's not right. It wouldn't be right to be angry at you. But I sure would like to scream, Ben, *I sure would like* to tear some things apart. Cheers, Ben," and he lifted his glass back and drank off most of it. Then he set it down on a bureau. "That's the nice thing about a hotel. You don't have to worry about ruining things." Ben realized that George was crying. The sound of sucking air in through his nose to clear it. "At home, with Ceil, another pleasure was, it was taking care of things. Not putting a drink down on something. Because the something mattered. Here the furniture doesn't matter. Oh shit . . ." George sat down. He sat very straight and, his head up, let tears come.

Ben stood still, not wanting to violate the man's privacy. Wanting to go to him and put his hand on his shoulder, not knowing whether George could accept that.

"But I'll tell you this," George said, running a handkerchief roughly and quickly on his face, blowing in it, and stuffing it angrily away, "I'll tell you this. I'll tell you something about being a big fighter pilot *and* a colonel. You've got a hell of a lot to learn about flying. Oh, you handle an airplane okay. Better than most. Not as good as some. But you did a good job out there today. On instruments. For the time you've had. And you did a good job on top. For all I know, you saved our lives. Do you know we might have been hypoxic up there? Never mind. I want to keep to the point. You still have got a hell of a lot to learn about flying. The most important part. Sure, you can fly the airplane. But you've got to be *in charge.* You've got to learn *to be in charge.* You can't let *anyone* tell you what to do. Not me, not Jonah, not an airline captain, not Falun Aigborg himself. *You're* in command. You've got to learn *command.*"

Ben began to become angry again. "I told you, George, I told you this *wasn't* a mission. I'm flying a lightplane. Most of the time I'm flying alone. What has command got to do with that?"

"You think about it," George said. "And maybe this flight will be worth something to you after all."

119

It was hot in the cabin of Fifty Pop and Hilary left the door cracked as he taxied over to the terminal ramp to pick up Laura.

He was doing everything precisely. Of course, it was only start-up and taxi, but he felt the sure confidence in his fingers, his eyes saw the way his fingers went to the knobs and toggle switches and controls, he felt how *in control* he was and, yes, it was just the way he'd imagined it back in that winter room, New Year's Eve, in Queens, with the airplanes he couldn't see, but could only hear and feel, coming into La Guardia over the roof of his building.

Laura had attracted three men. And why shouldn't she? With her looks, and dressed the way she was in those shorts and that thin jersey? The four of them stood inside the fence at the New EnglandAir gate. Two of them were ground people who worked for New EnglandAir and the other one was a policeman. When Hilary taxied up, one of the New EnglandAir people opened the gate for Laura and she came striding out. He imagined their view of her, that rounded, oscillating behind in shorts. He felt the warmth of arousal. Somehow *imagining* what she looked like from behind was even more exciting than seeing her walking toward him or the reality of her face as she bent and slipped into the Cherokee and sat beside him. He pulled the door shut and locked it and hit it to make sure it was secure. Then, with a feeling of jollity and good old eroticism, he put his hand right between her legs and gave her a quick squeeze.

"Don't do that!"

"That's for luck!" Hilary said happily.

"Well, you keep your hands to yourself, do you hear?"

Hilary braked hard. "You can get out right here."

[311]

"What?" Laura said. Her voice was considerably softened.

"I said *you* can get out right here."

"I heard that." She looked down at her lap. "I just wasn't ready for that."

"Well, you just better *get* ready for that. That's what you were talking about before, weren't you? Flying and fucking?"

"Don't be crude."

"Wasn't it?"

"Well, fly, boy. We're sitting here *still.*"

"You're just crazy to go off into that wild blue yonder."

"Yes, I am. And I'm sitting here still waiting for someone to *do* it. Now *do* it or I'm getting out and going home."

"Oh, lady. I'm going to do it."

Hilary lined up with the runway stripe. It seemed to stretch off into infinity. Way out there somewhere it seemed to dissolve in golden light. The tops of the trees beyond the runway were bathed in what looked like golden smoke. It was one of the most beautiful sights he had ever seen, as thrilling as Laura's nudity the night she had undressed to her waist.

He was hardly aware of his takeoff, it was that good. The numbers on the instruments fitted together with the wheels on the runway and then with the wings' passage into and through the air. The airplane climbed like a magic carpet, as sure as daylight, as easy as daylight. It just wanted to climb and climb . . .

Hilary was as happy as he had ever been in his life.

And going back to the ground soon.

No one had ever had as much fun flying as he was having just then. No one had ever been so *in control.*

He leveled at the proper altitude and made a left turn, gentle, slow, smooth, and sure, back into the pattern. He was downwind, parallel to the runway, but he couldn't exactly see it. It wasn't *obscured* exactly, but the only thing he could see clearly was if he looked straight down, and then the ground could be clearly seen, but the ground had gotten dark. The yellow light was brilliant around them. Like the glow from the halos of saints in old paintings he liked to go and look at in the museums in New York. It was so beautiful.

Laura had placed her hand on his leg. Softly, lightly, but her touch overwhelmed him with sexual eagerness. "Hil, just fly me over my house."

"I don't know where it is."

"I'll show you. I think I can find it. But that's the important thing. I want you to fly me over my house."

"Okay. If you can show me where to go."

"It's over there somewhere," Laura said.

Hilary turned the airplane to where she had pointed. He had gained two hundred feet without noticing, Hilary saw. He leveled off. The funny thing was, he realized, he had to look straight down to fly the airplane. That was how he kept it straight and level. Odd. Very odd.

Then he looked down and could not see the ground.

The terror in him was like an electric shock.

The airplane made strange noises, cryings out, horror screams from the engine, the feeling of hurtling down in his body and he couldn't *see* anything, just golden light streaming by, as if it had substance, like in the saints' pictures . . .

Above he saw blue. It looked clear up there. It looked as if he was flying in golden smoke and up above was a large hazy blue circle, but where he was, he was in the middle of the circle but beneath it and all he had to do was climb and he'd be up there, out of this murky stuff . . .

He was wrestling the airplane, twisting it, twisting controls, instruments pointing at each other and nodding off erratically to places they should not be, the stall warnings coming on, going off, coming on . . .

He had full power on and the one instrument he could read fully he concentrated on, the artificial horizon, and when he pulled back too much on the yoke the red-light stall warning came on and he could control that by keeping his airspeed up, up about eighty or above and he concentrated on that, the airplane wings of the artificial horizon just up in a climb position but not too far up, and the airspeed back and forth up and down *65 72 75 70 90* as he dove and then slowed to *70* again as the airspeed fell off . . .

He knew that if the airspeed got too low they would stall and they would die. There would be nothing he could do about it.

He had imagined himself in a movie at the controls in a stall situation on instruments many times. But this was real. He wasn't the hero here. He was helpless. The best he could hope for was to keep the airplane flying. He had no idea how they would get down again. He looked down. All clouded over. He had no idea how he'd ever see the earth again. If he couldn't see the earth again, he could never get down to it again. He had learned enough about flying to know that.

120

"Jonah's out in the garden, Ev," Yvonne said. She didn't know what was wrong between Jonah and Ev. She only knew that Jonah no longer would talk about Ev. That was unlike Jonah. She didn't know anyone that Jonah disliked, of the people he knew well. "Do you want me to get him?"

"Yes and quickly," Ev said over the phone.

Jonah's hands were damp with earth and sweat when he came in and he hesitated before he picked up the phone. "What, Ev?"

"Your student. Amory. Or whatever his name is. He's in trouble. He took off, Jonah. In this. He, look, he taxied over to the terminal in Fifty Pop—"

"How the hell did he get Fifty Pop? He called me and I told him—"

"Never mind about that, Jonah, *never mind about it!* He's out there. He's flying."

"He's flying? *He's flying?* In this?"

"For Christsake, Jonah, *what have I been saying?*"

Jonah hung up.

Yvonne watched Jonah run to the car. Her husband. The pains were regular now. It *was* the baby coming. And there he was out there, the *bastard,* going to the airport. As usual. Yvonne sat down and cried. She cried for a minute, maybe two minutes. *And that's it,* she said to herself. She sniffled, stood up, and went to the phone and called Dr. Glynn. She told him her signs and symptoms. He said come in right away.

121

Jonah stood still. He stood as still as he could keep himself and listened to everything Ev could tell him.

"He's got Fifty Pop. I left the keys in it. Don't I *always* leave the keys in airplanes *here?* But he's flying around out there and I can't get him on the *radio.* And you know, that's instruments out there, Jonah. *Instruments.* How much instrument time does he have?"

"Forty-five minutes."

"Sure." Ev had always argued that the government requirement of thirty minutes of instrument time before solo was both too little and too much. It was too little because it wasn't enough to teach anyone how to fly instruments. And it was too, too goddamn much, because after their thirty minutes of orientation people thought they could go ahead and fly instruments on it. "Sid, over at New EnglandAir, said he took on a passenger. Laura Sullivan."

"Jesus shit Christ."

"I can't get him to answer on the radio, Jonah."

"Well, why the fuck not, Ev? Maybe he's got the fucking thing sitting there not turned on?"

"Look, Jonah, no one's ever been killed in this operation."

"Oh, Ev, shut up. C'mon, Ev, let's all . . . just try and *think* about this."

"Can he fly in this?"

"I don't know . . . No, Ev, he can't. He can't fly in this. He doesn't know enough instruments. He'll get terrified. The best we can hope for is he doesn't kill someone on the ground."

"He could climb out," Falun said.

"Yes," Jonah said. "Yes, by God, Falun. He *could* climb out. If there was a hole. He wouldn't even know he couldn't do that. What are the tops, Ev?"

"Locally?"

"Well, shit, I don't mean Chicago, Ev!"

Adele came in from the parking lot. She went to the secretary's desk and got out some papers.

"They were at fourteen around two o'clock."

"Get on the horn and find out where they are now."

Falun said, "How high can that Cherokee One-forty climb? What is its service ceiling? What is its absolute ceiling?"

"Falun," Jonah said, "the book says—the way it's loaded, two passengers, no baggage, maybe three hundred pounds aboard, in passengers—they can go to fifteen thousand, seventeen if they really work at it. But it's going to be damn slow above eight, you know that."

"Can this fellow fly, Jonah?"

"No." Jonah stopped. "A little. He's got a talent. But goddamn little training."

Adele looked up and listened.

"He'll become hypoxic at fourteen thousand," Falun said. Jonah went to the doorway and looked out. "He'll become subject to hypoxia, if he gets there. Do you know what? With my emphysema, that is exactly what I'm suffering from. Hypoxia. Insufficient oxygen. I can't get sufficient oxygen into me just as if I were at too high an altitude. He and I are dying of the same thing," Falun said. "He doesn't know it, of course." Falun looked down at his hands. "Damn waste. Young man. Young woman."

Jonah turned back from the door. "Have we got IFR minimums now?"

"That's what New EnglandAir says," Ev said.

Jonah said to Falun, "That young man—someone's going to have to fly the airplane for him. One way or another."

"Your student?" Adele said. "Amory?"

"Hilary. His name is Hilary."

"No one knows what the tops are now, Jonah," Ev said. "Last pirep was about two o'clock this afternoon. But nothing's flying around those levels now. There's cooler air moving in on top. They could be breaking up on top, lowering."

"Adele," Jonah said, "you try to raise him."

"You ought to do it, Jonah. Your voice might help him. He doesn't know me very well."

"I know, I know. But get started on it. I've got to call ATC."

"Maybe he doesn't realize he's in Fifty Pop," Adele said. "What's his last name."

"Blane. Good point, Adele. Get started. I'll take it in a few minutes." Jonah had picked up the telephone and dialed. "This is the Cornwall airport," Jonah said, "and we have an emergency here. Get me the watch supervisor."

Adele was saying into the microphone, "Hilary Blane, this is Cornwall. Five-zero Papa, this is Cornwall. Do you read?" She let go the button, waited a few seconds, and then keyed it again. "Cherokee Fifty Pop, do you read Cornwall?" Again she waited.

Over the phone Jonah heard, "Watch supervisor. Gillis speaking."

Jonah said, "Mr. Gillis, this is Jonah Jaquith. I'm an instructor at Cornwall. We have a possible emergency here. Student took off in a Cherokee at—approximately what time did he take off, Ev, and get me the fuel on board."

"Off at about five o'clock. I don't know how much fuel's on board, all I did was taxi it out. It hasn't been flown today, I guess it was topped off last night—"

"Well, look in the goddamn records."

"Hilary Blane," Adele said, "I say again, pilot Hilary Blane, can you hear me? If you hear this transmission, key your microphone button. Just press the button on the microphone, Hilary, I'll hear it on this end."

There was silence.

Jonah said, "Off at approximately twenty hundred hours Zulu. Not qualified on instruments. Has about forty-five minutes' instrument instruction, half an hour of solo, eight hours total. We believe he has a passenger. We can't make radio contact."

"*Sonofabitch!*" Ev said. "Who was lineboy last night?"

"Cherokee Fifty Pop, Hilary Blane, if you read Cornwall, key your mike twice." She released her own mike button and said to Ev, "Tommy was."

"Shit, I sent him home."

Jonah said, "He's been up about twenty-five minutes. Hold on . . . Ev, get on another phone and call Sauer and see if the police have any reports of loud explosions, anything that would indicate an airplane down locally . . ."

Jonah listened as the watch supervisor spoke to him. "Okay," Gillis said. "I've got the word out, the boys are looking." In his mind Jonah saw the interior of Boston Center, the huge room, dark and windowless, a couple of hundred men looking at radar screens and talking, over microphones, to other men in the air, sometimes hundreds of miles away, men who were white blips on the screens in front of them, blips that widened and enlarged every few seconds as a scanning line swept through them. "In particular," Gillis said, "I've asked the radar controller for your sector if he can pick up a target in the vicinity of the Cornwall airport."

Gillis was silent for a few seconds and Jonah almost spoke. But then Gillis said, "In a panic situation—and we may as well assume we're going to be dealing with a panic situation, *if* he's still up there—in a panic situation, where the student isn't qualified to handle the airplane, we want an instructor who is completely familiar with the student so he can tell the student how to fly it. Are you his instructor?"

"Yes, I am."

"You on good terms with him? Does he trust you?"

"Yes to both."

"Okay, what's his name?"

"Hilary Blane. That's Hotel India Lima Alpha . . ."

"Fifty Pop, if you read Cornwall, key your mike, or talk to us. Press the microphone button *down,* Hilary."

"If I can talk to him," Jonah said, "I'm going to concentrate on getting him to keep it straight and level, that and calming him down."

"That's right. Get him in reference to minimal instrumentation. We want to get him to a safe altitude with the wings level and then work on him from there."

"Cherokee Five-zero Papa, Fifty Pop, Hilary Blane, if you can hear me, push your microphone button down twice. Go ahead."

The radio speaker went *click click.*

The sound of it was surrounded by silence in the room.

Jonah said, "Hold on, we may have him."

Adele spoke very carefully. "That was good, Hilary, very good, Cherokee Fifty Pop. I heard you. Now do it again. Key your microphone button twice. Go ahead."

There was silence.

Ev said, "The sonofabitch wasn't topped off last night. Or else, if it was, no one wrote it down. Looking at the records, the most he could have had on board, I figure an hour and a half at the outside."

Click. Click.

Jonah nodded. "We figure he can stay airborne for about another hour," Jonah said to the phone. "That's his fuel supply."

"All right, Cherokee Fifty Pop," Adele was saying. "Good work. Now Hilary, when I tell you to do it, I want you to hold the microphone up to your mouth and push the button down and tell me you hear me. Then release the button. All right, Hilary, go ahead, talk to me."

The words were rushed—*"I hear you."*

"Good work, Hilary. What are your flight conditions?"

"We've got him, we're talking to him," Jonah said.

"Can you help me? Can you help me?"

"We're going to help you, Hilary. Tell me your flight conditions."

Gillis said, "We've alerted the direction-finding stations, we've got the DF network alerted. Is he transponder equipped?"

"Negative on transponder."

"What frequency have you got him on?"

"One twenty-two eight."

"We haven't got it. We'd like to put him on a discreet frequency, if we can. But we don't want to confuse him."

"I'll start working him in a couple of minutes. We'll see."

"I say again, Fifty Pop, Hilary, talk to me, what are your flying conditions?"

"I think I'm in a turn." Again terribly rushed.

"Okay, Jonah. The Gardner radar man has picked up a target. We don't have any other traffic and no known IFR traffic in your vicinity. He has a target fifteen miles northwest of the Cornwall airport. The target looks like he's heading in a northwesterly direction."

"Hilary, can you see the ground? Over."

"The plane keeps getting away from me!"

"We'd like to ask him to make some turns for identification," Gillis said. "When you think he's ready."

"I'm going to start talking to him now. He's panicked, all right."

"Jonah," Gillis said, "the instructor has got to be very careful about how he talks to the pilot, how he tells him what action to take. So he doesn't confuse the pilot further or cause him to do something to put the aircraft out of control."

"Jesus Christ. I know what to do."

"Okay, good luck. Stay with me?"

"Yes."

"No, no. Can't see ground."

"Hilary, I'm handing the microphone to Jonah now. Jonah's going to talk to you. Listen to him."

Adele handed Jonah the microphone.

"Hilary, this is Jonah. Talk to me, man. Over."

"Hi, Jonah."

"You're doing a good job, Hilary. Christ, I taught you, didn't I? You're going to get down okay. Your left hand hurting?"

"Shit yes!"

"Okay, okay there, white knuckles. Relax it, just for a second. What do you see, Hilary? Can you see outside the airplane?"

"Oh, Jesus—"

Jonah listened. "He's gone," Jonah said to the phone. "You guys still got him?"

"We have the target."

"Jonah!"

"I'm listening, Hilary. Hilary, look at the artificial horizon. Forget everything else. Look at the artificial horizon. Get the wings of the little white airplane resting on top of the white line of the horizon. Concentrate on getting the wings on the horizon. Tell me when you've done that."

There was silence. Then, "Okay, Jonah. Okay. Things are better here."

"Keep your eyes on that instrument, Hilary. Keep the wings on the white line and everything else will take care of itself. Now keep watching that. I'm going to ask you some questions. But I don't want you to look outside. Just watch the artificial horizon. Have you been able to see the ground recently?"

"No. Couldn't see ground. Not for a long time. I've been climbing. Up toward the light. It's okay now. I'm okay. I can look up and see blue. Jonah? Jonah?"

"Hilary? Do you read me, Hilary?"

"I'm losing altitude, I'm climbing, I think I'm in a spin!"

"Shit, he wouldn't know if he was upside down," Ev said.

"Look at the artificial horizon, Hilary."

"The stall light's on!"

"Push the nose down. Push the nose down, Hilary."

"I'm diving!"

"Artificial horizon. Wings on white line. Artificial horizon. Wings on white line."

Again silence. Jonah waited, letting him concentrate on the one task.

"Jonah?"

"I'm with you, Hilary."

"It's okay again. Everything under control. I'm up above it now. All the clouds are underneath."

"Okay, then you feel okay, Hilary? You can fly visually?"

"Yeah, I'm okay, Jonah. This is okay here."

"Keep looking at your artificial horizon anyway. It hasn't tumbled has it?"

"Tumbled?" Hilary laughed. "Shit, we've taken a lot of tumbles. But I kept getting it back. Over."

"Do you have an altitude on him?" Gillis said.

"Not yet," Jonah said to the phone, and then to Hilary, "Okay, *okay,* Hilary, my man. Stay cool. What's your altitude? Say your altitude."

". . . That's hard, Jonah . . . I'm looking at it . . . but it doesn't make sense, I've forgotten how to do it . . ."

"Hilary, we'll do this simple. What's the big hand pointing at?"

"It's between eight and nine. The little hand is up toward three."

"That's good, Hilary."

"Shit," Ev said, "he couldn't be coming up on three thousand. Could he? Not on top he couldn't."

"Hilary, there's a tiny little hand. Is it pointing at zero or off to the side?"

"It's not pointing right *at* zero. It's hard to tell, Jonah."

Jonah said into the phone, "He's between thirteen thousand eight hundred and thirteen nine and he's on top." Into the microphone he said, "Hilary, you got a lot of eyes on you now, radar eyes, a lot of people are helping you. Now I'm going to ask you to do some things they want you to do. Simple things, like when you first started flying. Just remember you've done them hundreds of times now. Anyway, I'm talking to the radar people on the phone the same time I'm talking to you. If you don't hear me come back to you right away, stay cool, I'm talking to the radar people on the phone the same time I'm talking to you. If you don't hear me come back to you right away, stay cool, I'm talking with the radar people. Now you stand by while I ask them what they want you to do."

"Okay, Jonah," the watch supervisor said, "that was well done. Ask him to make a ninety-degree turn to the left. No, hold that. All right. Ask him to make a standard rate turn to the left. Can he do that? Does he know what a standard rate turn is?"

"Hilary, I want you to make a gentle bank to the left. Just make a long turn, like you were doing a one-eighty for me. Tell me when you start the turn."

"Starting turn." The tightness was back, the words jammed together.

There was silence on the telephone. Then, "Yes, Jonah, the target we're watching *is* turning."

"Good work, Hilary. They think they see you turning. Keep turning. Nice level turn, maintain your altitude." To the phone Jonah said, "If I try to get him over to your frequency there's a chance we might lose him entirely."

"Okay, keep him on unicom. Now tell him to make a standard rate turn to the right."

"Hilary, you're looking good, real good they say. Now level off. Tell me when you're level."

"Level."

Adele said, "He sounds relieved."

Ev said, "Christ, he's scared doing a turn. Can you imagine trying to come down? *The poor bastard.*" He bit his cigar.

"Hilary, they'd like a turn to the right now. Give me a real nice turn to the right. Keep it gentle."

There was no response.

"Okay there, Jonah, we have him. He's now eighteen miles northwest of Cornwall bearing three-four-zero degrees. Now we have a helluva problem. What do we do with him?"

"Stand by," Jonah said. "I want to talk to him . . . Hilary, Jonah. Say hello, man."

"Hello, man."

"Hilary, fly straight and level. They've got you, a confirmed radar target less than twenty miles from here. Hell, man, you're on television."

"I've been there before." His speech is slowing up, Jonah thought. "I'm flying level, Jonah."

"Good work. Stand by while the radar guys and I talk." He unkeyed the microphone. "Okay, Gillis, what are the options?"

"We've got to get him someplace where we can get him on the ground. That's what our helluva problem is. Every place is socked in. The nearest place we've got that might be VFR is Albany and we've got radar assistance there. Albany's marginal."

"Negative on Albany. He hasn't got the fuel."

"How're you?"

"We might have IFR minimums. Hold on. Hilary, how you doin'?"

"*. . . I don't know.*"

"Tell me about that. What do you mean about 'I don't know'?"

"*Goddamn it, Jonah! I don't know.*" Jonah waited in case he might say more. Then Hilary's voice came back. "*. . . I'm scared . . .* I've got a headache . . ."

"Hilary, I'm going to come and get you. Can you fly the airplane all right? For a few minutes? Talk to me, Hilary. Over?"

". . . Yeah, Jonah . . . You gonna be here soon?"

"I'm coming right up." He said to Adele, "Try to get him turned around. Just give him a standard turn and wait till ATC says he's pointed in the right direction." Jonah said to the phone, "Gillis, I want you to clear me up and steer me to him."

122

The Skymaster was oxygen-equipped, and before takeoff Jonah quickly checked the pressure gauge in the console above him. Then he was climbing out and on instruments—visual contact with the ground came and went erratically. Coming back he might have to cheat the airport minimums for landing. That was all right. He could cheat. Given the circumstances. Coming back. He never cheated. Not like that. No reason why he couldn't kill himself, cheating. He forgot about it. No student of his had ever hurt himself. Wasn't going to happen now.

ATC gave him vectors, and when he broke out and told them he was on top, the controller said, "Roger, Two-two Charlie, on top at thirteen thousand. Target aircraft is five miles at eleven o'clock and closing."

"Thank you, sir, I haven't got him yet."

"ATC would like to give you a thousand feet vertical separation."

"Negative, Boston."

"Roger, we understand. Five miles' separation is required. Or one thousand feet vertically."

"Two-two Charlie understands."

"Roger, Two-two Charlie. Your target is two miles now at twelve o'clock."

"I've got him. I'm going wide of him and then try to join him. I'm leaving your frequency for one-twenty-two point eight now."

"Two-two Charlie, frequency change approved. Good luck."

The blue of the sky to the east was already tending toward soft gray. The clouds below were orange-glazed to the west, stark white immediately below, and chilly darkening to the east.

"—doing fine, Hilary. Good work. Center tells us you're heading right back toward us. Now look ahead of you. Straight ahead. Jonah is about two miles away. Do you see him?"

". . . don't see nothin' . . . Looking at . . . art . . . rizon . . . Don't see Jonah . . ."

Jonah said, "Hilary, I'm right beside you. Look to your left."

"Jonah . . . *Hey there, Jonah* . . ."

There was a girl on the other side of Hilary.

"Hilary, I want you to concentrate on your flying. I'm going to come in beside you. You just keep watching me and do what I say. Try to watch me as much as you can. And listen to me. Every so often I'll be silent and I won't transmit. You can talk to me then if you want to. This is just like a lesson except we're in different airplanes. But I'm going to talk to you and you listen to me just like we were sitting next to each other. Okay? Over."

". . . God *damn* you, Jonah . . . this *fucking* broad sitting . . ."

Jonah waited until he was sure there was nothing more. "Say again, Hilary." But he knew what it was. Belligerence, anger—hypoxia. With his throat dry and cold from the supplemental pure oxygen, and with the intense lucidity it always seemed to create in him, Jonah looked over at the man who was starving to death for air. He would be trying to chew the oxygen out of the low-pressure air, his heart racing from hyperventilation

—there would be dizziness and fatigue and terror and the headache he had mentioned and . . .

Adele said, "Center has had you as a single target for some time now."

"Roger."

"—*fuck you, fuck you all* . . . Jesus . . . Jonah . . . What can I do?"

"Easy, Hilary. We're going down now, I'm going to take you down. When we get lower you'll feel better. Stay right close to me . . . I'm tucking in now, Adele. Stay right close to me, Hilary, and we'll go to the VOR and then fly an approach together so you can land in Cornwall. Your head will clear as we go down. All right, Cornwall, I've set up a formation situation, more or less wingtip to wingtip. That's it, Hilary, stay there. Now ease back on your power. If you can read your rpm indicator, it's over there to your right, just above the copilot wheel, do you see it?"

". . . rpm's . . . I see them . . ."

"Pull back your throttle till you're showing nineteen hundred rpm's. Till the needle is at nineteen. Can you do that?"

". . . Got nineteen, Jonah . . ."

"Okay, Hilary, that's fine. Now we're going down. You watch me. Just like under the hood, but you get to watch outside. Cornwall, we're going down to ten as quickly as I can take him, get some oxygen in him. Okay, Hilary, put your nose down a little. I'm putting my nose down, see me?" Jonah pulled back further on his power. The engines were pulled back so far that Jonah thought he could hear the air slip by now. "We'll go down at a hundred and twenty miles per hour, Hilary. That's twelve on the airspeed. The airspeed indicator is just to your left. It's the first instrument on top to your left. Do you see it?"

"I see it, Jonah . . . I've got the needle on twelve, Jonah."

"Fine, Hilary. That's it. Looks good, looks good, looks real good. Remember, just like we practiced. Gentle on the controls. You're doing fine." They slipped into the silver dancing air and then into grayness.

"*I can't think! I can't concentrate!*"

"You're doing fine. Keep your airspeed at one-twenty. How's the airspeed?"

". . . twelve . . ."

"Good deal. The twelve is one-twenty. Keep it there and we'll stay side by side. Okay now, Hilary, you're too close to me, you're moving in too close," Jonah said, his voice as calm as he could make it. The prop of the other airplane was coming up on the tip of the Skymaster's wing. Jonah tried to pull out in front of it and off to the side. The spinning prop seemed to throw off vapor. "Just maintain your present airspeed, Hilary." Jonah added power.

"*You're pulling away—pulling away!*"

"I'm not going anywhere, Hilary. You're doing a good job. Maintain your present airspeed. Good. We're at a safe distance and we're good and close in now, Hilary. You're flying *great.* We're going through, we're almost at eleven five now and you should be feeling better. You feel better, Hilary?"

There was no answer, but Hilary was holding the course and descent rate and relative position. *Christ,* there he came again! This time his wingtip caught Jonah's, and Jonah put on a burst of power and slipped to the side.

He readjusted, slowed, and eased back in closer to the Cherokee. The Cherokee seemed to be porpoising now, nosing up and down, its left wing rising up steeply.

"Hilary. Straight and level. Level off. Use the artificial horizon. *Hilary, the artificial horizon. Forget everything else, the artificial horizon!*"

Jonah checked his instruments and maintained his flight path. He looked back out to Hilary. He said into the microphone, "He's not there."

"Two-two Charlie, say again?"

"He's not there." The Cherokee was gone. There was nothing but darkening grayness, the grayness darkening in the descent.

"Hilary, do you read me?"

Silence.

"Hilary, do you read me?"

Silence.

Then Adele's voice. "Jonah, Center wants you to sqawk ident. They have two targets now."

Jonah was about to key the microphone to call Hilary again when, over his speaker, he heard Hilary's voice.

"—eeeeeeeeeeeeeeeeeeeeee—"

Five seconds, ten seconds. Then silence.

123

Adele was standing by the radio.

"Nothing," she said, when Jonah came in.

Sauer, the police chief, was there, too. "Did you hear him?" Sauer said to Jonah. "He was screaming, wasn't he?"

Jonah nodded.

Ev said, "They lost him on radar about ten miles west of here."

"That's all trees and hills," Sauer said.

"The worst of it is," Ev said, "Monadnock's in the middle of it."

"When can we get a search started?" Jonah said.

Sauer said, "The state police are out already. They're calling houses over there. The radio station is asking for information, sounds of a low-flying airplane, that sort of thing. We're getting some volunteer climbers, but they haven't got much daylight left. We can't do very much till dawn."

Jonah looked at his watch. Six-thirty. An hour and a half ago, Hilary and Laura Sullivan had been alive. Been on the ground. Hell, *fifteen minutes ago* they'd been alive.

"*Jonah,*" Adele said, "no one's told you. Yvonne's gone to the hospital."

124

Ben lay in the dark in his hotel room in Albany. He felt as if there were compressed stillness all around him. And within him. In the darkness he saw black instruments, white hands, white numbers, white calibrations and lines. It was like the flight coming up toward Albany.

He and George and Randy had gone out to dinner. They hadn't discussed the flight again. Afterwards Randy had gone up to bed, and he and George had had some drinks in the hotel bar. Several drinks.

When they were ready to go to their rooms, George had said, "I want to apologize for this afternoon, Ben. I should have shut up and done whatever you wanted, stayed on the ground, whatever. It's your airplane and you were kind enough to let me use it with you." George held out his hand.

The gesture surprised Ben, and it was a second or two before he responded, so George had stood there in the lobby with his hand out, a statue, a model of farcical courtesy.

Ben shook hands with him. "Thank you, George. Let's forget it. When the weather clears, you and Randy fly back with me."

"No. No, Ben. Thank you. I'll rent a car. We'll go home by car. I think I'll go out for a walk now." He'd left Ben then.

The thing was, Ben thought, it *was* his airplane, it *had* been his decision all along. That was terribly important. Terribly, terribly important. So simple and so important . . . He *was* in command. He could tell himself to go to his studio and do his work.

125

Falun lay on the couch in the dark living room of his house. He had asked Marion not to leave any lights on when she went to bed. He wanted to be alone in the darkness as times before he had wanted to be alone in the air. Darkness came in the windows that he could barely see, blackness spilled in and blurred his vision, the warm night air brought in the smell of pine forest. That smell was one of the earliest memories Falun had of the house. Thirty years ago? A little longer?

. . . He thought of a spring when their child, their Helga, their glorious Helga had been born. He thought of Helga and of her children. It was a gladdening thought and then a sad one. To leave them. But what he is leaving, Falun thought, is complete. That is enough. He felt proud. The bird of pain plummeted. He was terrified for the instant, but found the pride still there, a nourishment.

He found himself surrounded by others who were not here alone with him in the darkness. The ones whom he had read about who had died during these allotted months left to him to live. Claude Dornier, died December fifth . . . Then "Lefty" O'Doul, first name Frank. Batting champion. Saw him play . . . somewhere. In the thirties. Early thirties. Flying a Stinson S.M. 6000B passenger carrier then, on Long Island. Carried eleven passengers. Went Long Island to Newark to Boston and back to Long Island. Brooklyn, that was it. Played for Brooklyn. But saw him in Boston first, playing for Boston. Braves or Red Sox. I think he was American League first. Saw him at Fenway. The 6000B was a good airplane and half the price of the other trimotors. Got a cruise of a hundred and ten out of her sometimes. O'Doul had died December seventh. I was flying a DC-3 over Nebraska for United Airlines on December seventh, *the* December seventh. They told me about Pearl Harbor over the radio. I went back and told the passengers myself, one by one, because that was how it had happened to me over the radio.

I can remember the past so well, Falun thought, why do I have so much difficulty staying in the present?

He went back to the beginning, to his first log, going back to when, with the bequest of a departed uncle in hand, he had run away from home in New York City and gone all the way to Garden City, Long Island, and there, looking much older than his twelve years, had enrolled in Moisant's flying school. Four hours later he had soloed. In a Wright B, a cumbersome airplane. And a few air hours later he had flown all the way to five hundred feet and demonstrated a set of figure eights and had been licensed by the Aero Club of America, probably its youngest licensed member. And then a certificate from the Fédération Aéronautique Internationale, making him the youngest recognized pilot in the world, though no one knew it. He had been found and brought home by his understandably frightened and displeased parents when a night demonstration flight of his had attracted a crowd of—he was told—some five thousand people and there had been photographs of him in the New York newspapers. The people at the school had believed him to be sixteen. Everyone thought it very daring to go into the air, Falun remembered, but, as he had told many people over the years, really he had never done anything that he had thought daring. He had been in trouble at times, in danger, a sudden mechanical difficulty, angry winds, but he had never dared himself to do anything, or let anyone else dare him. He had told that to many people. That he had never himself done anything daring. People did not believe him. He could not understand that. Always he remembered the times when he had stayed on the ground while others went into the air. Many of them not to know the earth as a living person again after many such sorties, or after only one.

He had been reading his own log books. He had kept track, kept logs, even when no one else bothered. It was as if he had known that someday it would be important to him to know where he had been and with whom and how the weather had been in order to know where he had gotten to, where it was, finally, he was at.

The book he looked at now no longer existed anywhere but in his mind. It was a scrapbook of pictures and accounts of flights and pilots and airplanes carefully cut from newspapers and pasted onto butcher's paper. Stacks of pages, never bound, for he could never figure out how to bind them, the child back then. But now he could see each page, read it, remember the emotions, wondrous exultations and strivings he had felt. The very exultations he later experienced in the air. There was a photograph of Wilbur Wright flying over a hay wagon in France. A man on top of the wagon leant on a pitchfork and looked up. The animals pulling the wagon —longhorns by their look—bent to their work, stared at the ground . . . Herbert Latham trying to cross the English Channel and ending in it less than a mile out. Blériot. Yes, Blériot. What had he written of his flight that Falun had found so important? He had always remembered it, could see the page it was on, the typography . . . And now it was gone from him . . . What was it about Blériot? It had been after his Channel crossing. After having beaten Latham. Falun thought of spring, this last spring. No one can be so ignorant, so totally ignorant, that he does not know when he is seeing for the last time that which has been a part of every year of his life and which he will never see again . . .

Well, he has been to strange places. Falun remembers flying the Caribbean when almost no one else was, when there were no fields to land on and you went on floats or stayed to hard beaches and trusted your luck, and when you carried your own fuel or stayed within range of fuel. On one island he had broken a prop and then had discovered that, not only was he the first to bring an airplane to the island, but no ships called there regularly at all. Three months later he went off on a U.S. Navy coalburner which had happened by. Two months later he was back with a new prop. A shrine of sorts had been built around the airplane. It had to be torn down and the aircraft intricately neated and revived before he could take off. Lindbergh had been down there then. Looking around for Pan Am, as it turned out.

Blériot . . . Blériot . . . ? Falun remembered carrying souvenir mail for stamp collectors to help pay his expenses down there. And drawing maps for the Army Air Corps. And being afraid of headhunters, though of course there were none. He loved the *separateness* out over the water . . .

Falun remembered the words of Blériot describing his flight, his adventure across the Channel . . . *I turn my head to see whether I am proceeding in the right direction. I am amazed. There is nothing to be seen, neither destroyer, nor France, nor England. I am alone. I see nothing at all. For ten minutes I am lost. It is a strange position, to be alone, unguided, without a compass, in the air over the middle of the Channel.*

. . . a very long time ago . . . a very, very long time ago . . .

Falun wondered if perhaps he had experienced it all before, if perhaps he may be among the best prepared to die:

For . . . *I am amazed. There is nothing to be seen. I am alone. I see nothing at all. It is a strange position. To be alone. Unguided.*

Falun has spent a lifetime so. He is comforted by the familiarity.

126

When Jonah got to the hospital a few minutes before seven, Yvonne was lying in bed looking up at the ceiling. When she saw him she smiled and then she cried, smiling all the time. Jonah sat by her and they began to do the timing of the contractions together. A nurse came in and spent several minutes trying to find an artery from which her needle might draw blood. "When will the doctor be in?" Yvonne said.

"You mean Glynn hasn't been in yet?" Jonah said.

"Her contractions haven't been regular enough," the nurse said. "He'll be in after his dinner, I'm sure. He usually makes rounds between seven and eight."

The nurse went away and Jonah timed the contractions and the intervals between them and kept a meticulous accounting. Sometimes the contractions were strong and Yvonne used her breathing technique while Jonah coached her. But mostly the contractions were irregular and mild, varying between two and three minutes apart, though sometimes they came at only a minute apart.

"What happened at the airport?" Yvonne said.

Jonah, without thinking, just shook his head vaguely.

"Oh, my God. Something bad."

"We don't know yet. I'll tell you about it later."

"Jonah, now."

"I'd rather not, Yvie, really."

"Someone we know? Ev was on the phone. My God, Adele? Ben? George Det— Jonah, you have to tell me."

"A student. A student may have killed himself. And a passenger. That's it."

"A student? One of your students? . . . Hilary. Your student Hilary. The one I was scared of."

Jonah nodded.

"Who was the passenger?"

"We're not sure."

"Jonah . . . the contractions are starting. *Who was the passenger?*"

Yvonne breathed deeply and regularly, then paused and took a long cleansing breath. "There. That was a good one, Jonah. Strong." She put her hand on his. "Who was the passenger?"

"We think it was Laura Sullivan."

"Oh, God," Yvonne said quietly. "Oh, God. You thought you saw them downtown together one night, didn't you?"

"Yes."

"The night you went down to get me ice cream." She smiled. "But you don't know yet whether they're dead, whether they crashed?"

"They were trapped in instrument conditions, Yvie. We know they ran out of fuel about six-thirty. That's all we know."

"Then maybe they could still be all right? Somewhere?"

"Maybe."

When Dr. Glynn came in he asked Jonah to wait outside while he examined Yvonne and then he called Jonah back in. "Frankly, Mrs. Jaquith, I'm not terribly impressed. There is, as we say, a baby in there, and it does, as we say, want to come out. But, for the present, you're only middling dilated and the mechanism is not yet making a terribly sincere effort to present us with the little fellow. Patience, I advise patience. I'll stop in later. Keep the nurse advised, Jonah, there's a good fellow, you Lamaze people are most impressive—awfully useful, you husbands, and I don't say that idly. I'll be looking back in, Yvonne, keep up the good work."

When he was gone, Yvonne smiled and said, "I think Dr. Glynn is full of crap. Do you think he *meant* any of that?"

"I thought so."

"Oh." Yvonne looked pleased. She took Jonah's hand, started to speak, and then was interrupted by a contraction. Afterwards she said, "Jonah, as one Lamaze person to another, I'd like to ask you about a name we haven't discussed."

"Go ahead."

"I know you don't want Jonah for a boy. I appreciate that you want him to be his own person with his own name. But, Jonah? I've been thinking

[329]

all day. Of a name we didn't even discuss for a girl. The name feels so *right* to me."

"Well?"

"Joanna." She waited for him to speak. "It's important to me, Jonah." Jonah smiled. "Whatever you say."

At ten-thirty Dr. Glynn came back to make another examination and told Jonah to take a few minutes off. Jonah realized he hadn't eaten in many hours, but there was nothing he wanted. He went downstairs and outside. It was a small hospital, not quite two hundred beds, sixteen of them for maternity. Many of the lights were already off—except for a concentration of lights on the main floor and up on the second floor where the maternity facilities were. Sitting up there with Yvonne, Jonah had become aware of the aseptic qualities of the room and its furnishings, the strips of tape on Yvonne's arm. Nothing had much changed since Yvonne had come into the hospital. The contractions had remained irregular both in interval and intensity, though there had been more of them at the one-minute separation as the evening had grown later. Jonah walked back to the hospital entrance. The summer night was hot. Moths and smaller flying things sounded and darted about in the light near the door.

Dr. Glynn sat with Jonah in the near-darkened sandwich shop and gave him a cup of coffee.

"Now here is the situation, Jonah. As best I see it. I won't be technical, not necessary. Yvonne is not making progress. The labor is not increasing significantly. But neither is there any indication of cessation. I have two choices. I may stimulate the labor—that is, give Yvonne medicine which will intensify the contractions. Or, on the other hand, I may give her a bit of sedative so that the contractions will slow and she may rest. The better to fight the battle tomorrow."

"Why not leave her alone?"

"I'm afraid, from my experience, I'm afraid she will stay in just this condition and tire herself rather much, expend all her energy on labor at this stage, and I *would* like her to have her childbirth fully aware, as she wants it, without anesthesia, do you see? This sort of thing, middling labor, can go on for a considerable time, sometimes a day, sometimes as much as three days, and then of course the poor woman is exhausted.

"But if I rest her, with sedative, the baby receives the sedative as well, through the mother's bloodstream, and then the baby is sedated as well, and I don't like that. The little critter needs to help as well, do a bit of struggle, and, as well, we want him fully awake as soon as possible so he can get on with his breathing.

"So I say, let's get things going."

"Shouldn't we ask Yvonne?"

"The very thing."

Jonah sat with Yvonne, timing and notating contractions. From time to time he wiped her forehead with a washcloth. She was receiving intravenous fluid and had been given an injection to stimulate contractions. Dr. Glynn came in a few minutes before two. He was dressed in a scrub suit and had been sleeping in the doctors' room down the hall. He sent Jonah away.

Jonah went to the solarium and sat down. The television set was on though there was no one in the room. The two o'clock news wrap-up came on. Israeli jets had attacked near the Suez Canal and in Jordan and Lebanon. The Jordanian and Lebanese targets had been guerrilla bases. In the Suez area the Israelis had attacked missile emplacements. All the Israeli aircraft had come back safely. A number of one-hundred-pound rockets had been launched into Saigon by enemy forces. American B-52's had bombed both sides of Vietnam's border with Laos as they went after the Ho Chi Minh Trail.

"Houston. Tranquility Base here. The Eagle has landed."

Jonah watched the jumpy, intensely white film of the astronaut's boots making imprints on the moon.

"One year ago today," the newsman said.

Eleven people had been injured when a United 737 had skidded during an aborted takeoff at Philadelphia International.

Boston had beaten Oakland 9–4 and was 7½ games out.

The weatherman was calling for a complete break in the weather, initially poor and unsettled, with clouds, showers, and high winds, turning later to clearing visibility and steady rain well into the next night.

Dr. Glynn sat beside him.

"Jonah, I'm going to take Yvonne into the delivery room now. She's speeded up some and she's almost dilated."

"How many fingers? How often are the contractions?"

"Look, my fellow, I'd just like to have a look at her in the delivery room. There's more equipment there."

Jonah stood up. "Is there some danger?"

Dr. Glynn paused, a hesitation in his answer. "No. I wouldn't say so."

Jonah watched twenty minutes of a movie called *Cattle Country.* He got up and walked down the corridor. Through a set of windows, with blue fluorescent light at the walls in the background, he could see the infants bundled in their careful little bedclothes, intense in sleep, as if they were studying it. He went to the nurse's station. The light at the desk was on, carefully angled at some paperwork in progress, but no one was there. Down the hall was the delivery room.

He thought he heard Yvonne moan in anguish, call out for him.

The sweat started out of him.

He'd go to her. If she called out once more.

She did.

Except that you have to be scrubbed and gowned around people who were having babies . . .

Christ, he'd lost one person today. Hilary. No, two. Laura Sullivan. Two ought to be enough. Two ought to be enough for anybody. That ought to be enough for Yvonne. And the baby.

Dear God, the baby. He loved that baby *so*.

He wanted to cry. Hilary. Laura. Yvonne. The baby.

Dr. Glynn came out. He peeled off transparent ocher gloves. "Jonah, the baby's coming down in an odd position. I'm calling Dr. Albuther. He's our anesthesiologist."

"What do you need—"

Dr. Glynn had already dialed the number. "Donald? Llew Glynn here. Look, I've got an occip post here, and I think I ought to assist the birth . . . Thank you . . ." He hung up and hurried away.

Jonah stood at the counter at the nurses' station. He walked and returned. Minutes on his watch were so slow in passing that he wound his watch.

He sat down in the chair at the nurse's desk. He was being excluded. Glynn had said he didn't exclude Lamaze people. Jonah got up.

Once again he thought he heard Yvonne. Christ. Twenty minutes since Glynn had called Albuther. Where the hell did he live?

A nurse came out of the delivery room.

She passed Jonah and said, "She's doing fine, Mr. Jaquith."

Jonah heard Yvonne cry out.

"Where the hell does Albuther live?" Jonah shouted after her.

"Dr. Albuther lives in Antrim," the nurse said, hurrying away.

Why was she hurrying? What for? Jonah thought about Albuther. Albuther gets the call. Few minutes after three. He's got to dress. Okay, let's say he pulls clothes on over his pajamas. Twenty minutes' drive here. Should have *been* here by now. He thought he heard Yvonne again. He *had* heard her again. Yvonne *needs* an anesthesiologist?

Jonah turned around and hit the counter of the nurses' station with the side of his clenched fist. The sound resounded in the air-conditioned stillness and he did it again and felt better.

He looked at his watch. Twenty of four.

Dead people. That's what he was creating today.

My God, let the baby die let Yvonne live!

The horror of the thought left him without strength in his body or will in his mind.

After a while he walked unsteadily down the corridor. At the end of it he stood still and looked out a window. An ambulance, with flashing red-and-white toplights, stood below in the darkness. Someone motionless was being carried into the emergency entrance.

Jonah walked away quickly. Albuther was getting out of the self-service elevator. He looked inner-focused, concerned inside himself. He walked past Jonah without acknowledging him. Though Jonah was the only person there.

Jonah stood in the silence of the corridor. He looked down at the delivery room.

Albuther started to go in, but then stood there, the door pushed in. He didn't enter. He looked inside and then let the door come back at him and walked away from it.

He looked up at Jonah and smiled.

127

They wheeled Yvonne out. She looked jaundiced. Her face was compressed—lips, eyes. But compressed about a smile. She opened her eyes and smiled at Jonah. She tried to raise a hand, smiled when she couldn't. She said to the nurse, "Can I see again?"

They stopped outside the nursery windows and Yvonne rolled on her side and propped herself up on an elbow. The nurse moved a pillow under her side.

Inside the room, a nurse, masked and gowned, turned, raising an infant from a scalelike contrivance. She held the infant up. Wet, purple and white, its little head streaked with black hair.

"Joanna," Yvonne said. "Joanna Jaquith."

128

Jonah was going to his car. He was downstairs and about to use the outpatients' entrance to go to his car, and he just had to sit down. He didn't know how long he was there. He was alone in the bright, empty corridor. There was the sound of the fluorescent lights. Somewhere, not very near, a floor polisher was being used.

When he looked up it was because someone had sat beside him. It was Dr. Glynn. Glynn looked as if he might cry and Jonah didn't understand that—Yvonne and the baby were all right.

"You know, after the war, I thought I'd keep on flying. But I didn't. I don't know why." He pulled his breath in. But what he said sounded like something spoken by a very weak, tired man. "We have these sudden conclusions to our lives, Jonah. I find they happen every day as I get older." He stood up and sighed. "Falun is dead. They brought him in from his home a few minutes ago, and he's dead. Falun Aigborg is dead."

TURNING
FINAL

I feel at home thousands of metres high,
neither bird nor myth,
I take stock of my powers,
and I fly without mystery . . .

—Carlos Drummond de Andrade
(translation by Mark Strand)
From The New Yorker

I picked up the African continent at Bizerta and there I began
to drop earthward. I was at home. Here was a place where I
could dispense with altitude which, as every pilot knows, is our
particular store of wealth.

. . .

To come to man's estate it is not necessary to get oneself killed
round Madrid, or to fly mail planes, or to struggle wearily in the
snows out of respect for the dignity of life. The man who can see
the miraculous in a poem, who can take pure joy from music . . .
opens his window to the same refreshing wind off the sea.

—Antoine de Saint-Exupéry

Final Approach . . . The last part of the approach procedure,
from the time when the aircraft passes the airfield boundary to
the beginning of the final flare-out.

—*Elsevier's Dictionary of Aeronautics*

B

ecause the weather was clear, it was not a small funeral.

A few aircraft arrived under the pale-blue early evening sky of the night before the funeral. Some few more settled down from the black sky of the night into the parallel illuminations of the runway lights. But most of the aircraft set down at Cornwall the morning of the funeral. The sun was strong and the air untroublesome. The aircraft were lined up wing to wing in tiedown lines three deep and twenty and thirty airplanes long. There were small jets and two large piston-driven aircraft and two DC-3's and a converted B-26 and single and multiengine light aircraft and several rebuilt open monowings and biplanes. The pilots—except for the representatives from the airlines, who were in uniform—were dressed as if they were going to an office. They got down from their aircraft and stood on the grass and looked about, orienting themselves to being on the ground and to this place. Some had suitcases with them. There were more than a few women pilots. The ages of the pilots varied, though many of the men were in their fifties and sixties. Some few were in their seventies and had come as copilots or as passengers. There were three U.S. senators and an Air Force general. There were some well-known film people who had flown with or learned to fly from Falun. And there were some lesser-known, more important people—corporation chiefs. There were airline pilots—several of them chief pilots now—with whom Falun had planned and flown and charted new routes. And there were some few others who had never known Falun Aigborg, but had known *of him,* some of them for all their lives. After they had stood on the grass and felt the sun begin to get to their skin and the earth begin to hold on to their feet and the trembling or tiny quivering of their aircraft begin to leave their bodies, they started toward the building and hangar of Yancey Flying Service. Some nodded to each other. Some stopped and shook hands and began to talk and were joined by still others.

130

Ev had been crying inside himself for three days without a tear ever showing on his face. His wife, Charlotte, had been disturbed by the look of him. His body had changed in that brief time: his carriage had become bent. He had been sleepless most of that time. When, the night before the funeral, she had insisted on calling Dr. Glynn, if only to get him a sedative, Ev had become furious and left the house. He had driven for a while and then stopped at a roadhouse. He had drunk some beer there. The owner had come and sat with him. "You look goddamn terrible, Ev." He had asked the owner to break the law and sell him a bottle of whiskey.

He had gone to the airport and parked his car behind the hangar where it couldn't be seen. There was some activity out on the field, a landing aircraft, an executive jet by the sound of it. Ev had gotten out his cumbersome ring of keys and let himself into the hangar. He had gotten into the Skymaster, the beautiful, still new Skymaster, and he had closed the door.

Even with the bottle there he hadn't done much drinking. That wasn't really what he wanted to do after all.

As the night went on and the silence in the hangar became a presence itself, the feeling inside him began to show itself to him.

It was a terror as deep as the sky.

He felt himself becoming colder and colder.

He found he would rather die than live with so much terror.

He only knew one good way of dying, and that was in an airplane, because that was where he had done most of his living.

He had a pretty good idea of what would happen the next day, the pilots coming in from all over. That would be during the morning. By noon, when everyone had gone to the funeral, the field ought to be quiet. He could see the silent field, all those airplanes lined up empty and motionless in the sunlight. He would taxi out past them in the Skymaster. And then he would take off. There were mountainsides convenient enough. Or he could turn east and in an hour he'd be out over the ocean. Then he could just fly east until all the horizons were ocean. Until there was the silence of fuel exhaustion.

*　　　　　*　　　　　*

Someone, sometime, opened the hangar doors, and the night inside the hangar was streaked with sunshine. Later, through the windscreen, Ev saw the pilots walking by, going to the office—his office. Some of them were old friends. Ev finally began to cry, a crying that shook him and ran tears down his face. He felt colder and colder and as if he were disappearing from the people walking by outside.

131

Jonah glanced down the workbench at his fellow workers. He was still not used to it—working in a restricted situation, and at repetitive work, and with other people around him. But then it was only his third day. The work was similar to the building of electronics kits which he liked to do as a hobby —soldering transistors and diodes and resistors and other small pieces into a circuitboard. But it was the same board over and over. Barney Raab had said he would find Jonah something else with his own company or another one—why didn't Jonah wait a while, take it easy at home? Jonah had just said he couldn't do that. With the baby born he needed the sense that he was working productively, earning money.

Jonah felt a tap on his shoulder and looked up from the workbench.

Barney said, "At least you give a man total concentration. But I've seen better soldering."

"I'll learn."

"It's one-thirty."

Jonah got up and followed Barney out of the room.

"You want to ride with Sylvia and me?"

"I guess not, Barney. I thought I'd go over to the hospital afterwards. If it's over that late. I don't expect to draw any pay for this afternoon."

"Of course you don't. I think some people will come back to our place afterwards. His local friends and a few others. We'll have some food and drinks. You come after you see Yvonne. If you want. When does she come home?"

"Tomorrow, maybe."

"They don't keep them very long nowadays."

"No, it doesn't seem like it, does it?"

"You going to have any help at home?"

"I guess not. Neither of us have anyone. I mean, anyone like a mother to come and help."

"You want the day off tomorrow?"

Jonah stopped. "For Christsake, Barney, *am I working for you or not?*"

"Okay, okay."

"I'll pick Yvie up after work and then we'll have the weekend to settle in with the baby. With Joanna."

Jonah thought again of something Yvonne had said when he visited her the night after Joanna was born. She had said, "It's like a little play toy, but it's serious."

132

The funeral, Jonah thought, was ponderous, ornate with biblical quotation and sentiment that did not touch the memory of the man. The stone church was not the place for Falun, not even the place to think about Falun. He was glad that only a few people had been asked to go to the graveside and that he was one of them. He wondered who the others would be. He was surprised that Ev was not at the funeral. His wife Charlotte was there.

There were not twenty at the graveside. The minister and Marion Aigborg. Mrs. Yancey. Dr. Glynn and his wife. Charlotte Goodsom. Adele Fortune. Sylvia and Barney Raab. Ben Cain. Tony Bergeron, the chief pilot of New EnglandAir, and standing a little apart from everyone but, like Bergeron, wearing the airline uniform with a black armband, Perry Sullivan. George Detwiler. Two older men who had flown almost as early as Falun himself. And Jonah Jaquith. The people who had been Falun's daily friends, or nearly so, in his last years, and the two men who had been his colleagues and friends in his early years.

The sky had a gentle blueness. The first red of fall was high up in the leaves of some very few trees, trees that were dying up near the sky.

Marion Aigborg let go the minister's arm and stood as straight as she might, all thin and pale. She smiled at the people she had asked to come to the graveside.

"We needn't mourn here," she said. "We can mourn by ourselves, in our own ways. But here we come together, all friends, to celebrate a life. A good life."

She looked at the sky and then cocked her head back and smiled again and said, "The White House wanted to send jet fighter planes here just about now. They said they wanted to fly over the gravesite in the Missing Man Formation while we were gathered here. I said no. Falun would have said no. You all know how gentle he was."

Marion Aigborg unfolded a piece of paper. "I can't tell you, you all know much better than I, what Falun meant to aviation. He never called it aviation, of course. He called it *flying.* But a man who knew Falun for many years and who now is chief pilot of an airline wrote me this, and I would like to read it to you. I have been asked by several publications to submit an obituary, and I think he would like this one. I quote to you now from the letter. 'Falun Aigborg was, in himself, the history of every man who has flown an airplane since the early years of this century. His death now nearly completes the death of all the pilots who flew when the air was an element entirely foreign to man. These pilots were men who learned the moods and behavior of that other ocean, the ocean of air, with the intimacy the early navigators aship had with the watery oceans of the world. It was a world and an ocean and an element that those of us who fly in it now never knew.' Well.

"I would like to read to you something Falun wrote to me years ago, when he had that crash in Greenland, and did not know whether he would live to get away from there. There he was in the cold and he wrote me that he had been waiting and hoping for rescue and that he had been thinking about emergency procedures, but not the emergency procedures he was accustomed to using in airplanes. He wrote, 'No, I am thinking about the slight adjustments that everyone makes day to day that are really emergency procedures one initiates to control one's emotions, one's personal flight, to bring one's aircraft and oneself to a safe rendezvous with oneself.' "
Marion Aigborg cried at that. "Falun is one of the few people I have ever known, I believe, who years ago brought himself to a safe rendezvous with himself. Now, one last letter that Falun wrote. He must have written it the afternoon before he died. If we have to have final memories, I am glad of this one. I can think of him writing this letter." She nodded to Jonah.

Jonah took the letter carefully out of his inside jacket pocket. It was two pages on lined paper of ballpoint pen in very careful, overly large longhand. Jonah read, " 'Dear Yvonne and Jonah, I have been thinking about the child who is going to join you. I think the only really good thing in life these days, in this world where we live, is the young children. I find very little decency and mutual respect in the world. What saddens me is that I find so little respect for our shared experience of being human. Hopefully, by the time your child is grown, there will have been some changes so that your child's world will not be dimmed by pollution and wars. And the lying and the hatred. I have always thought that flying, in whatever way one conceives it, is a way of getting nearer to ourselves. I would like to wish your child a happy journey, a long and happy flight, with many happy rendezvous. Your friend, Falun Aigborg.' "

As he folded the piece of paper he found that it was blurred and that he was crying.

133

In her room at home, Lou-Ann Ralsan was making her preparations. She had the gun and the bullets. She had the loan of a car from a friend of hers who had had his license removed for ninety days for driving while intoxicated. She had a box in which she would put food. She had a thermos. She had bought the clothes Conrad had asked for and the extra changes of shirts and underwear and socks, and she had packed them along with a new toilet kit in an overnight bag. Finding out about when Mrs. Jaquith was going to come home with the baby and when would be the first Thursday that she probably wouldn't have company around had been difficult. But a friend of hers who worked at the hospital had just called and said Mrs. Jaquith and the baby were scheduled to go home tomorrow afternoon, Friday. So Lou-Ann thought that the Thursday after next ought to be safe, thirteen days away. The company should be over by then. Conrad had specified a Thursday. No other day but a Thursday, and it had to be a *clear* day. She was just to write to him with the news of the baby's birth, as if it were personal news. And then she was to say what Thursday she might go and call on Mrs. Jaquith. And if that day turned out to be clear, she was to show up with the car at nine o'clock in the morning at a place near Attridge. She didn't know what else he wanted her to do or what else he himself was going to do. She had just promised Conrad that whatever he asked her to do, she would do.

"*Whatever?*" he had said to her.

"Whatever at all, Conrad."

134

Food and drink had been set out on the terrace at the Raabs'. The sky to the west was still blue softened by white, but the sky overhead was dark blue and the sky to the east was black. There were stars in the east and overhead and a few appearing to the west. George Detwiler looked at them and remembered something about a man falling down the sky.

Sylvia Raab said to George, "Charlotte Goodsom is near *despair* about Ev."

"Ev has always come and gone without much concern for Charlotte. Long as I've known him," George said.

"That, I think, is what's keeping her from becoming frantic *now*. But she knows something is very wrong. We all do. Ev failing to come to Falun's funeral?"

"I don't know. I don't know." George walked away.

The evening was warm. The conversation was quiet. The guests, at times, did not seem to want to raise their voices above the sound levels of their own thoughts.

Sylvia Raab had remained standing alone after George Detwiler had left, and then she went over and joined her husband and New EnglandAir's chief pilot, Tony Bergeron.

Sylvia said, "Look at Perry over there. No, don't turn around. I didn't really mean *look* at him. He's just sitting over there on the wall. He's had the same drink for an hour. I'm glad he came, but he might as well be home. *Almost.* Someone ought to . . ."

"Ought to what?" Barney said.

"I don't know. Distract him. I couldn't."

"I spoke to Jonah Jaquith," Bergeron said. "About Laura Sullivan."

"That's right. Jonah organized the search flights," Sylvia said.

"But not a trace," Bergeron said.

"None. Nothing," Sylvia said.

"Maybe they kept flying. Even after ATC lost them on radar. They weren't transponder equipped. Maybe they went down miles away," Bergeron said.

"Maybe ATC didn't have the right target. Maybe it was a false target, the one they lost," Barney said.

Bergeron shrugged. "It wouldn't be the first time something turned up on a screen that wasn't there."

"Are you two going to do anything about Perry?"

"What can we do, Sylvia?" Bergeron said. "I guess everyone's tried. He's in a null. Maybe it's the best thing for him."

"Anyway, he's with us," Barney said. "That's something."

Ben went over and sat on the wall by Perry. He didn't say anything. He drank from his gin and tonic, and when he did, the sound of the ice cubes was unreasonably loud. The sky to the west was a deep, hard blue now, like the blue of gun metal, and stars in the blue looked hard and sharp. Ben thought again of his lying on the bed in the motel in Palm Beach the night before he went out over the Caribbean. He remembered watching the stars there as the blackness climbed up the sky and absorbed the blue. All that fear that night, he thought. All that running. If I had the courage, I'd quit flying.

[343]

Perry said, "You didn't see anything, Ben, did you? I mean *anything at all.*"

"No."

"You were up by Pack Monadnock."

"Yeah. That's trackless up there, Perry, you know that?"

"I don't know that area as well as you do now."

"Where I was looking—it's a swath running northwest. I figure it's about twenty-five miles long and three miles wide, five miles in some places, and there's nothing in those boundaries, Perry. No village, no house, no road, no path. Not that I could see. I've been asking around. Even the hunters don't go in there. It's literally trackless."

Perry was silent for a long while. "That's where they'd have to be." He was silent again. "I mean, if they're anywhere near here. Everything else has been checked. Ben?"

"Yeah?"

"Did you know him? The actor?"

"Just met him once. Briefly."

"Know anything about him?"

"No. Just what everyone knows now. The television commercial and all that."

"Did you ever see them together?"

"No, I don't think I did."

Perry was silent again. When Ben had finished his drink and Perry had said nothing more, Ben got down from the wall. "Call me, if you feel like it, Perry."

Perry remained silent. Ben went back to the others.

When he saw that she was finally alone, George walked across the lawn and stood by Adele. Everyone else was up on the stone terrace. "I've been wanting to call you," George said, "since I got back. Randy and me." Adele looked at him. "I wanted to say it's no good thinking about marriage."

Adele said, "That's all right, George."

There was a distant sound of a jet, and George was silent until he had located its navigation lights in the night sky. He watched it disappear. He drank off all of his Scotch and soda, the half of it that had been left. He continued to look at the sky. "For a long time, for a very long time, ever since Ceil died . . . *Die?* Did I say *die?* I don't know that. *Disappeared.* For a long time I was studying to find some sort of . . . of *mystical* conjunction. Between technology and nature. Did you know that?" Adele said nothing. George said, "I really worked at it."

"What did you find?"

[344]

George laughed very hard. "I don't know. That's just it. I don't know." He looked at Adele. "I nearly killed Randy." He tipped the glass back and drank the emptiness in it, the little bit of melted ice in it, like some few, cold tears. "Look what happened to Ceil. Sometimes I think I killed her. Not murder. Not with a knife or a gun. But by *failure*. That I *failed* to do something. I don't know what. Something to protect her maybe. And that's why she disappeared." His hand squeezed the empty glass till Adele thought he might break it. She was about to reach her hand to his to stop him from hurting himself when he went on, saying, "I really don't think I ought to be around people. Not close to them. Not you. Not Randy." He walked away.

After a while Adele followed George. He was leaning heavily on one straight, stiff arm propped on the liquor table. He was pouring a drink into himself.

"George."

He took the drink from his mouth. "I'm here. Hello. I'm here."

"What you had to say about not staying close to Randy."

"What about it?"

"That was stupid, George. Stupid. Can you hear me?"

"I hear you."

Jonah drove up the Raabs' long gravel driveway. For an instant he thought a trick of his headlights made the black shape of a tree move. But then he saw that it was a man out there. He slowed. It was Ev. Jonah stopped and got out.

Standing in the light of the headlights, Ev looked old, older than even Falun had looked that last day. His hands shook. He looked thin and puffy at once, hunched over, waiting like a dying animal there in the night.

"Want a ride, Ev? What're you walking for?"

"Lost my keys. Keys to my car. Lots of other keys, too. I heard the old friends were coming out here. I just started walking. I don't know why. I could have called, someone could have picked me up, I guess. Charlotte. Someone."

He turned around and walked back and got into Jonah's station wagon.

"Don't start the car," he said when Jonah got in. "I was going to kill myself today. In the Skymaster. I was that afraid, that goddamn afraid," he said, almost not speaking out loud at all. "I was that scared by Falun's death. By Falun leaving me alone. Can you understand that? Well, what if you can't. But I didn't do it." Ev began to laugh. A hard laugh, a laughter that struggled to get out of his throat. "No, I didn't do it. Because I had too fuckin' much respect for the airplane. I wouldn't smash it up. Or drown it . . . Haven't got the guts or the interest to do myself in any other way . . . You ever mention that to a soul, I'll kill you. Now you can drive if you're going to."

135

Barney Raab was coming back from a business trip to Montreal. Sylvia was in the copilot's seat. She had gone along for the fun of the flight. It was a brilliantly clear day and Barney had not tuned in the navigational radios. He could hit the VORs by pilotage, he said. He had brought them down visually from Montreal, crossing each VOR without fault.

"Barney?"

"What?"

They were several miles northwest of Cornwall. Sylvia was looking down. "I think I see it."

"What?"

"The Cherokee," Sylvia said.

Barney made a steep bank.

136

Lou-Ann Ralsan was parked off a secondary road in the parking lot of a hamburger stand that wasn't open yet. On the other side of the road there was nothing but trees. Behind the hamburger stand there was an open field. She had no idea where Attridge Correctional Facility was relative to where she was. She kept looking from the field to the trees and back.

Lou-Ann Ralsan diagnosed herself. I'm nervous sick, that's what I am. I could throw up. She was where she was supposed to be, but Conrad wasn't there. It was *the* Thursday, it was a clear day, it was nine o'clock in the morning—the time when the work details left the fences at Attridge, Conrad had said—but Conrad wasn't there. She had everything he had asked for in the back seat, the way he had said. Everything but the gun and the bullets. They were in her handbag, the way he had said.

It got to be nine thirty, quarter to ten. The day was scalding already.

She was looking through the windshield to the field when she heard the door behind her open. Conrad slipped down on the floor behind the front seat.

"How y'doin', Lou-Ann? Nice of you to pick me up. Now let's head back toward Cornwall kinda easylike."

She started the car, backed up, and then swung out on the road. "What if they have, you know, roadblocks? Like that."

"I'll be mighty surprised. Mighty surprised. I don't think there's goin' to be anyone even *knows* I'm gone till a couple hours from now. And shit, baby, we'll be at Jonah Jaquith's in an hour."

137

Jonah hadn't once had a telephone call since he'd come to work for Barney, and when he was told to go to the phone it scared him. All he could think of was that something had happened to the baby.

Yvonne's voice said, "Don't talk to anyone. Just come home right away."

"So that's the way it is," Conrad said to Jonah. "Far as you're concerned, what you're witnessin' here is step one."

Yvonne was seated on the couch holding the baby. The baby had been crying frantically and Yvonne was quieting her by giving her the breast. Opposite Yvonne and Joanna, in a straightback chair facing them, Lou-Ann sat with a pistol in her hand and resting on her lap.

Conrad had his hands on his hips. He was dressed in neat, fresh clothes. "Step two," he said, "is you get an airplane and take me flyin'."

"What if I can't get an airplane? I don't work there any more."

"There is no *what if,* Mr. Jaquith, sir. You do as I tell you for the next few hours or it's tough titty for the baby." He laughed. "A might apropos turn of speech, Mr. Jaquith, sir. Tough titty for the baby. And of course for the missus, too. Now what I'd like is that plane you came and fetched me from Poughkeepsie in? A *Skymaster* airyplane, I believe?"

"Yes," Jonah said.

"Yes. Well, you get that one. You get it all filled up with gas. Order it now."

"What if it's not at the airport?"

"We'll wait till it is. Long as the wait's not too long. You jes call now, Mr. Jaquith, sir."

Jonah dialed and waited and then said, "Lucy, is Ev there? . . . Well, no. Is Two-two Charlie on the ramp? . . . All right. This is an emergency. You understand? Emergency. You get the tanks topped off, I've got a sick man's got to be flown out right away. I'm on my way over."

"Good enough," Conrad said. "I think we're gonna make out jes fine." He turned to Lou-Ann. "Now honey, you jes sit tight with little mother here till you hear from me, right?"

"Yes, Con."

"That's a girl. You appreciate the situation, Mr. Jaquith, sir? Lou-Ann's gonna sit with the little one and the missus till she hears from me. If anything *untoward* happens, Mr. Jaquith, sir, I've asked Lou-Ann to make bang-bang, you understand?"

"Yes."

"You see, I have no weapon. Nothing. My weapon's gonna babysit till I tell her different. Now, if she doesn't hear anythin' *reassuring* from me by six this evenin', it's gonna be bang-bang anyway, Mr. Jaquith, sir. You understand?"

"Yes."

"I thought you'd catch on."

Yvonne was crying. Soundlessly crying. "Can't we just . . . ? Does the baby have to . . . ?"

"Now you take it easy, darlin'," Lou-Ann said. "Everythin's goin' to be all right. I'm just *sure* of it. The boys'll take care of everythin'."

"But the baby . . ."

"No need to worry. Soon's they go, we're goin' to travel ourselves. You need anythin' for the baby, diapers, like that, you just go fetch it. I'll just stay right here with the little thing. I been a babysitter most of my life, darlin'."

138

"Is this a good place to circle the field?" Conrad said.

"It's as good as any."

"Then you jes circle the field right here, Jonah. I think I'll call you Jonah now. My, it sure is pretty up here. So free and fresh. You can see so far. I sure am enjoyin' it. Now, have I got this right? I push this button down and talk into the microphone and I'll be broadcastin' to the airport?"

"That's right. But just a minute, Conrad. I don't know what you're going to say. But you ought to know this. In case it affects the safety of my wife and baby. There's a monitor at the police station. In case of emergencies at the airport. I don't know if it's on or not. Someone may tell them to turn it on."

"*Dee*-lightful." Conrad smiled. "That is most helpful, Jonah. I hadn't figured on such a fine audience. Okay, here I go . . . You know what? I'm *nervous* about talkin' into a microphone. Can you beat that?" He waited a few seconds. "Okay, I'm gonna do it." He keyed the microphone button. "Hello, you folks down there on the ground. This is Conrad Whittier up here in the Skymaster airyplane called Two-two Charlie. Can you hear me down there?"

There was silence for a few seconds. "Two-two Charlie, is that you, Jonah? Over." It was Adele's voice.

"No, no, this isn't Jonah. Jonah's flyin' the plane. This is Conrad Whittier speakin'. You got that? Conrad Whittier."

"Conrad Whittier. All right. Cornwall reads you. Over."

"Well, what I'd like you to do is, get the po-lice to listen in and get my father, Mr. Gilbert Whittier himself, get him to . . . Wait a minute." He unkeyed the mike and said to Jonah, "Can he broadcast from the police station?"

"Yeah. On this frequency he can."

"Good, good. Okay down there. You tell Gilbert Whittier to hustle hisself over to the police radio. Now you jes call me back when he's there and ready to talk to me on the radio."

"Okay, Two-two Charlie. Let me talk to Jonah."

"You jes hustle up my father. Quicklike."

"Okay, Two-two Charlie. Stand by."

"Nice girl?" Conrad said. "Sounds kinda sexy."

139

"Conrad, this is your father."

"Why, hello there, *Dah*-dee. Listen up. Now you jes hurry back to the bank and fetch me a hundred thousand dollars in cash and bring it out to the airport."

"—can't do that."

"If it's more than a hundred thou, that's okay, too. But not less."

"—crazy. I can't do that. You know it."

"Yes, you can, Dah-dee. You know it and I know it and we both know why. Now if you want everyone else to know it, I can sit here and make a very interesting broadcast about it." Conrad waited. He said to Jonah, "I do believe he's thinkin' it over."

"Conrad?"

"Yes, Dah-dee."

"You just control yourself. It will take half an hour."

"Yes, Dah-dee. And leave it in whatever it came in—you know, something plain, nothing ostentatious. And now, is the big chief there? Mr. Harvey Sauer?"

Another pause. "Sauer here. Over."

"Well, goodness gracious. Hello there. Now, Chief, sir, Captain Jonah Jaquith, here on my left, flying this airplane, he's going to get on the radio and tell you, in his own words, how things are. *Heerz Jonah!*"

"Harvey? Over."

"Listening. Over."

"Got a problem, Harvey," Jonah said. "I wish you'd do nothing about it. You do anything but what Conrad here tells you to do and Yvonne and the baby will be killed. I say again, Yvonne and the baby will be killed. Over."

"I understand, Jonah. Over."

"No tricks, no attempts, nothing. You understand? There's nothing you can do. I know what the situation is, and there's nothing you can do. I want you to understand, Harvey. This situation is like a hair trigger, it's like a booby trap. You don't know how you might trigger it. Just accidentally. Don't do anything. Just get Whittier to the airport with the money and stay away from the airplane. Send him out alone with the money to the airplane. Now read all that back. Over."

Sauer repeated the instructions. He finished and said, "All right, I'm going to do everything the way you say. What about after you get the money?"

"I don't know. He hasn't told me yet. Stand by." Jonah looked at Conrad.

"Just tell him the situation will remain the same. As long as he doesn't do anything to upset it. If nothing gets upset, then in a few hours everything will be cool."

140

Over unicom Jonah heard Adele close the field to all other traffic. Normally that would have been Ev's decision and job as the airport manager. But Ev hadn't been around for days, Lucy had told Jonah.

He looked at the fuel gauges. "Conrad, I don't know what you have in mind after this. We'll have been up about forty-five minutes. That's forty-five minutes of fuel used up. You want me to top off when we land? Fill the tanks to the top?"

"How much fuel will you have left?"

"About five hours."

"How many miles is that?"

"Depending on the winds, say, nine hundred," Jonah lied.

"Why, then we're jes fine the way we are."

Jonah slow-flew the airplane around the pattern. "You sure your father can get the money?"

"As sure as it's Thursday he can. You remember that congressman that got killed?"

"Lyman Dougherty?"

[350]

"Yeah. I was in the lockup then, but I can tell you the circumstances just as sure as if I'd been here. Every Thursday now, since as long as I can remember, there's a man—one man or another—he comes into the bank on Thursdays. Usually he's got a suitcase or a couple of briefcases, something like that. He goes into my daddy's office, and then my daddy takes him down to the vault, they go into a storage room inside the vault, and they leave the satchels or whatever it is. Then the man goes away—usually. Sometimes the money goes into accounts in the bank. And sometimes it gets transferred out in cashier's checks. Not one big one, of course. A lot of little ones. And sometimes someone else jes happens by and my daddy gives him the bags and the someone else takes the bags somewhere else? You follow?"

"I think so."

"Well, it's not terribly difficult. A hundred thou a week comes in and gets cleaned up, one way or another. *Laundered* is the preferred parlance. Sometimes, though, there's a need for that cash money someplace. That's when they send someone for it."

"They?"

"Oh, didn't you figure? You know, old man Gilbert Whittier, staunch Republican, granite Yankee, family goes back to the founding of the hills, bank started by *his* granddaddy. Well, old Gilbert Whittier assumed the presidency of the family bank back in nineteen and thirty-two, not a good year for banks. I think he was still on the first of the four wives then, my mother being number three."

"Well?"

"Well what?"

"Nineteen thirty-two. Bad year for banks. He was president."

"Ohhhh, yeah. Almost went under, the bank did, and of course Daddy would have gone down with it. As I surmise, Mob money financed him out of it. Gave him buoyancy, don't you see. Been operating as a clearing house ever since. You have no idea how much Mob money there is in New Hampshire."

"Is there?"

"Go ask your local greenback laundromat."

"Two-two Charlie."

Jonah looked at Conrad. Conrad nodded. "Two-two Charlie," Jonah said.

"Mr. Whittier is here with some baggage," Adele said over the radio.

"Tell her we're coming down," Conrad said.

Jonah did so and followed the pattern around and began his descent.

"I bet there're some Fish and Game people over in New York State lookin' forward to expensive sports cars, fancy vacations, things like that."

"I don't get you."

"Sure you do—if you think about it. Wasn't it Fish and Game people found the airplane that had the congressman in it? Now why would my father be in such an all-fired *hurry* to get the congressman over to some private dude ranch in the middle of a snowstorm? I'll tell you why. Because someone called him and said, 'Gilbert, that fellow who just brought you all the money, that congressman, you jes get his ass and that cash money right over here.' And so he went. Carrying a satchel or two. About one hundred thou. Now there wasn't any fire after that airplane crashed. It was just covered up with snow all winter. Preserved-like. I don't recall any of the Fish and Game people—three guys, wasn't it? I don't recall any of them making a statement about 'Gee whiz, you'll never guess what we found in that airplane.' No, sir. And no one's gonna go *claim* the money either. No one's gonna go admit to its existence. Those guys said to each other here's all this money, no one knows about it, let's just hang on to it, don't say anything and see if we don't just get to keep it by default."

141

"Well now, Captain Jaquith, that was a nice right landing. And looky there. It's dear old Dad. And the police of chief hisself. Just hold it here and let Dah-dee come over to us . . . *Hey. Sauer's coming too!*"

Jonah jumped out. "*Get back, you sonofabitch. Get back, Sauer! I'll kill you!*"

Sauer stopped. He spread his hands wide. Whittier had stopped, too. Sauer said something to him. Whittier started walking toward the airplane.

Conrad had the microphone. "*You hear me in there?*"

"Roger, Two-two Charlie. Listening. Over."

"You tell Sauer *one more thing like that* and *that woman and kid get dead.*"

"Roger, Two-two Charlie. I understand. Over."

Conrad replaced the microphone. "Get back in here," he said to Jonah.

Jonah got back into his seat, harnessed himself in. They watched the older man come slowly toward them. He carried two cylindrical cloth bags, one in each hand.

When the old man got to them and was standing under the wing looking into the cabin, he was breathing hard.

"*Hello,* Dah-dee," Conrad said. "Hand me one." He opened it.

Jonah looked at the money. It was old money, neatly bound with rubber bands. Conrad dug through it to make sure it was real money all the way to the bottom and to the ends.

"The other," Conrad said. He began to go through the second bag.

"I believe there's an extra twenty thousand dollars in there. I wouldn't want my son to go needy."

Conrad finished with the second bag and looked at the money. "How sweet it is," he said.

"A hundred thousand dollars, even a hundred and twenty thousand dollars doesn't go far. Doesn't last as long as you think, Conrad."

"I don't plan to live as well as you, Dah-dee. Now get your ass out of here."

The old man backed away and then turned and walked toward the flying service buildings. He was not holding himself as erect as he usually did.

"Take off," Conrad said.

142

When they were well into the air, Conrad said, "Keep climbing, keep climbing."

"What direction?"

"I don't care for now. Just keep climbing till they can't see us any more."

After a few minutes, Jonah said, "We're at eight thousand feet. I don't think they can see us any more anyway, but you look down. There's a bit of white haze and low cirrus. They can't see us."

"Fly north."

Jonah turned. "Any particular place north?"

"Canada."

"All right. But where in Canada?"

"Toward Montreal. There are some small fields up there. Grass fields. Between the river and Montreal. I want to go into one of them. Something that doesn't look busy."

Jonah was silent. He thought hard about keeping his voice even, not insistent. "Is that all the thinking you've done?"

"What do you mean?"

"You don't even know if there'll be a telephone at the field. To call Lou-Ann and tell her you're all right."

"I'll find one. I'm not out to screw *you,* Jonah."

"You won't have a chance to find one."

"Why not?"

"Because the police will be there."

"Maybe later."

"Maybe before we land."

"Yeah?"

"Yeah. We're on radar right now, Conrad. Air Traffic Control has us as a target and they're following every move we make."

"That may be, or it may not. See, I've done some studying about this, Jonah. We may be a blip on a radar screen, but there're lots of other blips on a day like this. And a lot of them don't have any identification either. We're just another unidentified blip."

"Maybe, but we won't be for long."

"You tell me, Jonah."

"You're going to violate Canadian air space. They'll have us on radar, and they'll send up a couple of jet jockeys to look us over and rock us around a bit. When they get the numbers of the aircraft, they'll know who's in it. You. And they'll stick with us like glue. When we set down, there'll be a whole bunch of folks waiting."

Conrad thought about it. "Start to circle." Then he said, "No, don't do that. Keep going. We got a ways yet before Canada."

"Twenty minutes."

"Yeah, okay. What do you suggest? Remember, it's your wife and kid, you remember that."

"I'm remembering." Jonah thought. "All I can do is put you down somewhere now. Before we're an identified target. Now the state police and a lot of airports are going to have the numbers of this airplane, I think. I know a couple of small fields that are mostly unattended. You might be able to walk away from one of them. Or maybe they haven't got the word yet. One I can think of has a telephone booth, an outdoor telephone booth. That's the best I can do. Set you down there. But I'll expect you to call Lou-Ann. You'll have to do that. I'm staying with you till you do . . . The best I can do, Conrad."

Conrad was silent again. After a while he said, "I thought I'd get free up here."

"A lot of people do."

143

It was minutes before Conrad agreed to it and then he said, "All right, take me down, take me to that place . . . Oh, fuck it, *fuck it!* I've made this flight so many times . . . in my dreams, in my daydreams . . . there at Attridge. Yeah, take me down, that's all I can do, right? Fuck you, Jaquith."

"I'm doing the best I can for you. There's the field. There's no activity. I'm not going to call in—"

"Sure you're doing the best you can for me. You've *got* to. Because of your wife and kid. You know nobody ever did anything, said anything,

nothing my whole life, it wasn't ever anything had to do with me . . .
Anything ever said to me, done to me or done for me, always because of
someone else, always because of my father, the great Gilbert Whittier. No
one ever saw *me*. I never existed for anyone, *he's* the one who exists. *Can
you understand what it is not to exist?*"

They landed and rolled to a stop on the grass and swung around and went
back toward the single small hangar and single pump.

A lineboy came out. He rubbed his eyes and stretched and scratched. "Do
you anything?"

"No," Jonah said. "Just use your phone."

"Didn't hear you call in. I been sleepin'."

"Don't let us interrupt," Conrad said. He was carrying the two cloth bags
and the overnight bag.

"Phone booth's over by the road."

"I know," Jonah said.

Conrad went over to the booth. He looked uncertain but then put the bags
down. He entered the booth and started to close the door. Jonah prevented
the door from closing.

"I want to hear," Jonah said. "I'm going to make damn sure."

Conrad hesitated, then nodded. He placed a collect call to a Cornwall
area number. When he was through he said, "It's me . . . Everything cool?"
He looked at Jonah and nodded. "We can't meet where I planned. Now I
been thinkin' about it, sugar. I think the best place would be, you remember
that place I told you about? Where I have a friend who could put me up
if I needed it? . . . Right, sugar. I guess I can get there in a day, maybe two.
You come right along. You leave those people right there and—" Jonah put
his hand on Conrad. Conrad said to him, "I got my reasons. For them being
left where they are. Don't sweat it. They're perfectly safe . . . Or I can hang
up." He waited. Jonah released him. "As I was saying, sugar baby, you leave
those people there and git. You think they saw the license plate? . . . All
right. Can they see the car when you drive away? . . . Well, everythin's cool
then. Have a nice trip. Be seein' you, sugar baby." He hung up.

Jonah said, "You were wrong about no one ever doin' anything for you."

"Yeah?"

"What about Lou-Ann?"

"Now do you really think she counts?"

Conrad walked away.

Jonah thought, I can stop him. I can stop him now. I can try and stop
him.

As Jonah started toward him, Conrad turned and bent to one knee as if
to tie a shoe. From beneath a pants leg he removed a long and narrow blade.

It reflected light dully, a crude length of metal, pointed and ground sharp on a wheel and wrapped with black electrician's tape at one end for a handle. Conrad looked at Jonah and slipped the knife, blade first, up the sleeve of his shirt. The handle remained butted in his curled fingers. He turned and called to the lineboy. "Hey, you got any transportation here?"

"I got a courtesy car. To take people to town."

"Okay, give me a hand with these bags. They'll be five bucks in it for you. Maybe more. Maybe we won't go to town."

Jonah climbed the Skymaster out. He hadn't seen the courtesy car on the ground, so he didn't know what to look for from the air. He looked for *any* moving car on a road near the airport. There was only one road in and there was nothing moving on that. He really didn't care.

He climbed high enough to get the Berlin Flight Service Station and asked them to relay a message to the state police and then another one to the Cornwall police.

144

The night brought some coolness with it, an unexpected suggestion of coming fall. Yvonne and Jonah sat in the kitchen. Jonah held the baby and made a gentle, rocking cradle of his arms.

"She's nearly asleep," Yvonne said.

"I know."

"She's fighting it. She keeps trying to look at you."

Jonah looked down at the baby. She looked back at him briefly and then closed her eyes.

Yvonne said, "Let me put her to bed."

"All right." Jonah completed the—to him—terribly hazardous transfer of the baby from one person's arms to another's. He drank deeply from his glass of beer. The telephone rang and he talked for a while.

When Yvonne came back she said, "Who was that?"

"Harvey Sauer. The state police picked up the Ralsan girl."

"What about the other one? Conrad."

"No trace so far. But Lou-Ann, she's got to be a dummy," Jonah said without smiling. "She's got a perfect getaway and she blows it. The police didn't have her license-plate number and they didn't have a description of the car—"

"I told them. When we went out to her car, from our house, from *here* —she was holding *Joanna* and the gun. I wasn't *looking* at her car."

"I know, Yvie. They didn't have anything but her name and she still managed to get herself picked up. She ran out of gas. The dumb little bitch ran out of gas. A state cop stopped because there was this car stopped with its lights on. She explained she was out of gas. The cop asked her for her license." Jonah got up and got another beer. "Can you imagine anyone that dumb . . . Christ, pointing a gun at you and Joanna? Harvey says we'll be witnesses. At the trial."

Yvonne shook her head slightly. "I don't know. It scares me."

"It should scare you. You want someone like that wandering around? Maybe she'll decide to come back."

"Maybe your friend Conrad will, too."

The knock on the kitchen door startled them. They looked at each other. Jonah said, "We can't start living as if he's on the other side of every door."

He went to the door and opened it.

"Evening, Jonah. Evening, Yvonne," Ev said.

"Good evening, Ev," Yvonne said.

"You had a little flight today, huh, Jonah?"

"A little one."

"You want me to stand here outside? While I talk to you?"

"I didn't know you wanted to talk to me, Ev." He stood aside. In spite of what he had said to Yvonne, he found himself looking around the outside of the house before he closed the door.

"I'll have a beer, if anyone offers one."

"No one's offering, Ev."

"Jonah—" Yvonne said.

"No one's offering, Ev."

"Wasn't feeling too well, last time I saw you, Jonah."

"You look okay now. Look like the same old Ev. That's the major reason why I hope you're about to be on your way."

"I got some things to say, Jonah. You think I could say them to you in private?"

"No. I tell you plain, Ev, I don't like you."

"Be that as it may, I'm goin' to say what I got to say."

"Keep your goddamn voice down, Ev, you'll wake the baby."

"This is the goddamn way I talk, Jonah! You know that. This is my goddamn normal tone of voice. Now, God damn it, let me sit down."

He stood there, the older man, a man becoming an old man, as Jonah saw him, waiting like a schoolboy to be allowed to sit down.

"Sit down, Ev," Jonah said.

"Thank God," Yvonne said. "One baby in this house is enough."

"I think I'll try and ignore that," Jonah said, but he didn't smile.

"A beer would make this easier," Ev said.

"Oh, shit. Have a beer."

"I'll get it," Yvonne said.

Ev looked at the beer for a long time before he drank some of it. "That's good. That's awful damn good. I haven't had any booze since . . . Since a couple days after they laid Falun to rest." He drank some more.

Jonah was silent.

"Good. Awful damn good. Sorry about what happened to you today. Must have scared the shit out of you."

Jonah remained silent.

"Well, Jonah . . . Before I say what I'm goin' to say, I got to preface it. I've gotten the idea that if my business stays in good health, maybe I'll stay in good health a while longer myself. That's my preface. The substance is, I guess you're right about the way things should be done now. Getting students and all that. I'll give you twenty percent to start with and I'll give you five percent more at the end of one year, *if* things keep going the way they are. You'll get five percent more the year after. That will give you thirty percent of the business. I've consulted with lawyers about this and they assure me it's fair and equitable. Upon my death," Ev said rapidly, "you will have the option of purchasing from my widow enough equity in the business to give you controlling interest. Now, God damn it, Jonah, I think that was worth a beer to listen to."

"I think so, too, Ev."

"Now you just bear this in mind, Jonah, you accept this, you're *in this with me,* just like you wanted. The business makes money, you make money. Otherwise you sweat."

"I understand." He looked over at Yvonne. He looked at her for seconds and seconds of silence, Jonah thought.

She said, "Jonah, I accept your flying."

Jonah put out his hand to Ev. Ev took it, but he spoke to Yvonne. The loud voice had become a whisper of words. "I thought, if your husband joined me, I thought it might kill me. I actually thought that. I never thought it might help me live."

145

Perry Sullivan sat in the left-hand seat and looked out ahead. He had just brought New EnglandAir Flight number One-six-five to a company gate at La Guardia and was remaining aboard while passengers were filing off. It was a bright, golden September day, sky hazy blue, temperature in New York, as he had announced, sixty-seven degrees, fall moving down and touching the city.

Perry's copilot and chief pilot, Tony Bergeron, said, "You're hanging tight, aren't you, Perry?"

"Yes, sir."

"*Yes, sir,* shit. How's it going? I can't tell a goddamn thing by your flying. Your flying's fine. I couldn't criticize a damn thing you did. How do you feel?"

"I went through all that with the company shrink. You've got the report."

"Jesus, you're wise-ass, Sullivan. If the report could speak for you, I'd ask *it,* and I wouldn't go flying with you. That stuff's *interpretive* and you know it."

"You mean there's some doubt—"

"Stop screwing around, Perry. How do you feel? You feel okay flying?"

"Yes."

Bergeron tapped his fingers. "On the ground, you feel . . . different sometimes."

"I get thinking about Laura. Hell, yes, on the ground I feel *different* sometimes."

"No one's suggested it incapacitates you in any way. I just want to make sure you don't start brooding about it when the weather's down to minimums and you're making an approach."

"You saw how I functioned. Yesterday. Instrument approaches all day long."

"It crosses your mind? Laura trying to get down through?"

"Well, how the hell wouldn't it, Tony?"

"Okay." Bergeron stood up. "Long as you're not hiding it from yourself." Bergeron left the flight deck.

Oh, no, Perry thought, I'm not hiding anything from myself. It just worries the shit out of me sometimes now that there are all those people back there flying with me, my passengers, like Laura was my passenger.

He heard the maintenance people coming on.

"Can I take it now, Captain?" a mechanic said behind him.

"Sure," Perry said, "I'm through with it. For today."

146

Ben and Adele were at a private tennis court. The day was dry. It was hot and fragrant with the smell of fallen, brittle leaves. The colors around Ben and Adele rose up against the cloudless blue sky like varicolored fires frozen still. Ben and Adele each wore whites. A white tennis dress. White shorts and white shirt. White wristband. The clay court was brick red. The ball was yellow.

When Ben had been in the studio ideas had been flying about him like birds. This was the third day of it. Or the fourth or fifth. When he'd left the studio to meet Adele here at the private court, the birds had not gone away.

Adele looked so pretty in the short-skirted tennis dress, the white band tying her hair back.

There was only the sound of the ball against the rackets and *punck* against the court. Thwack. Punck.

They used to practice like this. Silently. It was something that had become an intimacy between them. The long silence except for the hitting, the long rhythm of the stroking as they sent the ball back and forth.

They rarely played a game. It was just this. The silence. Watching the ball. Hitting it. Watching for the next one. Back and forth, back and forth.

They hadn't done this since Ben had told Adele he didn't want to get married.

Slowly the rhythm took hold of him. The birds in his mind became manageable.

Ben hadn't known whether Adele would accept his invitation back to his house or not. They hadn't spoken much. He had been in the office the day before to settle his hangar and maintenance and gas account; she had been there and he had asked her if she'd like to play tennis. Adele had thought about it and then said, "All right, I guess—okay."

Ben said, "We could go out to dinner after the tennis. We could go back to the house and have a swim and go out to dinner later."

"All right," she said.

He took her by her place and waited while she went up to get a swimsuit and a dress for the evening. It was September and Ben watched the students back on Adele's street. At first he was surprised at how young they were.

When Ben and Adele came up from the water, Adele walked across the deck and into the bedroom and went on into the bath and got a towel. She came out into the bedroom. Ben came in and sat on the bed. Adele got undressed and dried herself. Ben took the towel and did the same.

The blue light was like the light in the Florida motel room by the sea— but it was a deeper blue.

"I gave up flying," Ben said. "I sold Zero-niner Whiskey to Ev and Jonah."

Adele lay next to him, and though they had made love, their hands continued to touch and caress each other shortly, as if they had never known each other's bodies, as if it were all discovery.

"When?"

"Yesterday. But the finish of it was when we were playing tennis today."

Adele was silent for a while. "Forever?"

"I don't know."

Adele was silent as the room turned darker and then to darkness and the chill fall air settled into it. She drew the sheet up and moved closer against the warmth of his body. "I wish I could," she said.

147

"Goddamn rich just sit around and read all day," Ev said.

Jonah looked up from the magazine. "I'm waiting for a charter."

"Who is it?"

"Me."

"*Jesus Christ,*" Ev said. "I *knew* it'd be like this. I *knew* it'd be terrible." He went into his office and closed the door.

Pirates in the Sky said the cover of *Time.* September 21, 1970. Joanna had been born two months and one day before the date of the magazine. *All week the nation fixed its agonized attention on Qa Khanna, the stretch of Jordanian desert where three hijacked airliners rested improbably, like a mirage of beached whales,* Jonah read. *The terrifying juxtaposition of technology and barbarism . . .*

Jonah turned the page. It was something he *ought* to read. But he wasn't going to do it just now. He didn't feel like it. He was waiting for something splendid.

Out of the desert and the juxtaposition of technology and barbarism, he read *Excerpts from Spiro Agnew's speech last week: We have more than our share of the nattering nabobs of negativism. They have formed their own 4-H Club—the hopeless, hysterical, hypochondriacs of history. These men are hard up for hard times. They can only make hay when the sun does not shine.*

Outside the sun was bright. A safe, calm air, cool and buoyant and steady.

Jonah skipped through Judge Carswell, President Nixon's earlier nomination to the Supreme Court, trying to be a senator from Florida and failing. He turned the page. *Deep in the timeless Jordanian desert, the three silvery jetcraft glinted like metallic mirages in the afternoon sun, their finned tails emblazoned with the insignia of three famed airlines: TWA, BOAC, and Swissair . . .*

Jonah stopped reading again. The aircraft had been blown up. He knew that. He didn't want to read more just then.

"Jonah?"

He looked up and smiled. Yvonne stood there with Joanna in her arms.

[361]

*   *   *

In Ben's Cherokee Zero-niner Whiskey, they lifted off, Jonah flying and Yvonne beside him in the copilot's seat with the baby in her arms.

He was joyful, Yvonne could see. He kept looking over at her and little Joanna, and he was joyful.

He had promised that it would be just once around the pattern, and when Yvonne had, hesitantly, said he could fly them over their house, Jonah had said no, some other time if she wanted, this time they'd stick to their flight plan.

Downwind, parallel to the runway, he cut back some on power and looked over at Joanna as if she could see what he was doing, learn from it. His hands set up a sure, steady glide and, with the end of the runway off his wing and eight hundred feet below him, he pulled back more power and notched on flaps, just as he taught students, and turned base. The runway was ahead to his left, stretching straight out toward the hills, pointing out in the same direction as the wing. He put the nose further down and added more flaps, hearing the whistle of air outside, feeling the airplane buck, for an instant, in resistance to the airload hitting the increased flaps. He added a little power and turned final, all smooth and trimmed up, steady, just where he ought to be.

ACKNOWLEDGMENTS

I am grateful and indebted to a number of people who over the course of several years lent me their expertise and sometimes, as well, shared with me their flight decks and cockpits.

My thanks to Captain Delbert L. Combs of Pan Am; Captain Christopher Hart and Captain Reginald Tibble of BOAC; Captain J. J. O'Donnell, president of the Air Line Pilots Association; Dr. D. Glynn Millard; Mr. J. V. Connelly, chief, Boston Tower; Mr. H. Leverett Jacobi, General Aviation Divisions, North American Rockwell; Captain Joe Green, WBZ Radio; Major Alfred J. Pratt, USAF, Physiological Training; Mr. Lee Bowman, Bowman Flying Service; Colonel Douglas D. Brenner, commanding officer of the 49th Fighter Interceptor Squadron, Aerospace Defense Command; and Major Larry D. Waldron, Captain Jac Suzanne, Captain Joe Vojir, and Lieutenant Jay Stretch, also of the 49th FIS; Lieutenant Colonel H. James Greene, ADC; Mr. Peter Garland; Mr. Christopher Barnes and members of the staff of the Keene State College Library; and the staff of the Peterborough Town Library.

Special assistance was given me by Mr. Frank Leary, executive pilot; Mr. Jim Lucas, chief training officer, ATC's Boston Center; Mr. Martin Mooney, also of Boston Center; Mr. Alfred T. LeRoy, assistant chief, Albany Tower; Mr. Stephen P. Stone, also of Albany Tower; and Captain R. O. Loranger, chief pilot, Northeast Airlines (Delta).

I am particularly grateful to Nils Floren, First Officer, American Airlines. As I am also particularly grateful to Bob Loomis, my friend and editor and fellow pilot who served this book in all three capacities.

R. F.

ABOUT THE AUTHOR

RICHARD FREDE was born in Albany, New York, in 1934, but grew up in Chattanooga, Tennessee, and New York City. A graduate of Yale, he was a Scholar of the House in English his senior year. He has been six times a Fellow of the MacDowell Colony. He is the author of several novels and short pieces of fiction and nonfiction, and poetry. He is a licensed pilot.